Heldin

Heldin

Coming to Terms

a novel

MILLY JANZEN BALZER

iUniverse, Inc.
Bloomington

Heldin
Coming to Terms

iUniverse books may be ordered through booksellers or by contacting:

iUniverse
1663 Liberty Drive
Bloomington, IN 47403
www.iuniverse.com
1-800-Authors (1-800-288-4677)

ISBN: 978-1-4620-0168-2 (sc)
ISBN: 978-1-4620-0169-9 (dj)
ISBN: 978-1-4620-0170-5 (ebook)

Library of Congress Control Number: 2011903798

Printed in the United States of America

iUniverse rev. date: 03/31/2011

For those *Heldin* and *Helden*:
Brave women and men
who ask questions that cannot be answered.

Kyemt teet, kyemt raut.
Time comes with a solution.

Acknowledgments

Most of the incidents in *Heldin: Coming to Terms* are from my mother's anecdotes and accounts. To her—Sara Wall Janzen (who died in 1967 at age seventy-seven)—I owe my sincere thanks. I was eleven when my father, Henry F. Janzen, died at age fifty-four. He is my model for Franz Lober.

Thanks are also due to my mentor in college, Alan Swallow of the University of Denver Press. Poet Allen Tate, of the University of Minnesota, arranged for Joseph McCrindle to act as my agent when I was a Fulbright scholar at the Universität zu Köln in Germany. They encouraged me to begin work on—and complete—this novel while I was still a student. I regret laying it aside for some years. I wish they were still living so I could show them what I finally did.

My siblings: Justina, Jacob, Elizabeth, Clara, Henry, Annetta, William, and Gladys participated in much of the action. Only William and Gladys still live.

David, my husband, allowed me alone time to work while he pursued his own interests. My son Edward took time to read and critique the manuscript, while my other children, Naomi and Daniel, cheered me on. Members of the Quaker Writing Group at Gwynedd Meeting—Beverly, Mimsy, Christine, Chuck, Janet, and Faith—pushed me to finish and polish what I started.

Introduction

In the valley of Martins Creek, not suitable for farming, was land owned by a man who immigrated from Ukraine in 1875. The rich black earth teemed with wildlife, and native grasses and willow and poplar trees tolerated occasional flooding.

The immigrant was Aaron Wall, a skilled farmer. As a diligent member and elder of a Mennonite church in the nearby village, Aaron participated in congregational business. Known for physical and medical care he provided for injuries and ailments, he manipulated dislocated joints and prescribed exercises, poultices, and herbs, practices he had learned from his father in the old country and passed on to his son, Jacob.

He came to differ with other members of the church concerning the Sunday school. It seemed the church was becoming liberal, almost worldly. He looked at the worthless land adjoining his arable fields and felt called to lead those who agreed with him to establish a new church there. They named it *"Bruderthaler"* or "Valley Brothers," and it came to be called "Valley Church." Members also spoke of it as the *"Bayd Hus,"* or "house of prayer."

It had space for the church with balcony, and a side room with an exit for mothers and their small children. Separate buildings comprised a dining hall with kitchen, a German-language boarding school, and a stable for horses. Across the road, they soon had a cemetery. The creek was usually not too deep for adult catechists to kneel in for baptism.

The wood clapboard buildings were painted white. Inside, no images or decorations distracted the congregants. The clear glass windows would be wide open in summer, and birdsong was the only accompaniment to the congregants' enthusiastic singing. In winter, several Round Oak wood-burning stoves broke the chill. Evening prayer meetings were illuminated by gaslights that puffed as they were lit and hissed softly throughout the service.

Water was heated on the kitchen stoves and carried, steaming, in tubs to the sanctuary for foot-washing rites.

This was where I learned early to sit quietly during the worship service, to whisper and not wiggle. It was comforting and comfortable to be next to my mother, who sat on the women's side during church services. I could lean my head and rub my face against her soft plush coat, and I would sometimes nap a while. She always carried a *"tvaybak"*[1] in her purse in case I was hungry. My father, who sat across the aisle on the men's side, did not carry a snack for me, and his woolen clothes felt too scratchy for me to lean on.

When I was old enough, I went to the dining hall to attend Sunday school. I would sit on a bench with a dozen or so other girls my age to learn about sin and redemption, and to discuss that week's Bible lesson under the direction of a young woman. Here we felt free to fidget and giggle, and sometimes to question the teaching of the day's Scripture. The curtain hiding us did not quell the chatter of all the other classes who met in that hall. After class, we walked together to the sanctuary, where we sat in the front two rows, across the aisle from the boys.

Whenever the adults had business to discuss, we children were excused back to the dining house where we could visit or chase each other. Before long, when our noise reached people inside the church, someone—usually my mother— came to organize singing; she drew the line and refused to let us sing "Yankee Doodle."

Business was conducted by men in private meetings, but sometimes the entire congregation heard confessions by members who had transgressed the stern and uncompromising tenets of the church. I was too young to attend these but overheard the talk: a man had confessed to infidelity to his wife; his wife divorced him—though divorce was not acceptable either—and both left the community. A young single woman became pregnant and refused to identify the father. She was repudiated and expelled from membership in the church.

Otherwise, members helped each other, celebrating happy events with them and supporting them in hard times, through prayer and with practical assistance.

*   *   *

Heldin: Coming to Terms is the imagined life story of a brave woman who tries to conform—*held in* by the teachings of a rural Mennonite church community like mine. Major events in her life were my mother's: death of her young mother and remarriage of her father soon after. Her own marriage to a farmer. Hilda's children and other relatives are composites of real persons;

---

1   A traditional Ukrainian yeast bread.

several are invented because they contend with problems—questions—of her faith. Most of all, dealing with her faith, and trying to come to terms with it, govern her life.

Heldin is the German word meaning "female heroes." Male heroes are *Helden*.

CHAPTER ONE: 1906

Years later, Hilda remembered this rare day in 1906, when she was fourteen and had faith Ma would continue to be well. It was the day she thought of making a proposal to God, an offer for an agreement.

How contented she felt as she stretched, reaching with her toes to the foot of the bed, careful not to nudge Liesebet sleeping next to her. *I can smell cracklings. That means Ma feels well enough to cook, even after her trip to Canada.*

She didn't hurry. Her muscles ached where the plowshare had bruised her a few days before. She had thought it a good idea to post a sapling onto the plow handles in such a way that it tapped the horse on the hip with each step he took. It kept him moving—if not faster, then at least regularly. It worked for a few rounds of the field. When the sapling fell off, she wrapped the reins around the handles of the plow and went to the front of the plow to retrieve it. Old Klaus, startled, pulled forward and knocked her to the ground; he continued pulling, scraping the share over Hilda's shoulder. Then he stopped and waited for her to get up and take hold of the reins again.

She sat behind the plow for a minute. The share hadn't cut her, and there had been no blood. She was alone. John was working in the back forty, too far to have seen what had happened, and their parents were somewhere between home and Saskatchewan. There was nothing to do about it but to brush off the dirt and continue plowing. Luckily, all her joints worked, probably thanks to the softness of the rich black ground. As she finished plowing the field she had been assigned to do, she got somewhat used to the pain. She decided not to tell John or her parents what had happened. It was her own fault. Easier not to mention the pain than to explain why she had rigged up the goad. Besides, it hadn't hurt the horse.

Still sunk in the comfort of two featherbeds—one under and one over her—Hilda pulled up her legs and hugged them with her arms. Then she drew down a corner of the cover and listened to the sound of the wind blowing through the tops of the huge cottonwood trees, the windbreak north of the farmstead. The sound was not constant; it paused, hummed, and rose and fell in tone; she could almost sing along with it. Warm in her bed, Hilda felt soothed and at peace. *I wonder if that's really how the ocean sounds, as Ma says so often. Some day, I'll find out.*

Little sister Liesebet, nine years younger, gave Hilda a sense of ownership. Not only did she enjoy being looked up to, she was well aware of the siblings she could have had. Hilda did not know the sex of her mother's new baby—if it was old enough to be a baby—recently miscarried. Only she, Liesebet, and John had survived; and John, five years older than she, would soon marry and live on a farm some miles away.

During Ma's frequent illnesses, Hilda found ways to comfort her little sister as she worked, to make up for Ma being bedridden. She and Liesebet would pretend to be royalty, putting away rich pewter knives and three-tined forks after washing them. As imaginary schoolteachers, they went over the latest reading lesson. When there was leisure time, Hilda helped Liesebet climb trees, where they fancied seeing places as far away as Iowa or South Dakota. Or other countries they might visit someday for fun, or even as missionaries. She comforted her little sister when she fell and skinned her knee, and held her hand when they crossed the stepping stones in the creek while herding the cows home from pasture. On those walks, they could look to the sky and laugh at what they imagined the clouds portrayed: animals, trains, even just pans of *tvaybak*.

Saturdays, when Ma ailed, Hilda was especially busy. Those days, the house had to be cleaned more than ever—the kitchen floor washed on her knees and all the chairs dusted—for there could be guests Sunday afternoons: people from the congregation or relatives. Hilda included Liesebet in the work she had to do, giving her a small-sized dust-rag that could be her own. She suggested a game of blowing the dust—to Heaven, or just to a castle—from the corners of the stairway. Saturdays, Hilda followed Ma's directions for mixing flour, milk, lard, and yeast to make tvaybak that they always served their guests, and she soon managed results almost as good as Ma's. She let Liesebet help make the little balls, one on top of the other, to make the "tvay" of the tvaybak.

Now, Hilda could hear the familiar squeal of the back door heralding Pa's return from the barn for breakfast. *I guess I should get up. Oh well. I might as well enjoy the warm nest I'm in... Maybe if I make an agreement with God, Ma will not get sick again. I can promise to give my heart to Jesus if one year from now, Ma is still well. If I keep my word, maybe God will let her stay healthy longer. Maybe until I'm grown up. I know somewhere the Bible says, "God is not mocked." I'm not mocking. I'm not trying to bribe God. I just think I want to make a bargain. A secret one—just between me and God. I mean, between God and me.*

But then other thoughts intruded. *How many miscarriages has she had anyhow? Why does it keep happening? I wish she'd stop getting pregnant. I heard Grosspa telling Pa that she shouldn't have any more babies. How does it happen that she has so many pregnancies—I mean miscarriages?*

How are babies made? I know how calves are made—and puppies and kittens. The bull just jumps on the cow's back and does it. And hangs on for a while. And the cow can't get away. Same with dogs and cats. I've heard the cat shriek so that it woke me up at night. Does a man do the same: jump on his wife, and she can't get away? Does Pa jump on Ma? Why doesn't she stop him?

Anyhow, when I marry, I'm not going to have any babies for a long time. Maybe I won't marry. Maybe if I do marry, I won't have any babies. Or just one or two. Eventually.

Well, it's time and, if Ma is well, I can go to school today. I hope I haven't fallen too far behind this time.

Hilda turned to her side and pushed her feet out from under the covers. The floor was cold. She grabbed for her clothes, pulling them on swiftly in the unheated upstairs bedroom as she continued her musings. *It's fun when she's healthy.*

*   *   *

Having missed school for a month while her mother recuperated from blood loss after this most recent miscarriage, Hilda settled in to make up the lessons she had missed. Arithmetic wasn't hard, and she felt able to help plan the grocery list, prioritizing those basic foods needed for the family. She enjoyed biology, copying into her copy-book diagrams of the various body systems from the drawings on the large oil-cloth scroll the teacher hung from a nail in the wall. She could trace the route food takes from the mouth through the esophagus to the stomach and so on. The heart was an interesting muscle, especially interesting because Ma's heart was in trouble.

So far, there hadn't been any lessons about how babies came to be. She wondered when—or how—the teacher would introduce that subject. One day, when the teacher went outside for recess with the other children, Hilda managed to stay behind. It was a chance to peek behind the pages of the scroll; perhaps there was a page showing the insides of a woman. There wasn't.

Who knows, she told herself, *maybe I can be a nurse some day. Then I'll find out. Then I'll be able to help Ma keep healthy.*

But when the time came that Ma was ill again—could she be pregnant again?—Hilda again had to miss school, and now she had to do all of the cooking, with Ma sometimes not even in the room to give her directions. Liesebet helped with the dishes, drying those not too big for her. Those days, she also clung to Hilda, following her around and sometimes actually holding on to her skirt. Pa helped in the house too, but he and John did all the outdoor work by themselves, now that the harvest was in and they had let the itinerant boys go back to their homes farther south.

Normally, Hilda milked a couple of cows twice each day—before school and before supper. She had been milking since she was nine years old. She loved the time, precious to her for the quiet talks she, John, and their father could share. She believed Pa also valued those talks. He sometimes even discussed with them his choice of a sermon topic for the following Sunday.

This time, Pa spoke to her alone. "Hilda." This time, Hilda noticed a break in his usually strong, steady voice. "Hilda," he started again, "Hilda, you—we—must be strong. Your mother is not going to get well. We must pray that she doesn't have too much pain." He was silent as they finished milking.

Back in the house, Hilda looked at the calendar on the kitchen wall, an annual gift from the grocery store. It was not a year since she had thought of offering a bargain—a promise—to God. Her stomach hurt. *I didn't make an agreement with God. Why didn't I? What if I had? I only thought of it. Why did I keep putting it off?*

I'll do it now. I'll show God I believe. That I trust Him. Really. Sincerely. Silently, she mouthed the words that came to her, "God, Thou art almighty. Thou canst heal her. Make her well, I beg Thee. Then I will give my heart to Jesus."

She walked to the quiet bedroom, and for some minutes, she stood at her mother's bedside. "Ma, are you awake? I want to tell you something. I've asked God to heal you. I've prayed very hard. Now you have to try to get well."

She bent closer and heard what she thought was, "I can't. God doesn't always give you what you want."

Hilda dropped to her knees, cradling her head next to her mother's arm, and continued her prayer silently. *God, don't you* want *my heart? I need* my *mother.* Then she felt a warm, firm hand on her shoulder. It was Pa's. "Come, child. Let her rest."

*   *   *

A week later, Hilda stood alone in the parlor with the wooden coffin holding a dead woman. She tightened her lips and felt her body, arms, and legs tense as she whispered, "How do you talk to a God who doesn't hear you? Or hear him say, 'Yes, child. I want your heart.'" Sadly, she realized, *Now I don't have to keep my side of the bargain. I'll just have to forget the idea.*

Still standing, Hilda decided, *That lady doesn't look like Ma. She never had such an expression, even asleep. Besides, she's not really here. Her soul is in heaven. And she never wore that dress in bed. She sewed it herself and wore it only for special church days. I helped her sew those little buttons onto the sleeves. When we finished, I sat at the table while Ma spread it so we could admire it together.*

Now, with Pa and John outside and Liesebet in the kitchen, Hilda felt in her apron pocket for her sewing scissors. She quickly reached below the cover hiding Ma's legs, snipped a piece out of the dress, and pushed the cut edge under the body. *No one will see.* She held the relic to her nose, remembering the smell of Ma's closet, and then folded it neatly and tucked it into her pocket. *I'll find a place to hide it, but if anybody comes across it, if I don't label it, they won't know what it is or what it's there for. It's my secret. My forever part of Ma.* She also considered cutting a bit of Ma's hair but decided people would notice.

CHAPTER TWO: 1907

Reverend Heldin sat on his rocking chair in the parlor, a quiet refuge where he could be alone or think about his next sermon topic. There, he kept his large Martin Luther Bible, written in the German he could best understand. The children seemed to respect his being there, finding hushed or gentle things to do until he emerged. Usually he came out refreshed. This time he went to sort out his circumstances, his feelings. His mind went in circles, like a continuous belt that ran around two pulleys, without an end.

I'm lonely. The children are all right, I think. The older two don't say much. John plans to marry and is starting to work on his farm. Hilda helps with the little one. She learned to bake good bread during Katherine's many illnesses. Poor Hilda, she's missed a lot of school. She shouldn't have to be a substitute mother for Liesebet. In no time, Hilda will be old enough to marry too. If she forgets about becoming a nurse.

Then other thoughts broke through the circle, making another ring. *Katherine died only three months ago, but I just have to remarry. Liesebet needs a mother. And a sister. Not a sister who mothers her. I'm not so good at patching trousers, and I don't know how to bake bread. And, oh God, I need a wife.*

He shuddered and realized he was praying. *How could it happen that she should die so young? She was healthy enough when I married her; maybe she shouldn't have been pregnant so often, but what could we do? She always welcomed me when I approached her; she loved her babies, even the ones who died before they were born.*

She taught the living ones. Not just the good works from the Bible, but also how to have a sense of humor, to love pretty things. Look at the flounces and ruffles she invented for the girls' dresses, the clever neckties she made for me and John. Her baking was inventive; she might hide a sweet nut or candy inside her tvaybak to surprise the children. She could create a new dish from leftover food, that we might enjoy as much as we did the original one. She could turn an event into a joke; she was even a bit vulgar or bawdy at times. But she was never irreverent.

She put a new perspective on what seemed sad. When I felt downhearted about something, she could come up with something even worse, like, "What if you couldn't move your bowels?" She paid close attention to my work; when I was exacting and tried to see that our church services were flawless, she lightened my mood by mimicking the vorsinger,[2] the congregation following him like sheep. How I laughed when she chanted, a little off key, "Was ist los mit meine Brille? Die ist ganz mit Fett beschmiert."[3] She claimed the congregation dutifully repeated this nonsense.

She sang as she worked. It will be hard to find a woman as vitally alert.

Oh, God, I've been praying and praying, but I can't get over my anguish. I'm supposed to be the pastor, the minister, the reverend. I'm the one who should interpret Thy ways to my church, to my family, to myself. What shall I do?

He sat up, no longer praying. *I know of available spinsters—here in the community and in Canada. If I used my brain, thought practically, I would choose the school teacher, even though she has had only basic education. I remember her from the general conference in Manitoba last summer. Came from Ukraine like me. I think she knows some English, as well as Low- and High-German. As a teacher, she likely knows how to manage children. She looks to be around ten years younger than Katherine was. Seems physically strong. Sturdily built. If she were a cow, the vet would say she was built for breeding. Very serious minded, and a member of a traditional Mennonite church She wore a simple, almost somber dress. But I only saw her. Didn't talk with her. I haven't heard her sing. I don't know how well she cooks.*

From the next room, he heard the sound of music. Whatever they were doing, the girls were singing as they worked. He didn't recognize the number; it was likely one from school.

Reverend Heldin felt it was safe to continue his prayer. *Dear God, my Father, should I use my practical brain? Act as if remarrying is a business? Maybe that is what I should do. Go and meet her. Wilt Thou intervene—point out a flaw in my business if Thou dost not approve? If Thou dost approve, help me to*

---

2   A song-leader for people who don't read music. He sings a line and the congregation repeats it.

3   "What is the matter with my glasses? They are completely smeared with grease."

figure out how to approach the children, how to introduce her. That is, if she will have me.

Of course she will; she is, after all, a spinster. There aren't so very many eligible single men. Any spinster would be pleased, even flattered by the attention of the pastor of a thriving Mennonite church. Even me.

That is what I must do. Surely Thou wilt intervene if she is not the right choice for me. I must believe what I preach. Thou dost not allow things to happen that Thou dost not wish to happen. Even the death of Katherine. Thou allowed that to happen. She was too good for me. I need someone plainer. My children will be all right. Somehow, I'll tell them. But later, after I know for sure.

Realizing that he had been rocking hard, each swing of the rocker squeaking over the hardwood floor, Reverend Heldin wondered what the children might be thinking. When he noticed that the singing had stopped, he went across the room to look out the window. The girls were outside, Hilda watching Liesebet, who was climbing the boxelder tree.

Now was time to write a letter. Before he might change his mind, he took out his writing paper and a pen. The mailman had not yet come by their driveway, and he decided to mail it as soon as possible. Not knowing if postage to Canada was the same as that in the United States, he decided to add another penny stamp to the envelope.

*   *   *

It was Friday, and Leah Loewen found a letter in her mailbox at the post office. She did not get many letters; usually all she found was *Die Rundschau*, the weekly German-language periodical that brought her up-to-date on events around the world, including the United States. She did not recognize the handwriting. *Probably wants money*, she thought.

The writing was neat and clear, the message short. The writer wrote that his wife had died, and that he had three children, living. He asked if he could come visit next week. It was signed, "John Heldin." She recognized his name; he had been a speaker last summer at the conference meeting she'd attended.

Her friend Sophie had shared gossip about him: he had a sickly wife who had bad luck, losing baby after baby. Three living children. They speculated and even giggled about what his wife must have been like. Always pregnant. Loved babies. What was he thinking?

"Now what can he want?" she muttered to herself, though she actually guessed what he wanted. She pictured him standing in front of the audience; she had been near the back. *Handsome in a way. Full head of dark hair. Erect—I mean his back.*

Well, why not? What can it hurt? We can have a nice talk, and then he can go back home.

But here I am, getting close to spinster age. Teaching children not my own in a clapboard room, heated with coal that I shovel into the potbelly. One privy down the path under a cottonwood tree; children take turns. Ignore the rime outlining the seats in winter. Try to keep the mud-dauber wasps from building nests on the rafters in summer. An open barn for my horses, with stalls for the children's horses.

What choices do I have? There's Kurt. Has two feebleminded brothers. Not too bright himself. Might run in the family. I wonder if I could teach him to read. Our children might be dull too. Dete is brighter, but rough. Kicks his dog, horse, cow—whatever is in the way. Hasn't kicked me yet. I haven't been in the way. Yet.

I could always keep on teaching. Wipe a new crop of runny noses each year.

Then there is Reverend Heldin. I can't call him "John." He addressed this letter "Dear Miss Loewen."

If I marry him, if—when—we have children, how many more does he want? As babies, they will be uncle or aunt to Hilda's and John's babies when they have some. Assuming they marry soon and have babies.

Leah decided to answer his letter. "Come, if you want. I am here." She signed it, "Yours truly, Leah Loewen." Then she re-copied her letter to sign it "Sincerely," since she wasn't "his truly." At least not yet. She sealed the envelope and mailed it.

CHAPTER THREE: 1908

Everyone had gone home at last. Hilda sat on the top step of the back porch. Tiredness had been creeping into her limbs all afternoon, seeming to reach her cheekbones and the hollows behind her blue eyes. She looked at the brilliant sunset that promised a good day tomorrow, framed by newly leaved trees. Crickets had begun to sing for the first time and, here and there, a bird chattered to itself.

From the front of the house came the voices of her father and his new bride. Hilda shifted her foot in order to lean more comfortably, hoping they would not stop to talk to her.

A soft touch startled her—Liesebet, almost seven years old. *It was for you that Father remarried. You need a mother, and I couldn't be more than a sister, even if I tried. Will she love you as much as Ma did? Does she love Pa as much as Ma did? Does Pa love her as much as he loved Ma?*

The child had been asking something. "I'm sorry," Hilda said. "What did you say?"

"I was a good girl today, wasn't I? I didn't fidget at all."

"Yes, you were a good girl. You're growing up. But you ought to change out of your new dress."

Liesebet thought about it and was about to go into the house when she brightened. "You didn't change either. Why should I change if you don't, just because you're fifteen? I won't dirty it."

"You'd better. She wouldn't like it if you got something on it. And I'm almost sixteen."

"I don't care. If you can wear your new dress, I can too. Besides, it's not so pretty. It's not nearly as pretty as the one Ma made me, and I wear that at home even if I don't want to."

Funny how Liesebet remembers Ma. She thinks Ma made prettier things too. She'd rather have Ma too. "You'd better change. I'll change too. We have to do some things differently now."

"Is she really our ma now, or did he only marry her?"

"Pa married her, so that makes her our *muttah*[4] now—not our *ma*."

Liesebet settled her elbows on her knees, which she had braced far apart. "Did he marry her because our mama died?"

"In a way, yes."

"Why did Ma die—did she die so he could marry Muttah?"

"No. No. She died because she was very sick. Too sick to get well, so God took her," Hilda answered. She thought of her offer to God. *The offer God—who knows our every thought—didn't listen to, or agree to.* Her stomach lurched, remembering.

"Is she better now?"

"Yes, she is well. And in Heaven with Jesus and the angels."

"Where is Heaven?"

"Liesebet, you're asking questions you already know the answer to. You know it's somewhere in the sky. Where everyone who dies and is saved goes to."

"Then I wish *I* could be saved and die and be with her."

"Don't say that. It's a sin to say that. You won't die until God decides you should die," Hilda said, thinking of her own wish.

Liesebet was silent and picked at a scab on her knee. "Are you glad that Pa married Muttah?"

"I guess so. Yes, of course." Hilda felt a stab, trying to say what she knew she had to say to her little sister. If she could only pack her things, and Liesebet's, and get along by themselves, or maybe go to live with John. Except that wouldn't be a good life either. John was married since about six months ago.

"I'm not glad. I don't like her. She made me sit next to her in church last Sunday and I wanted to sit with you. Why did Pa marry *her*?"

"You mustn't say that. She's nice, and she wants you to love her. She said that, you know—remember? And you promised."

"James said she's my *step*mother, and he said stepmothers are wicked and cruel. He said she'd probably beat me because his mother said so."

"No, she won't beat you, especially if you're a good girl. Besides, nobody *beats* in our family."

"Hilda, why *did* Pa marry her?"

Why did he? Hilda tried to take the deep breath she had been trying to breathe all afternoon but found something still keeping her from it. She

---

4 A formal name for "mother." More formal than "ma."

prayed a little to herself, hoping that she would be able to say the things she hadn't quite taught herself to believe.

The child sat still and waited for Hilda to tell a story that would be comforting and happy and true. She would be able to tell James, and he would tell his mother. And maybe Muttah would learn to sew things as pretty as Ma had.

It was good that the sun had almost set. Flowers nearby were losing their color. Seeing that, Hilda knew her own lack of color would not be evident to her little sister, who always mirrored her attitudes and feelings. It gave her the words with which to start. She decided to start with the months after Ma died, and she had to do the work Ma had always done. She told of the days when Pa had come in from fieldwork or from a visit to people of his congregation and found her not finished with the work she had set out to do. How he tried to be patient with them all. She mentioned that he started the long lonely prayers he prayed at their daily devotions, both morning and evening.

Then Hilda said to her, "Remember how attached you were to your doll, until you lost it in the woods? You couldn't stop crying until I wrapped a corn cob in a blanket so you could pretend it was a doll. That was like Pa's loneliness after Ma died. He had love he wanted to give someone, not the kind of love he can give us. So he had to find another wife to love, and now he can be happy again."

Almost as if she hadn't been listening, Liesebet kept on with her questions. "Did Pa preach at the wedding?"

In a way, Hilda wished Liesebet had been allowed to attend the wedding. Pa had said something about her not being able to behave, and that she might get a big impression from it. Now she had to be told many things. *Does it really make a difference to her, or is it just a story?* "No, Pa didn't preach, because he was the bridegroom. Pa just walked in with Muttah, and when they got to the front of the church, Brother Schmidt asked them a few questions. Then the choir sang, and I recited a poem, and then Reverend Schmidt preached about husbands loving their wives and wives obeying their husbands, and then he married Pa and Muttah."

Liesebet sat still for a while. "Is that all?"

"That's almost all." *Isn't it enough?* Hilda wondered, but she added, "Then we all went to the dining hall to eat."

"Was it good? What did you have?"

"I hardly remember. I was too excited to eat much, but they had potato salad, ham, pickles, coffee. You know, what they have for Children's Day dinner."

"Did Pa and Muttah eat there too?"

"Yes, they sat at a special table so the people could see them and wish them well."

"Then what happened?"

"You know the rest. We all came home here, or rather all the relatives came, to visit and welcome the new bride into the family. That's when you said your little piece."

"Is Muttah going to stay with us always?"

"Yes, of course. She's our muttah now."

"Is she going to cook for us and go to church with us, and sleep in Pa's room, and do I have to kiss her when I go to bed?"

A mosquito bit Hilda's arm. She let it bite, feeling an enjoyment from the little pinprick, knowing it was bloating itself with a red drop of her blood. Then, with her hand, she slowly crushed it and felt the wetness under her finger. She stood up, removing the support against which Liesebet had been leaning. "We'll have to be going in now. It's getting late, and the mosquitoes are getting hungry. We'll get used to Muttah here, Liesebet, and we won't even think about it anymore."

Helping Liesebet into her nightgown, and hearing her prayers as she had done since Ma died, Hilda wished she could believe what she had told Liesebet. But knowing—hoping—that did not make the hurt less now. She blew out the lamp and was about to leave the room when she impulsively reached down to give Liesebet one more hug. With a start, she realized the child was silently crying. There seemed to be nothing to say.

*   *   *

It was only a few minutes to the place where the creek widened and deepened into a small bathing hole. Ma used to get water from here to wash clothes when the cistern water was low, and she didn't know Hilda and John had come here to swim after they were supposed to be in bed. Or if she knew, she didn't say anything. It was several years since Hilda had come here to swim, or even to look at it much. The hole hadn't changed during the years. It was always full in spring and almost dry in fall; now it was still full from the melted winter snows and the recent spring rains.

Hilda looked at it for a while, trying to pretend she was thirteen again and that Ma was at home going to sleep, thinking she and John were in their beds. Maybe if John was here it would be possible to pretend. Except John lived miles away and hadn't even come for their father's wedding.

The water felt cool on Hilda's toes. She let one foot sink into the silky mud as she arched her other foot. It made the tired ache disappear.

For a minute, she wished she would fall and soak mud into the fabric of her new dress, specially made for Pa's wedding. She hadn't changed out of it after all. Perhaps it would be ruined, and she would not have to wear it again. However, she removed it carefully and laid it neatly on the soft green grass nearby. Then the cooling water played its way up her limbs, replacing the humid warmth of the air; as she lowered herself slowly, she felt the calm of relaxation for the first time that day. Without convulsive sobs, and without pain, she allowed the tears to come.

She floated on her back; through the moisture of her tears, she looked at the sparkling stars. *Up there*, she thought, *is Ma. Is she looking down? Can she see me? Does she think about my offer to bargain with God? Why didn't God respond to my proposal? How can I believe in a God who doesn't reply? How can I now give my heart to Jesus? I can't.*

She shivered as she waited for her body to dry before she dressed again in her new dress. Her hair hung dripping on her neck, though she had wrung and shaken it; she hoped it would not show on the dress after it dried.

She walked slowly to make the walk home seem longer, and she soon reached the back door of their newly remodeled house that had been built for Ma; the house Ma had had the chance to live in after so many years in the old house, with its uneven floors and drafty walls. It had been so much fun to move the furniture into each room as it was ready, and then help Ma move into her new kitchen.

How happy Ma looked then, when she saw the new cook-stove, which was our surprise to her. Then we all knew Ma would soon get better. She had been better too, until she got pregnant again. Then, just as Grosspa Heldin said—if she got pregnant once more, she'd die—she did die. Hilda found herself asking again, *Why did God make her get pregnant?* But she stopped herself as she remembered her father's answer when she asked him that question once. "It was God's will and we must not question it." *Just the same*, she wondered, *why did Grosspa, who was just as religious as Pa—and a doctor—say Ma shouldn't get pregnant? I wish I hadn't heard that conversation.*

The sky seemed to be becoming lighter again, and Hilda thought vaguely that the sun might be rising soon. In a minute, however, she realized it was the moon, now slightly past the full point, and she soon found herself completely illuminated and almost warmed from the light of it. She looked at the summer kitchen now, almost imagining Ma calling for her to come help.

Years ago—maybe just months but it seemed like years—she had liked to sit outside and look at the stars, and it seemed as though Ma would tell her it was time to go to bed just when her imagination was taking her beyond the Big Dipper. Later, she had always come inside without being called, and still later, there had been no Ma to call.

There, beyond the summer kitchen, was the shortcut she and John always took to the district school. John was lucky to be a boy, because he had been able to go to school much more than she. It might have been different if Ma hadn't been sickly. But maybe not, because when she was twelve and Pa discovered that the schoolteacher was male and only eighteen years old, Pa had kept her back from school. Did he think she would fall in love with the teacher?

It had been fun to play and talk with children her age there, some she didn't see at the Meadow Church. Also, she was able to read many books available only at school.

Ma had helped her learn to read the primer, *Die Fibel*, and to memorize some verse in it. She especially liked two poems: "Fuchs, du hast die Ganz gestohlen"[5] and "Im Winter, wenn es frieret."[6] She helped Hilda practice writing the ornate German script. Ma hadn't had much education herself, but she had done well in helping her and John over those first humps of alphabet and vocabulary. It wasn't long before they were able to read to her those tales of fancy or of religion, which Hilda's mother had read so often. When Pa was not out on a call, and the evenings were not given to discussions of farming or of parish problems, Ma took out the big parlor Bible and, as she read, she translated into Low German favorite stories that she knew so well. Almost invariably they would ask her to repeat that same story when she finished it because she told it so well. But, with a little laugh, she would answer that she would, but not today. When the sun sank too low to read by, she taught them songs they could sing together until it was necessary to light the kerosene lamp, which she would turn up to make it possible for them to read after sundown.

Hilda pictured the scene around the table. *John, trying so hard to look grown up, and little Liesebet, deep in her cradle, kicking the foot of her cradle so only her feet were visible.* She tried to picture them as if all the sisters and brothers who had died had been there too, but she could not imagine their being anything but funny-looking, undersized babies.

Ma. What a friend she was. I could ask her any questions, even trifling, unimportant ones, and she always answered with respect, as if I was old enough to deserve respect. But she never talked about having babies. I guess I never asked her.

Beggar came silently to the doorstep, not wagging his tail or even sniffing the ground. Ma had named him; before he had a name, she had often given Hilda or John a crust of bread with the words, "Give the beggar at the door a crust." Soon his name became "Beggar." He sat a moment, looking across the yard, almost in imitation of Hilda; then, just as quietly, he walked away.

A sense of satisfaction came as the spasms of sobs and tears shook her

---

5   Fox, you have stolen the goose.
6   In winter, when it's freezing.

recently thinner body. She let them come voicelessly. Then there was a hand on her shoulder, saying nothing. Without being able to see that it was her father, whose hand she recognized, she found her way to the room she shared with Liesebet. She looked into the back of her Bible and fingered the bit of cloth from Ma's last dress.

*   *   *

Awake, Leah heard Reverend Heldin quietly close the door of his bedroom after him. The bed was comfortable enough. The room was warm enough. She wondered whether she would sleep this night. So many things to think about.

Why didn't John and Marie come to our wedding? Said they were too busy with farm work. Huh. One day they could have given me—or at least their father.

And that Hilda. Doesn't meet my eyes when she talks to me. Hasn't said anything off-putting. Does what she's told to do. Then leaves for her room.

Liesebet? Seems to be afraid. I'm not sure if she's afraid of me, or just afraid. Shies away like a rabbit. Follows Hilda around. They call me Muttah. Formal. Will I ever be "Ma" to them?

Buried under these thoughts was more frank unease. Leah had never before been with—lain with—a man. She had never seen an undressed adult man. Oh, she had seen the little boys when they had accidents at school and had to be cleaned and have their trousers changed. But that wasn't the same. Once, in a library book, she saw a picture of a statue named David, but she had closed the book quickly for fear that she would be seen looking at it.

She decided to be firm with herself. *I'll make it somehow.*

*   *   *

She found she slept after all. Morning brought a new day. The first day of her marriage. It wasn't so bad, she thought.

Would she remember this night? Would she always remember how he came to bed wearing a calf-length nightshirt? New. It still had the fold-creases from its package. He said something like *"gode nacht,"* and she wondered if he meant that she should turn over and go to sleep. However, he lay next to her, face up, not touching. She waited. Somewhere, in the next room, a clock ticked. Outside, crickets chirped, and a night owl called. Would it chase after the crickets?

When he didn't move, Leah turned to her side. "Are you asleep?"

"No. I don't want to bother you."

"You aren't bothering me. We're married."

She remembered, *Then he turned to face me, and I could feel his manhood*

16

between our bodies, through his nightshirt and my gown. He made a little sound, like a chuckle, or he could have been clearing his throat. And I answered with a matching sound. He knew what to do, and he did it slowly and gently. And I figured out what to do.

What should I call him now? I can't call him "Reverend Heldin" like before.

He doesn't call me anything. Yet. At least not "Miss Loewen" anymore.

I'll call him "Father" when I have children.

CHAPTER FOUR: 1909

Strange child, Reverend Heldin had thought when he found Hilda crying on the back doorstep. As he thought on occasions before that. Now, again, he studied her. Hoping she was not aware of his watching her, he held his *Quarterly* higher and pretended to read it.

She was drying dishes—first one side of a plate and then the other side. He didn't blame her for following her old pattern, of placing the plates on the second shelf where Katherine had always kept them. After all, it was a habit. *But I can see how much more efficient it is to keep them on the bottom shelf, as Leah planned. After all, what difference does it make? There's no need to cry about being reminded to change things.*

The child shouldn't be so set in her ways; she's acting like a settled, mature woman resenting a stranger in her kitchen. She does work hard. She's almost grown up enough to be a wife and mother soon herself. If—when—she gets married we'll miss her help, both indoors and outdoors.

He tried to remember what it was like being her age. *I'd been in this country almost five years when I was going on seventeen. I had to get used to big things like different climate and landscape. Even farming methods were different. I worked hard too. Of course, my parents helped me get used to the new life, but she has at least me—her father—and a stepmother who's doing her best.*

Leah's a good woman. My luck is remarkable—finding a mature woman, capable in her housework and pleasant mannered. God truly answered my prayer...

Reverend Heldin watched his wife working quietly and efficiently. She carried herself well, though she was thirty and had not had a child before. He counted on his fingers, wondering, *Isn't the baby due about now? Well, she hasn't had any cramps so far—at least she hasn't said. I surely hope she'll have less trouble bearing children than Katherine had. Hope the baby will be a son and, this time, a son who'll stay with me to help keep up the farm work. And express an interest in the farming of souls. Not that John isn't religious enough.*

Liesebet has adapted to the new life well. It's good that she's turned to Leah as a mother; the relationship between her and Hilda is now more like sisters than like a mother and child. She even told Hilda to stop bossing her; I heard her say, "You're not my boss."

Hilda will be all right soon too, if only she would talk more. It takes so much longer when people keep to themselves.

The dishes were done. Hilda folded the dishtowel neatly, hung it on the old rack, and walked immediately to her room. *A little stooped. Reads too much. How should I talk to her to make her understand, to accept her new mother?*

"Have you finished?" His wife smiled at him; was it tiredly?

"No, I've been thinking. I can't find a topic to talk about Sunday. I want to talk about something that will interest people. That they will discuss, and think about all week. Something they don't hear all the time." He closed the *Quarterly* he hadn't started to read.

"How about the 'Love Chapter' in *Corinthians*?"

"I spoke about that already this year." He bowed his head over his Bible, hoping she wouldn't talk just now. *She's not able to give me ideas the way Katherine always did.*

She sat down heavily and picked up her crocheting. It was to be a cap, to train the baby's ears back so they wouldn't stand out.

*   *   *

Glad when it was chore time, Reverend Heldin inhaled the sweet smell of the fresh hay that pervaded the barn. He had put it up himself. Hilda helped, but she didn't have the strength to do as much as John had. Leah, in her condition, could not help.

A few stanchions away, Hilda silently milked Rosena, her usual cow. Reverend Heldin milked old Susibelle. With no flies to annoy the cows now, he could concentrate on his thinking instead of on avoiding the switching of her tail.

The pail filled gradually with foaming milk, becoming warm against his legs. When it was full and the cow could give no more, he poured half of it into a clean container for the cream to rise. He gave some to the waiting cats and dog. The cats drank in turn, each one pushing her head between the bowl and the other cat. Beggar had his own bowl; he had learned not to drink out of the cats' pan. Then he offered the rest to the calf, teaching him to drink—by submerging his hand in the pail, he gave the calf his finger to suckle. Eventually, the calf wouldn't need his finger any more. The calf—it didn't have a name yet—had recently been weaned from its mother; now it had stopped its continual bawling.

When the Reverend Heldin started to pick up his containers of milk to take to the house, he remembered the waiting horses. They were quiet, blowing small plumes of steam from their nostrils as they nuzzled around in their oats. With their sensitive muscles, they twitched away imaginary flies and insects and, when he rubbed and scraped their already shining bodies, they held very still.

It was later than usual when he finished his evening chores; yet when he started for the house, he realized he still had no inspiration for tomorrow's sermon.

"It's late. Did you have trouble? I thought of coming to the barn to see," Leah said, standing up immediately when he came in. She rolled up her crocheting to start preparing for evening devotions.

"I couldn't think of a topic."

"But you always have one ready before this," was her answer, as if that would make him ready for tomorrow.

"Maybe I *will* use an old one. One I preached some years ago. No one will remember."

Hilda had come in quietly. "But, Pa, you *never* use old sermons. I know the Lutherans have something they call a 'lectionary' so every three years they can use the same text. But we don't. You told me that once." Before he could reply, she continued, "How about 'God answers prayers'? Or, 'Deals God makes with his followers'?"

Leah spoke up. "Respect your father, Hilda."

As if he hadn't heard his wife, he turned to his daughter. "Hilda, what makes you think of that?"

"In the Bible, it declares that God made covenants. With Moses. And Noah. And Joseph."

He replied, "Those are topics I might speak on some day, but there isn't time to think them out before tomorrow. And just because I haven't ever reused a sermon's no reason for me not to do it tomorrow. Maybe it won't hurt people to hear something more than once." He pulled out his Bible and started to read aloud before they could think of more to say to him.

He ended the reading, a portion of the Old Testament; then they prayed in turn, in thanks for one more day and in preparation for the next.

*　　　*　　　*

As they were praying, Hilda felt Muttah looking at her. Respect, she'd said. How could I talk with Pa and show the respect I feel? Why would my remark be disrespectful? Maybe if he took my suggestion, his sermon could explain why God didn't respond to my offer to give my heart to Jesus.

She decided not to voice her opinion again; still, she was perplexed. *I hate her!* she thought with a momentary feeling of relief but then was horrified by that feeling. Quickly, she substituted a silent prayer, hoping it would neutralize what she had thought. Then it was bedtime.

*   *   *

When the water broke, there wasn't time to send for the village midwife to help Reverend Heldin deliver his bride's first child. "Hilda, lend me a hand!" he called. "I need you to help here."

Groggy and pale, awakened by his urgent call, Hilda came from her room to hear her stepmother moaning, still calling him "Reverend Heldin" while cursing her father. Hilda had never heard such words before, not even in town where there were rough characters. She stood, arms at her sides. What did he want her to do? She wished she hadn't eaten supper the night before.

Hilda didn't know Pa had never witnessed the birth of a child. For every baby born to Katherine, alive or not, he had been sent out of the room—even out of the house—so he wouldn't hear Katherine scream, if she did. "Get a clean basin, and some hot water. First wash your hands really clean. Bring scissors. Some clean string. Grocery string is fine—but not if it's been on the floor."

He sat down, ashen-faced and sweaty. She followed his directions, not looking at her stepmother's face, trying not to see what her hands were doing between those thick legs. The baby came out, lustily crying, turning a bright red. Alive. A boy, Hilda guessed, though she had never seen a boy or man before.

"Now tie the cord close to his body. Then snip the cord. That's all."

Hilda held the baby, wrapped him in a clean old blanket. He was wet and bloody.

Her stepmother groaned again, and out came another bundle—not a baby this time. Quickly, Hilda handed the baby to her father—his father. "Afterbirth," Pa called it. "Just collect it in the basin."

It was finished, Hilda's responsibility. Leah took over, giving directions. "Wash the baby. We'll call him 'Hermann,' after my father." Then she took Hermann into her bed and put him to her breast.

Hilda returned to her bed, next to Liesebet, who stirred a bit and kept on sleeping, but Hilda lay awake.

*   *   *

Leah thought about the previous evening's interchange with Hilda. *That girl. She always does what I and her father tell her to do—work I mean. Never says much. Nevertheless, I can see in her eyes that she doesn't like me… I don't care. I shouldn't care. You can't make someone like you, but you can demand respect… She sure did help with Hermann, though. What a sissy Reverend Heldin turned out to be. Proud of being a healer. A healer of bodies and a healer of souls. And I've got a son. My Hermann… From now on, I'm going to call Reverend Heldin "Father."*

*   *   *

Reverend Heldin left the house to tend the cows and horses, forgetting that he and Hilda had done chores earlier. He gulped the outside air and gazed at the stars that appeared to be flying behind clouds that looked stationary. In the barn, he checked for anything or everything that needed to be done. All was still. The cows were quietly chewing their cuds; some were lying on the fresh straw he had put down. One of the horses blew "fpbfpbfpb" with his flabby lips. He thought of letting them out, but it was cold outside; their water tank would have ice on it. Then he realized there was nothing to do.

I have another son, he repeated to himself. *Born alive.* When he returned to the house, he found Leah and the baby asleep. Since he still couldn't think of an appropriate topic for the morning's sermon, he decided not to preach that day at all, in recognition of the birth of his son. That ought to be reason enough.

He thought of his daughter. *Not yet seventeen. Delivered her brother. Half-brother. Stood between her stepmother's legs. Saw what she saw. Did what she did in my presence. Did what I couldn't do.*

CHAPTER FIVE: 1910

An elegant team trotted slowly with their shiny, almost-new surrey, as if showing off for a Sunday role. When they turned, they came into view of Liesebet playing with her half-brother in the sand pile Pa had prepared for them. Hermann had recently learned to walk; he ignored the newcomer, for he was busy filling his moist mouth with fine, silky sand.

Liesebet got up to run for the house, but noting Hermann's appetite, she yanked his hand from his mouth before darting toward the kitchen steps.

"Hilda, someone's here!" she announced. "Who is it—should I tell him Pa and Muttah went away?"

Hilda didn't answer immediately. She peered out from behind new curtains to see a young gentleman pick up the screaming, sand-covered Hermann, who added thrashing kicks to his verbal protest at being left by his sister and was now being grabbed hold of by someone he didn't know.

"Go out and get Hermann. Tell the man that Pa will be home late tonight." Hilda realized she should probably go out herself but felt held back by the sight of the careful grooming of the man's horses, and of the man himself.

"I'm scared. Who is he?"

"Go! Hermann's crying and you said you'd take care of him. It's only Abe Geppert. He did business with Pa last week."

Liesebet went. Hilda watched her eight-year-old sister lift her crying, chunky, year-old brother from the sand pile where Abe had set him. A heavy load for a skinny girl. He was still crying, now in anger.

The man was speaking and smiling at Liesebet, who dug her toes into the sun-warmed sand. While he spoke, Hermann flavored the batter of sand in his mouth with his forefinger and then went to chase the cat that dared look out from under the kitchen steps.

They were coming to the back door. Liesebet called, but she did not come in herself, "He says he wants to talk to you."

Hilda thought of chores she would have to do by herself tonight, and that she would have to begin soon, before the cows' distended udders started dripping milk. Perhaps he wouldn't stay long.

"I think you remember me, don't you?" He didn't look as suave and confident as he had through the window. He held his hand behind his back, but not before Hilda noticed that the pores were lined with stubborn work grime. His hair was oiled and combed, not accustomed to the kind of grooming the expensive horses had. His shoes gleamed and, except for the shoulders, the suit fit him well. The shoulders, too, would fit after he became a little older and finished maturing completely.

He straightened and took a formal pose. "I am Abe Geppert. I was here last week to buy steers from your father. I saw you carrying fuel cobs to the house."

"Yes, I know," Hilda answered. "Are they all right? Pa won't be home until tonight. He and Muttah are doing their Sunday visitations"

"Yes, they're all right. They're fine. But I came to see you." His ruddy complexion deepened and spread up to his white forehead, not tanned because, like all farmers, he usually wore a straw hat.

Slowly, Hilda realized why he had come. Before she decided whether she was pleased or not, she thought, *He's my first beau. This is what it's like.* Then her mind went on, blending stories she had read while her parents assumed she was studying her Sunday school lesson, with her own dreams of what might be someday. *Will he take me riding on his surrey, and tell me about his work, his crops, his horses? And will he kiss me, and will I like it? Then will he marry me, and will Muttah let me have a white dress with a few ruffles if I don't put any lace on them?*

He spoke again. "You have a nice farm here. Your father has a nice herd of cattle. Your yard is nice too."

"Yes, he works hard. We all work." Hilda realized she had never thought about her work in this way and wondered why she couldn't find something else to say. "We work hard too. All farmers work hard, I guess. Nevertheless, it is the best life."

Hilda saw him looking for a place to sit. "Come into the parlor and sit down," she said, not without a qualm, for her parents did not open the parlor except for their best entertaining when there were no children. It was the room that held the family's finest things: the pump organ, Pa's rocking chair, and their two upholstered chairs. The shiny brass samovar, brought all the way from the Ukraine, stood on the center table that had claw-feet gripping glass balls. Doilies Ma once finely crocheted decorated the organ, tabletops, and the backs of the chairs.

Hilda knew that courting must be done in the parlor and hoped Pa would understand and not mind. If he didn't mind, and spoke to Muttah about it, Hilda knew she wouldn't mind either.

She looked down at her dress, her Sunday dress that she hadn't changed out of after church. It was appropriate for the front room. But if she had known she would have a guest, she would have re-combed her hair. Anyway, she was wearing shoes, though she had changed from her good ones. As she sat, she tucked her feet under her chair.

After he sat down and said they had a nice parlor, Liesebet came in, weighted down by the hefty Hermann. "He's wet his pants again." She was about to bring him to Hilda, for it took Liesebet a long time to change the wriggly boy.

"You know what to do."

Her little sister now struggled into their parents' bedroom, where Hermann performed his usual crying protest.

Abe's previous blush hadn't yet left his face. He spoke quickly. "I had my twenty-first birthday last week. That was what the steers were for. My pa promised me three steers for when I would come of age. I had to pick them out myself, so if there would be anything wrong, I would learn to pick out steers."

"You said they were fine." Hilda wished they could discuss a book maybe, or religion, or the way the sun looked when it set, or maybe even fishing.

"Oh, yes, they're fine. But I don't know much about them yet. Your father is a good man, and he sold me good steers." He now held his grimy hands folded in front of him, between his knees.

Hilda saw her chance. "Pa is good because he is religious."

Abe added, "I'm religious too. I try to be good too."

"Some people are better than others, even if they are religious." Hilda wished she could remember Pa's answer when Ma said that.

"Not really," he responded. "In God's eye, no one is better than anyone else, as long as they believe in the Lord Jesus Christ as their own personal savior."

There was nothing more to say; Hilda regretted bringing up the subject and dreaded his next question that she knew he would ask.

Liesebet came in, letting Hermann toddle his way across the parlor floor toward Hilda.

"Are you saved?" Abe asked.

"Yes." Hilda felt Liesebet's concentration on her answer and did not say more, though she wanted to say more—what, she didn't know, just so it was more and so it would tell him exactly what she thought.

Then, because her first yes had not been spontaneous, she lied again. "Yes," she said, this time more definitely. As soon as she said it and knew she had lied, she wondered whether she had really lied. She had thought so often about giving her heart to Jesus, and had prayed so often to him—or God—or both, that she felt as if she actually had a kind of relationship with Jesus. Or with them. A dull ache returned to Hilda's stomach; it was an ache she often felt when she thought about salvation.

Abe seemed satisfied with her answer but unnerved by its unembellished brevity. With his hands still folded in front of him, he offered another subject. "I hear you brought your little brother into the world. I hear you did a good job. People say you may be the next local midwife." Then he blushed again.

Having been allowed to stay in the room, Liesebet enthusiastically volunteered, "Ya, she did practically the whole job!" And Hermann echoed, "Ya."

Overcome and humiliated, Hilda stood, took her little brother by the arm, and looking at Liesebet with her sternest look, walked them both out of the room. *What nerve of him! It's not a subject for mixed company. Or in front of my little sister and brother!*

When she returned, Abe was standing, still red-faced. "Um, if you have to do chores, I can help you. Pa said I don't have to come home in time for chores tonight."

Hilda saw his blush. *How could he be comfortable talking with me if he doesn't have sisters? He doesn't know girls. Maybe that's why he's so red-faced talking with me, even though he's grown up and twenty-one. I wonder how long he planned this visit. I never noticed him before. Has he been watching me in church? Where did he get the idea of calling on me?*

He spoke, "Um, how many cows do you milk?"

"Six," Hilda said, and accepted his offer. "I really could do them all by myself."

*   *   *

Watching Abe, who had shed his coat and, with rolled-up Sunday shirt sleeves, was forking over some newly threshed straw bedding for the calves, she tried to imagine him twenty years from now. His family must be rich to give him three steers and have those fine horses. So he will be well-off too.

Still, the picture did not come. She wished it to come, and inside herself said a little prayer that he would ask her to marry him so he could help her be able to say yes honestly to his question of whether she was saved.

Hilda and Abe had both milked since they were small children, and because the cows were soft milkers,[7] the chore was quickly done. Not until she had given the pets their due of bottom milk did Hilda notice Liesebet, who had come to the barn.

"You have on your Sunday dress for milking," she stated.

"Where did you leave Hermann?" Hilda was glad for the chance to change the subject, which was, this time, more important than what she was wearing.

"He went to sleep on the parlor floor. So I picked him up and put him in his cradle. But what will Muttah say when she sees you have on your Sunday dress?"

"She won't know unless you tell her."

"She said you couldn't have another new dress this year—you know she did. She said so just yesterday."

It was true. A glance at Abe showed Hilda that he was trying to appear busy and not listening. She did not say more, and Hilda decided to wait until he left before she bargained with Liesebet not to speak of her dress to Muttah.

He carried the heavy pails to the milk house for her but did not come into the house when she opened the door for him. "I gotta go before it gets dark. Will you shake hands with me?"

She gave him her hand.

"May I come again?" he asked.

"Yes," she answered, and she watched him untie his shiny, eager horses and climb into his buggy. He turned once to wave, and then his surrey turned off the driveway.

Liesebet was waiting on the back doorstep, where they usually sat until the twilight was completely hidden behind the trees. They would discuss church, or Liesebet's school, or any other questions Liesebet had, like growing up. Tonight, however, Hilda felt too restless to sit, and the knowledge of what Liesebet would ask about Abe's visit had not brought with it knowledge of what Hilda would say in response. She hardly knew what she herself thought.

"Did you undress Hermann?"

"No, I didn't want to wake him."

Hilda went to the baby's cradle. It made sense; yet in spite of Liesebet's protests, Hilda slowly undid Hermann's clothes and extended the work of putting him to bed until the elder Heldins returned home.

After they put aside their traveling wraps, Pa and Muttah decided that it was time for evening devotions and Liesebet's bedtime. They were tired and did not mind when Hilda excused herself to do some reading in her room.

---

7   A soft milker has soft, plump teats; milk flows easily.

*　　　*　　　*

No one said a word at breakfast, except about the work of the beginning day. Hilda remembered that she had had a visitor, but she pushed it aside. It was not until afternoon, after Muttah, Hermann, and Liesebet were taking their naps and Hilda had begun a new book, that Pa sat next to her on the bench.

He did not speak immediately. Then he said, "Why didn't you tell us of your visit yesterday? Why must we ask you of it first?"

"I didn't think you would be concerned. Did Liesebet tell?"

"That should not interest you. What should interest you is telling me about it and not keeping it from me." He was well used to speaking of personal matters to the souls of his congregation, yet not to his young daughter.

"I'm sorry, Pa. I would have told you, only I didn't know what to tell."

"The truth. That is all I want to know." The expression on his face was one Hilda had never seen before.

It was bewildering. Hilda started thinking over Abe's coming, *his picking up the baby, his rough grimy hands.* His slow talk, and the only question she could remember—*are you saved? His mentioning my part in Hermann's birth—did he think I'm grown up enough to know all the facts of life? Did he think I would talk about it with him?*

"He came, and he picked Hermann up because he was crying. Then Liesebet told him to come in, and he came in. Then we talked a little bit, and he said the steers you sold him were fine. And after we had talked a while, he helped me do the chores because it was time. After chores, he shook my hand and asked if he could come again. Then he went home. That's all." Try as she might, Hilda could think of nothing more that she wanted to add.

"Did you sit in the parlor?" Reverend Heldin shifted in his hard chair.

"Yes. It's for company, isn't it?" Hilda knew she shouldn't have added that, out of respect for her father, but Muttah wasn't there to hear.

"Of course it is. Some day, when you start keeping company, you may use it every Sunday. But you aren't keeping company with Abe. Or is that what he wants?"

Hilda knew that was what Abe wanted, but she said only, "I think that is what he wants. I don't know him very well. He said he is saved."

"Of course he is saved. He is most likely a good boy. But I have to tell you a little bit about him. There is trouble in his family. A stain. His parents committed a great sin by marrying. It can result in problems for future generations. Muttah and I would not like for you to marry into that family."

In spite of the way she truly felt, Hilda found herself defending poor Abe with almost the words he had used himself: "God makes no distinction between people so long as they are saved." Inside her own soul, Hilda wished with all her being that she could say without a doubt that she, herself, was saved. *Washed perfectly whole.*

Reverend Heldin gave Hilda the best answer his Bible offered. "Yes, in the eyes of God, those who accept him are *all* precious in his sight. But we are human. We are not God. We must make distinctions sometimes for our own good and protection. We must obey Psalm 1 that says, 'Blessed is the man that walketh not in the counsel of the ungodly, nor sitteth in the seat of sinners,' and so on."

"He said he is saved."

"He has a weakness in his inheritance. If you keep company with him, and marry him after you are of age, you will be going against the wishes of your father and muttah. We want you to have a happy life; we are older than you. You must learn from our experience."

"I shall do as you wish, Pa." Hilda rushed from the room, but when she came into the privacy of her room, she did not cry. Instead, she felt a great relief, the relief of having a choice lifted from her and with it the responsibility that would inevitably accompany a choice, should that choice be the wrong one.

*   *   *

The following days were happy, and Hilda forgot the visit of last Sunday, as well as the promised one for the following Sunday. Not until she saw Abe in church did she remember her duty to ask him not to come, and she waited for the privacy of the after-church visiting period to talk with him.

He was flushed with hurt. "Is that how you feel? Do you always do what your parents say?"

Hilda felt a sudden impulse to marry him, simply for his sake. Yet she was grateful for Pa's words and remained firm. "I respect the wishes of my father. If he does not bless my plans, my friends, I will not be happy."

That should have been the end of their conversation. But when he looked at her through his pain, saying, "I'll see you in church," strange electricity struck through Hilda's entire body, touching even her fingertips, the backs of her ears, and the heels of her feet. She thought of Abe's words a long time, though to her parents she merely said, "I told Abe not to come any more," and continued in weeks that were happier. She did not try to think why.

*   *   *

Leah decided not to voice her thoughts. *So she's got a beau. Somebody is interested in her. Seems like an all-right young man. Wonder what Father has against him. Won't tell me, even when I ask directly. Some family trouble, he says.*

29

I can think of all sorts of trouble—some awful, some not so bad. Insanity? Feeble minds? Incest? Robbery? Murder? Just odd?

Whatever. They're church people. Even members of our church. For sure, he's good enough for Hilda. She's not so hoity toity that she can marry anybody she wants. Even with all her frilly dresses. Better to take what she can get. Then she can move out from under my thumb and do as she pleases. Not that she's been under my thumb. Just does what I ask her, no more than that. Tries not to bump into me in our—my—kitchen. Leah sighed.

CHAPTER SIX: 1910

"You could send for Hilda," Marie repeated to John, who was frightened at the imminent birth of their first child. Neither had had much contact with young children, and they knew little about labor, except for the births of the farm animals.

Though it was several weeks until the expected arrival of the child, they had to make arrangements so they wouldn't forget something quite important at the last moment. Marie was strong and didn't anticipate trouble, but they wisely decided not to be alone during this, their first time. He might be able to attend to her, from what he knew about animals, but John could not imagine applying his experience of delivering calves to the delivery of a baby—especially his own.

"Hilda's only eighteen. She's my little sister." He could remember so well some of the games they had played when they were children—their swimming naked in the hole at the creek, their whispered discussions of new kittens, and their examination of little Liesebet when she was a new baby. *Now for Hilda to help at the birth of my child? It's embarrassing.*

"She knows about childbirth better than old Mrs. Schmutz. I'd rather have her. Mrs. Schmutz isn't clean. That's why the Wolson baby died of lockjaw[8]—because Mrs. Schmutz used dirty string on the cord. Hilda knows about delivering *and* taking care of new babies. You know she delivered Hermann and also helped take care of him. Besides, I'd also like some help during the first week after, or so." Not used to begging, Marie pled this time, "I really want Hilda."

"Pa might not let her come. He might need her, or he might think she's too young."

"Why, John, you know Hermann came too soon and there wasn't time to

8   Tetanus.

31

get anyone else. You know Hilda did most of the work. She wasn't too young then. And that was a year ago."

"Well, we'll talk about this again later. I have to do chores now. I'll try to think of another older woman who can come over to help."

"Today. Today we have to decide. We've put it off for so long. We have to ask in time so she can make ready." Marie planted herself in front of the doorway, as if to stand siege until John would agree. He picked up his milk pails, set them loudly inside each other, and then slowly pulled his work jacket on over his already thickly-clothed shoulders. He did not look at Marie as he walked toward the door she was guarding; she stepped aside and let him pass.

*   *   *

When Hilda finished reading the letter from John and Marie, she put it down and said nothing. Her father picked it up and read it. At last he said, "I guess you'd better go. After all, he is your brother and my son, even if he did move so far away.

"Liesebet is big enough to do some of your work, and Muttah is stronger now too. You can ride Klaus; he's not too fast, and he'll get you there. Stop at each neighbor's house so you will be sure to get there safely. If it gets dark, you must stop for the night somewhere, but only with people we know. Don't even consider sleeping on a haystack out in a field."

He didn't ask her if she wanted to go, but Hilda remembered their conversation just a week before. She had spoken to him while they were milking. "Pa, I've thought about what I want to do with my life. I want to be a nurse. That way, I can serve God and help other people."

He replied, "Well, we'll have to wait and see. I don't much like for you to leave the farm to go to the town hospital. You would get pale from being inside smelly hospitals instead of out in fresh air that's so much healthier."

"I want to be a country nurse, going to people when they need me."

"You would still have training inside the hospital."

Hilda dared to add, "You objected to my keeping company with Abe. That would have been assurance of my staying on a farm."

He ended the conversation then. "Abe is not the only eligible young man in the congregation."

Hilda was sorry now for bringing up the subject. It interrupted her original idea—of asking Pa whether she could take nurses' training.

*   *   *

Now, though Pa didn't ask whether she wanted to help Marie, he decided she would go. There wasn't much to pack except some everyday clothes and a church dress.

Hilda had ridden spirited, prancing horses of every color, but this time she would ride old Klaus. He was a plodder, never fast, never tricky, never independent, but always sure. His dependability had been proved since he was a young colt, faithfully trotting alongside his mother as she did her harvesting duties. That was why he was the horse Hilda had been allowed to hitch to the plow when she did the plowing. He was patient as she harnessed him in his worn riding saddle, and he calmly opened his mouth for the bit; Hilda noticed that the sides of his mouth were calloused from a lifetime use of a rubbing bit, and his teeth were wearing down.

Hilda hugged her little sister and wiped her tears when she left in the coldness of the early morning. "Don't cry, Liesebet. I won't be gone long. It'll be only a month. At most."

The ride was long. As she was bade, Hilda stopped in at neighbors' homes to give the horse a drink, take a drink herself, and rest her legs that were not used to hugging the round belly of a horse for long periods at a time. But when she neared the Geppert farm she skirted it, hoping there was no one in the field to see her.

Suddenly Klaus stopped short. Startled, Hilda looked to the side; there was Abe, astride a bareback horse, smiling at her. "Hello."

"I didn't see you." Hilda wished he wouldn't be so friendly when there was no point to it.

He looked more poised on his horse than he had been in his Sunday clothes in their parlor. "Why don't you stop in, or are you in an awful hurry? Your horse might need a drink."

"I just stopped a little bit ago. I must get on. I'm going to John's."

"Are you mad at me?" It was a directness Hilda had known from home since she was a child. Now, however, she needed to answer in the same direct way, and she knew of no polite direct answer. "No," she said. She felt as if she should answer more, to make it more comfortable.

Abe pushed on. "Why don't you even want to talk to me? Don't you remember we had a friendly visit that time at your place?"

"I'm sorry. But I have to go on. My horse has now rested, and I want to get to John's before it's dark tonight."

*   *   *

It was slightly after dark when Hilda arrived at John's farm home. She had been there only once before, to help Marie clean the old place shortly after they were married. It had been a job to clean: the old bachelor who had lived there before them had not cared much whether he washed dishes after each use, or that they crusted sour from previous meals, and he hadn't cleaned spilled food off the pantry shelves. The farmyard had also been unkempt; whatever he had dropped stayed where it fell. Now the farm looked almost unfamiliar to Hilda. In the grove of trees, north of the house and around the outbuildings, was evidence of John's industry. There was even a fence encircling the house to keep the chickens out, and to give the native grass a chance to become lush and green in summer.

Somewhere a dog barked; soon it came running from the barn and smelled at the horse, which reached toward the dog with his nose. At the same time, a lamp came moving from one of the windows, past a hall window, and to the front door as Hilda reached it. In its halo, she saw John's face. He looked much older, with shadows outlining new wrinkles.

"I'm here!" Hilda felt almost incapable of walking; her legs did not seem to want to straighten out. She had ridden on past all recent farms in order to make it to her brother's house, and she hoped Pa would not find out.

"Already. Good." John led Klaus away into the barn for his much-needed oats and rest.

The tired Marie had already gone to bed. In whispers, as the door between their bedroom and the dining room was just a curtain, John and Hilda talked a bit. "How's everybody?"

"They are well. Send you their greetings."

"Liesebet? Every time I see her she's bigger."

"You wouldn't notice that so much if you came to church every week."

John looked at his sister and remembered that she used to speak to him quite forwardly—so why not now? "Hilda, I'm glad you came. I miss our frank talks. Sometimes we were just playing, but we also were open with each other."

"I miss you too. I feel lonely sometimes."

He led her to the kitchen where they could sit for a while and drink warm milk with honey. "Tell me what it's like to have a new mother. I haven't met her yet. They were married just when I was very busy planting, and Marie was in her early pregnancy that she lost."

"I didn't know …"

"Ya, well, that isn't something people talk about much. So how is Muttah?"

"She's fine, I think. Tries to be a good wife. Works hard."

"Is she good to you?"

Tears welled in Hilda's eyes. "She tries."

"You can talk to me, Hilda, I'm your brother. Are you happy?"

"She's not Ma. She never can be. She never will be. No matter how hard she tries. If she tries… I just want to get away. I want to be a nurse."

"You want to be a nurse just so you can get away?"

"No, I want to get away. And I want to be a nurse."

"You know, Hilda, since I've been on my own, married to a woman I love deeply, and soon to be a father, I've done a lot of thinking. About our parents. Life as a family. I love Pa, and I loved Ma very much. But I want my family life to be different. I don't want my Marie to have to work as hard as Ma did. To get worn out having babies. I don't like to see my sister working as hard as you are. That is why I don't always go to church, even to hear my father preach. I can consider Sunday a day of rest, even from having to worship."

Since Hilda had nothing to say, he continued. "I hope you know that nurses work very, very hard. Is that the kind of life you want?"

"Well, I'm managing to work hard on the farm, and it's not too bad."

"No matter what you decide to do—nurse, teach, or get married, I hope you find work—or a husband—who helps you have a better life than Ma had. And now you'll get a chance to see whether or not you'll like nursing at all," John said with a wry smile. "Though Marie won't be an average patient. She doesn't like to have people wait on her."

"I hope I won't be in the way." Hilda couldn't help being modest with her big brother; ever since they were children, he had been authority—the leader—and she had submitted, had followed. Now she again studied his new facial lines, and in her mind he became one of another generation. *What caused his "transition"? Was it marriage?* Hilda thought again of marriage for herself.

"Don't worry about being in the way. There'll be too much else to do. And don't worry about nursing. Some nice farmer will come and take that idea out of your head and give you the chance to nurse some babies." John laughed at his own joke.

"I don't think Pa wants me to marry at all."

Surprised, John paid attention to her sudden remark. "Why not? What makes you think so? What's been happening?"

"Abe Geppert seemed interested in me. I don't know him. But I didn't have a chance to find out what he's like. Pa told me of some sin, but he wasn't definite, and I almost wonder whether there really was a reason. He told me not to see Abe again."

"Oh, that," John chuckled. "Yes, that's a funny family."

"John, what's *funny* about them?"

"It's not really *funny*." John stopped a moment and looked hard at his sister. "I guess you're old enough to hear this: Abe's parents are first cousins. He has a couple of brothers who aren't 'all right' in the head. Feeble minded. Not only that, they're deaf and dumb. That's what can happen when cousins marry."

"Are you sure about the brothers? I've never seen them in church."

"They're kept at home. You'll never see them in public. I think one of them actually died a year or two ago."

"But Abe seems to be fine. He looks fine. He talks like a normal person."

"People think it can run in the family. Abe might be all right, but his children might not be."

"So is it a sin to marry your cousin?"

"I think it's against the law, and breaking the law is a sin. Ask Pa."

That, Hilda doubted she'd ever do, or at least not yet.

Their cups were empty and the parlor clock struck. John rose and patted her shoulder. "You'll get lots more chances to meet the right person. Now, you'd better go to bed. You can have the spare bedroom. You know where it is. It might be cold at first, but the featherbeds are there, and you can use what you want. If it will help you go to sleep, you can read one of the books or magazines on the bookcase."

"If I do that, I might want to take it home to finish."

"Fine. Just return it later. Most of those books are Marie's."

*   *   *

Hilda slipped between the featherbeds, closed her eyes, and imagined herself being at home in her own room here, or some day in her own home. She stretched and relaxed, except for the aching of her legs from the stirrups, and the throbbing behind her eyes from squinting against the setting sun. She wondered how she would fit in, here in John and Marie's home. She hoped the baby would not come early, or at least not until she had rested from her ride.

Then she thought again of the change in John. *Is marriage a threshold? Do people, when they cross that threshold, change? Has John really changed, or will I find him tomorrow as he always has been and always will be? Do all people change when they marry?*

She thought of Pa. *Has he, too, changed because of marriage with his new wife? Is that why we don't understand each other now? I'm not sure I know exactly how he's changed. Or how John's changed. He looks different. Maybe after he shaves, he'll be as I remember him. Something about his manner is different too, something I can't see, or name, except his strong feelings about Ma and her hard life.*

The down-filled duvets were warm and comforting. Her tired limbs seemed to melt and diffuse among the feathers. The feeling that she would marry and change some day too melted and didn't matter so much. She gave herself up to sleep.

*　　　*　　　*

Marie had breakfast ready when Hilda woke. While she ate, Marie showed her the layette she had ready: shirts, nightgowns, receiving blankets, and a stack of diapers all neatly hemmed. She had started knitting a sweater, but she was a beginner at knitting and would need some help or advice that she hoped Hilda could give her.

"Furthermore," Marie said, "I think I have had some pains, so maybe the baby will be born soon. They aren't very frequent, and I'm told the first baby takes longer to be born, but maybe we can get things ready—the room and the bed. I think we'll use the narrow bed for the actual birth—it's one we let the hired man use during the harvest—not our double bed. We can cover it with some old sheets and blankets."

The delivery, several days later, was not a difficult one. Hilda's hardest task was to keep John occupied. She kept him heating pail after pail of water that she did not use. Marie, indeed, seemed well in control. She marshaled her strength for pushing, not wasting her breath on outcry. Hilda thought about Muttah's shouts, and determined that, some day, when she had babies she would try to be like Marie.

When John was admiring and complimenting the new mother, Hilda handed him his son, though the baby could have been laid into his waiting cradle. He would be John J. Heldin, whose father was also John J. Heldin, whose father was also John J. Heldin. There was no middle name: the "J" simply represented the father's name.

*　　　*　　　*

After a couple of weeks, the new mother was able to bathe and care for her own baby. Hilda, remembering Liesebet's tears as she left home, asked, "Do you think you can manage without me in a week or so?"

Marie declared, "I love having you here, Hilda, but I'll be able to manage sooner. And I hope you will come often to see how Johnny grows."

The next day, John announced at supper, "I don't like that you should go home by yourself, especially now that the days are shorter and the weather is colder, so I sent word to Mrs. Lober to send one of her boys to go with you. He will come here tomorrow night, and you can start back the day after, early in the morning. He can handle a gun if there should be any wolves or fierce dogs." John gave her a direct look. "He's a decent sort; we've helped each other out plowing and hay making. I like him."

Mrs. Lober, Hilda knew, had a son named Franz. Even so, why should she be accompanied? After all, she had come here by herself. It took only a day. Well, it was arranged. So be it.

As he came into the house, John led Franz to the wash basin, where he bent to wash his hands and smooth back his plenteous dark hair. "This is Franz Lober," John said, leading Hilda toward him and, in giving him her hand to clasp, she noted that his was warm and strong. She felt his hand even after he had released hers.

He ate heartily, saying nothing. *Does he know I cooked the food?* Hilda watched him furtively, but when she noticed his unembarrassed attention on her in return, she concentrated on her own meal and did not dare to look up at him again. Yet she was conscious of the air about him. It enveloped her.

When the meal was finished, she washed the dishes for the last time; beginning tomorrow, Marie would be doing all the cooking and cleaning up. There was little conversation, for they were all tired, and they had to get up early the next day.

But Hilda could not sleep. She felt the pressure of his hand, as it had almost hurt her—a hand that was used to strenuous work. It was not that pressure that kept her awake. *It was the realization that he was the one.* She would marry him, and she would bear his children, cook his meals. They would love each other; he would kiss her, and she would like it.

The next morning, she took a last look at her new nephew, sleeping in his mother's arms, and then turned to her brother, who said, "Remember our talk. Keep well. Go with God."

She answered, "I'll remember." She did remember his wish for her to have a better life than their ma had had. That would be up to her. And God.

Marie stepped forward and shifted little Johnny to her left arm so she could embrace her sister-in-law. Almost tearfully, she whispered, "Thank you. Thank you." Turning to Franz, she spoke more clearly. "Take care of my sister. Don't let any wolves get near her."

Franz grinned. "I will. I won't." Then he helped Hilda onto Klaus's back, even though she did not need his help. They turned and waved farewell.

CHAPTER SEVEN: 1911

All members of the Meadow Church knew about customs followed by courting couples. Whatever the chemistry, a young woman would know in her heart when she recognized a young man as her future. She did not think of it as love at first sight; it was simply knowing. A time of learning followed: sharing of thoughts and feelings. The man might send a few notes by mail, perhaps decorated with a picture of a flower or heart, and signed merely with his initials to avoid satisfying the post office sorter's curiosity. He might come in person, on an urgent—or not—errand. All that could happen before the woman's father acknowledged his suitability.

When he came to call, the woman could invite him in or, if she wanted to avoid facing her family, would step out for a walk with him through the orchard or along the lane to the farm fields.

How had it happened that Franz was the Lober son who escorted Hilda home? Was it that he was the elder of the Lober widow's sons? Amos was closer in age to Hilda. Was it a deliberate ruse of Hilda's brother John to introduce the two?

Somehow, although Hilda and Franz did not talk much on their way to the Heldin home, a look between them exchanged a message. It was sent, and it was answered.

The question now was, Would Franz meet Pa's approval? It was important to face that question, Hilda knew, before she encouraged Franz wholeheartedly, before he actually called on her at her home. Still, she felt, this time she would use her best negotiating skills. She would wait until she and her father were milking, when they had their best chats.

"Is he a born-again Christian?" was Reverend Heldin's expected first and ultimate question.

Hilda cringed inwardly, thinking of her offer to God. The promise she hadn't had to keep. But she answered simply, "Yes," though she didn't know, and hadn't asked Franz directly.

"Will he join the Meadow Church? He will have to be baptized again in our creek. Will he do that?"

"I'll ask him when I know him better. Why would he have to be baptized again if he's already been baptized at his church—it's a Mennonite church too."

"Mennonite churches are not alike. His church is more easygoing, more liberal. They baptize using a pitcher of pump water, not a living stream. It's not the same thing."

"Are you saying that all those seven Mennonite churches around here differ only because they baptize differently? Don't they all baptize only grownups?"

"Yes, they—and we—are all Anabaptists. We all baptize adults because they have reached the age of understanding, of responsibility, unlike babies. People who are already right with God. To some churches, it is important to completely submerge a catechist in a lake or river, and some even require that the submersion be forward, not backward. Sometimes the differences seem to be trivial. Originally, we probably all came from the same roots."

"Is Franz's church different only because they use pump water for baptism?"

"No, there are other differences. One is that families sit together in church, where we keep the men and women on different sides of the sanctuary. They are more lenient about some worldly pleasures, like attending movies, dancing, even smoking."

"I don't think Franz does any of those things… What if he asks me to join *his* church?" As soon as she said this, Hilda recoiled inwardly, in fear of jeopardizing her case. *Why did I even suggest this?*

Now it was Pa, her father, answering—not Reverend Heldin, pastor of her church. "I would like to keep you with me—with us. My child. But you have to work that out with Franz. You're both old enough to make decisions. Even so, you first have to be sure that he is the man you want to marry. Pray about it. When you know him better, when you both decide, you may send him to me, and I will question him."

Hilda remembered what Abe had said about all men being the same in God's eyes. But all men were not the same in *her* eyes.

*　　　*　　　*

Some weeks later, Pa, sitting in his parlor rocking chair where he could count on privacy, reviewed his impressions of the young man who had asked to court his daughter. *He came to me, looked me in the eye, and asked for* her hand. *I like it when people look you in the eye. It means they are honest, straightforward. They know who they are and who you are.*

He realized he was rocking, the floor squeaking each time he leaned forward. *The man who marries my daughter must be a Christian. Franz was baptized by the standards of his church. I believe he met those standards. I did suggest to Hilda that he would have to be re-baptized, but, on the other hand, I may make an exception for him. It seems a lot to ask a grown man to have to do.*

He reminds me a little of Katherine. She had a sense of humor. Could see the bright side of life, of people. Sure, he is a man, not a woman or even womanly. But there seems to be a sparkle in his eyes. His face shows laugh-lines.

I looked at his hands. They are calloused. Clean, except for some pores. He is a worker. He looks strong and healthy. He's been the man of the house since his father died so young, of cancer. I hope that doesn't run in their family.

Franz's family is well respected in the community. No scandals that I heard of. You might say they were of a "higher class" than we were in the old country; more of them were merchants. But our family has doctors—bone setters. My father was able to correct club feet; my eye exercises have straightened cross eyes, and I've also set broken bones.

I hope—I believe—this young man is the right one for Hilda. Yes, I think Franz is a good match for Hilda. He will be good to her and for her. She is a little young, but she needs to get out of our house, I think. And she loves him, I think.

*   *   *

Back in the house, Leah thought about what Father told her, that he had given permission to this Franz Lober to court Hilda. *He didn't ask me, of course, but that's all right… No more snooty ideas of nursing school. Wait till she starts having babies. No more time to lose herself in books or daydreaming out her window or making dandelion-chains for Liesebet.*

Franz is "good enough" for her, according to Father. Actually, what he said was, "He's a good match." I have to keep this straight. Be fair… He seems bold. He looks me in the eyes—it feels a little as if he thinks he's my equal. He hasn't done or said anything disrespectful, but I feel as if it's right there under the surface.

Well, we are peasants. My family in Canada are peasants, and the Heldin family are also peasants, although they may think they are better peasants than my family. And the Lober family is no better.

Now, maybe, I can feel more relaxed being the mother of Father's other children, Liesebet, Hermann, and the one coming soon.

*   *   *

Hilda wished she knew how Franz had answered her father when he came to ask for permission to call on her. She knew only that her father had accepted him. She was glad she was the one to fetch the mail when a valentine appeared in the Heldin mailbox, and she had time to hide it until milking time so she could tell her father privately. She knew that Franz was quiet with his family, especially his sisters, Mathilda and Esther. They teased him about his interest in her, he said, and ridiculed what they described as the narrow-mindedness of the Meadow Church.

He called on her, usually Sunday afternoons, arriving on his bicycle, which he leaned against the barn. They walked side by side, along the lane toward the pasture where they could sit on some stones underneath a tree. They could see in all directions: the neighbors' fields and homesteads.

At first, their conversations were general, about people they both knew, about their own siblings, what they had done that week. Thus, Franz learned that Hilda knew a lot about child-rearing, while Hilda could tell that he knew very little about young children. She told him, "You have to be firm, sometimes, but you can also have fun. Teach them things through the games you play with them."

"Maybe I can practice on your little sister and brother and John's little Johnny," Franz suggested. "But I feel like a clumsy oaf next to them. They're so little."

"It'll be different when you have your own," Hilda countered, and then, shocked at what she had just said—suggested—blushed and covered her mouth.

It was enough for Franz to grin widely and then reach out to push at her shoulder. Gently. And gently, he changed the subject. "What's your favorite food?"

"I like *pluma mos*—the Christmas one with prunes, raisins, and other dried fruit like peaches, apricots, and pears."

"I like it too. But speaking of prunes, my favorite food is *perischke*."

"Which kind?"

"Made from prunes stewed with sauerkraut and baked into a kind of bread pocket. Then it's heated, smothered with fresh cream. I could eat those every day."

Hilda tried not to shudder. "I've never had that. It sounds odd. Ma never made those."

"You've missed something very good. It's food my ma learned to eat in Ukraine."

"Well, maybe she can make them for you every time you visit her."

"You mean you aren't willing to try? I'm sure my ma would be proud to teach you."

Hilda's stomach contracted—didn't exactly feel nauseated, just uncomfortable. Here was a challenge. Did she love Franz? Love him enough to marry him and learn to make this concoction?

But they went on exploring, studying each other. Knowing she had told Franz she wanted to be a nurse, he looked at her intently. "What about nursing school? Are you really considering it?"

"I have thought about it seriously," she said. "I'm not sure if it's just a way to get away. Out of our house. Be on my own, not subjected to Muttah. I think I *would* like to take care of people. But in a way, I could still help people who need it. Pa has taught me a lot about poultices, bandaging, how to lower fever. I wouldn't have to go to nursing school to help some people who need help."

"I don't want you to marry me and regret not being a nurse at the same time. Be sorry the rest of your life."

"I love you, Franz. More than I could ever love formal nursing."

They found what they had in common: a love of school and learning, even from incidental reading. They both enjoyed music although he said he couldn't sing, until she pointed out that he could. "I heard you when you were leaving on your bicycle last week."

They both loved to read. Franz would bring to their home his stack of *National Geographics* that he had collected, and some history books. Hilda tended to read novels and biographies she borrowed from school.

They discovered differences: Franz was concerned about the threatening relations between the United States and Germany that he read about in the newspaper. "I am opposed to killing anyone, but the thought of shooting someone I can carry on a conversation with is even more distressing. We might still have kindred living in Germany. I know Mennonites are excused from active involvement in war, should the things come to that. Anyway, if it comes to a vote, I will vote against war."

They both knew that many Mennonite men didn't vote at all, choosing to leave the future to God. Many decisions—in local government as well as in the church—were made by drawing lots. The Bible said that God shows his will through the casting of lots.

Hilda was not really interested in politics; Franz was old enough to vote. She was not old enough; and besides, as a woman, she was not eligible. "I will pray," she said.

They surveyed farms that were for sale, and talked about the advantages and disadvantages of location. One was handy to Franz's mother's farm; it would be easy to borrow machinery from her. An alternative that his mother hadn't (yet?) offered was for her to move to town and let him take over the farm. Or for him and Hilda to move in with her, or to build another house on the farmyard. That idea didn't appeal to Hilda—from one woman's kitchen to another? Franz didn't like the idea either. Then Mrs. Lober decided to buy the farm near hers, for them. She would continue to live on her farm for a few more years until her son, Amos, was ready to settle down on his own.

One subject they did not delve into was their personal beliefs. Franz didn't ask Hilda whether she was saved, and she didn't ask him where he stood. It was a subject that was part of her private life, and when she let herself think about it, she wondered if Franz had the same secret. Did he? Could he?

They had not prayed together; they would expect to do that in the mornings and perhaps again in the evenings after they married. When Hilda finally had the courage to ask him how he felt about joining the Meadow Church, he replied, "What do you want? Do you want me to, or…?"

"I wish we could decide that later. Maybe take turns going to each other's church for a while. After we're married."

Thus, they decided. Franz would attend the Meadow Church before he formally joined as member. "I do like your Pa. I'm comfortable with him. Furthermore, belonging to one church or another isn't like living in another country."

"I'll visit your church too, from time to time," Hilda replied.

*   *   *

On one of his visits, Franz handed her a small box.

"What is it?"

"Open it. You'll see."

"A watch pin." She held it to her ear to hear its delicate tick. "You shouldn't spend so much. I can always look at the kitchen clock."

He laughed. "And when you're not in the kitchen?"

"Well, I read that the Indians say 'Only white people need clocks to know when they are hungry.' Now I will know when I'm hungry… But, wait—I have something for you too."

"Now I have to ask what it is. It looks like a twisted cord of some kind."

"It's a pocket-watch fob. It's made from my hair. Now you will have something of me whenever you wear your watch."

"It's coffee colored, like your hair. But I don't see any hair missing from your head."

"It took me a long time to collect it. I couldn't just cut a hunk out. It would look odd."

The gifts made a kind of seal, a personal one that they invented. All the other dealings were public.

*   *   *

Now, soon, on three successive Sundays, Reverend Heldin would announce their plan to marry. Then would come their Sunday afternoon visits with all their nearest relatives—his mother and grandparents, his aunts and uncles, and her parents and grandparents, aunts and uncles.

Hilda could tell what an ordeal it was for Franz, whose shyness with her kinfolk seemed almost painful; she felt quite speechless at his people's homes also, especially when his sisters were present.

CHAPTER EIGHT: 1912

Slowly, setting each long-haired foot down as though they had to think each step, Klaus and Dolly drew the Heldin buggy closer, closer to the Meadow Church. Their hooves made a wet sucking sound as they stepped in the freshly thawed-out earth that was the road. Now and then they bent over a pale leaf of grass that had dared up from its winter bed. Also pale, as if it, too, was sheltered in the earth during the winter, the morning sky outlined the greening branches of the willow trees.

With his wife at his side, holding their young baby, Marta, on her lap, Pa looked down on the smooth muscular flanks of his team. He thought back to more than six years before when he married his namesake, John, to Marie. *It wasn't easy, so soon after Katherine died and before I married Leah. Since their marriage, I have joined dozens of other couples. Now it's hard to marry off my daughter. How can I slip in my love and care for her with the same words I use when I join other young people in matrimony? Will she catch my message when she catches my eyes as I speak?*

After his silent meditation, Pa said, "Soon the crocuses will be out."

"Can I go pick some?" asked Liesebet. "Then Hilda will wear them." She was getting up to scramble over the side of the buggy.

"Sit still. I said *soon* they will be out. That might still be a month from now."

If not for the pudgy Hermann sitting between them, Hilda would have reached to give Liesebet a caress. "I don't need flowers, Liesebet, when such nice things are said. I'll just think of your idea."

Hermann stared at Hilda, whose face was clean as always, framed by smoothly-combed, pulled-back hair. He lifted her coat to look at her white dress and poked his finger underneath one of the skirt ruffles to feel its crinkly stiffness.

*   *   *

Hilda had sewn her wedding dress, hiding her tears as she thought of how Ma would have enjoyed helping her make the ruffles and pleats, and tat the lace. All the strong, tiny stitches were even and hidden, as Ma had taught her. She had not asked Muttah to help; her sewing was practical and quite plain, not festive. She knew Muttah considered the dress to be a kind of waste. *I'll probably never wear it again. It's not appropriate for regular church or even Christmas, and certainly not as an everyday dress for housework.*

Hilda had enjoyed the long ride to church almost every Sunday since she could remember. She knew every turn in the road and the creek they came upon suddenly after one of the turns. Red-winged blackbirds sang in the trees, wild ducks and geese found homes, and bullheads swam in the creek water. It was where she had knelt for baptism when she was fifteen and Ma was still alive, and where she still expected Franz to be baptized in due time, when the water was warmer. As seasons changed, the creek never changed. It might be under ice, it might be swollen with spring rains and melted snow, but it was always there.

Today, she felt almost sad when she saw it. Today, she would look at the creek on their way from church. Would it seem different to her? If it seemed unchanged, she would know that the marriage rite had not changed her. She recalled her time at John's house last year when she noticed a difference in her brother. Would she know that difference in herself today? Or would change come gradually to her so she would not be aware of it?

"Can I sit with you in church, Hilda?" asked Liesebet, who had sat with her ever since Ma had her frequent ailments and, then, since she died.

"Of course, Liesebet. Only in the afternoon you can't, but we can keep on sitting together in the worship service all the time."

"Can I too?" asked Hermann.

"You sit with me and Marta in the women's and babies' room," answered Muttah, who had seemed not to be listening. "You'll see Hilda lots after this. She won't live so far away."

When they arrived at the church, Hilda looked for Franz but didn't see him. His buggy was there, clean and with a new coat of blacking. It was standing next to his mother's buggy because they would go home separately after the wedding.

Sunday school met first as always. Hilda joined her class in the sanctuary, now separated by heavy curtains suspended from wires that spanned the room. Liesebet went to hers in the dining hall. Afterward, the sisters met in the main auditorium, as usual. It seemed to Hilda that the congregants were looking at her more sharply than ever before. She kept her coat on, which hid her wedding dress, for that morning service, though the church was warmed by the black stove. The congregation could have done without heat, now that it was spring, but firewood was plentiful, and some of the old folk were happy for the warmth.

They were singing. Carefully, trying not to turn her head too much, Hilda tried to see Franz on the men's side of the aisle. He must be sitting further back, she thought when she didn't see him. The older men who could not hear well sat in the very front, and behind them were the young boys who had permission to sit with their friends. Logically, Franz would be sitting about as far back as she was, and she did not dare to turn her head that far.

Reverend Heldin was preaching. As always, he spoke in simple High German, the language of the Meadow Church and of their hymnbook. The congregants, whose language at home was Low German, as his was, could follow him well enough. He spoke slowly, deliberately, clearly. Smiling inside, Hilda remembered her childhood when her parents questioned her about the sermon to see if she had listened. Now she knew no one would question her. She was glad, for she could not concentrate.

After he had spoken almost an hour, hints of coffee pervaded the church. "I'm hungry," whispered Liesebet, who had been as excited as she, so neither had eaten much breakfast that morning.

Generally, Hilda didn't answer Liesebet's whisperings during church, but today the noon meal was being prepared for her—and Franz. "Be patient. Church is almost over. Then we can all eat." She felt hungry too.

The Reverend Heldin was making an announcement. He had finished his sermon. "Now we, the parents of Miss Hilda Heldin, would like to invite the entire congregation to a fellowship meal in the dining hall, and to the wedding in the afternoon."

*   *   *

The dining hall, heated for the Sunday-school class, was still warm. The dividing curtains were now pushed aside. Long tables, set up on sawhorses, were covered with white tablecloths and loaded with customary wedding food, all homemade. Ham, potato salad, bread, cucumber pickles, and cookies had been prepared yesterday but were still fresh. Liesebet and Hilda sat with their parents after the Reverend Heldin offered a long table prayer. They filled their plates high; Liesebet said no more and began to eat hungrily.

Then John was there, with apologies for Marie, who had stayed home with a cranky Johnny, who was teething and had sniffles and had kept Marie sleepless through the night. "You're going to be happy, little sister. You're getting a fine husband."

"Eat now," Pa was saying. "It's a while until suppertime." To give her time to eat, he talked with people who came to congratulate her. Liesebet reached for seconds, and even Hermann had cleaned his plate. Hilda ate, though the food felt heavy in her.

Finally, the people returned to the church sanctuary. Muttah, carrying little Marta, left with Hermann and Liesebet. Then Franz was there, his dark eyes silently expressing his love. Pa pinned on their corsages: little wax flowers and berries. Then he left to take his place as pastor in the high-backed chair at the front of the church.

Hilda and Franz had each watched many weddings and had not needed a rehearsal. Now they climbed the stairs, and as she walked up the last step, her skirt caught on a nail. Franz stooped to release it and smiled up at her. When they crossed the threshold of the men's entrance into the sanctuary, Hilda realized she had never seen that room before. *It looks just like the women's entrance. I guess that isn't a surprise.*

Once in the meeting room, Hilda wished he would hold her arm while they walked toward the front, as he did when they went for walks on their farm. But she knew people would talk, and she knew she could walk alone, even though she felt shaky. *He's wearing the watch fob*, she noticed. *Does he see that I'm wearing the new watch?*

The congregation had never seemed so still when they walked down the aisle, and since windows were open, they could hear the spring songs of meadowlarks and robins. It was their only music, lovelier than any pump organ or orchestra. They reached the front, and two ushers set chairs behind them.

The Reverend Heldin stood. Simply, he raised his hands, and the congregation rose for prayer. "Great God, Thou hast gathered us together to witness the joining of these two, Thy children. Help them to be ever mindful of Thee, and keep them and their children under Thy watchful care."

He prayed long. He mentioned the needy of the congregation, the community, the country, and the world. He prayed for the heathens who did not have the opportunity to worship, or to have Christian weddings and burials. He prayed, and Hilda's new shoes, white for the occasion—but not the new-fashioned low kind—began to hurt her feet.

She wished her father had not mentioned children—but she wondered, *what will my and Franz's children be like, and how will they look? I hope the boys, at least, will look like him: dark haired and dark eyed, with strong jaws and straight foreheads. The girls can be blue eyed, and fair, and curly haired. But it will be acceptable if they also have dark hair and eyes.*

Her father had finished his prayers, and they sat down. It was the first time she and Franz sat together in public. From the corner of her eye, she could see his hands, folded in his lap. She could smell him—an essence of his mother's homemade soap. She felt his presence. She thought about her new white dress and wished she could put her hands back to straighten it and keep wrinkles from forming. She thought about the swatch cut from Ma's dress that she had pinned to her petticoat. *In a way, Ma is here today. I know she would like Franz.*

She knew what the sermon would be. It was preached at all weddings, though her father always rewrote it. But she should listen to this sermon, the only one for her—and Franz, of course—that she would ever hear, because naturally, she would not hear her funeral sermon.

"When a young person marries another young person, and both are born-again believers, there is great joy, for together, they will be able to serve God better than they could do singly. As Paul says, 'Be ye not unequally yoked together with unbelievers; for what fellowship has righteousness with unrighteousness? And what communion hath light with darkness?'"[9] He paused. "It is with a double joy that we celebrate this wedding: the joy of a pastor who is the representative of God, and joy of a father at the wedding of his daughter."

Oh, oh. He assumes we are both saved. I hope he's right. Then Hilda felt the same twinge she had felt when Abe asked her two years before, whether she was saved. Franz never asked her. Now she wished he had. *What if he isn't saved himself? How, then, can we help each other?*

Hilda was compelled to listen on. Her father was reading a long passage from the Pulpit Bible, the Martin Luther one. She missed the reference, and though she could recognize the words, she could not remember from which Book they came. "Therefore, as the church is subjected unto Christ, so let the wives be to their husbands in everything. Husbands, love your wives, even as Christ also loved the church, and gave himself for it …"

I can go along with that. I will always do whatever Franz asks, since I know he loves me.

When he quoted the Apostle Paul's definition of love, Hilda found herself mouthing the words that she had been required to memorize years before. "Charity suffereth long, and is kind."[10]

As Hilda reflected, he began the marriage ceremony. Inwardly, she winced as he read, "If there be any who can show just cause why these two should not be joined together, let him speak now, or forever hold his peace." *What if someone should speak now?* Hilda thought of Abe Geppert.

But no one spoke, and the Reverend Heldin continued. "Do you, Franz Lober, take this woman"—*I am this woman, and he standing next to me*

---

9   All English quotations from the Bible are from the King James Version.
10   I Corinthians 13: 1–13.

is Franz, almost my husband—"Hilda Heldin, to be your lawful wedded wife?"

"Yes," Franz replied. He did not hesitate, even to clear his throat.

"Do you, Hilda Heldin"—*that's my name, but it's the last time I will be called Heldin. My name will be Hilda Lober. Mrs. Franz Lober. Will I ever feel "held in" again?*—"take this man, Franz Lober, to be your lawful wedded husband? To love, to obey, to cherish. In sickness or health, in adversity?"

"Yes." She heard her own voice; confident, sure.

"What God hath joined together, let no man put asunder."

She was no longer single. She and Franz had become one person. As she took his hand and listened to her father bless their union, it came to her that she would now spend all her time with this man. She would love him as she did now, perhaps more. She would obey him in all things, but it would be willing, cooperative obedience. She would nurse him if he should become ill, though he was strong and healthy. If hard times should come, she would be help him. Hard times. What could be hard times?

The ceremony was over. Suddenly, Hilda wanted to be alone with Franz. To run out of the sanctuary, holding hands. To ride with his lively horses pulling his black buggy. To ride on and on, where only he and she would be.

She felt cramped when she rose from her hard chair, a married woman. People smiled and reached to shake her hand. She let them, and far away heard her voice responding appropriately. They came, left her, and made room for others who took her hand, and with their movement, kept it warm. She was being kissed on the cheek; it was Muttah. Then Pa and Liesebet. And when she stooped, Hermann. Muttah held Marta for her to plant a wet kiss. Next, the Lobers: Franz's mother and brother and even his lighthearted sisters—those teases—who only shook her hand and smiled.

But Franz led her outside to the freshly blackened buggy. Someone had hitched his horses, Minnie and Jerry, to it. The people outside watched Franz help her into the buggy, and the new couple drove toward the house that Ma Lober had bought for them.

*   *   *

The horses were well trained, and the ride behind them was smooth as it had been during the rides she and Franz had taken Sunday afternoons. The day was warm for the season, and not at all windy, even though it was March. They came to an intersection, and Franz reined for a turn. The realization that they were not going directly to her new home startled Hilda. More than that, she realized that they had passed the creek, and she had not noticed it. Is this, she wondered, change happening to me?

"I figured out a different route," Franz said. "Now, if they want to follow us, they won't know where we went."

Hilda looked at him. "Who? Who would follow us?"

He shrugged and smiled, showing the dimple in his cheek, "Anybody."

There was something beyond his symmetrical nose, forehead, and eyes. There was strength, definiteness, health that merged with kindness, intelligence, and warm wisdom. And a sense of playfulness. With her whole heart and being, she loved him. His lips were soft and warm and tender. As she felt something in her heart loosen and flood over all that was tired and lonely and afraid, she allowed her hands to bury themselves in his hair and then to travel down the back of his head, his neck, and to his muscled shoulders. She felt his tendons tighten as her breath left her in an almost painful sweetness.

The sky was a spectacle of colors and clouds when they came to their new farmyard. Slowly and nonchalantly, the team drew up in front of the house to let their owners out. They waited quietly as Hilda and Franz walked hand-in-hand across the threshold of their new home.

*   *   *

It was evening. Franz had put up the horses in their new stall. Inside the house, Hilda made their bed, using sheets she had hemmed, pillowcases she had embroidered, and a fine, deep feather comforter Liesebet had helped her fill with goose down and feathers.

Now it was time to climb into bed. Hilda sat up and smiled when she saw Franz in his nightshirt. It seemed too small, with his muscled arms and legs sticking out, his feet bare on the linoleum floor. *I must braid a rug for his bare feet,* she thought, but as she lifted the covers for him to get in next to her, they were interrupted by a loud roar with a banging, like shotgun blasts—and shouting—

Franz hurried to the window. "There's a gang out there—"

"Why? Who is it?"

"I can't see—maybe your cousin Henry—maybe people from my church. Or yours."

"Come on out!" someone shouted from amid the din, the clapping together of disc blades. Another shout.

"It's a *shivaree*—a crazy way to celebrate our wedding," he said. "People do that sometimes."

"What are you going to do—it sounds dangerous."

"Oh, they won't shoot at the house."

"What about the horses? They'll start bucking at their stall."

"They've heard loud noises before."

"You mean other shivarees?... So—you knew about this practice! Did you ever participate in such heathen ways?"

If he had wanted to answer that charge, he was interrupted by another shout. "Come out! Show us a kiss!"

"I'll tell them to go home... I thought no one would know where we went. That's why I took the roundabout route here."

Hilda scrunched under the covers.

Franz opened the window. "Go home! You should be in bed yourselves." And to Hilda, "We'll have to ignore them. They won't keep it up forever."

He blew out the lamp, slipped into bed beside Hilda, and held her tightly, and they listened to the ungodly commotion. It seemed to last a long time. No one entered their house.

Then Hilda noticed Franz's roaming hands.

"What are these, melons? Melons in bed with us?"

"Du, Franz. Don't be silly."

"There's even a little knob on them... Let me taste... Hmmm—good."

Giggling, Hilda joined the game. "That tickles. But, I think there are hard-boiled eggs and a sausage in bed, between your legs. Seems as if we can make a salad." She cupped them in her hands.

Then, Hilda knew what Franz would do next, and unlike what she had imagined as a child, that she would try to push him off or try to run away from him, she welcomed him. It was pain, but a slight pain, and it was mixed with pleasure that filled her core.

In the morning, all was still and the sun rose.

CHAPTER NINE: 1913

Quickly, because a field full of hay waited to be put up before gathering clouds in the west evolved into rain, Hilda made thin pancakes that would be their dinner. She piled them, hot and golden, onto a small plate, reserving the first burnt ones for herself. She set coarse sugar and tank-cooled milk on the table and waited for Franz to finish washing his hands and drying his fingers one by one on the circular hand towel.

She watched him eat. After strewing an even layer of sugar over the entire disc, he rolled it into a sausage shape. Then, using his fork and knife, he cut slices into neat packages. The part of the sugar that did not melt into the pancake made a slight crunching sound as he chewed. He did not speak of the food, but with his look, he told Hilda that she was a good cook, and he appreciated also that part of her.

Rising, not resting long enough to let his meal settle, Franz prepared to go back into the fields.

Though she was beginning to be aware of a new strangeness within her body, Hilda wasn't quite certain and decided not to mention anything to Franz until she was sure. Since she wasn't certain, and had all her young strength, she rose also to join him, saying, "Let's go. We'll be done before the rain starts."

Behind her apron, she counted on her fingers. *How many months ago was it that I had those same feelings? All that happened after was a heavy flow of blood and some cramps that lasted a day and a half. In a while it dwindled and stopped. It scared us a little, and we considered asking Pa about it. But we decided not to mention it. It was almost a year ago. I do hope I don't start another flood. Blut Flut.*[11] She almost laughed about her rhyme.

So, out they went. Minnie and Jerry, hitched to the hayrack Franz had

---

11 Blood flood.

recently built, walked slowly and ploddingly, fitting their gait to the type of work. They seemed different from the team that pulled the Sunday buggy. Even if they had not been wearing blinders, they probably would not have bothered looking around at the dried grass, cut just days before. They walked almost in step with each other, each pulling an equal share of the weight that increased as Franz and Hilda tossed light, fresh, full-flavored swathes into the rack.

When the wagon was full, they climbed atop the load and allowed the team to find their way easily to the shed, while they played in the loose, fresh hay.

Unloading was easier than loading. Hilda slid bunches of hay off the top for Franz to catch and toss onto the pile in the shed. They were working as fast as they could in hopes that they could get one more load in before the rain started. A calm had come, and with it a sultriness that the breeze had kept away before. Perspiring now partly from their previous romp, they spoke little.

Crops had been good last year and this year so far as well; a sign that God was blessing them in their marriage. Corn didn't yet have tassels, but it was showing promise with bright green, sturdy stalks. As they looked back at the few remaining loads of hay, now soon to be wetted in the field, Hilda sighed.

"Too bad," Franz said, "but that's farming for you. We take the weather as it is."

When the gusts of wind began, they quickly unhitched the horses and directed them into the barn. It was only a minute before the rain fell, sharply and heavily, without the usual, gradual increase from a few drops. Franz went to the back door of the barn and let in the already drenched cows, Mrs. Thick and Mrs. Thin, wedding presents from Hilda's parents. The cows went directly into their assigned stalls and waited stolidly for the wetness to run off them.

It was not yet time to milk. Franz returned to Hilda, who was seated on a pile of straw directly inside the door, where she watched the continuous sheet of rain.

"If this rain stops soon, and the sun shines tomorrow, we should be able to get the rest of the hay Saturday," he said. "I have always enjoyed rain," he continued. "Sometimes, even when it's causing damage, I forget all about that because it gives me so much pleasure."

Hilda didn't reply. *I can't forget the damage just to enjoy the rain. My faith isn't strong enough.*

He went on. "Perhaps some day, when we're depending on a crop and it rains, we won't feel this way."

Then Hilda reacted, "I'm glad *you* feel so sure. That encourages me. I wouldn't be optimistic if I weren't so lucky to have a Franz to watch over me."

He slid closer to Hilda, watching over her shoulder as the rain continued to slash at the earth. "I'm luckier. I have someone I love to watch over, and you don't. I'm thankful for the privilege of giving. I'd rather watch than be watched over."

At this point, Hilda felt herself almost hypnotized into telling him of her suspicion of the possibility of bearing a child soon. Then she *would* have someone to watch over. Someone she would be sure to love. True, he would then have two to watch over, but he could not then say that she had no one. Instead, she said only "Some day I will have someone to watch over." *Some day.*

He pressed on her arm. "Soon?" he asked. "I hope so."

Did he guess? It would be fun to plan for their children with him. "I hope so too," she answered. She was not lying, for how could she be sure so soon? Maybe she'd say something tonight. The words didn't come yet.

"How many children do you hope God sends us?" he asked.

"I've never thought of a definite number. I don't know. More than three. But not too many."

"I want five. Three boys and two girls. Boy, girl, boy, girl, boy." And they both laughed, knowing they wouldn't have a choice about such things. "Well, however many God sends us will be fine so long as there are some at least." He stopped as if finished, but then added another important point. "There must be a couple boys to help me with the farm work when I get old."

They laughed again, for they knew they would never grow old. Looking at each other, in the gloaming created by the now waning rain, she tried to imagine him after thirty years of married life. With her finger, Hilda traced along his forehead, where she thought he might some day have wrinkles. She pressed down his hair to see how his face would look if there were no shock of dark hair. Retaliating, he pulled in his lips over his teeth, to show how he would look without them.

"Oh, that's not fair! You can make such awful faces, and I can't. Some day you'll have to stop that. If you don't want your children to be making faces in church!"

"I think I'll teach them to make faces. We'll have face-making contests!" He laughed. He couldn't laugh as loudly as his brother Amos, who never laughed without infecting other people present, at least with mild smiles. Franz's laughter came from inside him somewhere, and when he began, he sometimes kept it up longer than seemed possible to Hilda.

Suddenly, he stopped laughing. "Why do you keep talking about our children today? Are we going to have one?"

It was hard to keep the truth from him when he looked at her as he did, squarely and directly. She blushed, and she hoped he would think it was because she wasn't used to speaking so freely about intimate subjects. She didn't lie directly. "Some day, I hope we'll have more than one."

"Of course. But what I mean is, are you pregnant now?"

Hilda liked that Franz seldom asked direct questions, unlike Abe Geppert. Abe would have asked her every day perhaps. With an inner shudder, Hilda wondered, *Why am I thinking of Abe now, of all times?*

It was easy to have a conversation with Franz; in the end, she always told him everything. And, discovering things was more interesting—so much better than having question, answer, question, answer. *He's never asked me whether I'm saved. Some people, if they knew, might ask whether he really cares if he doesn't ask. I wonder if he wonders. How long can I keep this secret?* She thought again about her offer to God of a bargain. A bargain she didn't have to keep.

With a feeling of panic, Hilda hoped he hadn't been able to guess that she wasn't sure about salvation. During the weeks of catechism before she was baptized, her father, Reverend Heldin, had asked the whole class if they wished to give their hearts to Jesus—to follow Jesus all their days. She simply joined all the others by saying, "Yes." Then he had prayed, holding his right hand high as he beseeched God's blessing on them. That was it. Afterward, she didn't feel different. Nothing had changed. *Shouldn't I feel something? Like being sure? Positive?*

She hoped Franz wouldn't question her until she could be sure. *When I'm sure, the answer will be certain to be yes. I know that. But would he ask me that question about salvation so directly? Now that he's asking me about having babies so directly, he might do it again.*

I wonder what Pa actually talked with Franz about. He must have catechized him about his soul for he changed his mind about requiring him to be baptized in our creek.

"Are you?"

Brought back to the question, Hilda felt her face flush. *How long was I off the topic? Is it obvious?* She answered, "Am I what?" Hilda had heard his question. Very plainly she had heard him, for he was sitting very close, and the warmth of his body radiated through his shirt. But this would give her time to think of an answer.

"Hilda, look at me. You're not answering me, and I know you hear me. Tell me, are you pregnant?" Something like fear, or at least unrest, was in his eyes.

She had had time enough. Still, she had to think as she talked. "No, I don't think so. How can I tell?" It was the truth. *I don't know for sure. Really, it's too soon.*

Again there rose in her core the pain of loss—the loss of her mother, who had never told her about the process of conception, of pregnancy. When she was twelve and found some spots of blood on her underwear, she had hid in the outhouse to look herself over, to see just what was bleeding. Since she didn't find an injury, she secretly took her underwear to the cattle trough to rinse. With the bleeding continuing, she finally asked Ma just what the matter was. Ma sighed, and called it the "curse of God for women, after Eve disobeyed him and ate the forbidden apple." Then Ma helped her fold some old flannel rags into shapes to pin inside her underwear. Ma never got around to telling her about how babies were formed in the first place, or how they were born.

Hilda never spoke of the subject with Muttah, who doubtless assumed Hilda knew the facts. She never talked about it with friends in church or school. Now it occurred to her that she knew all about the birth of a baby, helping Muttah with Hermann, and Marie with baby John. She knew how a baby came out, but not about how or when it actually started to grow inside the mother. She knew that there was a connection between lying with Franz and pregnancy. That the monthly bleeding was somehow involved. She knew that cows and horses joined their bodies sometimes, but it usually looked as if they were just cavorting. Lying with Franz was also such fun, also cavorting. It wasn't at all like she had feared when she was a child—that she would try to get away, as cows seemed to try to escape from bulls.

Franz did not press the issue with her. Hilda wondered what he knew about symptoms of pregnancy. *Had he talked with other boys about what they knew, there behind the stables? Or did his mother or sisters tell him anything?*

"You will tell me when you know, won't you?"

"Yes, Franz." And Hilda postponed telling him until after they finished all of the harvest and he had more time to be indoors with her. She wanted now to be able to keep on helping him with his work, so long as she felt fine. Maybe if he knew he would make her stay in the house to save her strength, even though housework was often as hard as the work she did helping him. Certainly, she did not *know* she was pregnant. She hoped she was, and when she thought about it, she felt a strange tickle inside her.

CHAPTER TEN: 1913

Franz worked in the barn during rainy days, mending harnesses, sharpening tools, cleaning the pens of the two young calves, and then coming into the house to eat hot, colorful, vegetable soups Hilda cooked for him.

A week passed before the remaining hay had dried enough to be hauled from the field. On rising from breakfast, he asked, "Do you feel well enough to make hay?"

"Why shouldn't I?" *Was he beginning to guess?* Hilda wasn't ready to tell him about her suspicions. Mornings, when she felt nauseated, she remembered that Ma had eaten soda crackers for breakfast sometimes. It had seemed an odd breakfast food, so she asked about it. Ma told her that crackers helped get over nausea. Her mother hadn't said why she felt sick.

Seeing her eat crackers, Franz, asked, "Are we out of oatmeal? Why are you eating crackers for breakfast?"

"Oh, I just saw them in the cupboard and decided to eat them." After that, Hilda made sure to eat the crackers in the pantry while she was finding other food to put onto the table. It shouldn't be so hard to share her suppositions with Franz, but she wasn't ready to start that conversation. *So many things to think about: What to name a baby. How to get the house ready. Borrowing or building a cradle. For now, just getting over the sickness each morning was enough.*

At the same time, she wondered whether evading his question was a form of lying. *If so, it's a sin of omission.* She added it to her load of secret guilt.

Franz looked at her. "You must say if you don't feel well sometimes. I don't want to be known as a man who works his wife too hard."

*　　*　　*

Picking up leftover hay was easier this time than it had been the week before. Today, with no deadline, they were sure to be through before sundown. With no clouds, the sun was warm, and Hilda soon felt moisture creeping through her sleeves and running along the creases in her neck. The hay had lost the sweetness of its former smell and no longer felt smooth and fresh. Underneath, it was still damp. On the way home, Hilda and Franz did not romp in the hay as they had done the previous week. They sat in the front of the wagon, not even chewing on the hay.

Hilda wondered whether the mustiness of the hay made her feel different. Something seemed different since that day in the rain. She hoped it was the rain that had spoiled their mood, not the fact that she hadn't been open with Franz. "Love, honor and obey," part of the marriage ceremony, meant many things, not only that when the husband asked questions should the wife answer directly. The words meant to follow, to love always, to agree. Besides, she had answered him truthfully; she did not know. Not for sure. Not yet.

But when they arrived at the hay shed, Hilda did not want to get up and go to work. Her arms weighed at her sides, and perspiration on her forehead had become cool, as though it was not perspiration at all, but moisture condensed on a cool container from the warm air.

Then she was in her bed. Franz, frightened at her side, asked, "Shall I call Father? Maybe he can give you some medicine. Maybe you worked too fast. Does it hurt anywhere?"

But all she could answer him was, "I love you, Franz."

Then he knew. "Why didn't you tell me? I almost guessed it several times, but then I knew you'd tell me if it was true. Why didn't you tell me?"

It was too hard to answer. That would have involved explaining that she didn't actually know which symptoms to watch for. More, he would insist she stay in the house instead of being with him all day. *Then, what if I wasn't pregnant after all?* She allowed herself the luxury of going to sleep, leaving Franz awake by himself.

When she woke, she spoke to Franz, who was still sitting at her bed. "The hay. Shall we unload it now, Franz?"

It was his first smile. "No, you stay in bed until I have asked Father Heldin what you shall do, what medicine you should take. It won't be too hard for me to unload the hay, and we'll leave the rest of it in the field for fertilizer. It isn't very good after the rain anyhow. I was considering leaving it."

*　　　　*　　　　*

Franz returned by himself. The trip to her father's house had not taken him long.

"Wasn't he at home, Franz?"

"He said Nature will take care of you. You are to stay in bed for a few days, and then not do any outside work, like pitching hay. Oh, and eat lots of carrots and drink lots of milk."

There was a small wrinkle between Franz's eyes. Hilda had not noticed it before; now she thought of John, and the wrinkles she had seen on his forehead. Were they the same kind of wrinkles? The old piece of tin hanging above the wash basin was not clear enough to show Hilda whether she had any wrinkles. She had tried to look many times since she was married but had never been able to tell. She then wished she had not left her tiny glass mirror with Liesebet when she married. Somehow, at that time, she had thought she would never need a mirror again.

Thankful that the haying and harvest season was almost over, Hilda tried to picture herself doing all the indoor work. If she didn't help Franz outside, he wouldn't have time or energy to help her inside the house either. That would mean they would have less time together.

They secretly did some things other families did not do. Franz dusted the carved curlicues of the chiming clock his mother gave him, one that she had brought from the Ukraine when she had immigrated as a sixteen-year-old girl. He wound it regularly, once a week. He dusted the writing desk that had been his father's, and arranged his collection of books and *Geographics* on top of it, since he hadn't yet built a bookcase. He helped make their bed—he on his side and Hilda on her side. He even took over some scrubbing of the uneven linoleum floor, pointing out that they had more time to sing their favorite songs together. He told Hilda he liked sitting next to her while she played their pump organ, a wedding gift from her grandmother, Ma's mother.

"I can milk though, can't I?"

"He didn't say. I suppose it wouldn't matter, and it would help a great deal. But for several days, you have to stay in bed." Franz's hands looked helpless, hanging down at his sides all by themselves.

"I'll cook, though. That isn't hard. I can sit while I peel potatoes and I won't carry pails. You don't have to cook."

Franz did not argue that. He had never cooked anything, and he was awkward even slicing bread.

"Some women can do all the work they ever did when they are in the family way. Aunt Mary even had her baby on top of a hay stack."

Franz snorted, "You don't say! That can't be true—right up on top of a big haystack?"

"Maybe not way on top. But on the hay. At a haystack out in the field."

"Was she by herself?"

"Well, I wasn't there, of course, but that's what Ma told me. Aunt Mary's quite proud of it. She had been helping with the haying at a field quite far from their house. And then the pains started." Franz was still bent over with laughter as she continued her story. "So she lay right down on the hay and gave birth!"

"I don't suppose it was so bad. The hay was fresh. Probably cleaner than some beds. Besides, think of how much less there was to clean up afterward. And, remember, Jesus was born in a stable, and was laid in a manger."

The story had brought some color to Hilda's face, and Franz, cheered by that, retorted, "Our baby won't be Jesus. And he won't be Mary's child. So you know, Hilda, her having a baby on a haystack isn't a good reason for you to be doing the same things. Aunt Mary is no ordinary woman, even if her name is 'Mary.' Besides, look at all the babies she miscarried."

"Franz, you talk so of my relative. Shame on you. She means well."

"Many a person has been driven to Hell because of someone's good intentions." It was the first time they had discussed Aunt Mary, Pa's sister. Until now, they had both been careful in Aunt Mary's presence and had not brought up the subject in her absence.

"Then we have to be better than she, and not debase ourselves by talking against her."

"Which means also that we must be better than she and not try to do what she does. Which means that you shouldn't try to do man's work, especially when you're pregnant," added Franz.

"Nevertheless, we have to be kind when we speak of her," Hilda insisted, aware that she had never been so persistent before. She wondered whether her pregnancy made her more than usually sensitive.

"Of course. Now, you sleep a while, and I'll unload the hay. When I come in, you can tell me how, and I'll try to make dinner."

He would not have needed to tell her to go to sleep, for she did not hear him close the door after him. When she woke, he was already trying to slice the ham for frying. Lazily, she told him to cut off the rind, to wash some potatoes, and to cover them with water in the kettle. To please him, she ate, though she was not hungry.

*   *   *

That evening, almost as if their conversation had conjured her, Aunt Mary appeared with her young son, Peter. Her husband had died some years before—a young man who, weakened by ulcers, had not been able to resist pneumonia. While he was living, it had appeared that she was the dominating person; she was a large-boned woman, amply covered with flesh and insulated with fat. The truth was, he had raised her. He had married her, an awkward young girl who had many sisters and was needed more in the fields than for more genteel housework. He had given her suggestions for her cooking, had taught her to read the Bible so they could take turns in their daily devotions, and had told her what to think. Almost fiercely, she learned to love him, who made her feel as if she deserved a lifetime just as other people did, and she felt it a sort of mission to spread his interpretation of life to anyone who would listen, and especially to those who would not. She was afraid of horses, so the only son she had been able to produce drove her where she wanted to go.

"Here's your chance to be kind, Hilda," announced Franz while Aunt Mary was cleaning her shoes on the shoe scraper that once was a plowshare. He was making a face, and in spite of it all, Hilda was laughing when Aunt Mary made her entrance.

"So you are going to be a mother!" Aunt Mary decided before they had a chance to tell her she was expecting, or that she had a slight case of the flu. Heavily, she seated herself on the strongest chair Franz was quickly able to find for her.

Franz said hastily, "It is early yet, so we aren't telling anyone."

"Of course, I'm your aunt. I won't mention it. But I'm glad I know. Now, Peter and I can pray for you." Peter was sitting in the corner; like a young apprentice, he was listening to the conversation, seemingly memorizing the words of his mother. "But you shouldn't stay in bed. That's bad for you. You should keep on having exercise to make your baby a strong one."

In spite of the sleep she'd had, Hilda's voice sounded weary. "Pa says I should stay in bed for a few days. He is a doctor."

Waiting for Hilda to finish, Aunt Mary continued. "Yes, yes. Respect your father. But he is a man, not a woman. How can he know about childbearing? My Peter was born one day on the haystack when we were very busy. Look how strong he is now. I wouldn't know what to do without him." She looked triumphantly at her son and then to Hilda.

Hilda smiled, wondering how many times Peter had heard this history of his origin. It wasn't possible to see just exactly what he was thinking, if anything.

"You smile because you don't believe me," Aunt Mary claimed. "Well, you ask your father. He was there to help with the haying. But we must go. We only wanted to stay a few minutes."

She started the closing devotions. Peter read from the Bible he carried with him at all times, and even said a prayer using words he likely could not understand. Then she prayed, commanding God to take charge of the fetus, and predestining it to be a missionary to the foreign lands where people did not have a chance to hear the gospel as she interpreted it. Or, rather, as her husband had interpreted it to her. When she finished, there was no need for Hilda and Franz to pray, as she had said everything there was to say.

Parting, she promised to come often to help Hilda in her pregnancy, and then repeated part of her prayer: "Remember, being parents is a great responsibility to God."

Like a well-trained puppy, her son followed her out the door, taking the same-sized footsteps.

"Tomorrow, it will be all over the country," predicted Franz as soon as he came back into the house.

Having known Aunt Mary as long as she could remember, Hilda had always accepted her for who she was: Aunt Mary. Simply, Aunt Mary. But for Franz, she was someone to get used to. He needed to be reminded. "Remember, Franz, she is my aunt. Pa's sister."

"That doesn't exempt her from acting her Christianity."

"She is doing as best she can."

"She promises to come often. You promise me you won't listen to her."

"Some of the things she says are good and right."

"We will get a good midwife when the time comes. I won't have her delivering it. She'd probably break all its bones just to make it hardy."

"Franz, you're exaggerating. It makes me uncomfortable. Besides, don't you have relatives who are different in ways?"

"Hilda, when you married me, you promised to cling to me and to leave your father and mother. That means your aunts and uncles too. You promised to obey me. I ask you now, not to listen to her advice. We can't turn her out of the house when she comes—that wouldn't be Christian. But I ask you not to let her influence us. I'm asking you to rest as your father said you should."

He left the room, and Hilda was happy he had spoken so. It felt good to turn all responsibility over to him. She'd let him be in charge of her health and the baby's. While she thought about it, for her soul and his. And the baby's.

CHAPTER ELEVEN: 1913

"You were so brave, Franz," Hilda whispered when she knew it was accomplished.

"You know I didn't do anything. Mrs. Harmes did all the work. I just stood here."

"You stayed with me. Most men don't. They have to go outside. You were brave staying here."

Still in charge, Mrs. Harmes said, "All right, you can leave now, Franz Lober." Color had crept over her face when he insisted on staying in the room during the entire delivery. Reared in complete privacy from the other sex, she never exposed herself even to her husband, waiting rather until he had blown out the lamp before she undressed. Obviously, his hands didn't bother her so much as his eyes, for she had borne seven children.

"But I don't have to do chores yet. I've lots of time," Franz answered, eager to share with his wife the joy of their first moments with the life of their firstborn.

Mrs. Harmes was firm. "She is going to feed the baby now. You must not discomfit her by looking."

*   *   *

Though it was much too early to milk, Franz went to the barn to feed the young calves, and when there was nothing else to do, he methodically began to prepare the cows. Now that he was milking by himself, his hands were getting used to the extra strain. He hoped Hilda, when she became stronger, would help with the milking again. A loneliness that was a sort of homesickness settled on him. He missed her—their companionship—as they shouted back and forth around the flanks of their respective cows.

The two cats came to him. Hilda had named them "Old Mur" and

"Young Mur," since one was the mother and the other the daughter—and, laughing, she called them "Murmur" for short. They sat expectantly, as Hilda had taught them, for their milk. Franz squirted at them, though inexpertly, and the warm liquid wet their entire faces and necks. They licked themselves well. Old Mur even stretched over to help Young Mur at a hard-to-reach place. Then they waited for more, as if to encourage Franz.

You greedy things, does it taste so much better squirted at you than from a pan? I can't believe you're so hungry that you can't wait until I finish one cow, Franz was thinking, for he hadn't learned to talk aloud to animals as Hilda often did. Before his marriage, he had never thought of conversation with animals, at least not in a companionable way. He might have said, "Come." He did say, "Come baas, Come baas" in a singsong way when he was calling the cows to the barn for milking. He spoke to the horses: "Giddap" or "Hoe." Or he clicked with his tongue. He called the pigs to the trough, "Soo-ee." Calling the dogs was "Heeyah," and the cats was a falsetto "Meetz." He did speak to the animals, and they understood. When he called the cows, the cows came—not the dogs or the cats. When he called the dogs, the cats ignored his call.

Franz chuckled, remembering the time Aunt Mary asked what the dogs were named. Pointing first to the larger one, Hilda had answered, "Which One." Mary, thinking it was a question—not the dog's name—then pointed to the smaller one, so Hilda had replied, "Ask Him." She explained the names she had given the dogs for fun to Aunt Mary, for she immediately regretted her seeming disrespect. Aunt Mary had even laughed.

As slowly as possible Franz finished milking and, finding nothing else to do, started back for the house. He hoped the midwife would be finished with her work and was ready for him to hitch up her team.

*　　*　　*

The baby was asleep. Franz reminded himself again, almost as if it was a lesson he was studying, Not "the baby." She. Grace. Not "it." Carefully, he washed his hands, even though the water was unheated, and then he filled the kettle, setting it on the heater where Hilda usually kept warm water for him.

"There you are. You may go in to her now." It was Mrs. Harmes. A sharp quick surge rebelled inside Franz, but he put it down immediately, remembering that they had long ago arranged with her to help Hilda with the delivery. He recognized her right to speak with the authority he now resented.

Hilda was smiling. "It wasn't so bad. Especially that you were with me."

"She didn't want me here. When she told me to go, and I said I had promised you to stay, she tried to send me out anyhow."

"She means well. I'm glad you stayed. Now it's over with."

"It's a fine baby."

"You mean, '*she*' is a fine baby." Hilda smiled. "Her name is 'Grace,' remember? She is here, thanks to the amazing grace of God."

"Yes, but I have to get used to her being a 'she.'"

Mrs. Harmes came in once more, not knocking, and Franz again had the feeling that she belonged here more than he did. She paused a bit and then said, "You must not kiss her for a while now."

"Why not?"

"It isn't good for her now. Not the kissing, but it isn't good for you to come too close to her now. Later, after she is healed, then it can be again as it was before she was pregnant."

Franz's only response was, "Oh."

Then she left, not asking for pay. Franz, in the glow of his happiness, did not think to pay her, after she had given a whole day's work to them.

*   *   *

Though she sneaked out occasionally, Hilda lay in bed most of the following days. Liesebet came to visit and, more, to help her bathe little Grace, bringing warm water and soap to her bedside so all Hilda had to do was sit up and dash water over the baby. Then Liesebet stood ready with a clean dishtowel. Franz also helped, even changing her diapers sometimes. Now he was outside, working on some machinery in preparation for spring work that would begin soon.

Hilda looked forward to the time when Grace would be old enough to take to the field. *That will be at least a year or two from now. Maybe by then there will be another child. And when the children are all here and big enough to be left alone, I'll be too old to enjoy helping with the fieldwork.*

To her surprise, Hilda didn't resent that idea. Holding the sleeping baby in the curve of her arm, she traced her little nose, the swollen lids of her tiny eyes, her mouth protruding as if permanently shaped for nursing, and her short, straight, fine dark hair.

Here I am, a mother. Looking at the small face, Hilda tried to imagine how Grace would look some day. Even the color of her eyes was obscure, though they would probably be like Franz's some day. *Aren't first babies usually like their fathers? If she were to favor me, wouldn't she have light brown hair like mine too? And what will her character be?*

With those thoughts, she remembered her wish—soon after Ma's death— that she could die. When he discovered that she had such wishes, Pa told her a story: *Once there was a young girl who always wished she would die. She never found the joy in life God intended for her. But always, Death answered, "No, not yet. Wait a while." But always she wished she could die. Then, one day, long after this girl had forgotten her wish and had married and had children, Death, remembering her wish, came to her and said, "Now." The girl pleaded and cried, saying, "Not now, Death, not now. I am happy now. I don't want to die now." But Death did not listen; he took that girl with him, leaving her child motherless and husband a widower.*

It was a horrible story, and Hilda had not been able to forget it. Never after that had she wished for death. Now, as she looked into the face of her daughter, the power of the story took hold of her until, tearfully, she began to pray. *Forgive me God, forgive my childish and entirely innocent wish of many years ago.*

The baby stirred, and with her eyes closed began nudging for milk. It was not necessary to move much to give her suck. With the milk, Hilda gave her love, and as she loved, her whole being flooded with warmth.

"You don't have to be a missionary if you don't want to," Hilda said aloud to her Grace, even though she knew that the baby ears could not understand, if they heard. "Aunt Mary is praying that you'll be a missionary. I'd be happy too, if you'd be one. I *think* I'd be happy, but I'd miss you if you went far away. If you don't *want* to be a missionary, I'm sure God wouldn't want you to be what you don't feel *called* to be."

When Hilda was a young child, a visiting missionary spoke in church, and afterward, came to their house for dinner. He talked of the strange countries he had visited, of the wild animals, the hot weather, and the naked heathen people who looked and acted almost like animals. He had brought back so many beautiful blankets, baskets, and trinkets that she wished he would give her some. But he simply packed them back into his satchel to show to other congregants, that they too might know how the godless peoples lived. At the time, she wanted to be a missionary for a chance to visit strange lands. But Pa explained to her that a missionary is anyone, even those who stay in their own country, so long as they brought others to a saving knowledge of Christ. That was when she decided she wanted to be a nurse—a kind of missionary. Then one thing after the other kept her from it—work at home, John's son's birth, and finally, Franz.

By a near-divine revelation, Hilda knew that this was her calling. Being a mother. This was her mission. She knew God would answer her prayer not to die until her mission was fulfilled. Then she prayed that her mission would not be complete for a long time, but that it would be done before Franz's so she would never have to live alone.

Grace had stopped feeding. She had fallen asleep with her mouth open and moist, and with her content, she lulled her young mother to sleep as well.

*   *   *

"I haven't really been sick. This is perfectly normal. Why should it be so hard for me to be up?" Hilda asked when she tried to make the first breakfast after her confinement. "I'm actually a little dizzy."

"Maybe you shouldn't get up yet. I can make breakfast if you tell me again what to do," was Franz's worried answer.

"But I have to get used to it sometime. I can't lie in bed for the rest of my life just because I've had a baby. Lots of people don't stay in bed as long as I have. Remember Aunt Mary?"

And they laughed. Hilda stayed up long enough to make and eat breakfast, but as soon as Franz left the house to do the morning chores, she lay down again to rest. Then, quickly, when she heard him coming in the door, she rose and busied herself with the dishes that had accumulated and become thickly crusted. "Too bad we can't throw these away and start over."

Franz continued. "Or that we don't have lots more dishes so we could keep on dirtying without washing. Then, when Grace is older, she can wash all the dishes that don't get washed because of her!"

"Can you picture that little body grown up and able to wash dishes? Those little fingers. That tiny nose, those closed eyes that aren't any color."

"And able to think, too. That's even harder than doing physical things. Imagine our daughter able to reason and judge?"

"Franz, think of Grace saying 'no' back to us when we ask her to do something. A person who has a mind of her own says 'no' sometimes."

"We'll have to show her who's boss," Franz said.

"I'm afraid, sometimes, when I think of all the obligations of parenthood— the work, the trust and faith placed in us… *We'll* be to blame if she doesn't turn out well. I can't answer all my *own* questions," Hilda added, thinking of the question that was so directly asked at revival meetings. "When I try to foresee some of the problems Grace will have, it scares me."

"I think we'll learn as we go along," Franz answered. "Her problems now are simple. When she's wet, we change her diapers; when she's hungry, you feed her; and every day we bathe her and put clean clothes on her, whether she likes it or not. As we go along, we'll learn with her, but we'll keep one step ahead."

"That makes me feel better, Franz. But what if we don't manage to stay one step ahead of her? What if she'll refuse to follow our steps one day?"

"I expect God will teach us patience to set a good example, and her to have judgment of her own. You know, you can get too engrossed in the matter

69

of perfect living, Hilda. That's what Aunt Mary has done. I'm sure she means well in everything she does. But you see how ridiculous she makes herself and her young son look. She doesn't allow for anything but what she believes to be concerned with the Kingdom, as she sees it. Every moment of her day is spent in pious thinking …

"And what's the result? She's fat because she doesn't think how bad it is for her health to overeat. She thinks only of the food she's not wasting. Her house isn't well cared for because she's forever riding out to see people she thinks need spiritual guidance. And in neglecting her house, she's also neglecting her son—his education, the fun of child play outside in the sun. Above all, what she doesn't realize is that she's doing harm with her solicitations. She's driving people to hell, out of sheer perversity. She doesn't realize that there are as many rights as there are wrongs, and that sometimes wrongs are rights and rights are wrongs. Some day, if she ever does realize that she has done a lot of harm in her intended help, I believe she'll go insane with remorse."

"Franz, she is Pa's sister. Our relative. She's given her life to Jesus."

"Yes, of course, and we tolerate—forgive—her. Others may not. What does your pa say about her?"

Hilda thought again about her many conversations with Pa, her forehead leaning against the hip of the cow she was milking; his leaning on the cow behind her; the warm milky fragrance in her nostrils; the feel of each teat in each of her strong hands as she pulled on them in turn; the purring sound each spurt made as it blended with the rising milk in her pail. "I don't know if I've ever asked him. I wonder what he would say if he was here, now, part of this conversation."

She went on. "You know there are many people in our church who want to do right all the time. Don't you want to? Is everyone who wants to do right all the time not normal?" She thought again of Abe Geppert. "Is everyone who is careless, normal?"

"I'm not saying that it's wrong to want to do right. I'm just saying that if it's an obsession, you will drive yourself crazy. We have to do our best, but beyond that, we have to trust God."

"Think about Mrs. Harmes. She is doing her best for God in her work for me and other new mothers. A full day's work always without pay."

"Oh, oh, I forgot all about paying her," Franz said.

"She doesn't want pay. I'll bring her some fresh bread, or eggs or a chicken when I'm able. And also help other people. 'Passing it on,' so to speak."

*   *   *

They could hear it beginning to rain—a warm slow rain that was certain to continue and to disintegrate the last of the dirty winter snow that had settled on the ground underneath the thicker growth of trees. Franz went out to let in the calves, unused to the soaking of the rain on their young pelts.

Warm air came in through the open window, and Hilda sat, resting her arm on the sill as she used to do on her father's farm. She watched as raindrops trickled off the dusty branches that swelled with buds in spite of the dryness of the ground. Everywhere a tiny drop fell, the dust curled itself upward around the moisture, as if trying to enclose it. Beyond the yard, cut through the heavy grove of trees, the earthen driveway was becoming the darker color of wetness, for the snow had lain there more recently.

A hen that had escaped the coop was walking slowly along the fence, tail down. Seemingly, moisture found its way through her feathers, for she began to run, clumsily stretching her neck forward and kicking her feet high, as if kicking would get her there faster. When she reached the closed gate of the coop, she paced back and forth, her beak trying to find a hole through which she could go. Franz had seen her too. He picked up the hen squatted before him in submission and tossed her fluttering body among the other clucking chickens.

It was raining harder. Underneath the gray-brown grass standing unevenly and brokenly around the buildings, fresh young light-green leaflets of grass began to show. Spring. The thought of it filled Hilda with excitement.

It was the awakening of beauty, life, hope, and faith in the future, and the love that she bore for her husband, her baby, her work, her environment, and yes, even for God. A greater excitement than she had felt in that earlier spring when she and Franz were married, for her love that had seemed perfect then, had grown many fold in those two years.

When Franz came silently to her side to share her reverie, placing his hands on hers without speaking, she felt she could not contain all that energy. She buried her head in the hollow between his chin and shoulders.

CHAPTER TWELVE: 1914

Franz, just back from visiting his father-in-law, excitedly told Hilda that Pa Heldin had shown him a legal paper. "I don't remember the exact words, but it's evidence that your parents have agreed to move to Montana. It looks like a very good arrangement." He stood just inside the door, still wearing his jacket and cap.

Hilda didn't look up from her potato peeler. "Then you have *decided*. To go. Also."

"Hilda, I don't want to make the decision alone. I don't want to do anything your heart is set against. You know that."

"But you are the husband. A wife promises to love and obey. If you decide to go, I shall not question but will go where you go."

They both stood now.

It seemed to be almost a sacred calling, this extravagant offer from the government, and many people, who had seemed settled for life, were made restless by it. John and Marie resolved to go, and land adjoining their claim and further away was still to be had. Pa became interested in moving to this new country, especially since the settlement requested he organize a Mennonite church there.

Franz continued. "If we go and aren't happy there, we can come back. We'll only have to promise to stay three years if we want the land—or the money for it. Then we'll own it."

He pulled out a chair for Hilda and sat himself. "We don't even have to stay three years if we don't mind losing out on the money we could get selling the land. And wasting the time. We'll be right where we started, less what it costs to make the moves."

He repeated, "And what's three years? If we can stick out three years, all the land we cultivate will be ours. We can stay there, owning our land, or we can sell it, and with the money, buy a new place—or add more land to this place here. Either way, we'll be ahead."

"I like this place. Why should we buy a new place?"

"I like this place too. But I can like more than one place."

"Why should we have more land?"

"It's not to get *more* land, not *much* more."

"And if crops aren't good in Montana?"

"They've been having good ones so far. All the reports are good. People are investing with the money they're making."

"Mennonites don't speculate: don't invest money to make more money."

"All right, I don't mean that *I* would invest. Though, you know, we don't follow *all* the Mennonite rules and regulations. Look at the decorations you have on your dresses. Lace and ruffles."

"That's a different subject. We need to talk out your idea of giving up what we've done here so far. Starting over. In a wilderness. The work would be so hard. We'd have to build a house, and what would we build it from? There aren't any trees."

"We're young. Hard work won't hurt us for a while. The settlers build their own houses, partly from sod."

"If Grace should get sick, or if I should have another baby, where would there be a doctor?"

"We're healthy. We mustn't borrow trouble. Especially since Father Heldin will be there—he can be our doctor if we need one. And you know so much about nursing yourself that you could take care of any little things."

"Our house here, and all the work we have done on it—"

"We'll rent it out, at least at first, until we're sure we aren't coming back."

"But you know what renters do to a place. It won't be as nice when we return… And, think about some other things: We live just two miles from town here—a short ride. You like to go to town often, if only to schmooze with the shopkeepers. You borrow books from the library…And the mail—the mailman comes by every day. We get a newspaper every day… A trip to the twin cities takes just four or five hours by train. All those things surely can't be available in the Montana wilderness."

"Hilda, think about it as an adventure. It can make us strong. We're young. We can invent new activities.

"An adventure, you say. With a small child. And who knows—maybe more children."

"Hilda, you're taking for granted that you won't like it in Montana, and that you'll want to come back as soon as the time is up. If that's the case, then we'd better not go at all."

"I'm sorry. I want to do what you want to do. I don't understand the technical things about it, so for your sake I'll not say any more. My happiness is doing your will, Franz." But, inside, she knew that answer to be more automatic than true.

Franz raised his voice. "That's not the happiness I want. I don't want demanded happiness. I want involuntary happiness, spontaneous happiness." He leaned forward now, his fingers pulling at the tufts of hair that needed cutting. "Let's not think about it for a while. Then, when we've become calm about it all, God will send us the answer. I don't want to do anything that keeps you from being happy."

Hilda was glad it was time to feed little Grace, who now had a few teeth and could eat mashed potatoes and ground meat; glad that if she cried, she could cry in the next room and the child wouldn't notice. Maybe Franz would forget about moving to the wilderness. It was so happy here. A change might be as happy, but it could not be happier, and it might not be as happy.

*   *   *

Franz, just back from town for the week's shopping, brought the news with the flour and sugar. "It's definite. Reverend Heldin will be pastor of the church they are organizing in Montana. His land will be convenient to where they are planning to build it."

"Is anyone else going too? Besides John and Marie?"

"Yes, the whole Geppert family—all the children, even the grown ones."

"Your mother is staying here?"

"Yes, she says she's too old to start fresh, and she wants to stay here. She says she isn't well enough for all that work."

"Your siblings?"

"Amos says our mother needs him here. Esther's Jonas isn't well enough to take on the move—you know about his heart. Mathilda says her Seth is making too much money, and he knows his business wouldn't succeed in Montana. He needs electricity for his machinery. He'd have to start a whole new business there—he's no farmer. Actually, those aren't her words, but that's what she meant."

"Are Aunt Mary and young Peter going also?"

"They are thinking about it—yes. So, Hilda, your father, brother, and aunt are going. Why would you want to stay behind?"

"Your mother and siblings are staying here. Why would you want to leave them? We have to make our own decisions. My heart is here. Here with you."

"I think you're more attached to your family than I am. That's maybe a difference between us; the difference between a man and a woman."

"Franz, doesn't it seem like an epidemic? They all think they're getting something for nothing. But there must be a catch to it somewhere. Your mother is wise for deciding not to go." Hilda prayed that God would not let them go, that he would make it impossible. Part of her prayer was thanks that the Geppert family was leaving, and she wouldn't have to avoid meeting Abe's eyes in church any more. Unless, of course, she and Franz also went.

"The government isn't trying to put anything over on us. They are just trying to encourage good farmers to settle the new land, and the only 'catch' is that it is lonesome, untamed land. If many families who are related by blood and by religion go together, then even that catch is removed."

"When is Pa moving to Montana?"

"As soon as his harvest is in. Before that, he'll go to choose a plot for their buildings and the church. Each family moving will bring lumber for the church building and will help construct it. When he comes, he won't have so much to do, in case winter sets in early."

Whenever he brought home news of more families deciding to move, his eyes glistened as though he forgot that it was others, not he, who were going to this remarkable land of promise.

Sooner or later, God will decide for us. Then I will go, or stay here, without a word. Hilda said, "I'll miss Liesebet. I hope she gets a chance for an education there—she always spoke of being a teacher."

"Liesebet will get along all right with your father as her mentor. She'll be able to teach the children of the settlers. With so many arriving, she'll fill a definite need."

*   *   *

So the others moved. Hilda and Franz helped them pack their utensils and better china that had been brought from the old country several decades before, using winter clothing as padding.

Her father's face looked younger, as if the spirit of adventure had given him a dose of energy. He took advantage of a quiet moment alone with Hilda to hand her the old samovar, saying, "I think this is better kept here. Our new home will be somewhat rough, and Muttah doesn't have the feeling for it that your ma had. That I know you have. Your ma always kept it polished, just as you did when you still lived with me."

Muttah did not speak of the move, and Hilda was not able to get from her either a warning to hold back or inspiration to follow. Fifteen-year-old Liesebet was crying.

Hilda tried comforting her; she felt none of the conviction in her heart but only a sense of loss that Liesebet was moving very far away. "Liesebet, it won't be so bad. You'll have Pa and Muttah—and John and Marie—with you, and you can play with Johnny, Hermann, and Marta. You'll be happy."

"Hilda, why don't you come too? If we could be neighbors, and I could see you in church every Sunday, it wouldn't be so bad. I could come to your place and help you with Grace when you're busy. Why don't you ask Franz if you can go too? Maybe he would agree if you wanted to." Liesebet's eyes shone more blue through her tears.

Then Hilda knew that Pa's family had talked of her and Franz's possible moving, or not moving, to Montana. They must know she didn't want to go. Since he gave her the samovar, he must not even be expecting her to go. Liesebet must have overheard that conversation and, from that, felt more fear at her own going. Franz was watching. Did he hope she would be touched by Liesebet's plea when Hilda had not been interested in going otherwise?

That evening, Hilda decided to tell Franz she thought she was pregnant. She hadn't had any symptoms yet: no nausea, no weakness. Still, she had little doubt about it. "I've missed the regular. You know—the monthly," she told him.

"Then that settles our staying here, for a while at least," Franz answered. "God has decided." He left the house, whistling.

*　　*　　*

It was a happy pregnancy. Grace no longer needed diapers and was talking. She knew the meaning of the word "no," both when it was said to her and when she said it to her parents. Franz seemed content, working on the already well-kept farm. The young crops were vigorous, promising to yield a bountiful harvest. Hilda worked hard; because it was her second time, she did not experience the fears and discomforts she'd had before Grace was born.

When the child was to be born, they again called Mrs. Harmes, who did not mind so much this time that Franz stayed in the room during the delivery.

Afterward, the room was very quiet, and Hilda even dropped off to sleep for a bit. When she opened her eyes, she saw that Franz was trembling. To reassure him, she said, "Papa, I love you."

"Hilda, he was a beautiful boy. A son."

"Was? Franz, tell me."

"He did not breathe. God did not see fit to give him to us." He wept.

Hilda could not cry. Her heart was dry with tiredness and submission. She did not, could not, did not want to say the words in her head: *God is speaking to us. It's my fault the boy did not live. I didn't want to move to*

Montana. God wants us to go. I should be willing, eager, to do God's will, so he won't have to punish us.

Those were the words in her head. In her heart were questions. *What kind of god takes a baby? What kind of god took babies from Ma? How did Ma deal with seven losses? Twins. Two girls. Four boys. All normal pregnancies, as far as I know. Fine-looking babies. One a six-year-old with diphtheria... How many babies will God take from me? Will Grace live to grow up? How will I cope? What can I do?"*

Mrs. Harmes, seeming to think it would comfort her, offered what another patient had said: "She cried at the birth of twins, on top of the other eight little children she has. She said she wished one of them wouldn't live. Or that she could give one—or even both—away."

"It's not fair," Hilda said quietly, though she wanted to shriek. "I'd be happy for a hundred babies if they lived!" *Why, O God... Why did you do it to me?*

In the next room, Grace was crying that she was hungry. Franz rose to help her. Mrs. Harmes left, taking the stained bedclothes with her to wash.

Later, when the day's work was done and Grace had gone to sleep for the night, Franz came to sit at Hilda's bedside. "What shall we name the boy? Shall we use the name we were thinking of when we thought he would live and be healthy?"

"I want to see him, to know what to name him. I think he should have his own name... Franz, does he have a soul? If he never drew a breath? Do you think he's in Heaven?"

"How should I know? You know more about the Bible than I do."

"I doubt that. Just because my father is a minister doesn't make *me* more informed. You've had more school than I've had... Where is he? Our son."

"I wrapped him in an old blanket and put him in the guest bedroom."

"You mean his body. Where is his *soul?*"

"Hilda, I don't know. Let's get some rest tonight. Let's think tomorrow."

*   *   *

They both slept fitfully. The next morning, Franz took care of chores that had to be done. When he returned to the house, Hilda was dressed, determined to show respect to this child, this boy who was an angel now. She was certain of that.

Together they studied him: his perfect fingers and toes and even his manhood. His face that looked so much like Grace, and like an old picture of Franz. They bathed him, with tears and water. Dressed him in the white dimity gown Hilda had sewed just last week, and swaddled him in a new flannel baby blanket that she had edged with a fine lace. The corner of the blanket would hide his face.

Franz found some good boards to build a small coffin. They placed a feather pillow inside it and laid their son on the pillow.

"I wish Pa were here to say a few words," Hilda said. "I'm not sure the new minister would know what to say about a baby that hasn't taken a breath." She entered Franz's outstretched arms.

Then they closed the box. They wrote "Cherub" on the lid. It would be his own name, not the name of any relative, living or dead. Franz dug a small grave north of the house, where it would never be disturbed.

Hilda's breasts smarted and ached, and the front of her dress was soaked with her milk. Inside the house, Grace was quietly playing.

CHAPTER THIRTEEN: 1915

Hilda's pregnancy justified staying behind when her parents and siblings took up new land in Montana. Now there seemed no reason to stay behind. It was settled. Believing the baby's death to be a message from God, Hilda relented.

During a nightmare of selling unneeded goods, packing, and saying goodbyes, Hilda arranged with the Heldins—cousin Henry and his wife, Emma—to keep safe the precious samovar while they were away. Not wanting to make work for Emma by asking her to maintain the tea urn's polish, Hilda wrapped it in paper. She folded her wedding dress carefully and packed both into a sturdy box. They were leaving another treasure behind: the grave of their infant, their Cherub. She was certain they would be back. It felt comforting, like insurance that this bad dream would end.

The day before leaving, Hilda took a long walk while Grace slept and Franz hauled a trailer-load of large furniture, including the cook stove, to the train depot. She went to stand at the crest of the hill where she could see as far as the town's water tower and grain elevators. Below was the creek, now a trickle, fringed with willow trees. A lone Russian olive tree stood halfway up the hill. Beyond the fence in the neighbor's pasture, grazing cows all faced the same direction. From the hill, she took the lane along the cornfield and observed that the corn was well eared. The renter would harvest it for them, as payment toward next year's rent. She looked at the grove, saw only one tree dying. Potential firewood. Other trees looked healthy.

She headed back to the house. One more night. They would sleep on the floor since their bed was disassembled and on the trailer in town. For the first year, maybe longer, the house would stand empty, or almost empty. They were leaving some things behind, things they would not need but didn't quite want to get rid of. The renter was leasing only the farm land; he lived in his own house on another farm.

Early the next morning, Cousin Henry arrived with his horses and wagon to carry the pig, cows, a crate of chickens, and some straw and feed. Franz, Hilda, and Grace rode in their own carriage, loaded with fragile items and the pets. Amos also came with a team and wagon to carry clothing and home-canned goods that didn't fit into the buggy. All together, they met the waiting boxcars at the Mound Lake train station. The station man gave directions and helped Franz lead the horses pulling the trailer up the ramp, where they were unhitched and tied to a rail on a wall. Franz took a moment to stroke them, their eyes wide with fear. The pig and cows had to be prodded, first to descend from Henry's wagon, and then to climb the ramp onto the train; chickens and cats were in cages. The leashed dogs would get on later, when Franz came aboard. The three men, with Hilda's help, unloaded the buggy that could quite easily be pushed up the ramp, where they reloaded it with household goods and clothing.

A bucket of water and sufficient oats and hay provided sustenance for the cows and horses, and the straw was enough bedding for the first days, perhaps for the entire trip. The pig would get leftover milk. They had considered leaving the cats behind to fend for themselves, but, well, why not take them? They and the dogs would likely have mice and rats to catch and eat right there in the boxcar. But when Franz opened the cats' cage, they fearfully huddled away from the opening.

Now another emigrant, Richard Jones, loaded his goods. Not Mennonites, he and his family were taking up land closer to Lone Wolf.

The train arrived from the east, just as the boxcar was finished loading. It passed beyond the yard and then changed tracks and backed hard, seeming to crash into the boxcar to couple it to the far end. The noisy monster blew black smoke from its stack above and hissed steam from below its side. Grace covered her ears and hid her face in Hilda's skirt. At that point, a conductor appeared to guide Hilda and Grace onto a passenger car, along with a lady and five children; she later introduced herself as Hattie Jones. They missed seeing Franz and Mr. Jones climb into the boxcar with their animals and goods. Their goodbyes were a hurried wave—Henry shouting, *"Gott befohlen!"*[12] and Amos seconding in Low German, *"Uht yay."*[13]

Hilda and Grace rode on upholstered benches, looking through large windows at the villages and cities and field after field of grain and herds of cattle. They caught sight of people—a woman throwing a pail of water out

12 [May] God keep you.
13 Adieu, go with God.

her back door, men standing at train depots smoking pipes, children on tire swings suspended from tall tree branches. Hilda allowed herself to imagine their lives, these people she had never seen before and would never see again. These strangers didn't see her or know her either, would never know her while they lived out their lives.

She opened her Bible and fingered the swatch of cloth from Ma's last dress hidden inside the back cover. Beside her, Grace played with her doll, Maggie, pulling off her clothes and asking for help when she put them on her backward. Grace watched the Jones children, who occupied two benches as they played with their toys. Before long, they included her in their play.

*   *   *

Franz could see through slats in the side of the boxcar where he and Richard tended their animals. They compared their hopes and expectations as they each faced a new life. Franz said, "I feel strong and healthy, and I look forward to my first harvest, with the help of my in-laws."

Richard sighed. "My wife and I aren't leaving anyone behind, and we aren't joining anyone in Montana." Franz didn't offer condolences, not being well-enough acquainted. *Who knows, maybe they like being alone*, he concluded.

The days and nights seemed long. The cows had to be milked regularly, so there was milk for everyone to drink, including the pig, cats, and dogs—even some to share with the trainmen, and some to keep in a jug so it would sour and clabber. The chickens did not lay eggs during the trip. During stops at rural or small-town stations, Franz and Richard cleaned from behind the livestock; local gardeners were happy to receive the manure.

Franz and Richard also took turns to check on their families. At one stop, as she handed Franz some tvaybak, cheese, and an apple, Hilda asked him, "How well can you sleep in that boxcar?"

He grinned, "Oh, very well. The straw is soft, and the dogs snuggle up next to me and keep me warm."

"I hope you don't plan to continue that when we get to our own home," Hilda warned him.

"You'll have to invite me politely," he teased.

*   *   *

When they reached Lone Wolf, the couples wished each other God's blessing and promised to keep in touch. Maybe they'd see each other when Franz came to Lone Wolf to shop.

Franz and Hilda decided not to take time to look around the town that seemed not much, if at all, bigger than Mound Lake. It was a railroad and highway hub, with mercantile stores, hotels, bars, and, of course, churches. The horses, fresh from the four-day trip, needed the exercise of pulling the furniture-laden wagon. Pa was there with his team to pull the buggy holding Hilda and Grace, as well as some fragile household goods. John had brought a sturdy wagon with a ramp that they coaxed the cows and pig onto. They were a parade, keeping track of each other on the thirty-mile trip to their homestead.

*　　*　　*

Now they were at Father Heldin's place until they could build their own house and barn. A bit like an usher, Muttah pointed Hilda to the smaller bedroom. "Grace will stay with you—I made her a little bed on the floor with some straw and a blanket over it. It will be quite cozy. Hermann and Marta will sleep in our room. Some of your things can stay in Liesebet's room, and large furniture will be safe in the barn stalls since the animals can all stay outdoors, now that it's still summer. It will be crowded, but we will get along."

Grace wandered around among the boxes and parcels. Turning to her own children, Muttah said, "Hermann, show Grace your blocks. You can teach her how to build a house." Then, to Hilda, she shared the news, "John and Marie have a new baby. Helena born just six months ago."

"We hadn't heard," Hilda said. "I guess we haven't kept in close-enough touch, what with our baby dying."

*　　*　　*

"And we'll live only six miles from you, Hilda," Liesebet was telling, as fast as she could, for she had so much to tell.

"What a change in you, Liesebet," Hilda replied, marveling at how quickly her body had changed from that of a girl to a woman. During just one year's separation. "But you're still young."

Liesebet blushed. "I'm sixteen. Pa says I'm grown up enough."

"But to get married. You were going to be a teacher. There is so much time in a lifetime. You can do many things *and* get married too, if you do them in the right order."

Her panic did not transfer to Liesebet, who couldn't conceal the glow within her. "You, yourself, gave up becoming a nurse to marry Franz."

"I know. Maybe we could have waited. But things were different. I felt our kitchen wasn't big enough for two cooks—two women. I wasn't used to Muttah. I wasn't used to Ma being gone. I needed to get out of the way. If Ma had lived… Oh." Hilda saw the look on Liesebet's face. "And you were

82

so young. You didn't remember Ma so well. You quickly adapted to Pa's new wife, your new mother."

"I was? I didn't? I did?" After exchanging a long look with her sister, Liesebet said, "Wait till you meet him. He's tall and strong, and as handsome as your Franz. He plays the guitar and sings very well."

A call from Muttah interrupted their getting-reacquainted conversation. "Liesebet, go get the some potatoes and wash them. It's time to make dinner." Liesebet's face registered a childish reaction to household chores, but her newfound maturity reasserted itself, and she left for the garden to dig. When Franz came in from releasing the horses, the cows, and the pig into the fenced pasture, Hilda took advantage of their privacy to tell him of Liesebet's engagement.

He smiled but raised his eyebrows. "That's nice. I don't know him, but I'm sure Father Heldin wouldn't give his permission unless he's a decent fellow."

"But Franz, she's so young. She's four years younger than I was when I married you. What does she know of whom she'll love when she *is* grown up?"

"You're borrowing trouble. Your father decided right when he agreed that you and I should marry, didn't he? Then we should trust his endorsement for Liesebet."

"You're probably right," Hilda said. Yet she could not help feeling anxious.

"Hilda, you know God always puts a barrier in the way of something He does not want to happen, so long as we trust Him," Franz said.

"But even if he *is* the right husband for her, and even if Father *likes* the match, she should *wait*. If the love is *real*, it will last even if they don't marry right away. She hasn't finished her childhood." How, Hilda wondered, could she talk with Pa about Liesebet's plans? Should she even try to talk with him?

He spoke again. "Think of two things before you ask her to wait to marry. One is that she does not have her real mother, and that, regardless of how good her stepmother is to her, she cannot replace a real mother. That, together with the reality of growing up in a pioneer country, makes her mature faster than other people. Actually, think of a third thing: What will you do if she won't listen to you?"

He went back to tending their animals. Hilda and Grace went with him to check on and comfort the cats, who were now locked in a small room of the barn where they would have to stay until they could be moved to their new place.

*   *   *

Meanwhile, the Heldin parents, noting Liesebet's happiness, shared their separate thoughts. Muttah, also getting used to the idea of Lieseet's engagement, said, "It hasn't been bad having Liesebet live with us. She helps me when I ask her. Hermann and Marta like her." To herself, she added, *On the other hand, I'll have my true, real children only in the house. It will be more like my family from here on. Flesh of my flesh.*

Pa brooded a bit: "I hope I'm doing the right thing in giving my blessing to Liesebet and her plans to marry Joe. She is young." To himself he said, *I think Leah will be more contented, even if she doesn't have the help in the house that Liesebet has been giving her. We've been happy enough with our combined family, but when I see the eagerness in Liesebet as she plans her future, I guess she'll be happier married to Joe.*

Aloud he said, "Joe's a fine fellow. He's a little more forceful—even forward—than I'm usually comfortable with. He's very confident of his belief in Jesus. And Liesebet's always been a follower: first of Hilda, then you."

"Now Joe. I don't know his parents or his other relatives. They're all back East somewhere. I wonder if they'll even come for the wedding. This is a different country, that's for sure. Everything is different. Except God. God is always the same. I trust God to watch over them."

*   *   *

After an overnight rest, Franz took Hilda and Grace to take their first look at what would be their new home. The land seemed flat. Oh, here and there were slight rises, but if Hilda swept her eyes sideways, it all looked flat. "It's so empty. Vacant."

"Of course, Hilda. It's vacant. That's why it's available for us to settle."

"I see cactuses. I know what they are. But what are those bushes?"

"I don't know. I think they're wild. Maybe the cattle or horses will eat them... But let's just close our eyes and imagine how it will look when we've built our house and planted a few things."

"I'll try, Franz," Hilda managed to say.

Far away on the horizon, they saw smoke they knew was from Muttah's kitchen, but they couldn't distinguish the house or even the chimney.

"Look, Grace," Franz said, "this is where we'll live. We're going to have a house here. And a barn."

But Grace was whining, "Wanna go home, Ma."

Hilda bit her lip to keep from crying herself.

*   *   *

Early the next morning, Franz returned to Lone Wolf to fetch lumber for their new home. The next day, he was back in time to mark out, with his father-in-law, where to start construction of a new home. Pa Heldin's fields didn't need much tilling at the time, so he lent a hand digging for a cellar and contributing fieldstones and boulders he had collected for the foundation. Both men worked long hours. When the roof was in place, Pa, saying he had some other errands to do in Lone Wolf, offered to bring back sheet metal for the roof. Franz could devote his time to putting up siding and even to start building an outhouse. They hoped, but weren't optimistic, to be able to move in before winter.

Living with Pa and Muttah challenged Hilda to combine her role as child and adult mother. She found herself working hard, helping to cook, clean house, gather cow- and buffalo-chips for fuel, and haul water from the well Pa had dug. She tried to anticipate whatever Muttah would need to have done, proving her adulthood, in a way—no longer a daydreaming child. She believed Muttah tried to let her be a grownup, but neither she nor Muttah found a way to discuss their relationship. It hung in the air between them like dust motes.

When she could leave Grace with Liesebet, Hilda rode the five miles to their homestead on one of Pa's horses. She could handle a hammer and followed Franz's direction in nailing inside boards in place; this offered the air between the outside and inside walls a kind of insulation. The house would have two rooms and a small entry room.

Other days, she took the three children for walks where the prairie grass had been cut for hay. She wasn't sure what to look for, but they saw an occasional prairie hen leading a brood of half-grown chicks, and sometimes a hawk circling overhead. Though they were careful not to step on cacti low in the grass, Hilda regretted not wearing shoes, especially when Grace cried and needed to be carried. Then Marta shouted, "Nake!" and Hermann corrected her, "Snake. Say snake." He looked for a stick. "I'll kill it," he announced.

"Better not." Hilda took his arm, this eight-year-old boy, the baby she had delivered. Her brother. "It's too dangerous—hear its rattle? We'll tell Pa about it."

Hermann reminded her, "Pa's away. Our dog can kill it too. I'll call the dog."

"No, no. It could bite the dog. You don't want the dog to die. Wait and tell Pa." Promising them she'd bake cookies, she led them back home. She hoped there were ingredients for cookies and that Muttah wouldn't mind.

*　　*　　*

On Sunday, they were all happy for a day of rest. Hilda longed to stay back while everyone else left for worship. But she did not. It would be unseemly.

Furthermore, it would be a chance to see John and Marie, provided they weren't "resting from church."

Still smelling of new wood and gaslights, the Prairie Mennonite Church seemed much like the Meadow Church. Why not? Planned and built by the same people, it was simple inside, almost stark, with plain glass windows and no decorations except for a German quotation from the Bible curved across the front: "Blessed are they who hear God's word and keep it." Pews were handmade rustic benches, to be sanded and varnished later. Men would sit on the left side, women on the right.

Hilda could see Franz sitting toward the middle of the men's side; she noted that he was asleep well before the sermon was begun. *Poor Franz. Works so hard.* Behind him was John, and not far away Abe Geppert, looking combed and pressed. *Oh, I had sort of forgotten about him.*

She reminded herself that letting her mind wander was as bad as sleeping during the service. Maybe worse. But she looked forward to chatting with John and Marie after church. Beside her, Grace fidgeted. Glad that she had brought enough for them all, she gave her half a tvaybak and half each to the other children in the row. Muttah seemed to be paying close attention to the words of her husband.

CHAPTER FOURTEEN: 1916–1917

The house and out-buildings stood ready. As soon as the ground dried enough that they could travel with heavy racks over the primitive road, they would move into it, and Hilda could again establish a home. They could smell spring in the air.

During the long winter, Franz went to work on it almost every day, taking loads of lumber, with the dogs chasing after. Some days—and even weeks—storms kept him restlessly at the Heldin home. Pa and other members of the church helped him, remembering their own problems of homebuilding in the new country. So it grew from a cellar to keep vegetables and a foundation made of boulders they found lying here and there on their own and Pa's land.

Some people had lived through their first winter with walls of only one layer, and others had only one room at first, so Franz and Hilda considered themselves lucky to have double walls with air space between them. She would wallpaper the walls later.

While they built their house, Joe was also building. Liesebet blushed, but she claimed that the one room their home was to be would be enough room for them, at least at first. They got married and moved into their little home.

Moving in took Hilda and Franz less than a day. The dogs knew their way around the yard, and the cats were already sleeping in the new shed on fresh hay, getting fat on mice they caught. Hilda hoped they would not go wild, being there on their own.

Grace, used to playing with Liesebet, Hermann, and Marta, whined that they would not keep on living in the same house together. She soon adapted to her new home, playing in the grassless soil around the house. Her face became brown with sun and dirt that would not come off in the hard well water.

"If there were trees here," Hilda said, wishing she could hold back her longing for the security of the protective-looking trees—windbreaks—they'd had on their former home back in Minnesota.

"There are some trees in the hollow of the creek that runs near town," Franz informed Hilda after a trip into Lone Wolf, where he had gone to get seed. "Their branches are turning a light green, and any day now they will have leaves. I broke off some branches when no one was looking and stuck them in the ground near the barn," Franz said, looking sheepish. "But we'll have to keep watering them until they get roots deep enough to support themselves."

"Why has no one else thought of planting trees?" Hilda wondered. "Don't people care?"

"I suspect they're hard to grow here. The climate is dryer, and perhaps colder in winter. Even the farming is done differently here. Some years crops fail too—not lately, but the Indians say some years are bad… Maybe times have changed; it's been many years since the last drought. Anyhow, we'll see if the trees grow."

*   *   *

At first, Hilda hand-carried pails of water from a spring some distance away. This was adequate for a while, although she wondered how clean the water was when she saw tracks of animals that drank there. Then, Muttah contributed her talent at dowsing. The water source she had found, and the well Pa had dug for their own use, dependably yielded fresh, clear water throughout the seasons. Now, she came to Hilda and Franz's place with her forked willow branch, walking back and forth near their home site. When the branch twisted and pointed downward, she tapped a peg into the ground to mark where Franz could dig.

As he deepened the hole, Franz placed a winch over it with a rope attached to a bucket. Hilda climbed into the hole and helped by filling the bucket with dirt for Franz to dump. Together they built a frame to shore up the walls of the well. Soon water appeared, and the digging was done. Franz placed a hand pump with a pipe down to the water and a platform over the well to keep the water clean, and animals and children from falling in.

Franz rigged up eaves-troughs with some tin sheets he found dumped behind an abandoned shack. The downspouts drained soft rainwater into a hogshead barrel for Hilda to collect and use for washing clothes and bathing. In winter, she would have to melt snow. When that water was not available, she'd have to use the well-water that was so hard that wash wouldn't look clean, and their hair would tangle in spite of the soap she made out of lard, lye, and water.

*   *   *

Without woods—dead trees to cut for fuel—the settlers became coal miners. The men went to an open mine a day's ride away, where they filled their wagons with coal. When they needed more fuel, Hilda, taking Grace with her, walked around the land carrying a gunny sack to collect dried cow- and buffalo-dung that she preferred calling "chips."

Franz worked hard, plowing the fresh virgin sod, getting up morning after morning, even before the time Grace usually woke them. When Pa was through seeding his fields, Franz borrowed his new drill,[14] finishing as quickly as possible so that Joe could borrow it too, in his turn.

Rains came when they were ready for them. As far as they could look, tender shoots of grain rose, and the branches Franz had broken off the trees in town put forth leaves.

The first harvest was good. Together with Muttah and Liesebet, Hilda served the threshers, young adventurous men who came from the East to see the new country for themselves, to make some money and, perhaps, to find young, unattached girls for whom it would be worthwhile to stay. They worked hard and ate heartily. Evenings, they entertained each other, singing and playing their guitars before they went comfortably to sleep in the fresh hay that Franz had spread out for them in the barn.

It snowed for the first time after all the crops were in and the fields had been plowed. The beautiful snow fell into the hollows of the furrows, catching a promise of moisture for the next year. The flakes that had fallen before were packed harder and further down, and a rising wind would not be able to sweep them away, providing insulation. The little house was warm and cozy. During the evenings, light from the kerosene lamp reached all parts of the room where they cooked, ate, and read. With surprise, Hilda realized it was possible to be happy even here, though she could not imagine any pleasure if it was not for Franz and Grace. She almost conceded but did not go over to him—she wasn't ready to admit anything to him, to grant him satisfaction for the decision of having made the move. Not that he would crow or lord it over her; he wasn't like that.

Whenever weather permitted, they drove their buggy, which was now beginning to show some wear, to the church to hear Reverend Heldin preach. There, they were able to spend time with John and Marie, who lived the same distance from the church as they, only in the opposite direction. Their Johnny was growing fast, his solemn face resembling his father and grandfather, as if to do justice to the name he inherited. Baby Helena wanted to crawl and get into things. Liesebet and Joe were also there, possibly expecting a baby,

---

14 A horse-drawn implement that plants seeds.

though they had not announced that yet. Aunt Mary sometimes missed attending if her arthritis was giving her trouble, but her son, Peter, attended faithfully. The Geppert family came regularly, including the still-unmarried Abe. Jonah, the surviving deaf and dumb boy who had been kept hidden back in Minnesota, never attended.

The congregation filled the small church. The people sang with energy gained from the exercise of work, obvious in the heartiness of their singing. Hilda's voice was not strong, but it was true—on pitch and sweet. Beside her, Grace joined in with her child voice, looking up at her mother as she sang.

After the service, as in Minnesota, the congregants gathered in small groups, sharing their thoughts and their news of the week. It was a bit late in the year to call on each other at their homes; such visits had to be short if they wanted to reach home before dark.

*   *   *

A spring-like thaw melted away most of the autumn snowfall and caused the air to smell of the earth and awakening life, even now, after Thanksgiving. Hilda opened the door and window, releasing stored-up warmth she had been hoarding in anticipation of the cold of winter, and letting in the fresh clean air. After a week of such weather, Franz could no longer restrain an idea, and early one evening, he suggested, "Hilda, we've had a pretty good harvest; don't you suppose I could go into town once more and get a few Christmas things for us? I know we're ready for winter and won't need anything until spring, but it's so nice, and we could have something special."

"What will you get?"

"That will be my surprise. You must be a good girl so the *Weihnachtsmann*[15] can bring you something you will like."

"I wish I could go with you to town. I haven't been for a long time." Hilda smiled, knowing she wouldn't leave Grace or take her on that thirty-mile trip to town.

They went to bed early so Franz could start at sunrise the next morning, and when he left, he kissed her, promising, "In spring, we'll both go, and we'll take Grace with us."

When he was gone, Hilda looked around for something to do; part of her felt something she chose not to name—a sense of freedom at being alone. Time to do whatever she felt like doing. Time to yield to impulse—she could spend the day reading a novel if she wanted, although she wasn't really alone. She couldn't read a novel and ignore Grace. Besides, she didn't have a novel to read. She did have the *National Geographics* Franz had brought, but found

---

15   Santa Claus. Literally, "Christmas man."

it hard to concentrate on her reading. Instead, she showed the photographs to Grace.

Other days, when he was away—helping at John's or Joe's or Pa's place—were always long, and Hilda felt a certain tension until he returned. This time, he was going farther, across a wilderness. There were no wild animals he could not defend himself against; the few wolves were easily shot by someone as sure as Franz. It was only a day's trip by buggy. Tomorrow he would shop, and the next evening he would be back. Still, Hilda felt useless talking to the child mind of Grace. She spent a good deal of time playing "catch me" outside with her. Then she dragged out the chores of feeding the hog, the dozen chickens, the dogs and cats, and the cattle—a pregnant heifer, a calf, and its mother, which she milked. When it was time to go to bed, she took Grace into her bed with her and, sleeping, she dreamt of Franz.

The second day, when she woke, she saw the snow, which had begun softly during the night and now covered everything. "Franz!" Hilda said aloud, and fell wildly on her knees to pray, but her prayer only woke Grace, who began to cry with fright. As she rose to dress her little girl, she realized she didn't dare cry because doing so would frighten Grace even more. Then it came to her that her prayers would be to no avail anyhow, for none of her prayers had ever been answered, except with a firm, "No."

It was surely because she had never been able to answer the question she had actually forgotten about for periods of time. Many times she had thought, *Yes, I am saved; I'm right with God,* but each time, new questions came. Questions like, *How do I know?* Or, *When?* Each time, she pushed away any thoughts of it in case an answer should come.

Hurriedly, she put out food for Grace and let the girl feed herself while she ran again into her bedroom to pray. "If you, I mean, Thou save Franz…" It was the wrong way to begin. Pa had warned her to never try to bribe God. She thought of the offer she had made to God in hopes of keeping Ma living and healthy. And of the baby, Cherub, whom God took when she had resisted leaving Minnesota. Now she was trying to think of some way to save Franz's life, some way to establish contact with God and, later, she would definitely attend to the question of the saving of her soul.

It occurred to her, that, always unbidden, she sometimes wondered how her life would be different if she had married Abe, who seemed so sure of the meaning of salvation. *Franz doesn't deserve thoughts like that. I love him. I'm absolutely, completely, entirely sure of that. No question about it.*

She thought back on the many prayers she had offered in her life. There were mealtime prayers, and memorized ones she had prayed as a child; she decided to eliminate them as an adult, as they did not represent her personal relationship with God. There were the prayers she was asked to pray at times in her Sunday school class at church. These too did not represent her private thoughts, as they had to be carefully composed to be as much a message to the other members of the class who were listening as they were to God directly. She eliminated them as well. The prayers with Franz were few, as so often they were too tired or did not go to bed at exactly the same time, or they just forgot to pray because there were so many other things to discuss. When they had devotions together, she still felt a little shy and never said as much as she would by herself. The only prayers left were the ones she sometimes prayed as she breathed in the sparkling air of a beautiful morning, and those were not spoken or composed of connected thoughts.

Again she tried to pray, this time omitting herself entirely, thinking only of the snow, and praying that God might stay it until Franz could get safely back to her. She prayed on, starting when she felt a touch. Grace had climbed out of her chair.

By noon, medium-sized snowflakes lazily and steadily fell in close succession. Impulsively, Hilda wrapped Grace in a large blanket and hurried out the door into the falling flakes. But she stopped and turned back toward the house, remembering that if she did run to Pa's house, Franz might come home directly and, missing her, become worried. The animals would need feeding if she was not here. Furthermore, if she set out those miles to Pa's house, she might get lost. Landmarks were not visible, and she could not rely on her sense of direction. Grace's short legs could not walk through the already foot-deep snow, and she wouldn't be able to carry her that far. Franz had taken both horses. If she set out, she would get tired, and being tired, she would rest and possibly—as she had heard people often did when they were lost in snow—fall asleep, freeze to death, and be covered with snow so no one would find her until it thawed, perhaps in spring.

Grace began to fuss and wriggle in her blanket, uncomfortable from having to breathe the warm wooly air. She loosed her, and together they slowly walked back into the house, where Grace scrambled immediately to her toys to play.

Trying to be slow to make the day seem shorter, Hilda fed the animals. They were eager for food, insensible to the dynamics of the world about them. There was not much to do. As she started toward their house with the full pail of milk, it occurred to Hilda that she had left Grace alone in the house, and the stove was heated to a glowing redness. She hurried, spilling milk along her long skirt, and the milk did not freeze but slapped coldly against her legs.

Grace was still playing with Maggie, sitting on her little bench that Franz had made before her birth, not doing anything but holding the doll upside down by one leg.

All the rest of the day Hilda worked, mending all the clothes she could find, darning Franz's socks, and even cleaning their bedroom from wall to wall. She did not allow herself to look out the window oftener than once every hour; each time she saw that the snowfall was not diminishing, but she didn't let herself consider that it might be denser. When evening came, she hardly knew it, for it wasn't much darker than day had been, with the snow giving off a kind of glow. Again she fed the animals, this time taking Grace with her to the barn, and still they ate, as hungrily as always. She let Grace feed the dogs and cats some table scraps.

She went to bed early, praying and believing that tomorrow the snow will have stopped and the sun would be shining. But she heard, faintly, a low moan that was wind, beginning far off, and coming nearer. She listened to it: it was not at all like the comforting roar of the Minnesota wind in the cottonwood grove. It was more of a distant shriek, a cry of pain. Not at all like waves of an ocean, even crashing waves as Ma had described them.

*   *   *

She could not see that it was morning, but she could tell from Grace's movements and her own wakefulness that morning must have come. The window was thick with heavy white snow, for it was not in direct wind. She sent Grace into the bedroom and told her to stay there so she would not have to worry about her getting near the stove. Then, dressing warmly, she left again for the barn and the animals. It was not cold, but the wind was strong and stung her face with the snow particles it hurled against her. Opening her eyes only moments at a time, she could hardly see the outline of the barn. She felt her way along, trying to ignore her skirt, once high above her waist. It occurred to her that they should have tied a rope from barn door to house door. There was grunting, meowing, and a quick warm lick of her hand that was one of the dogs; she tried to believe that all was well.

She poured water in the direction of the pig's trough and listened to it hit the wooden sides. Then she groped her way to the cows, feeding them hay and giving them water. She was glad they had sold one calf. Milking one cow by touch was not hard, and soon she felt that she could see at least the outlines of the barn furnishings. When she was finished, she headed out, but hating to leave the dogs to their boredom, coaxed them to follow her. They started, but they stopped when they felt the sharpness of the snow and turned back into the barn. Defiantly, Hilda scooped up one of the cats, put her inside her coat, and started toward the house.

The cat had never been inside the house before. It looked around, and when Grace ambled toward it, it scooted underneath the stove, from which it stared with stretched-out neck. "She'll come out, Grace, if we put some food down," Hilda said, placing a milk-soaked tvaybak into a dish on the floor.

The cat didn't move but continued to stare at Grace, who jumped up and down with excitement.

The day was long. That night, Hilda carried the cat back to the barn, and by feel, she again fed the hog and milked the cow. At bedtime, she was fatigued and hardly felt awake enough to pray that God had kept Franz from starting out homeward in weather such as this. In her heart, she knew that Franz had good sense, but she wondered whether the storm was just as bad in town.

The storm lingered on for days, not letting up noticeably, but not worsening, either. One day became as the others, and Hilda stopped looking in the mornings to see whether the storm had stopped. She caught herself wondering whether she would see Franz before spring, or even ever. Her prayers had become mechanical; to reinforce them, she began reading her Bible, but as she did, she caught her mind wandering. Even the swatch of Ma's dress inside the back cover didn't comfort her.

On the morning of the sixth day, she became aware of change. It was still. She could see nothing through the coated glass of the windows, so, with the caution she had learned from the wind when it snatched the door from her hands previously, she peeked through a crack of the door. Then she threw it wide. The storm was over. The sun was shining through a blue sky on dazzling snow that stretched into infinity. On the horizon was smoke coming from Pa's chimney. Hilda hoped he would come to see her, to check whether everything was all right; then she realized that he didn't know of Franz's going and would assume all was well.

Energetically, knowing that Franz would not be home until he had worked his way over the many miles of snow, Hilda began her chores. Even though the waiting was not over, at least now there was a change. The snow had formed a crust over which she could walk. The air was crisp but not yet cold, so she dressed Grace in many layers of clothing and took her along to watch her as she dug out the windows and door of the barn. It was hard work, and Hilda perspired inside her warm clothing.

When she walked into the barn to see more than faint outlines, she saw that sometime during the week of storm the hog, in its boredom, had overturned its trough. The water she had poured for it had indeed hit the wood, but it had hit the outside and gone to waste on the earthen floor. She found it funny. Something inside Hilda opened and let out laughter she did not try to control. Hearing her laugh, Which One came sideways to her, wagging his tail, and then jumping up at her, trying to reach her face in order to lick it.

Still laughing, Hilda finished her chores. She milked the cow and climbed into the pig's stall to right the trough that had sunk into the mire. She gave it an extra portion of water. But she stopped laughing when she remembered that all was not yet well and that she didn't know where Franz was. She started for the house with Grace but, looking toward the horizon, she saw a person walking toward the house. It was impossible to see who it was, and Hilda controlled an impulse to run toward him.

After she set the milk inside the house, she was better able to see details of the man's clothing. It came to her that it could not be Franz, as he had left with the buggy and two horses But still she prayed, "Let it be Franz, please let it be Franz."

It was. God had answered this prayer. Franz was running over the hardness of the snow, and then she was in his thickly-clothed arms. His lips were cold and almost hurt hers, and when he released her, she was fighting for air.

"I started right for home the day after I got to Lone Wolf. I drove the horses as far as Liesebet and Joe's, but when I saw that they couldn't hold out any more, I left them there and started out on foot because I was told it would be a long storm. By the time I reached Father Heldin's farm, I couldn't see any more. It was sheer luck that I found his place."

"I've been praying for you. I couldn't believe anything bad would happen."

"I worried about you. Father wouldn't let me try to come here when I thought I might make it. I wanted to come."

"I love you, Franz," Hilda managed to say before he again kissed her long and hard, in front of their house on the unbroken, snowy stretch that was Montana.

CHAPTER FIFTEEN: 1917

Even with much to talk about, Franz clearly couldn't concentrate. Insisting he was just resting his eyes, he dropped off to sleep, while Hilda tried to share her lonesome days. She gave up, fed him a quick meal of potato soup and fresh bread, and tucked him into their bed. She could hardly wait for Grace to get sleepy enough to be coaxed to bed so she could climb into bed with him.

Early the next morning, Franz took advantage of the hard-packed snow to fetch the horses and the wagon loaded with his purchases. When he returned, Joe was with him, on his own horse. Hilda saw that Franz needed an extra strong back to help wrestle a large wooden box off the wagon. The wagon also held lumber and some small wooden wheels that Franz explained he would turn into a doll buggy for Grace. He had remembered supplies on Hilda's list that included sugar and flour in large jolly-flowered cloth sacks that later could be sewed into dresses for her or Grace. He held up a small paper bag of chocolate-covered peanuts, his favorite.

Joe quickly pulled out the nails of the large box to show a sewing machine firmly packed inside it. A Singer. Then he stood next to Franz to see Hilda's reaction.

She held her breath. What was there to say? It had not occurred to her that she would ever—or so soon—have a sewing machine. Had she not prided herself on her work until now, her tiny, even stitches? She had sewed her wedding gown by hand, using a little needle and fine thread. She had stitched small, even hem-rows and embroidered abstract designs, flowers, and leaves onto strong white cotton sheets and pillowcases. She had not sewed Franz's shirts or trousers, but she had sewed all of her and Grace's—and Cherub's—clothes. All this she had learned as a child, practicing first on dresses and nightgowns for her doll.

She looked at the ornate cast-iron legs and treadle, the cabinet with four large drawers that could hold her measuring tape, straight-pins and pincushion, three scissors—straight ones, pinking shears, and button-hole scissors. A small center drawer was shaped to hold spools and thimbles and a tiny heart-shaped bag filled with graphite for sharpening needles. The heavy, black, cast-iron head—decorated with red, yellow and green scrolls, now lowered into the cabinet—could be raised and based on the top. It would be able to sew heavy-duty canvas cloth as well as delicate dimity, after a simple change of needles. The attachments would make ruffling, pleating, and piping easy, and a stitch guide would help keep the seams straight.

When open, the cover could serve as a platform for her work; when closed, it covered the hole where the head hung, and a doily on top of it could show off a blooming flower plant when she had one. Hilda raised it to a slant.

She allowed her imagination to ramble: *A fine runway for a toy car.* Then she reached with one foot to the treadle. With the belt loose, it moved easily. *Fun to see how fast it can go… Using feet. Or hands. Not for me—for the children. Some day.*

They'll have fun tracing the iron scrolls with their fingers. I'll teach all my daughters—and perhaps also my sons—to sew on that machine, to thread it, to wind the bobbins, to sew straight seams. But I won't allow them to tamper with the stitch tension. I'll do all the maintenance myself, keep it clean and oil its moving parts. If the leather belt becomes loose, I'll clip it and staple the ends.

Through the years, after my children are grown and leave to make their own lives, I'll keep on with my sewing projects. I'll make crazy-quilts for all my children and donate some to church for the missionaries.

And after? Where will the Singer go?

Hilda caught herself. Franz and Joe were still looking at her, watching her reaction, and here she had left the present—the gift and the now-time. Her thoughts had leapt from the just-unpacked machine through her lifetime and her old age! She rushed to Franz and threw her arms around him and Joe, who was standing next to Franz. And she realized that it was the first time she had ever hugged Joe.

The men carried the heavy cabinet into the house, and Hilda found a place near a window where daylight would illuminate her work. They set the head in place and stood together admiring the fine wood of the cabinet and the smooth works of the sewing mechanism. Tearing herself away from it, Hilda offered them prips[16] and cookies, and thought to ask about news from Joe's family and from Pa and Muttah.

That reminded Franz: "The biggest news is that Aunt Mary and her son, Peter, have gone home to Minnesota. They left just the day before I went

16 Hot drink brewed from roasted barley or wheat, and ground in a coffee grinder.

shopping. Father Heldin thinks the work was too hard for Peter, who really isn't much of a farmer, and Mary finally realized that."

"Why didn't we hear about her plans before she left?"

"Who knows? She has always been better at sniffing out other people's secrets than telling her own."

"But we would have had a farewell for them, in church, or at least at Pa's place."

"I don't know if Father would have had a sendoff party for her. I think Leah isn't very fond of Mary. Anyhow, they left suddenly. Once they decided, they found room on the train for what little they had brought in the first place. So off they went."

Hilda needed some time to mull over the news.

CHAPTER SIXTEEN: 1918–19

Spring planting was held up, first while they waited for the heavy snows to melt, and then because of a late frost. As if to atone for the delay, wildflowers emerged to adorn the virgin prairie land—large bunches of furry lavender crocuses, yellow snapdragons, and cacti with fragrant brilliant red blossoms.

Badgers and coyotes roamed the countryside, and chickens and children could not be permitted outdoors alone. Here and there, gophers dug holes; a horse stepping into them could break a leg. Moreover, they ate the seeds when Franz could finally plant, so he ordered the dogs to dig up the rodents' dens.

One warm day, while Hilda hung out wet wash, Grace, who was playing nearby, suddenly said, "Ma! Look! Big bird!" A hawk was struggling to lift off with a young rooster. Hilda chased after it, and the hawk dropped it, but the rooster's neck was broken. That day, she served fried chicken for dinner. Later, a mother hen with a brood of eight or ten chicks was proudly scratching the ground and calling her chicks to show them what she had found. Suddenly, she made a low crowing, a warning sound, and the chicks instantly ran to her. Looking up, Hilda saw another hawk circling lower and lower toward the chicks. She again chased it. After that, the hen and her chicks were not allowed outdoors alone.

Meanwhile, for days on end, Franz hauled and burned "*kurrei*"[17]. He now knew what those wild bushes Hilda had asked about were. That weed needed no care and very little water to grow huge. When uprooted, it rolled with the wind. Where there were fences, the weed tangled in the wires, making large walls. Contrary to what he had hoped, it was unpalatable; the animals could not or would not eat it when it was green and succulent; when it was

---

17   Russian thistle, a kind of tumbleweed.

old and dry, it was full of stickers, so it was useless for feed, and it took over the garden plot.

When Franz seeded the grains, it didn't rain until he became almost resigned to drought; then it rained hard, pounding the earth into clay. Some of the seed had been stubborn enough to germinate and even grow, but then grasshoppers came: not many of them, and they did not take it all.

Hilda yearned for some fresh lettuce, but birds ate those sprouts as they emerged. She told Grace to chase the birds away when she saw them, but Grace was soon bored and wandered off to play with the cats. "Why don't the birds eat the grasshoppers instead of my lettuce?" Hilda grumbled, not expecting an answer.

Through the long, hot summer, they concluded that the clouds had dropped all their moisture during the big blizzard. Then it was harvest time. "Sometimes, I think it doesn't pay to waste the energy of the horses on reaping those few kernels." Franz sat on the doorstep when he should have been out mowing the grain.

"That would not be right, Franz. We must be worthy of even the small crops that we get."

"If I had a herd of cattle, I'd turn them out on the field in order to let them harvest for themselves. There isn't so much out there that they'd overeat."

"It's a test. Now we'll find out what we are worth when things go a little wrong." Hilda knew her words were hardly consoling. She wondered why she was saying them and was glad that Franz seemed not to hear.

"I just wonder why you don't say anything about it being a mistake to come out here. It's worse when you don't say anything. Are you keeping silent because you know it's worse?"

"Franz, you know I'm happy where you are, and especially when I know you're happy. I'm not sorry we came here."

"Well, I am. It's silly to pretend that I'm not. If you're not sorry, you're either insensitive or stupid."

"You're upset. Don't let's speak when we're upset. We'll only say things—"

"Hilda, I don't see how you can keep from being upset. Or maybe you just don't realize the significance of this. This means that we can't buy new clothes for winter, for one thing—"

"It doesn't do any good, you know that."

"—Or celebrate Christmas, or fix the house, or even have enough seed to plant next year, or how we'll be able to buy groceries for winter, or next summer when we get a crop. If we get one."

Grace, hearing them and not used to their raised voices, started to cry.

"The Lord will provide," Hilda said. "The Bible says so. Now we will see."

"The Lord didn't provide for Aunt Mary ..."

"Her reasons for leaving were different ..."

"How different?"

"Oh, I don't know—she's getting old, and can't do the work that we can do," Hilda said. "The Lord provides, but people have to be able to do the work. If Peter's heart had been in the work, he might have succeeded. Or if he had a wife who worked at his side. Besides, we don't make plans to be like her."

Franz did not explode. He didn't raise his eyes, or show that he had heard her. "That is the Lord's way of providing. He sends the crops. When He doesn't send crops, it means we aren't doing the work, and He's not providing. Last year, He provided. This year He didn't. And because He is God, He doesn't have to have a reason for providing, or for not providing. Our capricious God."

"Franz, that's not so. You know it isn't." Hilda reached for Grace, and hugged her to her breast.

"How do you know that?" He didn't wait for her to think of an answer. He left the house, and when he came back in, he brought a chicken he had butchered, as if in defiance of the coming shortage.

The noodle soup was good, though Hilda began her frugality by using only one egg in the noodle dough, and she left out the butter, using instead a lot of thyme that she had dried in the abundance of last year. Eating it, they didn't speak. Even Grace, after a few attempts, gave up trying for attention by slurping noodles into her mouth. Once they had laughed at such antics; lately they scolded, but even scolding was attention.

They agreed not to talk about it. But when he brought home a rabbit he had shot, and brought it into the house, Hilda began to laugh. She stopped laughing when he spoke.

"When they start starving to death, their meat won't be as good."

"Franz, you always shot them for the dogs and cats. We aren't going to eat rabbits."

"Why not?"

"It's like eating rats and mice. They're just as much rodents."

"It's meat. Many people raise rabbits to eat."

"But not this kind. They're different. As different as hawks are different from turkeys. Franz, we aren't starving yet."

He laid the rabbit on the work table and left. He had skinned it outside. Its flesh was pink with health, smooth and moist. For some time, Hilda let it lie, trying to forget it was even there. When Franz didn't return, Hilda knew he expected her to have started cooking for their noontime meal.

Cut up, it looked like pieces of chicken, though Hilda was not quite sure whether parts of it didn't look like a cat. The long backbone, the full round chest, the un-chicken-like head. All the parts of it fit into her roaster. It was lean and needed fat. Water might keep it tender, but when it began to cook, it sputtered and splattered, and the smell of it was not one that made Hilda hungry.

Franz ate it, not speaking of food but of his plans for afternoon. Grace ate well, sucking on the bones as she did on chicken thighs. But the smell pervaded the entire room, and Hilda could not open her mouth to taste it. When she ate her potatoes, she thought the smell flavored them in spite of the salt and pepper she had used.

After supper, Franz declared he was tired and left for their bedroom. Without him there, Hilda could not find words to compose a prayer, to conduct evening devotions by herself. She knelt at her chair, took hold of the chair back, and clenched her eyes, but nothing came to her. It had been a long time since she had tried to deal with apprehension by herself, and she didn't know how.

Feeling too wrought to be able to sleep, she decided to write her cousins, trying not to voice her low spirits overmuch:

Dear Henry and Emma,

How are you? And how are your children?

Last week we were at the Cottonwood to pick June berries—a sort of blueberry—but there are very few. It is too hot and dry. Yesterday, we were in the Brethren Church for an installation. We drove thirty miles. Can your horses do that? Our horses this year are as good as last year, and also got no oats because we need the seed for planting. We think our mare may be pregnant from when she got out of her hobbles and joined a herd of wild horses until we found her.

The chickens are laying up to twenty eggs a day and we also have three roosters. We are selling cream to a farmer who has a big churn in a deep cellar. He takes the butter to town about once a week. He pays around $4.76 for five gallons.

The grain looks pathetic, and the yield is small. It's too dry and the plants are very small. We have enough coal here at home for the winter. Seven wagons full. We both work hard, but so far I haven't had to help Franz mine coal. Next week, we want to make hay.

People are beginning to move from here. You know about Aunt Mary. John's neighbors, the Stones and the Bergs, are going to North Dakota. Fausts want to leave this autumn. A while ago, we butchered a lot of chickens and a calf because we thought we could not feed them, but we find that they will eat the dry prairie grass. For us it goes also so, but everything considered, it is not yet time to give up.

Today it is again very hot. Being outside is not pleasant, but today there is no wind. Yesterday there was strong north wind. Then our faces burn, and by evening, they are very red.

We have no telephone at our home. The neighbors strung a wire along the top of their fence posts, a seven-mile stretch, and installed telephone boxes at their own house and one at Pa's, so there is some communication among people. We can go to the neighbors to call Pa if need be.

Greet our friends and relatives. Write soon.
Hilda

CHAPTER SEVENTEEN: 1919

Like other farmers of the area, Hilda and Franz looked forward to Sundays and felt, keenly, a sharp disappointment when illness or weather prevented them from spending the entire day at the church. The Reverend Heldin, whose own farming experiences kept him in sympathy with the problems of the other homesteaders, spoke words of encouragement and interpretation.

In slow, deliberate, clear High German he said, "Remember the fortitude of your grandparents and their grandparents before them. Our forebears had a good life in Prussia in the 1700s, thriving and rearing their children as Christian pacifists. Being prosperous, they strived to provide their sons with land, but because they were pacifist, the Prussian government would not allow them to expand to the frontiers unless they would defend the borders. When Tsarina Catherine invited them to South Russia and offered them freedom from conscription and freedom to worship as Mennonites, they undertook the journey.

"Our families worked the bleak plains of South Russia for a hundred years while keeping their faith. The land was much like Montana. They suffered hunger. They were cold. But they persevered until their faith was threatened by a new tsar who drafted men into his army and limited their schools and their native language. Again, they stood firm. They braved the voyage across the sea to America for all its promises.

"Here in Montana, we again face challenges, having moved from a more comfortable life in Minnesota. We work hard, and we don't always see what tomorrow will bring. We are facing difficulties. Nevertheless, we have food on our tables, and fuel to heat our homes. If this is a bad year for crops, we can't move our 'camp' to another area as the Indians can, but we can take a broader view. The Indians encourage us; they tell us that there are bad years and many good ones. Even though the government has given us reservation land, the Indians are friendly. Therefore, let us be courageous. Trust in God, who led us here."

The church did something more than provide support and help to bear hard times. It was the communion of the unspoken "fellow feeling" shared during their potluck meals, noisy with the chatter of women sharing recipes and quilt patterns and men talking of politics and animal husbandry. No one mentioned the drought or crop failure, though someone spoke of families who had given up and were heading back East before winter storms set in. Others brought up Aunt Mary's departure. No one condemned their actions and, from the looks on their faces, it was not possible to see whether they themselves would consider such action or wonder whether they were too stubborn to give up after one such failure.

When it was time for Sunday school, the children were too tired to fidget. They sat quietly, seeming to listen to every word their teachers had prepared during the long week. The younger ones accompanied their parents to their adult classes and fell asleep almost immediately, their heads perched precariously on the thin and rough-clothed legs of their young fathers.

Again after the classes, loud and garbled sounding to anyone who might be listening at the door, there was more talk, and even joking. But the conversations and jokes were more subdued after the lengthy prayer and benediction Reverend Heldin invoked for the coming week.

The men again turned to politics and a world war taking place far away that would not concern them much because they would not be drafted: they had children, and they were farmers. That made it easier to be the pacifists they were, though they were required to register for the draft. They obeyed the law, going to the county seat to fill out papers stating their ages, citizenship, and family status. To be sure, there were shortages of sugar, coffee, and white flour, but they ground their own wheat into flour. Officially, they were not allowed to do that, but no one explained why not, and no one checked. To buy white flour, they had to buy a certain amount of oatmeal as well, and again no one explained why. Later, they substituted barley flour that made a heavy and rather sour bread. Instead of sugar, they used syrup, and for a hot drink, they made prips.

Most ominous was news that a busybody had reported "dangerous Germans" living north of Lone Wolf, who spoke an unintelligible language amongst themselves and conducted their church services in German. As a consequence, the church services were to cease, or someone who could speak English should preach. The school, also mostly German speaking, would have to be suspended. So far, nothing had happened.

Another topic of conversation was about the automobile Reverend Heldin had traded a horse and two cows for: a second-hand Buick. How stern and dignified he and Leah looked as they sat tall in their seats, put-putting along the unpaved road. It was the only car in the area. Would buggies soon be outmoded?

As church was the bulwark against peril for the adults, it provided pleasure to the children, some of whom were old enough to be schooled but who saw other children their own ages only Sundays in church. They amused themselves, screaming back and forth from the church to the stables, and darting around and on the parked buggies. Some of the little ones, whose parents had allowed them to bring their dolls, were quietly dressing and undressing them in the privacy of their carriages. Others sitting very straight in other buggies were urging on imaginary horses, as if racing the other buggies parked there. No one watched them and, free from the feeling of supervision, they tirelessly and enthusiastically played.

It was time to go home. Already the sky was becoming languidly red, as if ashamed of the unproductive summer it had witnessed, hiding its most brilliant redness behind the squat bulk of the prairie church. Parents gathered their children together, packed them into the backs of their buggies, and started their miles toward their handmade homes.

Hilda and Franz seldom spoke much after those Sundays. Grace always slept all the way home, and they knew their speaking would not waken the child. It took a little time before they had sorted out new ideas they had gotten. During the week, a comment here and a bit of gossip there would fit itself into their conversation.

This Sunday, as always, they felt both tired and invigorated from the day's associations. Their team, rested after the shelter of the stable, steadily and surely drew them toward their own stalls. Behind them, when they turned to look, the sunset almost hurt their eyes. Hilda felt that it was a suitable ending to a faultless day but, as she was enjoying that feeling, Franz spoke.

"It isn't normal. See how it flickers?"

Before answering, Hilda tried to recall whether he had been speaking and, if so, what he had just said. She admitted she had not been listening.

"The sunset. We never have that kind. I wonder if something is wrong." His voice sounded alarmed and conveyed more than his words.

"What do you suppose? Is a storm coming? Will we get home? Have you ever seen anything like it before? It's so beautiful, can it mean anything bad?"

Grace stirred, affected by the tensed muscles of Hilda's arms around her.

"It may be beautiful, but it isn't pretty. I don't know. I don't know this country. I don't know what else can happen to us."

Nothing Hilda could say would have any meaning. Her mouth was becoming too dry to allow for speech.

By the time they reached their homestead, the sun was sinking further, though the brilliance of its setting did not diminish. The horses seemed to sense the human excitement, pacing and shaking their heads while they waited for their family to be unpacked so they could get to their stalls where they used to get oats.

"Usually, when unnatural weather comes, the animals sense it. They get restless and jumpy." Franz ran his hand along the back of one of the horses, and up along its neck to its nose. It moved, flicking its hide where his touch, moving softly as a fly would, was tickling it.

"Franz, did you hear something at church that excited you? Is it only the sunset?"

He turned sharply. "No, you know I was as calm and happy as you when we left the church. But, woman, look! Can't you see that it isn't natural? It's too red, even for a prairie fire!"

Grace was now awake, simpering and clinging to Hilda's coat. Her weight was becoming tiring, and Hilda pivoted to carry her into the house. As she walked, Hilda turned once more to look at the beautiful sunset, now frightening in its magnificence. There, framed in the center of it, was the silhouette of a horse, with a lumpy-shaped burden on its back, and with dust obscuring its running feet.

At risk of upsetting her child, Hilda shouted to Franz, who left off removing the harness from his team to join Hilda. When she came back out of the house, she could tell the rider was a woman with two children.

It was Marie, with Johnny and Helena. She was shouting that the splendor of the sunset was a giant prairie fire which, when she left their house on the opposite direction from the church, was heading toward their land and home. She hugged her silent children, whose eyes reflected their mother's terror.

Franz reacted with calm but commanding, words. "I'll ride Jerry over right away. Hilda, you get me all the old blankets you can spare, and then ride Minnie over to Father's. Tell him to load up his plow and then pick up my plow, and head toward the fire. Tell him to plow where he thinks he can go back and forth several times to form a firebreak. He can hitch several plows up if he does it right, and it won't hurt the horses to work hard for once.

"Marie, your horse is foaming. Rub her down; then go inside with your children and watch them and Grace. Hilda, tell Muttah to telephone everyone she can reach to come and help. Tell them to bring shovels and blankets. If we don't come home tomorrow, you might bring us out some food and coffee."

*   *   *

Franz could feel Jerry's response as he urged him cross-country. He seemed almost to enjoy the fast race to the fire. But when they neared the blaze, Franz found it necessary to blindfold the horse, which was frightened by the brilliant orange conflagration.

John and his neighbors scarcely looked up at Franz except to see that he had joined them, as they beat up and down with heavy wool rugs at the knee-high flames. Behind them, Abe Geppert urged his fine horses to plow one more row, to make the firebreak just a little wider so the fire would not be able to jump across to the house. Other neighbors—many of them but not all members of their church—followed, widening the furrows.

They exuded a sweat-soaked smell, even though they had had their usual Saturday night baths. No one spoke; almost in rhythm they beat at the persistent flames. Others joined them, forming a line to defend the little wood and sod buildings that John and Marie had so happily built almost two years before.

Gradually, they had to retreat from the heat of the fire, which a gentle breeze was encouraging and, from the ache of their muscles, used to work but not such strenuous work. When they saw that they could not protect the little out-buildings, John and a neighbor ran to them to pile what they could onto his wagon, which they then drove toward the horizon several miles away. Then they hurriedly started a new firebreak, this time a longer, wider one.

*   *   *

Franz felt his arms beat up and down mechanically, using now a blanket to replace the charred rug. As he worked, he allowed his mind to wander. He remembered when his mother had sewn it, during the long winter nights of his childhood back in the green vegetated country of southern Minnesota. *It has patches from my last short trousers, as well as from my first long ones. Some are of my father's clothes, my mother's dresses, and both my brothers' pants. I watched her sew it all by hand, her stitches painstakingly close together, as she bent over her work when we pulled the lamp from her toward our own drawings. The day she finished it, she proudly spread it over the table so we could see its pattern and remember the clothes it was made of.*

It was too good, too beautiful to use. At first she kept it folded, taking it out of the mothball-filled trunk only when visitors came to look at it. Then, when Paul became ill, and it was clear that he would not live, she began to use it, covering him with it, as if the blanket should perform some miracle. When he died, she aired it well and began to use it on the master bed. When I was old enough to sleep in the cold upstairs bedroom, she gave it to me and said I could keep it always.

Now it's an old blanket. As a child, I didn't always take off my shoes when I was on my bed. I took puppies and kittens to my room when Ma didn't notice, and I let them play on it. When they wet it, I hung it over a chair to dry and air. By the time I was grown, she replaced it with a new blanket. Hilda has used it since then, to cover the vegetables for early fall frosts, and to protect furniture when we move.

*   *   *

Looking down, remembering how pretty it once was, Franz saw that its bottom edge was becoming charred, and some of the wool batting was coming off with each beat of his numb arms.

At his side, Joe, who had arrived without Franz's noticing, was working hard, breathing with a grunt each time his heavy rug hit the persistent flames. Trickles of sweat formed paths through the sooty grime on his face, and he did not stop to wipe them except with the sides of his arms as he beat them up and down. Franz wondered whether his own face looked like that, and then felt perspiration running down, underneath his shirt collar, and even through the hair on his chest.

Presently, they had to step aside to let the rest of the buildings burn. They watched it. The flames did not burn furiously, nor were they large. Businesslike, they crawled up the sides of the dry grassy sod and to the roofs, one at a time. Not until they had eaten their way through the thick walls did they become high and powerful. After some time, the building slowly collapsed, as if the walls melted from the heat. Beyond it, John and his team were plowing, not even looking at his burning home.

By the time the buildings were burned, the flames became paler, and Franz realized that the sun was rising. Then Hilda was there, her arm around him, giving him a hot drink from an enameled mug.

"Where did you come from? What are you doing here?"

She could not take much time for him. "Drink this; we're out of coffee, but I made this barley prips. And rest for a while. We've sent for help from Lone Wolf, and they'll hurry here as fast as they can. Marie is sleeping now, finally. I had to heat water and order her to take a bath before she would relax enough even to go to bed."

"And John?" Franz saw him, sitting on the ground, his head on his knees.

"I'll take him home to us. He's not as strong as most men. He can't work this hard. You have to rest too. You can't do this work by yourself." Then she hurried on, giving prips to the other men who had worked the night through and did not realize they were thirsty until they drained large mugs.

To the West, the fire was still working, like grasshoppers crawling along the dry weeds and grass toward the freshly plowed land that was not wide enough to prevent its passing, and not long enough so the two ends of the fire reached around it. Automatically, Franz ran toward one of the ends and just as automatically started beating again. On the faces of the other firefighters, he could see the same fatigue that saturated his own body.

They took turns going to one of the parked wagons to sleep for an hour or so. That afternoon, as they were still retreating before the flames, someone noticed that help from Lone Wolf was arriving. They were mostly young men, eager for something to do, with bodies able to hold out for a long time. When they came, a capable leader directing them, Franz fell back with the others who, also tired, let youth—not so much younger than they—take the burden from their shoulders.

When Franz arrived at home, he saw Johnny and Helena playing happily with Grace. Marie and Hilda were preparing some kind of meal and urged him to go quietly to sleep in the same room with John, who was still sleeping.

CHAPTER EIGHTEEN: 1920

John and Marie did not give up. They waited the winter through at Hilda and Franz's warm little home, going with each opportunity to their own bare land with materials for a second house. When the first hints of spring appeared, and they had a makeshift roof over a thin-walled room, the Heldins left happily, because close quarters, especially with relatives, had become wearisome for them all. Their new home had only the barest of essentials, but neighbors were kind with their help and donations of spare blankets and utensils.

The animals had also been crowded in the barn; the dogs and cats—three dogs and six cats from the two families—had made their peace after some weeks of sorting things out. Which One had died during the winter after a skirmish with a wolf. Now the Heldins could return home, where their cows and horses could nibble on new grass coming up through the soot and ashes left by the fire. The chickens could chase bugs and flies, and the dogs and cats could hunt field mice that had survived the fire.

"I wonder if we'll ever be good friends again," Hilda mused even before John and Marie's wagon was out of sight. "Living communally just wouldn't be a happy life for me in the long run."

Franz was leaning inside the open door. "Yet, our forefathers did it all the time. Some of our people are still doing it."

"But no private life. It takes away the family feeling. I could always hear them in their bed, and I'm sure they could hear us."

"People can put up with a lot if they have to."

"But, Franz, you know how it was to see the children playing together. Johnny was always pushing Grace over, and I couldn't say anything for fear of hurting Marie's feelings. I know they could learn to play together, but before that, Marie and I would have to have a long talk. I can't talk with her about that. I'm not even sure what I would say. And baby Helena would start fussing just when we were busiest."

"I know how you feel. I'm relieved, too. But they're in a bad situation. They've lost everything and know they're obligated to us for the whole lot, even the clothes to wear. I wouldn't blame them for being a little touchy. I'm sure they're not angry with us for anything. I'm sure they love us very much, and after we've been separated a while, we'll find we understand each other so much the better for it."

Grace wandered around, not doing anything; then she teased Ask Him the way her cousin had teased her. The dog became angry and snapped at her, and she ran crying to her mother.

During the week, Hilda cleaned their entire small house thoroughly and found everywhere confirmation of the close living they had endured. Underneath the bed were the crumbs and a moldy chicken bone Johnny had left when he ate his snacks there. Behind the wood box was a dirty baby diaper. In cracks in the wall were stuffed bits of paper and a ruler, missing since the middle of winter. She felt guilty about cleaning so, as if she was trying to rid the house of some germ or insect. But when Franz didn't realize she was watching, she saw him sweep out the barn, raising large puffs of hay dust with each sweep.

Later in the week, when they finished their cleaning and Franz was beginning to prepare his seed for another try at a crop, Hilda said, "I wonder how the John Heldins are getting along."

"Probably as well as we are," was Franz's answer. "Maybe the fire has even done them good by burning off weed seeds and grasshopper eggs. Maybe their crops will be better than ours this year. Next fall, we'll see if it makes any difference."

"Now you're pessimistic. You sound as if you expect the same troubles we had last year."

"Our talking won't change anything. Either it happens or it doesn't."

"What have we done to deserve all this bad luck? Is God punishing us?"

"Now, Hilda, you know God sends sunshine and rain on sinners and saints alike. There isn't anything we can do about it. You know all the nonbelievers who live out here are having just as good or bad luck as we are."

"The Bible also says, 'Whom the Lord loveth, he chasteneth.' Therefore, it's more our fault than the unbelievers' because they are entirely out of God's field of interest."

"How can you say that? God sent his son to save those who are lost. He doesn't need those who are already righteous. The Bible also says, 'There is none righteous, no not one.'"

"You're as mixed-up as I am... But if you're saved ..."

"Sometimes I wonder if I *am* saved." Franz did not even appear concerned.

Something inside Hilda turned, the way it did when she was pregnant. For an instant, she wanted to shriek with laughter, but tears came to her eyes. "Franz, don't talk like that. It scares me."

"You've never said whether *you* were sure you're saved." He was smiling now.

Hilda thought, *God will strike us both down. Why didn't the prairie fire wipe us out, instead of Brother John, who is devout in his own quiet way? John introduced devotions twice daily into our home, and now that he's gone, we've unthinkingly dropped the practice.*

"You aren't answering, even now."

Hilda could not. Then he came to her, slowly, not saying anything. He looked at her steadily, without touching. To her, it was as if he had her in his arms, and from the back of her head, past her ears, down underneath her arms, along the outside of her body, and to her knees passed a sensation she did not will.

At last she could speak, for she knew he had forgotten his question, and she wanted to remind him of it. "I think so, but I'm not sure either. I don't know."

He ignored what she said. Frantically, she tried to finish the conversation she had so often expected, when she anticipated relief at knowing even the worst. To be sure, she had caught herself wondering what would be the worst to know.

But when he had her in his arms, using the strength of his muscles, she remembered with her whole body. She remembered the many nights that had made up the long winter. She remembered that those nights had been shared with John and Marie and their two small children in the only bedroom.

She did not protest. Not even when she could hear Grace calling her, or when she heard that call turn into a cry complaining at being left alone in the kitchen with the door to the bedroom closed. She wondered whether Marie experienced a relief such as hers, and if she was glad to be alone with her John, Hilda's brother.

*   *   *

Throughout the long winter, Franz and John together had watched Minnie as her belly grew. Neither man had ever witnessed the birth of a colt; their horses had been mature when they were acquired. Was the birth of a colt like that of a calf? When they asked Pa Heldin, he admitted that he had never helped a horse deliver. Surely, the horse would know what to do, but he would come to help if Franz let him know that it was time. This was Minnie's first foaling; she was not young anymore, though still not old.

Now, Franz tried to count the months since she wandered away to join the wild herd. She hadn't been gone long and had seemed unchanged when he found her and led her home. The stallion heading his herd hadn't menaced Franz, and Minnie was docile as usual when he haltered her. Had it been close to eleven months? Maybe there would be a foal soon.

When Minnie seemed ready to give birth, Franz rode Jerry to Pa Heldin's home; he immediately agreed to come witness the event, if not to help. Hilda longed to watch also, but decided it wasn't appropriate for Grace to see.

Minnie, indeed, knew what to do: the handsome little black body dropped to the ground and lay for a time while he submitted to his mother's licking. Then he raised his head, rose to his feet, and tottered closer to her. He nudged under her belly and began nursing while she nosed him to memorize his scent.

Together, Franz and his father-in-law admired the colt. "He's a prince," they agreed. And it had a name.

*   *   *

Franz sat at his desk, a piece of brown store paper in front of him. He drew a vertical line down the middle and wrote:

For returning to Minnesota:	Against:
Rain—better chance for good crops	Being a quitter
Better schools	Hilda's pa & siblings here
My ma & siblings there	Maybe better crops next time
Having a fine new colt	Moving a fine new colt
Closer to town, library	

What he didn't write about, in case she should see this list, was Hilda's clear unwillingness to have more children in Montana. He also wondered whether the birth of a foal should influence him one way or the other—a new beginning.

*   *   *

Franz planted seed, some leftover from last year and some he purchased with dwindling cash. Hilda planted carrots, lettuce, beans, and other soup-vegetable seeds; then, as she had done the previous year, she persuaded Grace to chase away any birds that looked as if they were eyeing the seeds and, later, the early sprouts. It again bored her, and she got Ask Him to chase them, saying, "Sic 'em." Even the dog was bored after a while and lay watching the birds, who were getting bolder.

Between Franz and Hilda hung the question of whether to stay or leave. The question was how to decide. What sign from God might there be? They tried some tests: close your eyes and spin the Bible a few times. Open the Bible and put your finger down somewhere. Read where your finger lands. Is there a message? Their first attempt brought up the Lamentations of Jeremiah 1, 13: "He hath spread a net for my feet; He hath turned me back: He hath made me desolate and faint all the day." That didn't help. It only described their feelings.

They spun it again. This time, Hilda's finger landed on Psalm 13, 6: "I will sing unto the Lord, because He hath dealt bountifully with me." That wasn't true. That didn't help either.

"You know," Franz said with a laugh, "next we'll get a list of 'begats.' We'll just have to figure out what we really want to do, and trust God will help us bring it to pass."

"Or not," Hilda finished for him.

So they decided. They would go *home*. Home to Minnesota. Next spring. That was what they really wanted. It felt good to have decided. Meanwhile, they'd wait before telling anyone, even Grace.

CHAPTER NINETEEN: 1920

Everybody in the congregation was curious. Nothing much had happened recently—no fire, flu epidemic, death, wedding, birth, or new neighbor. The World War did not reach their everyday lives: no men had been drafted, and they substituted available products for what was scarce or not to be had at all. Church services had reverted to the familiar German language.

As soon as Hilda and Franz let it be known that they would leave Montana next spring when their homesteading term was met, Pa—in his role as pastor—asked, "What decided you? Have you prayed for guidance?"

Hilda and Franz looked at each other. If you could count the unspoken prayers, the answer would be, "All the time." Trying to find Scripture that would guide them had felt almost like a game. They hadn't actually, or purposefully, knelt to pray about whether to stay or leave, but Franz answered for them both. "Yes, Father, we have."

Now everyone in church knew. Liesebet managed to see Hilda alone. "Hilda, is there something wrong between us that made you decide to leave? If there is, I wish you'd tell me so we can make it right."

"No, Liesebet, there's nothing. You have nothing to do with our decision to leave. Nobody does. We'll miss you very much."

"But we used to be so close. Lately, it seems as if there's a curtain between us, and I wonder if it's something I've done that I don't remember doing."

How could Hilda explain? The stories she had told to enchant their bleak childhood, when Ma was sick so much, had soothed and comforted Liesebet—and herself—with fantasy. Here in Montana, reality faced them. The stark, flat landscape. The severe winters, and the just-as-harsh summers. The reality of Liesebet's young marriage. There was no romance. No poetry. No fun.

Still, there were words to be found. The months of winter, the hope each spring. Hope that watered the potentially rich virgin earth, which then was sheared off by grasshoppers. Words describing the hard, deeply chapped hands of her little girl who called her world "Montana" and ate the infertile dirt she played in, whose interaction with the dog was to order him to "sic-em." Whose reaction to snakes was to kill them, to birds was to shoo them away. Or the evidently thinning hair of her young Franz, who ought not to age for many years, and her own substantial figure, thickening in spite of the hunger she felt after a meal of potato soup or flour pancakes.

It was easy to speak with Franz of these things now, for he agreed with her; but to the sturdy, staunchly loyal Liesebet, she felt she must have a more significant excuse for leaving. Wasn't Liesebet's Rachel also learning to live with this wilderness, and weren't her hands as chapped and hard as Grace's? Wasn't Liesebet's own face reddened, never softened by any kind of artificial balm, showing some tiny veins usually seen on the faces of middle-aged farmers?

"Haven't you thought of leaving?" Hilda asked. "Are you always loyal, in spite of the things that happen? Are you planning to stay here the rest of your life?"

Liesebet answered quietly, "Yes, we'll stay here. When our children are grown, this country will be to them what Minnesota is to us. By the time our children are grown, there might be nothing left for them there. Come to think of it, I wouldn't have met Joe, and our children wouldn't be born."

Right, Hilda thought.

Liesebet went on. "The Minnesota land will probably be worn out soon anyhow, Joe says."

"But that can't be. If land wears out so fast, this land will also be worn out. Then how will your grandchildren live?"

Liesebet replied, "Do you think this world will exist much longer? Didn't Christ say he is coming soon?" She smiled at her long-legged husband, who had come to help her reason with Hilda.

Joe spoke as he neared them. "What's this we hear? Are you going to be cowards just because you've done a bit of work without reward? Or is it as we imagine: is there something unforgiven between us?"

Hilda looked beyond him, wishing Franz was here to answer for her, or that they had left Montana silently in the night as soon as they decided. *Where is he anyhow, and who's talking to him of remembered or unremembered grudges?*

"I just talked to Franz, and his mind seems to be made up. He is stubborn, isn't he? I never realized what a cross you were bearing, married to him. We shall pray for you, that you can remain steadfast and a good influence on him."

Hilda fought sternly to keep tears from showing beyond her eyelids. Mostly her tears were for Liesebet, who had married a man unlike her Franz. She thought of something for which she should perhaps apologize to Liesebet: her domineering when they were children. *Maybe it's my fault that she needs a controlling husband.*

Except, am I so independent of spirit? At the moment, I can't think of anything Franz and I disagree about... Are Liesebet's inner beliefs unchanged from our childhood? I don't know what she believed then. We didn't discuss what we believed; we didn't openly question what we were taught. I know my beliefs have shifted—are shifting.

Franz joined them now; like a big brother, he said to Joe, "Leave off tormenting my wife, when she has enough to handle with moving and a new start."

*   *   *

Several evenings later, Liesebet and Joe arrived at the Lober home, with Rachel suffering from a severe cold.

"It was bothering us," Joe explained as his wife unbundled their wheezing child, "and we had trouble sleeping over it. So we decided to come talk with you."

Grace, anxious to play, dragged out her toys, but seeing that she didn't get much attention from her listless cousin, she resigned herself to playing alone in a corner. Liesebet balanced Rachel on her lap, cushioning her against the beginning life of a future brother or sister.

"Franz hasn't come in from chores yet," Hilda apologized. "Have you eaten?"

"Oh yes. We ate before we came," Liesebet answered politely, though it was obvious from the hungry look in Joe's eyes that they must have eaten quite some time before their long ride.

"How about some tea? Prips? Some bread and butter?"

"No, no," Joe replied. "We didn't come to break bread with you."

There was silence, for to start now would make it necessary to repeat the entire conversation when Franz came in. Joe finally found something to talk about and began to praise Grace for playing so quietly, and for being such a well-behaved girl. "It's too bad your baby died; she should have several siblings to play with."

"Yes, some day we hope she'll have brothers and sisters. But for the move, it would be too much," Hilda said, as if apologizing for not also being pregnant.

Franz came in. After some coaxing, Joe joined them in their meal, and

Liesebet ate some of the buttered dark bread, giving the soft, inside portions to her child.

They ate together, discussing impersonally at first the immediate plans for the church to have Sunday-school elections for teachers instead of having the minister appoint them.

"But the children, they aren't able to choose their own teachers," Hilda said, "and many of the parents don't know as well as the minister does which members are capable of teaching a class of little ones." She was thinking about how Pa carefully avoided asking people who had vivid methods of teaching, and who might frighten children with fearsome stories of the Bible. She also wondered whether Joe hoped he would be elected superintendent of the children's department, for he claimed to enjoy working with children. Indeed, his little daughter seemed to look up to him when she was feeling better.

Liesebet spoke before Joe was ready. "Oh, we parents know who gets along with children and who doesn't. Sometimes better than those whose children are already growing up."

"Hermann and Marta are still just children," Franz said quietly, and Hilda admired his ability to speak gently and unexcitedly when he disagreed with someone. "I'm sure Pastor Heldin will be able to choose teachers for children for some years to come—until his own are grown, and then he will learn through his grandchildren."

Joe was quick. "Oh, we didn't mean that we don't agree with Father's choices. But you know, he won't be able to keep up with everything. He isn't young anymore, even though he isn't old yet. He might not always be minister, either. Sometimes it is good to have a change, regardless of how good a minister is."

Joe had come to Montana hoping to start his own church. He had heard God call when he was a child in a state further east than Minnesota, and had practiced preaching before he was quite grown up. But when he got to the settlement in Montana, he found a church already established under the accepted leadership of the Reverend Heldin. He became an active member of the Mennonite church, and was chosen song leader of the congregational singing services with a more active and exuberant direction. At every opportunity outside the church, he expressed his own personal testimony of faith—to the Indians, to itinerant day workers, to shopkeepers.

The thought that Joe might some day replace her father as pastor of the congregation made Hilda glad they were planning to leave. *I wish I could remember Liesebet as I knew her in our childhood, playing with our dolls in the shade of cottonwood trees ...*

Or, perhaps, Franz and I ought to stay in Montana, if only to resist some of the newfangled and unconventional ideas that are coming into our isolated and self-

existing church. Is it running away when I feel relief at not having to participate in those new ways? Has our church in Minnesota also changed?

The dishes were easily done, though Liesebet did not help, excusing herself for not disturbing her child, now sleeping noisily. Joe became serious, beginning the topic they had come so far to discuss. He leaned toward Franz, who was so able to hide his emotions.

Hilda dawdled, wiping each dish thoroughly, realizing that she would finish eventually anyhow, but thinking, somehow, the pressure of what Joe had to say might become less as he had to sustain it longer.

She heard them anyhow. Franz was answering, "No, there is absolutely nothing we have against you. We aren't moving to leave you or anyone else in the congregation."

"There must be something," Joe persisted. "We have noticed that you aren't as cordial as you used to be. In fact, Liesebet says that it's happened ever since she and I were married. Before that, you were much more as brother and sisters. So I think you must have something against me personally." Tired of leaning forward, he sat back, sure he had his finger on the point.

"Why, if we seem to have been unfriendly, we must apologize," Franz said. "We haven't consciously started to feel any less love for either of you since you were married. In fact, I cannot imagine why you feel we have something against you."

Hilda bent over her dishpan, almost smiling when she remembered what they had just last night discussed about Liesebet and Joe. How they regretted that Liesebet had come here to Montana to meet him in the first place. *That doesn't mean we* love *Liesebet—or even Joe—any less.* When she was able, Hilda peeked over to the group. Franz's face was well composed, listening to Joe's tearful voice.

"There are many times that we don't agree, you and Hilda, and Liesebet and I. But what friends or relatives don't disagree sometimes? Shouldn't the love that we experience through Christ override all those disagreements?"

Liesebet was also weeping, wiping her eyes with the corner of her apron that she pulled up around her sleeping child. Hilda felt guilty that she was not crying, at least in sympathy, and that instead she even had to hide a smile.

Franz put his arm around the thin shoulders of his brother-in-law. "Let us say then, since we cannot sincerely think of anything that might be between us, we forgive any unknown grudges, and let us pray that God will take away even this feeling of suspicion that there might be something."

They knelt, turning to face their own warm chairs. Hilda joined them, drying her hands as she bent down. Only Liesebet, whose child needed the sleep she was getting, bowed forward as deeply as she could.

Joe prayed first, pouring out words with his tears as if he had found a release that he couldn't dam up. Listening to him, Hilda wasn't able to organize a prayer she'd be able to pray, one that would calm and satisfy him and Liesebet. As he prayed, she felt her mind wandering, thinking about her knees becoming tired of the hard floor, and wondering, *Why is Grace so quiet? Is she into something? I haven't really been watching her for the past ten minutes. She should be kneeling with me, or even at her own little chair.*

Joe was calmer now and digressing, asking blessings on each member of their church—all who had come to Montana. He prayed for future generations of children—those who were now playing and otherwise enjoying their young lives, and those unborn and not-yet-conceived ones who would some day make up the population of the world. He reminded them that God knew each heart and its needs. When he ended his prayer, it was as though he had tired his voice or run out of words. To Hilda, his voice generally sounded like the auctioneer who sold the goods Pa didn't want to take along to Montana.

Franz was now praying, and soon it would be her turn. She wondered whether she should let Liesebet pray first, or whether—as had always been the custom when they had both been young—she should pray first because she was the older sister. Franz's prayer was well composed, as if he had not been listening to Joe's prayer either but had spent that time preparing his own. Yet he was answering thoughts Joe admitted to. Franz could think as he was speaking, and *he* should have had the call to be a minister instead of Joe. *But he said he didn't even know for sure whether he had made things right with God. Had he truly meant what he said that night? Or was he trying to test me? Either way, it was no way to make a joke.*

It was her turn. Liesebet was waiting for her to pray first. "Kind heavenly Father," Hilda heard herself saying, for it was how she always started her public prayers. She managed to grope for and piece together words and phrases she had heard in church. "Thou seeest the heart, though we simple people only see the outside. Thou leadest, though we cannot always understand Thy reasons for things. Guide us, until we join Thee, together with those we love. In the name of Jesus Christ, amen."

Liesebet followed without hesitating. Now Hilda felt sad, sorry about the clichés she had used when she so rebelled against hearing them uttered by others, embarrassed at not being able to think of something more vital to say. In her heart, she wished for complete honesty among them all. That the strange, artificial wall between themselves and her sister would not be there.

Why does the world of prayer and of worship have to be so separate from the honest businesslike conversations I can have with myself or with Franz? I wish I could tell Joe what I object to in his personality. That once said, we would understand our differences and be friends in spite of them. Wasn't that what

Liesebet and Joe came for? Aren't they one step ahead of me and Franz, even if that step is held in by a restricting sense of religion?

She knew she would say nothing to Franz about the prayers when they were alone, and Franz would most likely think there was no need to discuss the evening, for they had known each other's minds.

When they rose from their knees, Hilda felt it difficult to straighten up, but she had to move quickly, for Grace had found a half-eaten jar molasses and was calmly but messily eating from it. She snatched the jar from the child, who reacted immediately, loudly, and stormily. It woke her cousin and invalidated all the kind words her Uncle Joe had said about her in the conversations that evening and in his prayers.

Joe and his family left then, tenderly kissing their sister and her husband. Watching them leave the yard, Hilda burst into tears. Franz's arms were strong. He didn't say anything but stroked her hair as if she had just had a serious shock.

That's how it was for some weeks. Others came, convinced there was something they had done to offend Hilda and Franz, wanting to make things right. Only John and Marie didn't come, and Hilda began to wonder whether they perhaps had a real grievance against them. When she suggested it to Franz, he laughed. "You've become quite experienced with your public prayers, but you won't need to practice on them. I think they have more sense than that. Besides, it's our turn to visit them."

CHAPTER TWENTY: 1921

"Du, Franz, it's our last winter here! Let's enjoy this storm. We may never in our lives have another blizzard like this one." Hilda poured hot water over the prips she had ground. The bread she baked the day before was still fresh, and there were still jars of ground-cherry jam left to sweeten their breakfast.

Franz reached for a piece of bread. "You said that last time—when was it—two weeks ago."

"Yep, and blizzards in Minnesota never last a whole week."

"This is a tough one. I'm glad we got rid of most of our livestock. Not so much mucking to do with just one cow and the horses in the barn."

"Do you know—how are they faring? Aren't they out on somebody's range?"

"There you go again. We can't worry about them now, Hilda. They're not ours to lose sleep over."

She sighed. "I know. But I do feel sorry for animals out in a storm. Especially if they're used to shelter."

"You *are* a softie," Franz declared, reaching to pat her arm.

"Does winter seem longer to you this year than other years?"

"This one's almost fun—I can feel its fury in my bones. Its doggedness."

Grace, just recovered from measles, came from her bed, still sleepy and holding her favorite raggedy blanket. Hilda reached for her. "Come and look at the feathery frosty swirls on the windows."

She picked up her daughter, "See what God painted while you were asleep? But no, don't lick it." For a quick moment, Hilda shuddered, remembering the death of her three-year-old brother who, Ma said, had contracted measles after licking frost off a window.

"Now that you're awake," Franz proclaimed, "let's all go outside and see what we can do. I think it isn't so cold now, and the wind has let down."

The little snow hills were fun for all three of them to slide down, with Ask Him running, barking, and sliding alongside. Only the cats were not amused and took advantage of the warmth under the kitchen stove, a place they were usually invited to only on the coldest of days.

*   *   *

The time had come. The imposing certificate signed January 6, 1921, by President Woodrow Wilson deeded two quarter sections of Montana land, comprising three hundred and twenty acres, to Franz J. Lober. Legal and customary, the deed was in the husband's name only. They had stayed and farmed it for a full three years, land thirty miles from Lone Wolf, the nearest railroad hub and shopping center. Now it belonged to them. To keep or sell.

All winter long, Hilda had used up canned goods so there would not be so much to pack when they prepared to move. She sorted out old, worn-out clothes and blankets to pad the better furniture. She again packed the dishes with the linens as she did before they had first moved there. As she handled each article they would no longer use here, she compared feelings she remembered from three years before—not that she now felt exultation. Then guilt followed immediately, guilt at being so happy to leave.

Looking back, she remembered only her excitement, being unable to sleep nights, once they made up their minds. She had not resisted coming here to Montana; the death of their infant son, Cherub, had persuaded them of God's direction. She had wondered what their new life would be like, and she had imagined it with a certain feeling of adventure and romance. At least that is how she thought of it now.

Now, looking forward, as she packed, she thought whether to replace everything in their old/new home where it had been: in the same cabinets, on the same shelves, as if they had never left? Or would it be better to find new ways to arrange things? Where should the new sewing machine be placed? She thought about the precious things they had left behind in Cousin Henry and Emma's care and on their farm—*the samovar, her wedding dress. Cherub in his grave*—which, she knew, wasn't a "thing."

The cow and remaining chickens were sold; Franz's brother, Amos, had a cow or two and some brooding hens for them to buy in Minnesota, and new chickens would soon be hatched there. Three horses, one dog, and three cats were going to ride the train back.

Leah suggested, "You can leave the cats at least; you can always get cats." But Grace cried when she heard that, and Hilda, thinking about coyotes, felt sad about the idea of just turning them loose to fend for themselves. So the cats would also travel, and Franz would tend to them all. He might even sleep on the straw near them as he had done on the trip to Montana three years before.

Now their plans for leaving were as a balm. Each day was one fewer in the little hut—she admitted to herself, *It's not only a hut, it's a shack*—and finally it was the last time to give it a thorough housecleaning. Hilda found herself laughing off little irritations that once were a "last straw." *What difference will it make a hundred years from now?*

She taught Grace new words, such as "Minnesota." It came out, "Soda."

*   *   *

Before they left, and after the cow was sold, the entire congregation met to have a farewell service for Franz and Hilda, and for another couple who had also decided to return to Minnesota. It was strangely like a funeral, though no obituaries were read, and weeping that there was was restrained and self-examining. It might be that those who stayed on wondered whether they ought also to leave—or were they merely postponing their own decisions until famine completely ruined them? Would their luck sooner or later turn, and Montana become a fertile fulfillment of their hopes?

Pa Heldin took Hilda aside to tell her, "Some day I will come to visit you in Minnesota. And when I die, I wish to be buried there, next to your ma, with my present wife at my other side."

*   *   *

Since the Lober's carriage could not hold all of their goods, several neighbors offered to load their buggies and hayracks, saying they would carry home shopping from Lone Wolf. Pa drove his Buick, taking Hilda and Grace and their more fragile articles. Joe also offered, hitching his horses to a hayrack carrying the larger furniture. Liesebet, whose pregnancy was advancing, was determined to go along, despite her condition. She said she wanted to be able to extend her time with her sister and help Joe keep his eye on the road. Their Rachel stayed behind with Muttah.

For spring, which could have changeable weather, the day started out fine. At daybreak, the caravan that started the thirty-mile trip was well underway. However, the morning sky was red, and the family felt some urgency to reach Lame Wolf before any storm might overcome them.

A few miles into their trip, the sky clouded, and what breeze there had been dropped. On the horizon, lightning flashed here and there. One of Joe's horses, a bronco he purchased recently, got nervous, perhaps sensing tension in air. Thus, Joe decided to walk alongside him. As he alighted from his seat, Liesebet, leaning forward and unbalanced by her pregnancy, reached for the reins. In overreaching, she fell off the front, over the buckboard and onto the ground in the path of the heavily loaded wheels. The bronco spooked and took off with his teammate, running over Liesebet, spilling furniture off the back of the hayrack. Joe did not see her immediately, but Pa stopped his car so Hilda could run to her injured sister.

I'm so glad Pa's here, was Hilda's first thought. Joe had now stopped and stood looking at his wife, as if she should just shake herself and get over whatever she felt. Franz took charge. "Joe, see to your horses, and let's reload your hayrack. Pa and Hilda will take care of Liesebet."

Her injuries were serious. Pa examined her and shook his head. "This is too much for me. We'll find room for her in our car and see if someone in Lone Wolf can help." He put up the roof of the car before the first raindrops fell.

By the time they reached Lone Wolf, Liesebet was talking, mostly in groans. When asked where she hurt, her reply was, "All over."

The only help in Lone Wolf was a preacher/healer, much like Reverend Heldin, who confirmed which bones were broken, and that he hoped they would heal sufficiently before the baby would be born.

The next train East would leave early the next morning, and Pa decided to send Liesebet to Minnesota. His brother, Jacob, was a well-known bonesetter. Joe stood forlornly by, unable to agree or disagree.

*   *   *

During the four-day journey, Hilda sat at her sister's side, swabbing her fever with a cool wet cloth, urging her to drink, and singing to her and Grace, both to calm her sister and to entertain her child. She sang every song she could think of, more than once: children's hymns—"I am Jesus's Little Lamb," "Jesus Loves Me," and "This Little Light of Mine"—as well as some folk songs she had learned in school—"Ich ging einmal in Brummels Wald,"[18] "Du, Du, liegst mir im Herzen[19] and "Die Schnitzelbank."[20] She chose these and other songs because they had many verses, with finger-games or handclaps. Her singing caught the attention of other children sitting on a nearby seat, and it even brought a smile to Liesebet who knew them from her childhood.

Hilda ignored, or tried to ignore, some nausea, wondering whether it was

18   "Once I Walked in Brummel's Woods."
19   "You, You, Live in my Heart."
20   "The Whittle Bench"

simply being upset about her sister's injury or if it could be morning sickness. *What a time to get pregnant!* she told herself firmly.

Whenever Franz felt he could leave the animals, he came to sit with Liesebet so Hilda could snatch a nap, or at least take her eyes off her sister.

By the time they arrived at the Mound Lake depot, Liesebet was delirious but alive. Hilda determined never to tell her some of the nonsense she spoke. *Was it really nonsense to say, "I miss my childhood?" Maybe what she meant was, "I miss my child." Or should have meant.*

*   *   *

Jacob Heldin came as soon as he heard and took over Liesebet's care. When the new baby arrived, Liesebet, remembering that she and Joe had agreed a boy should be named "Joseph," added "Jacob" as a second name.

Her time in Minnesota gave the sisters a chance to renew—even to mend or salvage—their bond. Hilda sometimes wondered whether that would have been possible if Joe had been there. *But he wasn't.*

CHAPTER TWENTY-ONE: 1922

Baby Andrew laughed, apparently enjoying the sweetness of his body after his bath in the warm kitchen. He kicked each leg and stretched each arm in turn, squirming his torso. It fascinated Hilda, and she laughed aloud in her own delight. Now almost three months old, he was beginning to respond to Grace's antics, who showed off to him, and to the smiles and baby talk of his parents.

Just a little more than a year before, the family—three of them—had returned to Minnesota, and how much had happened since then! Most important was Andrew's birth, a large healthy little boy, *alive*, with the eyes and hair of his handsome father. Andrew, named after one of Jesus' disciples: the younger brother of the Apostle Peter, now called *saint* in some churches. Baby Andrew's older brother was also a saint, a *Cherub*.

Hilda allowed herself to reflect on the tremendous feeling of *home* she had felt when they arrived, tired from the tedious train ride with her seriously injured sister. She would not forget her relief at handing Liesebet's care to Uncle Jacob, who could work miracles. How grateful she felt that not only would Liesebet recover and bear a healthy little boy but that they had had a chance to mend their sisterhood as adults, not as big sister/little sister. She found she could accept the direction Liesebet had taken, was taking, in her life with Joe in Montana.

The very day Hilda arrived, even before going into the house, she walked around the farmyard. She recalled each shrub and tree and patches where the grass would come out thicker than elsewhere, and she hoped that the renters or squirrels or field mice had not removed tulips she had planted earlier. Rhubarb and asparagus were still there, though they needed weeding. In a year, perhaps in just a few months, she would have it all in shape.

She visited Cherub's grave, the grass over it untouched, with trees shading it. Standing there, she thought of the baby who, so active and exuberant in the womb, had not taken a breath. *What might he have been had he lived? Why did he die? Was it truly God's doing? A deliberate, random, arbitrary act? Was it because of something I did or didn't do? Was it really God's way to send me and Franz to Montana for three hard years? If it was, what was it about Montana that God tried to tell us? Or about ourselves? Will I ever know? By and by, will I still care?*

His death could not be Cherub's own fault; babies are free of sin. She pictured him in Heaven, with other cherubim, surrounded by the seraphim as they sing to the glory of God, who sits on his throne... *Between songs, he might be cuddled in Ma's arms.* The thought comforted her. She wished she could send them a message. Would a prayer do that? She couldn't pray for his soul; that was not something Mennonites did. She could pray that she be worthy; yet she couldn't think what she should be worthy of.

In front of the house, she watched Grace, now a healthy eight-year-old, rolling in the uncut lush grass, imitating the frolicking half-grown cats, offspring of Old Mur. When they first returned to Minnesota, concerned about her safety, but maybe more because they were reluctant to face the reality of their firstborn's leaving the carefree years of her childhood, Hilda and Franz decided to keep her at home one more year. "Let her be a little girl a bit longer."

"Goody, goody," was Grace's response, happy to stay at home to play with her little brother, and to help at home. Franz taught her to milk, and Hilda let her break eggs and spoon cookie batter onto baking sheets, assuring her the privilege of licking the beaters. She also taught her to run simple seams—hemming a doll dress—on the Singer. "Don't pump the treadle too fast. You don't want to catch your finger under the needle."

*   *   *

The house, already old when she and Franz started their married life, had suffered considerably. After it had stood empty for a year, Franz agreed with the farmer who rented the land to allow his daughter and her family to live in it. Without people in it, the house had become a playground for mice and even rats. But the couple had obviously not restrained their several children in their savage games. It didn't disturb Franz so much as Hilda, however, for he said that the house had been ready to collapse at any slight jolt anyhow, and it was perhaps a good enough reason to start building a new permanent home.

Thus, slightly over the hill, he started to build, digging first an adequate basement that should hold vegetables and canned goods. He worked every day, using the team wherever possible but making the corners with his own spade. Sometimes Amos came to help, a silent boy-farmer who, though fully grown, was not yet married.

When the fields had to be seeded, the house did not grow at all, and to Hilda it seemed sad to see it stand there waiting. Sometimes she went to look at its shell, smelling so pleasantly of Minnesota wood. But she had her own work; with energy, she planted the largest garden she had ever had, and soon she was tanned from hoeing and weeding the quickly growing plants in the fertile black soil.

The house would not be completed this year, though Franz used every spare hour and every rainy day to work inside it. Hilda looked at it, planted between two healthy cottonwood trees, and tried to imagine herself doing her kitchen work in such a new clean place.

*   *   *

Tomorrow, a group of couples their age would come for "faspa."[21] Hilda would bake tvaybak. She would also make a cake, which she secretly got the recipe for from a lady in the sewing circle. She didn't want Franz to notice that she would use their limited eggs for that purpose.

This day, dinner dishes were cleared, Franz was out of the way, Andrew was napping, and Grace was observing her quiet time. Hilda pulled out her recipe and followed it word for word, sifting the flour several times and creaming the butter carefully and thoroughly—though she wondered whether lard might not do as well. While it was baking, she tried to read and resisted the temptation to look inside the oven to see whether it was rising. When it was time, she opened the door carefully. The cake was brown but strangely uneven, in spots no higher than it had been when she poured the batter into the pan. She hid it in a darkened corner of her pantry, hoping Franz would not come into the house until she had managed to air its smell. She wondered, *What did I do wrong?*

*   *   *

They had invited married couples, cousins of Franz and of Hilda both, as well as Franz's brother, Amos, and Anna Heldin, who were single. Playfully, Franz had suggested that they invite those two, just to see what might happen.

One cousin, Henry Heldin, had bought a Model T Ford car. He showed it, giving the other guests rides in it, and demonstrating its powers climbing hills and pushing a wagon about. Laughing, he mentioned how frightened horses became when they heard and saw them coming, and gleefully, he predicted that some day everyone might own a car like his. Franz tried to

---

21   Afternoon lunch or tea. The word is possibly derived from "vespers."

drive it, though he found it difficult to think of all the gadgets at one time, and he pretended to find it hard to walk a straight line after he got off. It was pretty, blacked, and shined. Ask Him sniffed around it, his neck stretched forward, his feet braced and stiff, and his tail straight back, half frightened that it might make some unexpected move.

After marveling at it, Hilda and the women went to inspect Hilda's garden, and the men to see the barn and the stand of the grain. And they all toured and admired the almost-finished new house.

The children played noisily in the shade of the trees near the house. In turn, when their honor had been hurt, they ran to their mothers, loudly crying, to be absentmindedly soothed and stroked. Then they hurried back to the group, afraid they might miss something. Even Grace, not yet used to playing with other children, was letting her guests handle her toys.

The meal Hilda set before them all was simple, the usual guest menu. Luckily, her tvaybak had turned out light, well-flavored, and slightly freckled from the shortening she had used. The guests heartily enjoyed them with the jelly she had cooked from last year's abundant wild grapes. It was not customary to talk about the quality of the food—for was not good food to be expected?

Amos said, "Do you know that some women are no longer learning to bake tvaybak?"

Anna Heldin sat quietly, not even looking up. Hilda reminded herself that Aunt Helen, Anna's mother, baked very good tvaybak and was undoubtedly teaching her daughters.

"You wait and see," Franz said with a laugh, "those will be girls who will be left old maids! Why, what will people eat for faspa? I wouldn't have married Hilda before I knew what kind of tvaybak she baked!"

They all laughed, except Hilda. The thought bothered her. *Is my tvaybak-baking so important? Is it? Really, Franz?*

"Have you tasted the new kind of baked food yet? It's called 'cake.'" That was Emma, always the one to step in when things turned unsafe. Emma, whose husband, Henry, had bought the car.

Hilda thought of the unsuccessful cake she had hidden in her pantry but listened closely to Emma, who said, "I haven't baked any yet." She watched her husband as she said the word *yet*. "But I want to try it when eggs get a little cheaper. If it's made right, it's very light, much lighter than bread or tvaybak."

"Have you tasted it?" Hilda asked. "How is it supposed to taste?"

Emma smiled, "Yes, our neighbors—they aren't Mennonites, they're English—made some and gave me a piece. It was very good but made me feel full right away."

"I hear it's not a new invention," Anna said. "They used to make it in the old country."

"But not our people," Peter, who seldom spoke much, said. "Remember, our rule is not 'What is not forbidden is allowed.' Our rule is 'What is not expressly commanded is forbidden.' I wouldn't say cake would be necessary. It is the simple, plain things that we must stick to."

When no one at the table responded, he expanded his contribution. "I'm so happy that I have given my life to Jesus. Aren't you all happy too? Isn't it wonderful how we cousins can fellowship in harmony like this? All of us born again. Saved."

They were all used to Peter's fervor—after all, he was Aunt Mary's son. They had all heard what he said, or something very much like it, many times. There was no response for a moment. Then, Amos, reaching for another tvaybak, broke the silence and finished the conversation with, "Well, anyhow, these tvaybak are good and don't call for anything more."

Hilda was glad she hadn't served a cake. Perhaps it was a good thing it had fallen. *Or would no one have said anything if I had served it?*

Henry, whose new car was not actually a necessity, laughed and added, "Well, I daresay that it is not the worst thing on earth to bake a cake, even if it *is* unnecessary."

After the women helped Hilda wash the dishes and the men finished discussing farming problems, the guests left to do their chores in time to go to evening service at church.

Emma stayed back a little and then confided, "I gave a piece of cake to Henry, and he liked it. But I'd know better than to serve it to other people. I mean Mennonites."

"Come," Hilda said softly, leading her to the pantry. She opened the pantry door and showed her the pan holding her clumsy attempt. "Do you know what's wrong?"

Emma bent over it. "It looks as if it rose all right and then fell. Did you put baking powder in it?"

"Yes, I'm sure I did. I read the directions over twice, and checked everything off," Hilda whispered, though the men were outside and could not hear anyhow. "I tried to keep it a secret and was afraid Franz would come into the house. But still, I thought I did everything right. The stove is old, but I've had good success with bread and such. We don't plan to get a new one for the new house. And the baking powder is new."

Emma patted Hilda's shoulder. "Come over to my house some weekday, and I'll bake one with you. Maybe we can work it out."

"I was beginning to think it fell because I was breaking a Mennonite rule."

Emma snorted and shoved her gently. "Sometimes it's fun to break a few rules. Who would really care?" When they heard the men returning to the house, they quickly left the pantry, giggling.

"What are you two up to?" Franz asked. "You're acting guilty."

"Women's secrets," Emma answered, as she wrapped a shawl around her hair to keep the wind from mussing it on their fast trip home in their open car.

*   *   *

"Do you think we will see results of the 'meeting'?" Franz had his arms around Hilda from behind and was looking over her shoulder at the shiny car leaving their yard.

"Maybe, maybe not," was Hilda's answer. "We might not know for a while. I'll have to ask Anna sometime whether she knows how to bake tvaybak." Then, changing the subject, she faced him directly. "Franz, I'm just thinking—are these cousins the same people who gave us that noisy scary shivaree on our wedding night?"

"Maybe... Some of them."

"Don't you know? I thought you recognized them."

"All right. Yes. Some of them, not all."

"Did *you* ever...?"

"Don't ask." Laughing, he left her to begin preparations for the milking.

While Grace paged through last season's Sears catalog, Hilda fed Andrew. When he was asleep, she put him into his cradle, gave it a couple of gentle pushes, and went to the barn to help with the milking.

As they were getting ready to leave for church, for there was to be a Christian Endeavor program, a visitor arrived. It was Aunt Mary who, now that they had returned to Minnesota and did not have Father Heldin there, considered it her duty to watch over them more than ever. It was easier to get along with her now, for she seemed to have adjusted to the idea that they were finally grown up. Peter had made it home in time to drive her back to call on them, but he did not participate, as he used to, in her long, patronizing prayer.

Though mellowed, she still inquired after the personal side of their lives and when, in turn, questioned as to her own health and well-being, she became immediately touched. Deeply grateful for the interest of others, she would answer with a break in her voice.

She did not approve of the house they were building. "It hardly seems necessary for you to build a new house when your own is still good for many years to come. Of course, it has scratches, but wait until your children are older and start their wild playing in the house. Grace is a girl, and she'll never be rough, but Andrew. He is a boy, and he will throw balls and pound on things with a hammer. You will hate to see that happen to a new house. Have you prayed about it?"

Hilda answered quietly, "Yes, Aunt Mary. And God made it possible for us to build it."

"Sometimes God gives us a possibility, even while He does not want us to do something."

Aunt Mary did not expect an answer, and she didn't stay long. She seldom did. But when she left, it was too late to go to church. Quietly, after the children were both asleep, Franz and Hilda felt the letdown after a full, busy, mostly happy day. Aunt Mary's words unsettled them, for she was the only one who said anything against their building a new home.

Franz was most direct: "Sometimes I think she is possessed. She always manages to bring in unpleasantness, even when she's in a good mood."

Hilda's responded quickly: "Franz, we must forgive her. She is an old woman. And she is Father's sister."

The following day, and each day after that, when Franz ate his lunch out in the field to save time, Hilda ate pieces of her cake. Even if it was hard and dry, it tasted good, and it wouldn't hurt her. She gave Grace pieces of it too, hoping she wouldn't speak of it, but Grace didn't like it and wouldn't eat it. She said it was bitter. Dry. Tough. Tasted like soap.

CHAPTER TWENTY-TWO: 1922

With a white sky heavy with humidity, and heat more oppressive than any they remembered, perspiration ran freely into Hilda's eyes and down her nose. It didn't evaporate. All day long the cats slept, ungracefully stretched out on the black dirt underneath the lilac bushes. Ask Him panted, restlessly moved from place to place, and snapped irritably at flies that disturbed him.

Hilda wondered whether the laundry she hung out would dry in the heavy air. She wore only a cotton dress with nothing on underneath and went barefoot as she often did, knowing shoes would hurt her feet Sunday. She let Grace run around wearing only panties, admonishing her to hide in case anyone should come to the yard. Despite their scanty clothing, the children were fretful. Andrew didn't nap, and it seemed nothing would stop his whining. Grace impulsively slapped him, and he screamed until Hilda gave him an extra cooling bath.

By early evening, far to the southwest low on the horizon, clouds sported a constant flicker of lightning. With the children in bed, Hilda and Franz sat on the back-door stoop watching the display. As the wall of clouds approached, tumbling and rolling, Franz spotted the funnel and knew it was time. Running to Grace's room, he grabbed her roughly and ordered Hilda to take Andrew, his diapers, and nothing else into their small dirt-walled storm cellar.

Almost as soon as they were safely there, they heard the storm strike, roaring loudly and wildly overhead. Grace clung silently to her father, not uttering even when a crack of lightning struck nearby. In her head, Hilda prayed. *God. God: Where are you now? Jesus! Jesus, stop the storm! As you did the tempest. Help*!

From the noise, and being held more tightly than he was accustomed to, Andrew began to scream; his fright gave Hilda something to do. She hugged him to her. With clenched teeth, she tried to center her attention. *Pray. "Pray without ceasing,"* the Bible says. *Who said that?—the Apostle Paul maybe.* Hilda tried to think which words to say. *Just Pray. God, preserve us. Save our farm. Save our house. Save our animals. In the barn and out in the pasture. Forgive my sins. Help my unbelief.*

They sat on a bench, heads bowed. The walls of the storm cellar, though dry, gave off its earth smell. Dug and furnished with a crude bench by the previous owner of their farm, this was the first time they had used it. They had laughed about it, imagining uses they could put it to, like storing wine they never made nor drank. Or to dump trash. Or to dig deeper for a well. Or as a shortcut to China.

Around the edges of the wooden trapdoor rainwater seeped, turning the walls into mud, and forcing Hilda and Franz to lean forward. They waited for a time after the height of the tornado passed, and they stayed in the cellar until the wind noticeably decreased. Not until the thunder gently growled in the distance, and the only sound left was the regular beat of heavy rain did they pull on their shawls and again go back to the house to return the children to their upstairs beds. They needed comforting—hard to do when the parents were themselves distressed.

Franz wanted to go back outside immediately, to see what damage the storm had done, but, afraid that there might be some freak return of the twister, Hilda persuaded him to stay with her and the children until she could safely go with him.

The rain had been cooling but was still warmer than the air the storm had brought with it. They did not attempt to shield themselves from the rain since it would be useless to try. Silently, they walked first to the site of their almost-finished house; though it was very dark with the lightning too far away and too infrequent to give them light, they found their way instinctively. As they walked, Hilda stumbled over a piece of wood. Knowing that it came from their new house, she held back, not wanting to know for sure, but Franz led her on, silently determined.

They had not seen it happen. In moments, it had devolved from a structure to a pile of its components. "It must be scattered over a large area," was all he said when they reached the place where the building had stood.

They did not return to the old house directly but went to see that the barn, with its few young animals, and the other buildings were all right. They would not know until morning whether the cattle and horses outdoors were still there.

When they went to bed, they could not sleep but lay tightly clasping each other. Presently, Franz spoke. "If only you'd cry. That would help me so much. Why don't you cry?"

Hilda did not answer. Neither could she cry. She was thinking of her prayers. *I should thank God for our lives. For the barn and this old house. He answered part of my prayer. But He took our new house. Who is God anyhow? How does God decide which prayer He responds to?*

The morning after the storm, the sunrise painted the last remnants of ugly clouds quietly dissolving. The sky sparkled pure, blued by a miracle washing product. Franz rose and pulled on the clothes that smelled of new wood, clothes he wore the day before while sanding the woodwork in preparation for varnishing. Now he walked over the soggy earth. Everywhere, the land had been washed clean; it smelled clean, like a freshly prepared salad: snippets of foliage—light green like iceberg lettuce, dark green like spinach—clung to fence posts and to those windows that remained intact. The ground crunched where he stepped.

Leaves on trees near the old house looked polished; trees further away—those still standing—were stripped of leaves. Beyond the clearing of the buildings, the grain lay wet and plastered together in bunches, like the too-wet hair of a farm boy on a Sunday morning. It was easy to see to all the grain fields, for the unfinished building, the new house, had been blocking the view.

*   *   *

Hilda did not open her eyes until she heard Franz leave the house. Then she pulled on her clothes to start the coffee and oatmeal that he would be sure to need when he returned. She kept herself from looking out the window, as if doing so would annul what had happened during the night.

The oatmeal was barely ready when he returned. "The animals are all there, though the fence is down in spots. I lifted the wires so it will do for a while, but I'll have to get at fixing it right away. Most of the grain will raise itself. We are lucky the storm came now rather than just before the harvest."

Hilda kept busy dressing and feeding Andrew while Franz and Grace finished their breakfast. But as she was working, she noticed how much older Franz looked when he was tired, and the smile wrinkles about his eyes and near his mouth did not seem to belong there.

When Hilda was able to sit down to her own breakfast, he stayed, as if the day was a holiday, or a Sunday. "Maybe your Aunt Mary was right," he finally said. "Maybe the Lord didn't want us to build. Maybe we wanted something we didn't need, and shouldn't have." With his fingers, he rubbed his scalp through the fine hair that needed cutting.

Though she had been hungry, Hilda found it hard to eat. "Now maybe we know how John and Marie felt after their house burned."

"Right. But I don't know why we needed to know how they felt."

"We're lucky we hadn't moved in yet," Hilda continued. Pa had often reminded her to look for the good, even in the bad.

Franz smiled bitterly. "That we are. There's a nice heap of junk in the new basement, and we'd be under that. That is, if we'd had time to get down into that basement."

"Is it *all* gone? I can hardly believe that we can't salvage at least some of it…"

A car put-putted at their driveway. As he rose to see who was coming, Franz answered, "The basement's all right. Even the drain is working. It's carrying off most of the water that filled it. And there's a lot of wood around that we can use again. But the two-by-fours and most of the larger pieces are in splinters. We'll have to keep children away when they're barefoot, because there are nails scattered all over, along with treacherous bits of wood. You'll have to wear shoes too."

The car had arrived. It was Henry and Emma Heldin with their two youngest children, who immediately ran to the house to look for Grace and her toys.

"We could see from home your new house wasn't standing. So we came right away to see if you were all right." For once, Henry had a serious expression on his face.

Emma said, "We weren't sure whether you had moved in yet. You said in church that you would soon, and we were afraid that you already had."

"We're almost wishing we *had* moved in," Franz said. "At least we wouldn't be alive to feel bad about losing the house."

"Don't say that," Emma gasped. "The Johnsons, you know, our neighbors—she was the one who taught me to bake cake. They're dead. The twister must have lifted and come back down, because there isn't much gone between here and there, but it took all their farm buildings. And them too. They were all killed, except the oldest boy, who was helping out at his brother's."

"We just came from their farmstead," Henry added. "There isn't much anyone can do there. We wouldn't know where to start."

Then Hilda saw that Emma had been weeping, and now she felt herself able to cry, for herself and Franz, and for the boy who had been left alone in the world.

"I'm sorry," Emma said, "I shouldn't be adding to your grief by scolding you."

And Hilda, thinking that the children might be watching from the house, forced herself to stop crying.

"How much damage did the storm do? How many other farms were hit?" Franz asked.

"Nothing big," Henry said, leaning against his black, now muddy automobile. "It took some of our trees and cut across through the big grove near the two-mile corner. But otherwise, we haven't seen or heard of anything. We haven't been to town or seen other farms. We came straight here."

Emma broke the silence that followed. "I kept my apron on. We thought we'd stay here today and help you if we could."

"What needs to be done first?" asked Henry, who was wearing overalls. "We can't do anything at home anyhow, with things as wet as they are."

"The fence," Franz said. "I suppose I'll have to keep the stock out of the grain if we want to have a harvest. God knows we'll need it."

Hilda had never heard him swear before. Yet, it didn't seem like swearing, for he had said it with reverence. She thought about it a bit: *When is a word "swearing"?*

They worked hard that day in the invigorating air, cleared of yesterday's sultry oppressiveness. By noon, Hilda and Emma had cleaned several rooms of the old house in which they would be living for some time longer than they had planned. The men had finished repairing the fence. They spent the afternoon clearing debris out of the basement of the new house, pulling nails carefully, and placing lumber that was still good into well-ordered piles.

Franz gave the children a game to play: "Sort the nails by size, and deposit them in separate boxes." It was fun; they scrambled further afield while Hilda reminded them, "Watch where you step. I don't want you getting lockjaw." She was immediately sorry, for Grace asked, "What's 'lockjaw'?"

That evening, when the Heldins had left, with a promise to come again the following day, Hilda and Franz prepared to go to bed early.

"Do you really think Aunt Mary was right, Franz? Has God taken the house from us because he didn't want us to have it? Or is it punishment for something we have done, or haven't done? Why did it happen?"

Franz's face was not visible, for they had not taken the kerosene lamp with them into the bedroom. He answered, "Let's not think of it that way, Hilda, or we'll despair. We mustn't confuse religion with superstition."

"But what is belief, and what is superstition? How can we know? If we don't believe that God punishes, then what power does God have? Why even believe in Him at all?"

"Do you have a guilty conscience, Hilda? Why do you think God should punish us?"

"No, the only things I can think of are the cake I baked—I didn't tell you about it because it fell and was spoiled—and the fact that we built the house when maybe it wasn't necessary. You said so just this morning."

"I guess I didn't really mean it. I'm just as upset as you are. Anyway, we have to be practical. You should look at the foundation of this house. It's been ready to fall apart for the last ten years… Aunt Mary's only a woman and doesn't know what this house is like underneath. Her one-track mind just always tries to find sin in what we—people—do."

"But why did God pick us out? And the Johnsons?"

"Why does anything happen? It just happens. You heard me read the article in *The Farmer* that explained how a cyclone is formed." He yawned loudly and—it seemed to Hilda—defiantly.

Disturbed for being wide awake, Hilda could not calm herself. "You know, though, the Johnsons aren't Mennonites. Maybe God had been warning them and finally took them. Maybe this is a warning to us, and we're lucky to be alive to do something about it."

"Now, Hilda. We mustn't think that just because they weren't Mennonites they were wicked people. Henry said they were good folk and went to their church every Sunday."

"But, you've said you're glad that you were raised Mennonite. That it's the best faith."

"Of course. I still say so. I wouldn't want our children, for instance, to leave our faith, or to marry outside the Mennonite church. But even so, that doesn't make the Johnsons lost people. You know, there are seven different Mennonite churches in this area. Seven different ways to look at the same thing. Some people say our church is too modernistic and worldly."

"But those are the Old Dispensation Mennonites. And some of their ideas of shunning worldliness are silly. Like not using buttons to fasten their shirts. Covering their arms by wearing long sleeves even in hot weather, wearing those funny little white caps that don't keep their heads warm or even cover their hair. Not to mention those messy, long beards that collect crumbs and sawdust."

"Even so, we have to respect their ideas, as well as the ideas of the non-Mennonite churches. And we must be firm in our own faith." He lay back.

"Franz, I just thought of something," Hilda said, raising herself in turn. "Maybe things have been going too well for us, and God sent us this cyclone as a sort of test. Like the story of Job. And if we prove steady and firm in our faith, he will reward us doubly in the end."

But Franz had fallen asleep, able at last to relax after the day's turmoil. Hilda, comforted by the idea, also slept.

*   *   *

During the following week, they worked hard. Until the saturated earth had dried enough for the farmers to resume their cultivation, Henry and other members of the church cheerfully organized and came to help Franz build. By the end of the week, the new house had a framework of new two-by-fours, as well as parts of walls, all firm on the foundation that had withstood the storm.

Though the house was growing again, Hilda felt that the work they did was not as good as the work Franz had put into it during the months of solitary building. That had been a labor of love, and this seemed to be more of a lark: work for the fun of being with a large group of people. Then she reminded herself that they were also working for love—love not for the house but for them: Franz and Hilda, which was perhaps a greater love. Besides, there was still a lot of work left to do: all the inside building, and the finishing.

CHAPTER TWENTY-THREE: 1923–26

"Du, Franz, what do you think? Was the tornado God's way of punishing us? Was it a test? Could it simply be a random happening, with God only standing by? Watching, maybe, as if we're just toys? Can God be so fickle?"

As he did whenever she brought up the matter, Franz shrugged.

"What I want to know is, is it our—my—fault?"

"Hilda, stop it. It has nothing to with what we did or didn't do. It's an act of Nature. Bad luck."

She had to let it go, at least for that time. Nevertheless, Hilda added it to her stockpile of personal guilt. Not being *right with God*. Her stomach hurt.

Their new house was turning out much like the first one. Not luxurious, but conforming to their commitment to Mennonite values. They weren't proud, but they were satisfied. Some work would wait until the third spring, since they couldn't work on it in cold weather or during planting or harvesting times.

Franz put his feet up onto the kitchen stool. "I feel as if I could build a whole row of houses, all alike, now that we've built two exactly the same way."

"Why does that idea even come to you?" was all Hilda could think to answer.

"Oh, I don't know. I know it isn't funny." He got up and studied the door and window frame of their "yet" home.

"Once we move out of here, we can use lumber from this place to build into a detached summer kitchen close to the new back door. There we can relocate things like the cauldron and cream separator."

"Except we'll have to bring the separator into the main house for winter," Hilda reminded him.

Franz went on. "Perhaps rooms in this old building can be turned into storage bins until we can build a proper granary. Then we'll raze it. Later."

The old house was snug enough, but Hilda realized that she was being careless about maintaining its appearance. She let her usually habitual Saturday dusting and cleaning chores go. "You can skip scrubbing the back hall floor today, Grace. It's cold in there, and the wet floor would just get icy. Slippery. And, Franz dump the corncobs in the corner of the summer kitchen. It's handier there."

Part of her carelessness was that her pregnancy was advancing. "This time," she told Franz, "the baby is taking up more room in my body. Probably bigger than either Grace or Andrew—or Cherub. It's harder for me to stoop or get down on my knees, so I can't ask you or Grace to do it either."

"Or in your mind, you're already moving out of this house," Franz suggested.

*   *   *

That fall, Grace attended the one-room country school a mile away. Hilda and Franz knew the long walk tired the young girl, but what could they do? It wasn't safe to trust her with a horse. Few people used their lonely county road, lonely because it didn't lead anywhere but to other isolated farms, so seldom would anyone drive by to offer her a lift. They knew there was no danger of wolves; but who knew what stray dogs might be around? They gave her a willow stick to swing hard if an unfriendly dog should come at her.

She didn't seem to mind the walk; Fritz, the new dog, always went with her to school and ran to meet her after school. When it was too cold for her to walk, Franz took her by buggy; when the road was blocked by snow, Franz replaced the buggy wheels with runners, turning it into a sleigh. School brought homework for her. Evenings, she welcomed being sent to bed early.

Winter was typically cold and snowy, and the only farm work was feeding the animals, mucking out the gutters behind the cows and horses, milking, and collecting eggs. For days, the temperature never rose above zero degrees.

During one of those days, labor pains started. Franz covered Prince with the old horse-blanket before harnessing him to the buggy, and wearing his warmest coat, he wrapped himself with an additional heavy blanket. "Good that Mrs. Harmes doesn't live so far away," he told Prince. "Hope she got the message last week that the time will be soon." It seemed—actually, he was sure—that Prince liked to be talked to. With no one to overhear, what did it matter if he talked to his horse?

*   *   *

Mrs. Harmes was ready, smiling. "Let me pick up my handy bag of

143

tools—well, really, my supplies. I always keep them in reach. I don't have, don't need, much more than my clean hands, and some string and my sewing scissors. I boiled them just this morning. I mean my scissors and string—not my hands."

Franz smiled at her joke. "Hilda's all set for you. Been ready for a week or so." He didn't remove his coat or sit down.

They arrived before dark, and Grace and Andrew were sent to bed soon after, but not before they came up with names they liked. Unlike most other parents, Hilda and Franz had informed them that there would soon be a baby in the family. The children knew that babies came from God, but they weren't aware of any connection between Mrs. Harmes's arrival and the coming event.

Perhaps trying to delay his bedtime, three-year-old Andrew proposed a name for the future baby: "*Jimmy.* The boy who sings and plays guitar on the radio with his papa. You know, *Asher and Little Jimmy.*"

Grace snorted, "What if it's a girl? You can't name a girl *Jimmy*! I think a girl should be *Jane.* Then I can play with her like the children in my English primer, *Fun with Dick and Jane.* Maybe if it's a boy we can call him *Dick.*"

"I guess *Dick* would be all right," Andrew allowed, "but I like J*immy* better. How about *Goldilocks* for a girl? Or *Little Red Riding Hood*?"

Hilda stepped in. "We'll wait and see if the baby is a girl or boy. Then God will help us decide what her name should be. Or his name... But, now off to bed, you two. And don't forget your prayers." She sat down, panting and perspiring.

"Off to bed you too, Hilda." Mrs. Harmes put on an apron and ushered Hilda to her bed after covering it with oilcloth. Franz, knowing she would ask for it, checked to see that Hilda had put water on to heat and added corncobs to the fire.

The baby was smaller than they had expected, but healthy. A girl. Hilda and Franz agreed: *Jane* was different. Not like so many Hildas and Huldahs and Saras, common in the area.

*   *   *

As soon as the weather of the following spring was warm enough, Amos came to help Franz load the cook stove onto the sledge that Prince pulled across the yard to the new back door. When the stove was installed, they hauled the beds and other furniture, with Fritz following each trip.

"How do we move the cats?" Grace was hugging Youngest Mur to her chest.

"They'll soon learn where they'll get their food," Hilda told her. "Besides, the old house will still be a source of mice. And they can keep on sleeping in the barn or under the lilac bushes."

As she carried coats and dresses draped over her arms, with Grace and Andrew at her side carrying some of their things, Hilda told them about another move to a new house, when she helped her pa move from their old one. "How happy my ma was. Then she died not long after."

It was a mistake. She caught the eyes of both children; it was Grace who asked, "Why did she die?" And Andrew asked, "Are *you* going to die?"

"No, no. I'm in robust health. My ma was frail. I'm going to live for a long time yet." She pushed the comparison away.

*   *   *

They settled in, and the house became a home.

When there was a lull in farm work, the whole family returned to the old house to take apart the good wood. The children were assigned to sort reusable nails by size into separate boxes, just as Grace had done after the tornado. They hurried, each trying to fill a box first.

Grace was bothered when Hilda interrupted her, saying, "Grace, mind the baby for a while. Let me know if she wakes up."

"Aw, Ma, Andrew will get ahead of me. Can't the baby just cry when she wakes up? I'll hear her."

Behind his mother, Andrew whispered, "Ha, ha. Now you can have your *Fun with Jane.*"

*   *   *

That evening, after supper, while Hilda washed dishes and Grace grudgingly dried, Hilda said to her, "When I was a child, my mother taught me this rhyme:

> *Frisch ans Werk, und nicht gesäumt.*
> *Was im Weg, ist weg geräumt.*
> *Was ihr fehlet, zuch geschwind*
> *Ordnung lehrne, früh mein Kind. "*

"I bet you can't say that in English," Grace said.

"Don't bet. Mennonites don't bet. But I can, and let's hear *you* do it." Grace could. She sing-sang:

> *"Fresh to work and no loitering.*
> *What's in the way, clear away.*
> *What you need, find right away.*
> *Learn order early, my child."*

145

Hilda sighed. "No need to put on an act, Grace. I just wanted to see how well you understood both German and English. And to get you past your reluctant kitchen help."

Andrew had been listening. "It sounds better in German."

"Yes, it does," Hilda replied. "I suppose a poem originally written in English sounds better in English than translated into German."

"I think some of the hymns we sing in church sound better in English than they do in German too," Grace said. "Is that because they were originally written in English?"

"It could well be." Hilda continued, "If you need a project for school sometime, why don't you find out which hymns were written in German and which ones in English? I'd like to know too."

*   *   *

Hilda and Franz did not seriously regret leaving Montana, though reports of the most recent years of crops there were good. John wrote them general information:

Other families also left after they met their three-year commitment. That took some attention off you. Those who stayed are starting to build new homes, or improving their starter shacks. Some have bought more land and are even taking trips, either back to their former homes or to other parts of the country. We're working hard, like everybody else. The children are healthy and growing well.

Whenever she thought about John and Marie, Hilda called up vivid memories of her weeks at John's home: not so much the birth of Johnny but John's wish for a good life for his wife and his family. Are *they having the good life he longed for? I do have the good life he wished for me. Now. And he did arrange for me to meet Franz.*

Pa didn't say much about the church. In his letters, written neatly in ink, he wrote: *I'm devoting my time to farming and to helping people who come to me for spiritual help. They still call me for medical help, to set broken bones or realign dislocated joints.*

It seemed to Hilda that Pa now considered her an adult, if not an equal. *He doesn't preach to me. Hardly mentioned any Christian admonitions, but he also doesn't share innermost feelings. Perhaps if I were to ask some direct questions, like, "How can you know if you're saved?"* he might answer. She did write that question one time and then tore up the page because it looked desperate. Deep inside, she also dreaded hearing from him words that would tell her how to find out: *A sort of formula, like an arithmetic problem. Then I would know the truth—but he would also know about my uncertainty.* She wondered, *Do I want him to know that I don't know?*

Muttah almost always included a letter in Pa's envelope. Hers, written in pencil, were devoted to what Hermann and Marta were doing: *Both of them are reading and writing in German and in English... The chickens are laying thirty to thirty-two eggs each day, and the cows average a full pail of milk each day. This summer, J canned tomatoes, green beans, and wild berries the children picked in the prairie.*

She never complained, but it seemed to Hilda as if she was working very hard. *Is she working as hard as Ma always did? How could anyone know? What's sure, she's healthier. On the other hand, she only has the two babies.*

One item of information surprised her: Abe Geppert died during a blizzard. He had never married and lived alone in a small hut. His farm work had seemed to fizzle, according to Joe. Hilda felt an ache in her chest upon hearing the news, a feeling she did not share with Franz. *How would things have been different?*

I wonder whether the Montanans are trying to make me and Franz regret leaving... Joe, just as I expected, has taken over the leadership of the church—that news had come from Liesebet; *of course, the congregation elected him after he used a transparent (to me and Franz, at least) campaign.*

Liesebet wrote frequently: *Rachel and Joey are doing well and growing tall and strong. Jn my spare time, when J have some, J help some neighbor children—not from our church but good neighbors—who are struggling with learning to read. Their parents are also learning English along with their children. Joe was hoping they might also be converted to join our church, but so far they haven't come forth, and J avoid talking about church while they work on reading.*

So, Liesebet isn't proselytizing. Good for her. She knows the difference between schooling and churching. And the rest of her letters are pensive—almost poetic, Hilda thought as she read them. *I'm so grateful for the months Liesebet spent in Minnesota after her dreadful accident. I'm very, very happy that our sistership has become a friendship.*

In her letters, and deep inside, and careful not to speak of any controversial subject, Hilda regretted the circumstances that had brought about Liesebet's marriage to Joe.

*　　　　*　　　　*

Hilda and her family had lived in their new home for more than three years, harvesting an abundant crop each autumn, and feeling happy in being almost debt free. Franz said on the fifth anniversary of their return to Minnesota, "This is a good life, and God is good to us."

Their healthy baby Jane was now toddling, vibrant, and starting to talk, Andrew was a sturdy, proud big brother, and Grace a usually serene adolescent. But on the back of Franz's head, where he once had an unmanageable cowlick, especially after the Saturday night bath, there was now a small cleanly shining bald spot. He joked about it, and giggled when Jane tickled him there, but Hilda did not like to see it any more than she liked to think about thick, ugly dark hairs she plucked from her upper lip and chin, or that she might soon need false teeth.

CHAPTER TWENTY-FOUR: 1928–29

Miss Friesen, the single teacher at the one-room country school, managed to teach twenty children. Some grades had several pupils; others had none. Some lessons could be taught across grade levels, but each child got direct and personal attention. She arrived early to build a fire in the potbelly stove until it was warm enough to take off her coat. The room was ready with the day's lessons chalked on the blackboard by the time children arrived on foot or horseback. She knew each child by name, and often knew more about their families than the children's parents would have been comfortable with, if they had known.

*   *   *

When Andrew was seven, and of two minds about going to school at all, he sometimes walked with Grace for his first two years—her last two at the country school. However, by then, Grace had learned to ride, and the two of them were trusted to ride old Minnie's broad back in good weather.

Grace was a good student—Miss Friesen guided her through the eight grades by the time she was fourteen. Then she encouraged Hilda and Franz to arrange for Grace to go to the high school in town. An obvious place for Grace to stay during the week was with Grossma Lober, who had moved to Mound Lake from her farm when Amos married. She welcomed her granddaughter, happy for her company and for the help she gave in the kitchen. Grossma Lober taught her some Russian, words she remembered from her own childhood: "dobre dyen," "rabota," and "sobaka." Of course, Grace already knew some Russian foods that Hilda cooked now and then: borscht, perischki, vereneki, and porzelki.[22]

---

22 Good day, work, dog. And cabbage soup, fruit-filled pockets, cottage cheese-filled pockets, New Year's fritters with raisins.

*   *   *

Hilda served Franz a large bowl of hot oatmeal before the children were up. They had gradually forgotten about daily morning devotions as they started to eat breakfast by themselves instead of waiting for all to sit around the table. Before sitting herself, she said, "It's strange. I dreamt again that I'm hurrying to finish my work because I need to start packing—I'm barefoot and working in the garden, or peeling potatoes in our fine new kitchen—something ordinary that makes me feel as if everything is the same as always. It's the same dream. Then I wake up, and find myself in bed, and I can't go back to sleep for a long time."

"Why do you keep dreaming it? Are you thinking about it a lot every day?"

"Not really. Oh, how can I forget?" Sighing, she took her own bowl to the table.

"I know you don't want to move. I wish you wouldn't keep reminding me."

"I'm sorry. I'll stop mentioning it. Maybe then the dreams will stop."

"You're really opposed to moving. Can't you think how it would be better?"

"Yes, Franz, but I'm not used to the idea. You say everything there is better than here. Except the house. And we can do something about that when we're able... But there's something about this farm, and *that* I shall keep with me. This house we put our love into as we built it. I won't—I don't think I can—learn to love a new place. I don't feel it inside, though I promise to try."

"You're very impractical," Franz said, shoving back his chair that screeched across the floor, as usual.

Hilda continued. "Don't you feel it, even a little? When you walk along the grove, toward the creek? When you sit near the bridge with your lunch, and Fritz comes to you begging for crusts that I know you give him? Or when you think that, after all the troubles we had at first, we finally have a change for the better? Why can't we be content with the happiness we have now?"

"Contentment and tradition are often names given to laziness," Franz answered. "We can be too lazy to make the moves that'll be better in the long run."

"But what are the shortcomings here? As I see it, this farm is only too small. Couldn't we just buy some more land to it? Or maybe rent some? It won't be many more years before you don't have all this excess energy, and you'll be glad you don't have so much land to farm."

"And Andrew? How shall we harness his energy? He's already beginning to help me so much. What will his inheritance be, Hilda—a run-down farm with a new house and a pretty little creek where he can sit and feed his dog the crusts from his lunch?"

"Franz. Please. You know that's not what I mean. You know that even the Bible says that man cannot live by bread alone."

"Neither can he live by pretty words. He must have bread too—every day, and enough of it."

Hilda persisted. "As a result, now that we have paid for this place, we'll again have a debt to work for. Can't we ever just live on the money we already have, instead of paying for things we bought before? This way, we have to depend so much on the crops we don't yet have, and every time the sky is dark we run outside to study it. To see whether there is hail or a high wind in the air."

"That has happened *once* in all the almost six years we've lived here. All the other times, we've had abundant crops as this land will give us. We have to trust in God, Hilda."

"Yes, we must trust to God as we throw ourselves off the pinnacle that Satan sets us on. And He will send us His angels to see that we don't dash our foot against a stone!"

"Hilda. Don't blaspheme."

"I'm sorry. I didn't mean to. But I did mean that we mustn't tempt God. Or fate. Or whatever. We're taking a big risk."

"Don't forget, at the new place, our children can ride the bus to the town school. Go to high school. They won't have to board. My ma isn't up to hosting children much longer, you know. Her knees and hips are giving out. She doesn't say much, but when I ask, she admits that it's getting harder."

"She hasn't said anything to me."

"Have you seen how she walks?"

"Maybe before long the town school will send buses *this* far."

"Or not."

"Well, we don't know the future. Only God knows. But maybe."

"All right. But back to the subject. We're still young, and our children are young and healthy. I've figured it very carefully. At the very most, it will take us seven years to finish paying for it. I have taken *everything* into consideration. Illness and doctor bills, crop failure, higher taxes. If things go well, it will take us half that long. Even if it takes us longer than seven years, we will still be young. By the time it's paid for, we will have plenty of time to get the children started on projects of their own. We'll be young enough to take a trip or two. Then we can start saving up for our old age, so by the time we're too old to work hard, we'll be comfortably off."

"And if we aren't?"

Franz rose to go out. But he didn't leave. "Faith, Hilda. Faith in ourselves as well as in God."

Hilda felt the need to say what she contained but found it hard to convey it in words. *Strange,* she thought, *once I believed that we understood everything between us; that there was nothing we would need to explain because our spirits were kindred.*

"I took a long walk with the children. It's over a month ago—before the first snow, or even the killing frost. I was through with my work, and the day was beautiful. The children seemed to be out of things to do. I was happy to enjoy things with them as I never could do before. When I was too busy with work, helping you struggle. So the four of us went for a walk along the creek. We took our time, stopping to examine a wildflower, or when Jane wanted Andrew to catch a butterfly for her. Of course, he never did; they were too fast for him. We walked slowly. Even Fritz caught the spirit of it and ran off only once. For a while we even sat until I was afraid Jane would fall asleep and I would have to carry her all the way home. When we got home, we found that we had been gone more than two hours.

"Then I made cocoa when we got home. And we drank it. After that, we pasted the leaves we had gathered into the old catalogue. It was a happening, an event that I can still experience, whenever I think of it. It makes me feel that this farm is alive, and that I love it."

"The new farm has a creek too." As Franz said it, on his way out the door, Hilda saw that there was no softness in his face, and that he would not look at her, even when he had to turn to take his jacket off the hook.

*   *   *

It was Saturday afternoon, the time Franz usually spent in the house during the late fall and winter, the time he usually used reading his books and magazines. From her window, Hilda saw him hitch the team to the drag sled—really, a heavy box with skids that slid easily over the frozen ground and snow. He used it in winter to haul manure and straw. He unhitched the horses and took them back to the barn. Grace and Andrew watched him climb into the box, which hurtled down the hill toward the creek.

Hilda busied herself with a cake she had learned to bake. It was no longer so difficult, but it still demanded concentration. At the moment, she didn't want to think, but silently so as not to disturb Jane who had gone to sleep over her paper dolls made out of Sears catalogue models, she prayed that God would make it impossible for them to move. Then, immediately, she begged forgiveness for her narrow-mindedness and tried to build within herself an attitude of childlike adventure.

One idea came to her. Though she had no doubt that she loved her husband and would love him wherever they lived, or in spite of whatever he decided, she imagined herself free, able to make her own choices. It was momentary; she did not wish it, but she imagined what it would be like. It did not displace her feeling of impotent dependence. She wished they had a spare bedroom that she could use occasionally. Not always. Not even often.

The cake was beautiful; it had good color. Hilda had learned to regulate the oven carefully, with a certain feel for direction of wind, the number of corncobs necessary to feed the flame, and at which intervals. She stifled a childish urge to taste it immediately. By the time Franz and the children came in, she'd serve them a special supper, with the cake as a surprise. She'd hidden it in the pantry until they would be ready for dessert. They seldom had dessert, so this would be a double surprise.

But when they came in, she was kept busy quieting Andrew, who was crying loudly. Franz did not explain more than, "I would not let them ride down the hill on the sledge alone. It would have been too dangerous."

Grace was quiet but looked angry. Andrew insisted on talking, trying to keep his sobs coming, one way or another. "First he asked us if we wanted to ride down, and we were too scared. Then he climbed on and rode it by himself, and when we saw how much fun it could be and wanted to ride down the next time, he wouldn't let us." He dug his knuckles into his eyes, as if to dip out more tears. Jane loyally went to stand next to him, her cheeks now wet with dirty tears, even though she hadn't been with them.

"Come on, Andrew." Franz gently pushed his shoulder. "Be a big boy. Stop crying."

But Hilda smiled. "He's just a child. He can have the privilege of crying long and hard when he's frustrated."

The lines in Franz's face eased somewhat. "Sometimes I forget they aren't grown up. When I asked them the first time, I didn't realize how dangerous it was until I tried it. I can't steer the thing, and I can't brake. If there had been a rock in the way, or a tree, or a ditch, I would have been hurt. I wouldn't even go down there a second time by myself. I only hope they don't try it by themselves sometime."

"Unless we give them cardboard boxes to slide on. They would tear before anything happened," Hilda added, happy to talk about something other than moving. She sent them to the sink to wash, tempted to bribe them to stop sniffling, but she stuck to her resolve that the cake was not a reward.

She had not intended the cake as a charm, and her only reason for baking it had been to keep her mind off their disagreement, but she felt disappointed after Franz ate it. She was more certain—though she had been certain before they started to discuss it—that they would move again. Still, she did not have the sense of relief she often had when a decision was lifted from her. Was not her life and Franz's irrevocably tied together no matter what happened?

It was difficult, but she went to him after the children had gone to bed, leaning her head against his muscular chest, telling him that his decision was hers also. In reply, he held her to him.

She pulled back and looked up at him. "One thing. It's important to me."

"All right. What is it?"

"I want to bring Cherub with us. Bury him at our new home."

"You can't mean that. It's been thirteen years. There won't be anything—"

"There will be. You can build a new coffin. I'll rewrap him. You won't have to see."

"Hilda, Hilda," was all he could say. He held her a while longer.

Monday morning, early, Hilda heard the sound of sawing and hammering. She went out to see. "I have some good lumber—it's nice new wood," Franz explained. "I'm making it now, while I have the time."

Her dreams continued, nevertheless, following her to their new farm and recurring for years until she could laugh at them. Eventually, they came at ridiculous times—during canning season or before a celebration, and her children learned laughingly to refer to "Ma's dream about yonder farm" as a family joke.

CHAPTER TWENTY-FIVE: 1929

On her first tour of their new home, just a mile from their present home—if you could fly—Hilda burst out, "Franz, look at the scratches on the woodwork! Those are gouges! You can't sand them out."

"They are ugly. But it's only looks. We'll get used to them and won't see them anymore."

"Huh. Everyone else will see. Think *we* did it... And—come. See the splintered cellar steps! You can trip on them. Break your neck."

"I'll plane them. And we can be careful where we step."

"The plaster's falling off one of the bedroom walls! There's mouse turds. I can smell them."

"The children can bring the cats into the house now and then."

"This house is much worse than the old one we replaced at yonder farm. We've got to build a new house!"

"You can stop now, Hilda." Franz had walked through the house on an earlier visit. "I checked over the foundation and pounded on the walls of all the rooms, both upstairs and downstairs. They're all sound and will last for a good many years. The roof is fine. It would be a waste to think of building before we do some other, more necessary, improvements."

"What can be more necessary than our living quarters?"

"For one thing, the house isn't drafty; the barn is. It's not healthy for the animals. We depend on having healthy animals. The machine shed needs shoring up; machinery has to be stored under roof to keep it from rusting. And I want to make sure the well water is pure."

"Well, if this is going to be our last move—a permanent home—why can't we enjoy it from the beginning? Turn it into a really fine place. "

"It will still be 'the beginning' next year. Let's see how it goes... We may

155

get lots of ideas of what we want for our 'permanent home.' Keep on thinking of what you'd like. Make a list. Write it. I'll make a list too."

Hilda gave up. "Oh. Well then, Franz... I'm grateful for one thing—living in our *permanent* home. I've always longed to find solid ground I could dare set my roots deep into. A place I can know so well that I can walk in the dark with my eyes closed without stumbling or getting lost."

She added, "This *permanent* home will also be an uninterrupted resting place for Cherub... I'll scout for a site that is sure to be undisturbed in the future. That would be the pasture—sheep and cows grazing; peaceful animals."

*   *   *

Hilda stood at the top of the hill above their new creek. Her eyes followed its journey to where it crossed the neighbor's land and on to yonder farm. It was the same creek. With identical willows fringing it. Turning around, she could see the town water tower and grain elevators. And to her right, was the graveled county road that would take her children's bus to the town school. It was good to be here, she admitted, with a sigh.

When she walked around, she found a grassy place slightly uphill from the creek for Cherub's grave. Franz agreed to her choice of a plot. Grace and Andrew helped dig, while Jane and Fritz ran up and down the hill chasing each other. When the hole was dug, Grace stayed behind while the others left to look at the cottonwood and willow growing along the creek. Grace took the opportunity to ask, "Why are you doing this? Why aren't you leaving the baby where you buried him in the first place?"

"Simply put, I want the family to be together."

"But the baby is dead. In my science book, I read that bodies that aren't embalmed decompose quickly. There are worms and insects. It's part of the cycle of life. Besides, he never lived. You said he never took a breath."

"Yes, that's true. But he was alive before he was born. And when he was born, his body was flawless. Complete. He had all his fingers and toes. His eyes, nose, mouth, and ears were perfect. His hair was an inch long, dark like his father's. I loved him before he was born, and I still love him. You might think of him as your brother. I know you can't understand that. And that's all right."

"Ma, I'll try. But why did you name him *Cherub*?"

"That is what he is. An angel in Heaven. Cherub is another word for angel. When our time comes, we will see him again—him and my mother and all the other people who were saved, whose sins were forgiven when they gave their hearts to Jesus."

"But how can a baby give his heart to Jesus? How can a baby's sins be forgiven when he never did anything, good or bad?"

"Babies are exempt. They haven't sinned, so they don't need to be forgiven. All babies go to heaven when they die." Hilda, saying this, knew she would have further conversations with Grace sometime.

Later, back at the yonder farm, now their former home, Franz and Hilda, alone, opened the thirteen-year-old coffin. Hilda picked up her child—only the skull was intact, with some hair, but she picked up all that was wrapped in fragile rags—and swathed him in a new blanket that she gently laid into the new coffin.

She and Franz didn't speak; there was nothing to say.

*   *   *

Hilda was happy for an early spring so she could devote herself to her gardening, instead of to cleaning those high-ceilinged rooms with so many doors. Franz had been right. The soil was good; even when she dug her bare toes into it, or pressed it over some seeds, she could tell its richness. It was almost a pleasure to wash it off her hands after a day's work in the garden, to feel it first smear into her pores and to see it color the water evenly, mixing with it rather than settling to the bottom of the basin.

The children too found enjoyment in the dirt. Shaded by the grove, Andrew and Jane had their own farms, using peach pits and plum pits to represent cows and sheep. They found twigs to build a log house and barn with leaf roofs. Elsewhere among the trees they found discarded buggy parts—buckboards and two-seaters—that they arranged in a row. With some grapevine for reins, they took imaginary rides to town, school, or church.

Andrew brought home wild asparagus and choke cherries, and eggs chickens had laid under some brush. Meanwhile, Grace collected leaves and included some three-leafed samples in her scrapbook. "Look, Pa," she said. "Do you know the name of the tree these come from?"

"Uh oh—that's poison ivy. There's a saying: 'Leaves of three—let it be.' Better go wash yourself. Use lots of soap, and show the plant to Andrew and Jane. To your ma, also. Warn them not to touch it."

When Franz, with Amos's help, sawed down a huge, dead cottonwood tree, the children found the branches to be a splendid obstacle course, with different ways to climb under and over the branches. They tried walking along the trunk, balancing themselves as long as they could in their smooth-soled shoes, finding it easier barefoot.

Discovering mushrooms in a circle arrangement among the trees, Grace declared it a fairy ring, an idea that immediately excited Jane. Andrew, catching a wink from Grace, helped her with the fantasy, and challenged Jane,

"You have to sit very, very still if you want the fairies to come out and play with you." Jane did her best sitting very still on the ground longer than she usually could, or until she needed to pee. But no fairies showed up.

Further on, Grace found a rock to sit on. She sometimes got ideas in the woods for poems she later wrote.

Andrew picked up a forked stick and worked on fashioning a slingshot. Here Jane threatened him: "You know what Ma will say if she sees you slinging stones at birds."

Elsewhere in grassless shade, Andrew and Jane established a cemetery to hold dead chickens and kittens that they buried with much feeling and ceremony, copying what they observed at church funerals. They started it and were consoled when their favorite kitten had died and Hilda set up a marker where they buried it. Later, when fewer animals died, the children began looking for corpses to bury, so Grace made a doll. She drew a face on a clothespin and dressed it in an old white handkerchief. Gleefully, with appropriate ceremony and pretend tears, they put it inside a matchbox and buried it. When Jane began crying in earnest because she wanted the pretty dolly back, Franz intervened and asked them to dig it up again. That stopped their care of their graveyard, and Hilda was happy to notice twigs and leaves collecting over the area.

*   *   *

In a way, Hilda longed to live out-of-doors with the growing things, on land that was not worn out from overuse by previous tenants. In good time, rains came. Soon, the leaves of new vegetables began to show, more vigorous and lush than Hilda had ever seen them. Franz built a fence around their house to keep out the chickens that otherwise scratched the ground and ate the seed, much like what birds had done in Montana. Next, he sowed grass seeds together with quick-growing oats to cover the lawn. Then, in soft, late-afternoon light, when they couldn't see the cheap, peeling yellow paint on the clapboard, the old house looked almost beautiful.

Franz worked and ignored the sticky humidity on days when his perspiration did not evaporate, and didn't take out time to rest during the hottest hours of the day. Andrew, and even Grace, went with him often to help, though their help was seasoned with frolicking play. They often returned home with collections of dead field mice and grasshoppers in their pockets—fragile ones compared with the ones Franz and Hilda had come to know in Montana—mixed with grass from the load of hay they had trampled down for Franz.

When she was able to leave her own work, Hilda would go with Franz and the children, pitching hay onto the rack, though not so steadily or with so big a bunch. Sometimes she thought about the games she and Franz played as they made hay, before the children were born, before the three years in Montana. At yonder farm. Now, instead of playing themselves, they watched the children play. When the weather was not so hot that they had to come into the cool shade of the house, they had a faspa picnic, eating the tvaybak and sugar lumps, and drinking the coffee Hilda had packed as she made their dinner.

Evenings, they did chores together, or when Franz was trying to finish something before an approaching rain, Hilda and the children did the work by themselves. They milked—all except Jane, who begged to learn. Hilda fed the hens, with Jane taking handfuls of wheat and corn to scatter on the ground for the hens to chase. They laughed as the only rooster clucked over a particular seed and called to his harem to receive his gift. Grace carried ground mash to the young chickens, and Andrew fed the hogs, cattle, and horses. When they came in for supper, which was often fresh bread, and milk cooled in the running water of the stock tank, they could smell the odor of the farm—animals, hay—but they did not mind, for they smelled it on themselves.

As the season progressed, grain ripened on schedule: winter wheat, oats, flax, and barley. Corn would ripen later. The yield was average—not too bad. Market prices were also average but worth the labor. When it was ready, Franz guided Minnie and her son Prince as they pulled the harvester that swept the standing grain onto its bed with its paddlewheel. There its sharp cutters, scissoring back and forth, cut grain that fell onto a conveyer belt, which fed it to the binding action. Shuttles wrapped the grain into bundles and tied each with a neat knot. These sheaves fell onto the ground and could then be stacked—five or six of them at a time—into teepee shapes, where they stood until the threshing machine arrived. When rain fell, it would glide off the stacks.

The whole family worked on the job, called "shocking." Franz could walk by himself, holding two bundles at a time, setting them down firmly, and surrounding them with four more. Hilda and Grace worked in tandem, building their teepees together. For a while, Andrew and Jane also tried their hands at the work, but they found it more fun to see how many grasshoppers they could catch without getting the grasshoppers' dark spit on their hands or clothes.

*   *   *

Second-cousin Esau had a threshing machine and a large noisy gasoline-powered engine that he took from farm to farm, in turn, to separate their grain seeds from straw. When it was the Lobers' turn, the massive threshing machine arrived and was set in place not too far from the waiting shocks of grain.

Grace was old enough to trust with a team of horses pulling a hayrack while itinerant farm workers pitched bundles of grain onto it. Minnie and Prince were so well trained that they actually did not need much guiding but walked from shock to shock, stopping at each one. When her hayrack was full, she steered the horses toward the thresher, where she waited in line behind another hayrack.

Looking at the huge thresher, Jane declared, "That machine looks like a giant cat. The maw eats the bundles the men pitch onto its conveyer. At its other end is the long cat's tail. Funny, it's pooping out the chaff from the end of the tail, not from—you know—where it's supposed to. It makes a little pile and finally the pile turns into a huge golden mountain that I can climb and slide down. The side of the machine spouts the clean grain into a trailer, like sideways tits of this cat. And the trailer is a kitten."

Andrew played around with her story. "So, what's the tractor that powers the threshing machine?"

"Well, it could be a dog, barking loudly at the cat."

"And the belt that goes 'round and 'round the two pulleys?"

"I don't know. Just a belt." Jane, now getting bored, turned away.

Andrew had the job of leveling the oats or wheat inside the waiting trailer. Flax, being slippery, slid into an even level without his help. When full enough, the trailer could be pulled to the village grain elevator.

Some grain was also stored in the farm granary, an old building converted from what people said had once been a church. Its cupola housed the top of a conveyer belt that brought grain high to a moveable spout that could be aimed toward one of several bins. The children were sometimes asked to help level the grain in the bins, just as Andrew had been doing in the trailers. It was great fun playing in the grain, pretending it was water to wade through, but when Franz caught them playing in the bin of flax, he became very stern: "Never, never, never, play in flax. I know of a little boy who slipped and sank so deep that he drowned in it. Nobody found him until it was too late."

Back in the house, Hilda was busy cooking for the help, as well as for the family. She did not invite the help inside the house; instead, she packed food into a dish pan tied up with a large white dishtowel to bring to them, along with a large kettle of coffee and a four-gallon pail of water freshly pumped from their well. To carry all that, she borrowed the children's red coaster wagon. Franz, Grace, and Andrew joined them as they ate in the shade of the threshing machine, with the tractor engine turned down to idle.

*   *   *

160

But never did they talk about the newly built house they had left. Sometimes Grace or Andrew did, but not at length, for neither Hilda nor Franz pursued the subject. They knew the people who had bought that farm from them, but they did not visit them. Sitting on the back-door stoop, Hilda wondered, *Will I ever get over loving that yonder home? Will Franz and I ever be close again? Frequently reminding each other of our love?*

She sighed, looked down at her dirty bare feet, at her broken fingernails, and then, remembering that she had not combed her hair that day, thought, *I never used to let myself go. Franz never used to see me looking like this. I don't think I ever used to see him look so, either. He needs a haircut. He's shaving only once a week, for church.*

Then she reconsidered. *What's so bad about that? We're used to each other. I'm getting over my longing for yonder farm. The new house we had there. Really.*

CHAPTER TWENTY-SIX: 1929–30

Shortly after her thirty-fourth birthday, Hilda bore another son. They named him John, though usually they called him Hans to distinguish him from his cousin.

After this pregnancy, Hilda's upper teeth became abscessed, and the dentist pulled them. While she waited for her mouth to heal, she cooked and chopped her vegetables and meat finely, and soaked bread in milk. She shared her food with Hans, who soon learned to eat soft foods with his toothless-so–far gums.

Jane, watching, declared, "I want my food chopped too. I want tvaybak dunked in milk."

When Franz snorted, "You'll have to wait until you have all your teeth pulled too," she opened her mouth, and pointing, said, "All right, pull my teeth now."

That brought guffaws from Andrew, who shouted, "Dummy!" and Grace, who added, "Silly baby!" With her feelings hurt, Jane buried her face in Hilda's apron for comfort.

Now Hilda's dentures were in place, and she had learned to eat with her false teeth fairly well. She had to concentrate on pronouncing some sounds, to keep the letter "s" from being a whistle and the "k" from turning into a click. It was much easier to brush those teeth: she could just take out the whole plate and brush it under the pump water. *Too bad*, she thought, *these teeth are better looking than my real ones were.*

*　　*　　*

They were able to make their first payments on the farm as Franz had predicted. Some money was even left over; they put that away to save for some unforeseen need. Hilda still thought, at times, of the fresh-smelling new home they had left yonder, but she was beginning to adjust her ideas of what *home* should be. Sometimes she wondered, *What are Franz's feelings, if he thinks of it at all?*

Hilda loved the summer Sunday evenings at home. When Franz had not yet come in from late chores, and it was not dark enough to light the lamps, she'd sit at the table with the children around her. *I'm just like my ma, she realized. This is what she did when I was a child. I'm glad my children are learning to love the Bible stories, as I did, and are asking to hear them, instead of my having to broach the idea.*

Occasionally, at the pump organ—Grace was learning to play the simpler songs—they would sing songs Ma had taught her and John and Liesebet when they were small. Hilda hoped she remembered the words. She taught them the song about Jesus fishing with his friends on the Sea of Galilee. When a storm came up, Peter, afraid that the boat might tip said, "Master, the tempest is raging, the billows are rolling high ..." and Jesus, seeming to be unaware of the danger, simply stood up in the boat and said, "Peace, be still." And the wind and the waters obeyed His will. Hilda was proud that the children had good, clear singing voices, though Hans's baby voice was still off key.

"Magic," Andrew called it.

"No, a miracle," Grace corrected him.

"I wish I'd been there," Jane added.

"In a way, we *are* there," Hilda suggested. "When we give our hearts to Jesus, we are there with him."

"How can I give my heart? I can't reach inside me to pull it out. Would I have to swallow a string with a hook on it? Do we pull it up like a fish?" Jane spoke the question the others might have thought about also.

Andrew laughed aloud. Grace smiled, and Hilda smiled also, wondering whether she would, herself, ever understand the concept.

But she repeated the words Pa and other ministers had always said: "Some things are hard to understand, even for us grownups." She remembered the old song lyrics: "By and by, when the morning comes. You will understand it better by and by." She decided not to teach them that song then. Maybe she would, by and by.

When it was dark enough to light the lamp, and the children were busily doing homework or playing with their toys, Hilda went to the mirror as if to prove to herself that Ma would not be coming into the room, that she was not still a child herself. She examined the face she had now. It was different from the one she remembered. She had been too busy to study it; her glances into the mirror had been to see whether her hair was smooth enough, or would she have to re-comb it.

She saw a few wrinkles in her cheeks and forehead, soft ones not yet sharp, though they would most likely be permanent. They were almost the same as Ma's were: horizontal ones of smiles and of squinting into the sunlight—not vertical ones of frowns or even worry. Like Ma's, her skin was dry, baked from going hatless when she worked in the garden. *It's a sin to use creams and rouges,* she reminded herself, *but no one would be the wiser if I used some of the oil I bought for the baby's skin.*

She looked at her eyes, softly gray ones. *I think they were once blue. I wonder what faded them, and when. Ma had gray eyes too; were her eyes blue when she was a child?*

At least I'm well and strong, and my children will have the chance I didn't have. But am I the kind of mother Ma was? One worth getting to know well? Sometimes I almost think it would be better for me to go—so the memories my children would have of me might be good ones. She shut that out of her mind, for it was not a good thought, and certainly not Christian.

Looking at the children, she wondered, *Where did they come from? By what mysterious power were they created?* When Grace asked where little babies came from, Hilda had answered that God brought them, and Grace was satisfied with the answer. Now, Hilda supposed the answer was more accurate than she thought at the time, for that was the only answer she could give herself now.

Thinking about her changed physical appearance didn't bother Hilda so much as knowledge that her inner self hadn't changed since she was a child. *Adult women have solved all the problems. They know what it is to be good. They make decisions. They comprehend the responsibilities of faith. They know what it means to be "saved."*

Whenever she allowed herself to think thus, Hilda felt frantic. So far, she had put off answering her children's questions about faith by asking them to be patient, for they would grasp the concept when they were older. She hoped.

*   *   *

It was particularly difficult during recent revival meetings in the school building. Reverend Bunker, the evangelist, may once have been handsome, but he had gathered considerable weight around his beltline and chin, and the fringe of hair around his head was a colorless mat. His looks were off-putting to Hilda and she tried, instead, to concentrate on his saxophone with which he seemed to excite fervor in his listeners. He spoke authoritatively of evil, and it seemed to Hilda that he was pleased to have had much experience so he could color his services with enticing accounts of his previous life: shoplifting, carousing, going to roadhouses, and worse: drinking beer, smoking, and dancing. He had not attended church. He had disappointed his mother, who cried and prayed for him daily.

Hilda reasoned, *What is goodness? Does goodness gain goodness the more wicked the evil it's compared with? I haven't lived a terribly wicked life so far. The worst I've done is keeping some secrets from Franz. And of course, from everybody else. That's not so bad, is it? Can't a person have some secret thoughts?*

Realizing that her thinking was not constructive, Hilda longed for peace—even if it was an acceptance of the religion Reverend Bunker preached. When, in the closing words of his daily meetings, he sounded more lovingly tender, speaking softly with tears in his voice—for there was no reason to believe that he wasn't sincere in his emotions—Hilda felt more and more rebellious.

When he started the altar call, the choir softly singing, "Just as I am, without one plea," he told of "a young man, just ready to marry his childhood sweetheart. He scoffed and rejected the call to come forward to give his heart to Jesus. He left the meeting, got in his car, the car his loving father had given him, and drove it fast toward the nearest tavern. As he reached the railroad tracks, though he saw the approaching train, he depended on his skill to beat the train. But the train was faster than his crossing. He died. It was too late. He forfeited salvation."

The audience was very still, but there was a rustling, as here and there, persons worked their way to the aisle to go to the front of the auditorium and make public their desire to give their hearts to Jesus. Hilda, her eyes closed, as were the eyes of most of the audience, peeked and caught, peripherally, sight of Andrew edging to the end of the pew where he had been sitting with his friends. *Uh oh*, she thought. *What next?* She watched more closely but did not see him follow the stream of people who were moving forward. It would not do to crane her neck, and she lost sight of him.

Actually, she felt strongly impelled to leave, knowing that she would not, even if she didn't mind the stares of others who were seemingly caught up into the spirit. She looked at Franz sitting beside her; his eyes were closed.

She wasn't sure whether the strength of her feelings was for herself or for her children. Thinking of the late hour, Hilda decided to postpone a discussion of the meeting until tomorrow morning, a Saturday, when they could talk by daylight.

*　　　*　　　*

As they were dressing the next morning, Hilda asked, "Franz, what did you think of last night's program?"

He responded, somewhat sheepishly, "I missed a lot of it. I was tired."

"So, when your eyes were closed, you weren't just praying? You didn't see Andrew leaving his seat during the altar call?"

"Did he really? He didn't say anything about it on the way home."

Usually, the children were allowed to sleep later Saturday mornings, and this day they appeared after Franz had gone out to start chores. After a few spoonfuls of oatmeal, Andrew and Grace wondered aloud who among their friends and acquaintances were saved and who were not. They each named a couple, adding that they were "just the type."

Before Hilda could ask, "What is 'just the type'?" Jane joined in, asking, "Have I been bad enough to be saved?"

Andrew quickly answered, "Ya, you're always bad enough," to which Grace spoke up for Jane with, "Speak for yourself."

Andrew's quip confirmed the Biblical verse that said, "All have sinned…"

To Hilda's question—where he had gone during the altar call—Andrew came back with, "Why do you ask? Your eyes were supposed to be closed."

She ignored that. "Where did you go?"

"Outside. For fresh air. My friends were playing kick-the-can, and I joined them."

The mood in the room was wrong for further questions, Hilda knew. It seemed that Franz always managed to be outdoors doing his chores when any questions about religion came up.

For herself, Hilda finally decided it would not make much difference after the meetings were over, but she disliked having the children learn that side of religion. She wondered, when she and Franz were dressing for another evening's meeting, "Do we have to go *every* night?"

He answered, "It won't do us any harm. Remember the adage, 'If the shoe fits, put it on.' It's easier to go every night for a few weeks than to have members of the congregation wondering, for a whole year following, why we didn't attend."

"I'm afraid the children might get a too-passionate picture of religion."

"Perhaps it will be good for them to pick up some emotion. Sometimes I wonder whether you and I aren't too matter-of-fact about it. In the end, they might come out of it with a nice balance."

To Hilda's comment, "Or they might turn completely against it," he said nothing. But he began, regularly, to hold evening devotions—a passage from the Bible, and a prayer each. For that, he had to call the family together. When Andrew began to retire early, Hilda hoped it was her imagination that he was doing so to avoid their vespers.

Gradually, Hilda came to realize why she had trouble answering questions, spoken or not, that her oldest children were facing. She, herself, had to face them by herself. While regretting that her mother had died when she needed her so, she wondered, *Would my mother have been able to answer those questions adequately? Am I trying to fit her into a pattern she would never have been able, or willing, to fill? Did she ever say anything about faith more than what little lessons came from the Bible stories she told me and my siblings? Did Pa ever say anything beyond his sermons in church?*

Hilda, aware of nostalgia for the things of her childhood, regretted not memorizing more truths of that time. She wondered, *Are changes since then so great, or is my attitude changing? If only my father were still pastor of the congregation here.*

Instead, he's thinking of moving even further west, to Oregon. To start over. In a recent letter, he wrote that he was beginning to feel inadequate to the rigors of the farm work and was interested in going to a milder climate. There, he would have the opportunity to serve a church, perhaps even for a salary.

Hilda knew she was not fair in her criticism of Mennonite principles as she understood them, though she liked to think that she was objectively critical. *Perhaps if I had the chance to get far away for a while. But I know that can't be.* She shut the idea from herself.

Franz, when she told him about her thoughts, her feelings about Mennonite doctrine, answered, "Life is too good for us. If we had a really serious problem to worry about, we wouldn't concern ourselves so much with these things. Surely, they aren't very significant."

It hurt.

Franz continued. "I'm not speaking of you alone. I include myself too, when we disagree with others in our congregation about, for example, how fast or slow our hymns should be sung. Or about leaving the old chorales that our forefathers sang for livelier gospel songs with their meaningless choruses. We're quibbling about little things... Maybe I go too far when I say that the choruses are meaningless, but they certainly are elementary. About the only appealing thing about them is their rhythm, and sometimes that is quite primitive, or—at the very best—something for our already wriggly little children to sing at their Sunday school classes."

Though Franz had not spoken words of consolation, Hilda felt release that comes with sharing. "Then you feel as I do, and I'm not being too sensitive."

"I'm afraid so, Hilda. I'm also afraid I don't have any idea of what to do about it. Some people just change churches, but I doubt they'll find their answers there."

"I think one trouble with the church is that people have too much voice in running it—"

Franz did not let her finish. "But that is a *basis* of our church. Our faith is based on each of us having a *personal* relationship with God. With Christ.

Otherwise, we might as well be Catholics if we want someone to rule over us. To be an intermediary between us and God. To tell us what to think."

"But the people who are the loudest in running the church are those younger immature ones who are just not very deep. They've never gone through anything hard. They don't know what deep worship is, because they don't know what deep despair is. Or anything deep."

"Yet, Hilda, they are sincere. When we judge them, we are exposing ourselves to judgment."

Hilda looked at her Franz, wondering if her love for him could be separate from her love of her church. Wondering if she did love her church.

CHAPTER TWENTY-SEVEN: 1931

"Our neighbors," Franz announced, "are having good luck raising turkeys. I haven't counted how many barns they have, but it's at least eight or ten. I think they're making good money. I wonder if we should learn how to raise them too."

He brought home a dozen cute, bright-eyed, brown-speckled babies. Six soon died; it wasn't clear why. Maybe they caught cold, had needed a cluck[23] to snuggle under; they had seemed old enough not to need that. Anyhow, the children quickly bonded with the survivors and named them all. Hans, still an unsteady toddler, accidentally stepped on the one they had named Elva. After squawking, it staggered crookedly away and seemed to be well enough, but always a bit bent.

As they grew, the turkeys followed the children around, and on warm days, would even sleep on their laps at the back-door stoop. At night, Grace and Andrew hand carried them to their roosts in the shed because they hung around the house, not knowing what turkeys should do at night.

When Hilda tired of having them underfoot, she asked Jane and Hans to lead them to the stubble fields to eat grasshoppers. Bored before long, they tried to sneak back to the house, but the turkeys, flapping their wings and chirping loudly, beat them to the back door.

One sunny day, Old Mur (the original Old Mur had died—thin and toothless—of old age, so the name had been passed down) and Young Mur and two turkeys, Hem and Haw, were basking on the summer-kitchen stoop. Hilda watched Hem stand up, stretch one leg behind it and then the other, and then reach over to peck Old Mur hard on the head before hunching down again. Old Mur abruptly sat up, looked around, and determined that Young Mur had assaulted her. She leapt at her, and the two cats took off across the

23 A broody hen

lawn in a fiercely loud tussle, leaving gobs of fur in the grass. For a long time, those cats wouldn't share that stoop, even though they were mother and daughter, leaving it for the turkeys.

By autumn, one turkey was left. Franz had quietly taken the others to market with some roaster-sized chickens. School started, and this year Jane joined Andrew and Grace on the orange wooden school bus. It was Grace's last year of high school, her last year at home.

*   *   *

Meanwhile, Hilda and Franz fretted.

The government called it "The Depression." The government defined the word in terms of stocks and currency. Workers lost their jobs, and people were hungry. Hilda experienced it firsthand when the geese honked the arrival of ragged, unshaven, middle-aged men—men who looked as if they could be more than middle aged. They came to the back door, one at a time, to ask for work. Or if not for work, for money. If not money, food.

She didn't invite them in but gave them food: tvaybak, coffee if she had it, or prips, and a leftover pork chop or chicken leg that they set out on the back-door stoop to eat. Meanwhile, Fritz, hiding under the stoop, yapped as fiercely as his terrier voice could bark.

As much as he could understand of it, Franz tried to explain the Depression to Hilda and the children. Weakly, he summed up by saying, "We'll learn to understand when we see what influence it'll have on us. Let us pray to God that we won't have to suffer too much."

"We have plenty of food to eat," Hilda said. "There are always eggs. During the summer, when we have lots of fresh cabbage and tomatoes, I put up vegetables and fruit as we went along. Cabbage, carrots, parsnips, and potatoes keep a long time in the cellar. We won't starve." She counted in her head the number of full jars of tomatoes, green beans, and spinach in the larder.

"We'll always have enough meat, too," Franz went on. "One of the hogs will be ready to be butchered soon, and all those geese and ducks should be good for something other than their feathers and honking when strangers come to the yard."

"And their nasty hissing at the children when they come near," Hilda added.

Throughout the months, Franz and Hilda began to learn what the Depression meant. They had a good crop—not a bumper crop, but good.

However, with that crop, they were barely able to meet the year's payment on the farm mortgage because market prices had dropped. There was little money left.

The evening he balanced their crop money against their expenses, his face was grave as he sat down to speak with Hilda and the children. "We have to be very careful with our money," he said. "Ask only for those things you absolutely have to have. We shall have to wear clothes until they wear out, not only until they begin to look worn, or are too small. Mother will have to make over even the old clothes. We must be very careful."

Jane joined in, "Do we always have to carry our lunches to school? Lots of children get free lunch every day. They get a plate with creamed salmon on toast, an orange, and a cute box of milk—all for nothing. We get the same old egg sandwich and canned tomatoes from home that we have to pack."

Grace quickly added, "It does get boring."

"You may be bored, but you're not hungering," was Hilda's rejoinder.

Franz returned to the question, "They get the free lunch because their parents have given up. They're on relief. The WPA.[24] The government is now supporting them."

"Why can't the government support us?" Andrew put in. "How are they better than us?"

Franz sighed. "They've given up. We haven't. We're hanging on to our farm. We'd have to leave this farm and all our livestock and chickens—yes, even our pets. We'd have to live in the cheapest rented house we could find in town, and I'd have to go to work somewhere else, like building roads or bridges. You, Andrew and Grace, would probably have to work too if you could find a job—maybe even have to leave school."

At that, Grace's shoulders sagged, but Andrew perked up, "Could I? Quit school, I mean?"

Franz clenched his fists and looked at Andrew as if he deserved a hearty swat. Instead, he turned to Hilda, who supported him. "We won't give up. We'll keep praying, and God will help us."

Grace came up with an idea. "Sometimes the kids don't even like what they're getting. We can trade lunches with them if we like their food."

"What does the lunchroom teacher say about that?" Hilda wondered.

"She won't know if we don't tell her."

Franz intervened then. "We don't want to hear from the school that you are interfering with rules. That free lunch program is a government program. Don't ask for trouble."

---

24 Works Progress Administration; later: Works Projects Administration. Government jobs such as road- and bridge-building for eligible men. This also provided school lunches and groceries.

The children had no more to say, but Hilda noticed the smiles and looks they exchanged.

Later, when they were talking privately, Hilda happily repeated, "At least we have something to eat. It's not as it was in Montana, when we thought we owned all that land yet didn't have enough to eat. And maybe we can vary how we make the egg sandwiches."

Franz was not so cheerful. "But if we can't make the payments on the land, we'll lose it *and* the privilege of raising our own food. It can't get any worse for us to survive."

"We mustn't be too pessimistic, Franz. Or is this Depression going to last long? Maybe it will be over soon, and next year we'll get good prices for our crops."

"I heard something in town, about how some people are coping with the Depression. It seems that a large number of people—they didn't say how many—are emigrating to the USSR. I don't think any are from this area. Stalin has promised them jobs. All kinds of jobs for engineers and even for farmers. Even for negroes. Also housing, schools for the children. I guess they promised them the moon. So whole groups of people—even some Mennonites—are selling and giving away all their things, if they have any, and are moving their entire families."

Hilda sat down to listen. "What is this USSR?"

Franz knew so much about geography and current events from the newspaper and radio. "It's the group of countries that Russia has annexed, countries like Estonia and Latvia and others. One 'S' stands for 'Socialist.'"

"Are those Christian countries?"

"No. You wouldn't call them Christian. I don't know if they are atheist, if they forbid Christianity, or are just neutral about religion."

"How are the people who went to Russia doing over there? What are they writing home? Have they been heard from since they left?"

"Not much. Some of their relatives are writing letters to Washington, asking for news, but it seems that the émigrés gave up their American citizenship and aren't on the embassy list any more. They aren't the concern of our government anymore."

"Can't they ask the Soviets for information about their relatives?"

"It's a sticky problem. The Soviet Union is now officially a friend of the United States, and our government doesn't want to offend them by hinting that the people may be in trouble. Besides, there are more important issues to deal with. War with Germany is brewing."

"That's scary. What will happen next? What's the world coming to?"

"I've told you all I heard."

"I wish them well. I hope we won't have to give up here. I don't want to live in an atheistic country."

"Pray that it will be so," he answered as he went outside to feed his stock: the animals that had recently been worth so much but were now a drain on feed. Gradually, he was weaning the cattle from the mash—ground corn and oats that made their milk richer—and the horses from oats—treats they liked. Instead, he fed them the hay that he and the children had harvested last summer. If he could, he would keep the stock until the prices were higher— but he might have to sell them for whatever money he could get.

They started to drink skim milk, selling most of the cream that the town creamery truck picked up, and holding some cream back to churn into butter. The children took turns cranking the beaters, quickly being bored when the cream was slow to turn, but eagerly drinking the buttermilk that was left after Hilda pulled out the curds and salted and kneaded them into a glistening yellow-gold mass. She let them spread it thickly on her rich whole-wheat bread. Some food tasted even better than it did before.

When Thanksgiving vacation came around, the children were happy for a break from school. For their Thanksgiving feast, most years, they had duck or goose. This year it was turkey. As they came to the bountiful meal on the table, the children took one look at the turkey with its crooked breastbone and, with one voice, cried, "Elva!"

Without a word, Hilda took the turkey off the table to the pantry and returned with a stack of homemade wurst.

Franz, looking sheepish, said so quietly that the others didn't hear, or didn't acknowledge hearing, "I couldn't sell a crooked bird to the market." The Sunset Home in town had a turkey dinner the next day, and Franz never again proposed raising turkeys.

*   *   *

A day came when a large sleek car arrived in the yard. In it was an assessor, who carried a notebook as he walked with Franz from barn to shed and back to his car where the two sat for a while. When Franz came in, he carried a carbon copy of the list the assessor had made. A list, by name if the animal had a name, or by description of each animal and farm implement:

Frau Schtrunk: black and white cow, pregnant

Frau Hultz: brown cow, milking

Rostov: calf, two-months old

Prince: eight-year-old gelding

Minnie: twenty-two-year old mare

Three hogs (additional one not listed—to be butchered)

Minneapolis-Moline tractor: lug wheels, about three years old

Corn planter

Manure spreader

Hayrack

"These are now mortgaged. Even the animals. He left us the chickens, ducks, and geese, and one hog," Franz explained. "We can't sell or butcher the others without checking with the assessor. So now we have the money to pay the interest on the farm for another year."

"Why isn't Jerry listed?"

"He looked at how old Jerry is and decided not to count on him for collateral." Old Jerry seemed too stiff with arthritis for heavy work and spent most days in the pasture. "He's earned it," Franz said, and Hilda agreed.

Hilda sighed. "Let's not tell the children."

*   *   *

It lasted for several years, the time called the Great Depression. More or less, most of the people of their community were affected, but most affected were those who, like themselves, had mortgages made when prices were high and land worth so much. The mortgages had been arranged in terms of cash, with no apparent regard to the varying worth of money.

Overhearing her father's account of the arrangement, Grace declared, "I'm sick and tired of hearing how poor we are! It's not fair! I wish we lived in a different country!"

Andrew announced, "When I grow up, I'm going to be rich!"

"Me too," echoed Jane, and then also Hans.

*   *   *

When a day came with Franz about ready to give up his fight, Hilda found that she had faith. It was a revelation to her, for she realized that the concept she had had of salvation was not the concept she had now. With that insight came a kind of peace in spite of her worry about daily bread.

It came to her when, with a heavy sigh, Franz said, "If we had stayed in Montana, this wouldn't have happened to us. We wouldn't have had the loss the storm made by destroying that house. We would be on our own land—"

At first, Hilda tried to reason with Franz materially, interrupting him. "But you know, they—the ones who stayed—aren't well off, either. They never yet have had a crop like the ones we usually get here. They will never have more than bare essentials. I think they get the same price for the grain they sell that we get."

He continued, "And they own their land. No one can take it away from them. They are sure of a roof over their tables. What more do we, as Mennonites, want than bare essentials? Sometimes you and I forget that."

But, Hilda continued her own line of reasoning: "What would happen to us if we gave up, Franz? We can't give up."

"We'd have to go on relief, just as I told the children. The government would put me to work on a railroad or other public project, but you and the children would have the food you need. We haven't bought oranges for many months. People on relief have oranges and bananas—all those things. They are better off than we, who are better off in name."

"That would mean that all the work we have done on this farm is worthless. All the money we have paid down would be lost, just because we couldn't go without some things long enough until times pick up."

Franz's head was bowed, held up only by his supporting hands. He did not look up as he said, "I am ready to admit defeat. Who knows how much longer these times will last?"

"You work, and I'll pray," was all Hilda could think to say.

Though she saw no logical reason for him to brighten—for hadn't they been praying for many years?—he answered, "I'll pray too."

Hilda prayed frequently for enough self-control never to mention that she had opposed moving to a farm they would have to spend years paying for. If they had stayed where they were, they would not have the present worries. She still occasionally had the dream of living back on yonder farm, but she never spoke of it.

Grimly, they toiled. The children came to terms with their home-packed lunches and mended clothes, and bravely helped with chores so they wouldn't have to hire men, or even women, who seemed to be constantly stopping at the door to ask for work.

Then one Monday, Jane came home from school, complaining of pain in her head and neck. Hilda tried to distract her, thinking she just wanted attention, but she felt her forehead, which seemed especially hot. "Well, go to bed; maybe you'll feel better soon." Without protest, Jane went to bed.

The next morning, she was surely sick, vomiting and crying, and the older two also complained of aches. Hilda kept them all home from school, hoping it was just a fast-moving flu. Grace and Andrew were better in a week and went back to school, and Hans seemed to have escaped catching whatever they had. However, Jane continued ill enough for Franz to call Dr. Fiddler. After listening to Hilda's description of the onset of her illness, Dr. Fiddler told her, "It looks very much like polio—usually known as 'infantile paralysis.' It's going around. There isn't any cure; it just has to run its course and maybe she won't suffer any permanent damage. Keep her in bed. You might try hot wet towels where it hurts. Give her oranges and have her drink lots of water. I'll check back in a day or two."

"How much can we bear?" Hilda asked, wondering whether she was asking God or a nameless thing in space. Franz, hearing her, gritted his teeth and clenched his fist but said nothing.

As Jane began to feel better, she tried to get up but wasn't able to stand or walk. She resorted to scooting on the floor, sideways, and then pulling herself up to a chair. Hans laughed at her and began to scoot also.

"It's not funny!" Jane told him, and Hilda picked him up and set him onto his highchair, saying, "You stay there." At which he cried and kicked the rungs of his chair.

On his next visit, Dr. Fiddler told them of place in St. Paul where they treated afflicted children like Jane. It was named "Hospital for Crippled Children."

Franz and Hilda looked at each other. Franz said, "Dr. Fiddler, we don't have money to pay for such a hospital."

Dr. Fiddler pulled out a form. "Just fill it out honestly. There is government help for her—and you."

CHAPTER TWENTY-EIGHT: 1931

Fat and sleek, the hog approached them, grunting, and reaching his snout toward them through the slats of the pen.

"Look how he comes to you. He knows you." Hilda walked by Franz's side as he carried fresh slops to the hog's trough. He was separated from the other pigs to make tomorrow's task easier.

"Now don't get all silly and sentimental, Hilda. It's the food, not me that he knows. Deep in his little brain, he also knows that he is food for us."

"The Bible rules against eating pig meat."

"The Bible lists lots of rules. Some are against foods that in those days were dangerous because of disease, like trichinosis. Our pigs don't carry that disease. They're clean. Those rules made sense then. Remember, the Bible lists more rules that we don't pay attention to: women had to stay in a separate hut during their 'unclean' time of the month. Men shouldn't cut their hair—remember Samson? Or how about making burnt offerings?" He had her there.

"Still, I wish I hadn't come here with you today."

"Stop it, Hilda. You've eaten pork all your life. That is what we do."

She sighed. "At least we didn't name him."

"So go inside and bake your pies."

*   *   *

Before long, two apple and two glumz[25] pies were ready for tomorrow. Hilda prepared the crusts as Ma had taught her years before: first mix flour, lard, salt, and a bit of baking power for tenderness and then rub them between your hands until the mixture resembled cornmeal. She broke in a couple of

---

25 Cottage cheese, home-made by keeping (unpasteurized) milk warm until it clabbers. Then it is heated until curds separate from whey.

egg whites and some cold water to moisten the mixture. Gently she rolled each separate portion into circles that fit into her four pie pans. Next, she doled apples she had peeled and sliced into two pans, meanwhile eating the peels herself, interrupted by Hans, who begged for some also. She chuckled, thinking of how he usually had to be cajoled into eating apples—after she peeled them.

When she had generously spooned dollops of sugar over the fruit, and covered each filled pan with another pastry circle, she crimped the edges with her three-tined fork. Holding each pie over her left hand, she cut the excess pastry from the edges; she would sprinkle a little sugar over these scraps and bake them separately, as treats for the children. Then she cut slits in the top of each pie to let out steam, and sprinkled some sugar over the tops.

For the glumz pies, she mixed her cottage cheese with the egg yolks (left from the whites used in the crusts), sugar, and cinnamon and poured the mixture into two other pastry-lined pans. These would bake into a custardy dessert, a rich brown on top.

When the oven was hot, burning the corncobs Andrew had brought in, she inserted the pies—the apple ones in back since they took longer to bake. The large oven could hold all four pies at one time, though she had to watch closely since it didn't bake evenly in all the corners.

That much was ready by six the next morning, when the Henry Heldins and the Amos Lobers arrived, each bringing their youngest children. Grossma Lober, now living with Amos's family, also came to help.

While they were just beginning to unwrap their children and remove their own coats, the three women started asking for news about Jane. "What's the latest? Is she walking yet? When is she coming home?"

"Well," Hilda said with a sigh, "she's quite homesick. Asks about what everybody is doing. I wish we could afford to call her every day, let alone go to see her more often. We've gone up only once so far. She's found some friends, girls in beds on either side of hers, and they tell stories and sing songs. One of them is teaching her to play the ukulele. The doctors and nurses are friendly but very strict."

Emma wondered, "What would they be strict about?"

"She has to eat what they serve, even if she doesn't like it or isn't hungry. They tell her it will make her stronger. And she has to practice walking—on crutches so far—even if it hurts. So I guess I'm glad they are strict."

Anna spoke up. "When you write her, tell her we're praying for her, to get completely well soon." Grossma Lober nodded at that.

"I will, Hilda said. "And before you go, let me give you her address so you can write her yourselves. She would be very happy to get a letter from you. You know, she's learning to read quite well."

By that time they were wearing their aprons, ready to go to work.

*　　*　　*

Now it was time. With strong help from Henry and Amos, Franz caught the loudly squealing hog, tied the hind legs together, and used the freshly honed knife to cut deep into its throat. Then all was quiet, except for the grunting exertion of the men as they dragged the carcass onto a wooden sledge.

Hearing the squealing, Hans begged, "Can I go watch?" His cousins stood by, hoping they could tag along.

"No—no," his mother said firmly. "That's not for children. You go play together. Take out your blocks and invite your cousins to help build a farmstead. Be sure you have separate barns for the chickens and the sheep. And don't forget a silo."

*　　*　　*

Franz hitched Prince to the sledge, to drag it to the large tree where he had earlier rigged up a pulley so the carcass could be hoisted by its hind legs. Meanwhile, the women brought out steaming pails of hot water dipped from the wood-burning cauldron[26] so the men could quickly use it to scrape[27] the stiff hairs off the skin. One of the men had already slit the belly, easing the entrails, stomach, and liver into one of the large empty pans for the women to take into the house to clean and separate.

By that time, the sun had risen. While the carcass was cooling, they all went to the house for breakfast. There was not much talk, for eating was hurried; what talk there was concerned the weather. They were happy for the cold—better for keeping the meat—and glad it wasn't snowing so they could work outdoors. Andrew and Grace left for school, happy they did not have to help.

Grossma Lober busied herself keeping an eye on her grandchildren. She was still spry enough to sit on a low stool to be engaged with their play. Emma and Anna energetically scraped fat off the liver and entrails and emptied the contents of the intestines into a large old tin pail. This could later be dumped over the garden area. They turned the intestines inside out by pouring cold water through them, much like turning a cloth belt.

With the cauldron now empty and still hot, and a fire still going underneath it, the women tossed all the fatty pieces into it. They took turns,

---

26 Water had to be hot, just as hot water is used by men to shave. In a sense, the hog was "shaved."

27 The scraper was much like scrapers used to prepare wood surfaces for painting, though these scrapers were strictly used for hogs.

179

using a wooden paddle, to stir lean trimmings and whatever else was in it, including the ribs, to render the lard and keep the bits of meat from burning. Before long, they could skim out the bits, called cracklings, and ladle the clear lard into stoneware crocks where it would keep for months.

Meanwhile, Hilda prepared noon dinner—roast chicken, potatoes, and cabbage-carrot slaw. She made separate carrot circles for the children, expecting that the visiting children would like them as much as Hans did. While she peeled potatoes, she cut slivers of the raw white vegetable, sprinkled them with salt, and offered them to the children, who liked them as she had when she was a child and still did.

At noon, the men came inside, bringing with them the head meat, including the scraped ears, lips, and snout, to be boiled while they took out time to eat dinner. This time, Hilda served the pies, eliciting comments like, "Now we'll have to take naps." But they all ate quickly and returned to their work.

Franz set up a meat grinder to chop up the cooked head meat and other trimmings that included gristle and skin, and started turning the handle. He salted and peppered the mixture and put it aside to be pressed into a block, called headcheese, that could later be sliced and fried.[28]

He also ground up raw trimmings, as from the hams; these he seasoned before they would be ready to be forced into the clean intestines, when Grace and Andrew came home from school. They could alternate turning the handle of the extruder, producing long sausages that Hilda twisted from time to time to make separate wursts.

When they learned that the casings were indeed intestines, Grace and Andrew both brought out loud "Eee-yooos."

Franz later hung the long ropes up to smoke in the seldom-used smokehouse, next to the hams. The liver, also ground, would turn into liverwurst.

Before sundown, the work of the butchering was done. The tired helpers were given a good share of liverwurst, some ribs and chops to take home, and a promise to return the favor in a few weeks. That left Franz, Grace, and Andrew to do the evening chores and take down the tackle. Rain and snow would eventually clean up the area. Hilda was left to clean the kitchen and the cauldron. Some of that work could wait until tomorrow.

*　　　*　　　*

In bed that evening, Franz and Hilda, though exhausted, felt wide awake. "That pig must have weighed four hundred pounds. It took all three of us to lug it onto the sledge."

---

28 Since the skin was "shaved," head cheese looked spotted because it contained bits of hair roots, distasteful to some people.

"We did get a lot of lard from it. Maybe we can sell some—you can take it with you next time you go to the grocery store, along with the eggs."

He stretched. "Either this one was bigger than the one last year, or I'm not as strong as I once was."

"Well, for your age, it's a good thing all three of you are strong. And fit."

"I could use a good backrub. If you give me one, I'll give you one after—you were working pretty hard too."

Hilda sighed a bit, having just settled into the nest of the featherbed, but knelt at his side to start massaging him. "Just don't fall asleep before you rub my back."

To keep him awake, she continued talking. "You know, in a way I'm sorry that we eat meat at all. When I see a fine, healthy pig greeting me as I come toward it, I cringe inside knowing we will kill it, cut it up, and eat it."

She could feel his muscles tighten as he replied, "You sound like one of those vegetable eaters—vegetarians. You know pigs are food. That's why we raise them."

"I've read that pigs are very intelligent. As smart as dogs. Pigs are known to have saved people's lives, letting them know about intruders, or fires."

"Would you rather eat dogs? Some people do, you know."

"'No, no. I just wonder how we can have the right to eat other beings, just because we have the power. I really think animals have souls, just as we do."

"Do you expect to see pigs in Heaven?"

"Why not? I expect to see all kinds of animals in Heaven. I don't think I could be happy in a Heaven without animals. Remember the promise of the 'lion lying down with the lamb.'"

"Now you're getting out of my depth. It's pointless to speculate about what Heaven is like, if there is such a place as Heaven."

A familiar pain found its way into Hilda's chest. *Why had this subject come up?* She did not reply, except to say, "It's your turn to rub my back..." Then she asked, "Did the men ask about Jane at all?"

"As a matter of fact, they did. Maybe I shouldn't tell you this, but people have been talking ... wondering how we could be so hardhearted to turn our little girl over to big-city doctors."

Hilda tightened. "You mean Henry and Amos think we're hardhearted?"

"No, they were just repeating what other people said. They said they didn't blame us. They'd want what was best for their children too."

"Well, I hope whoever's been talking will try to say that to me! I'll give them a good lesson in mother love!"

Franz continued rubbing Hilda's back. Added a kiss.

CHAPTER TWENTY-NINE: 1931

Butchering day provided respite from the heavy cloud that had hovered over Hilda and Franz. Fear of possible doom had tempered each meal, each chore, each decision. If the crops failed. If the next rain cloud turned into another tornado. If Jane should be permanently crippled. If one of the mortgaged animals died. If they couldn't meet the next interest payment. If there wouldn't be enough money for Grace to go to nursing school. Or pay their taxes.

The next morning, Franz remarked, "You know, nobody mentioned the Depression all day yesterday. It was almost as if times were good again."

Hilda nodded. "We women laughed and sang and told jokes. The children played and argued and shared their toys. And everybody ate all the food on the table." It felt good, except for Jane's absence.

Furthermore, Hilda found support she could hold onto through threats of despair: *God. I can feel His helping hand. I can share it with Franz. While I've been leaning on Franz, he's had to carry the weight of everything—and me.*

She knew Franz had come to depend on her unyielding strength, a strength she hoped would last.

*　　*　　*

They renewed their interest in their church, and with that, they found tolerance for what other members of the congregation believed or did. With increased participation, they found greater satisfaction. Franz seemed to enjoy his job as teacher of a Sunday school class even though he had likely not anticipated it. The women had chosen him. As he went over next Sunday's lesson, he remarked to Hilda, "I never thought I would be able to stand in front of a group of women, much less venture an idea in front of them."

Hilda teased, "You didn't seem to be shy when we were courting."

He replied, "Huh! You did all the courting. Besides, you weren't as important as these women are. So why should I have been afraid of you?"

"*I* did the courting? *I* courted *you*? *Who* sent me that valentine? *Who* asked Pa for my hand in marriage?"

"All right. *You* win. Still, it was easier to court you than to stand in front of a bunch of women in church."

Hilda also found work to do in the church. The class she attended in the church nursery elected her substitute teacher. She had many chances to teach, for the regular teacher had young children and could not attend every Sunday. "My job is harder than yours, when I do teach," she said. "The women with small children can't pay close attention when the youngsters are wriggling, crying, and hungry."

The children too found activities in church that kept them eager to attend, especially the last month before Christmas, when they had afternoon practice sessions. To be sure, they had to memorize passages that didn't make much sense to them: a short one for Hans, and fairly long ones for Grace and Andrew, verses directly from the German-language Bible. There was time, however, for them to visit and have fun with friends.

To add to the family happiness was Jane's coming home for good, if all went well. Yes, she had crutches, but they were mainly to be used when she was tired, or if the walk was uneven or long. For the first few days at least, her siblings were especially kind and gentle with her.

To the family, spending the entire Sunday at church was something special. Even the lunch they took with them was matchless, almost like a festival. The fried wurst was cold, with the fat of it congealed hard, but it was flavorful: smoked and salty. They learned almost to prefer it cold. They drank coffee that was half milk, lukewarm because the round-oak heater was crowded with other people's tin pails of coffee. It had a taste to it that they came to identify as "Christmas practice coffee."

Families gathered in small groups over their own lunches, sitting on the backless benches. They wore their overcoats because even the church finances were limited and could not pay for more than minimum heat. The mothers busily poured coffee and handed out food. The children shouted to each other, eating a piece of homemade wurst from one hand and a tvaybak and pickle from the other. After eating, the children began their games, and the older people gathered in groups to catch up on the previous week's happenings, until the Sunday-school teachers were ready to start their practice sessions.

When it was time to go home, the children were tired from practice and from play that was, at times, unsupervised and unrestrained. Though it was still mid afternoon, daylight would soon be fading. With a sense of well being,

Franz and Hilda agreed that what they enjoyed most about these Sundays was that they were able to forget the realities of the economic Depression.

However, after those days, when they mostly forgot themselves, came days they were mostly disturbed. Then it was a special hardship to Franz to see that their cows didn't look as good or well cared for as the herd they once had. Or to realize that Minnie was getting older and weaker, and to wish that he could replace her with a better tractor than the old Minneapolis-Moline. Then she could join Jerry at his retirement home in the pasture. Franz was fond of the horses and dreaded the day he would have to shoot them: Jerry and Minnie and, later, Prince—the colt whose birth he had watched.

Bitterly, he suggested to Hilda that they ought not go to church any more if the letdown was so much worse the following days.

But Hilda was quick with her answer: "We must get strength during our Sundays and make it last us through the week. We mustn't let church be only an escape for us. Who knows how much worse our discouragement would be if we didn't attend church at all?"

*   *   *

Yield from grains that year was again average. It didn't quite pay the mortgage interest, for they had to hold back some grain for next year's seeding, and keep out money for taxes and emergencies. Franz started taking a few chickens to town with him when he went to buy the groceries. He had found a merchant willing to accept them instead of money. By getting rid of some chickens, they were able to save on feed.

Hilda and Franz were preoccupied with financial worries, but the children, it turned out, had their own concerns. Thus, Grace came to Hilda, very quietly after several days of noticeable stillness. Since adolescence, when she learned to understand her body, she felt confident to speak with Hilda about other personal or intimate questions. She now had the courage to ask for spiritual help: she wanted to be saved. As if for support, she had convinced Andrew to come with her, and when Hilda asked him if he also wanted to be saved, he said "Ya." Nothing more.

It was a strange feeling. Her children were mature enough to face problems she had had for so long; the question she had just begun to deal with. Hilda tried to remember her own outlook toward religion when she was Grace's age and hoped she could speak to them in those terms: words that would be sufficient for their young minds, yet not words they would reject.

Simply, she said, "A conversion would be different for you than it would be for someone who has just heard the story of Christianity, or for someone who has ignored that story for many years even though he's known it." She reminded them of Reverend Bunker's story about his wicked past, and suggested to them, "I'm sure you haven't indulged in such wickedness, but being 'saved'—being 'converted'—still means a kind of turning away from sin. It means a decision, when you make an agreement with yourselves and with God to try honestly and willingly to follow him. It means being unselfish, and showing that unselfishness to God by being kind and considerate to each other and to other people. It means thinking of your Christian duties at all times, never forgetting that you are Christians. That might be hard."

When Hilda asked them, "Do you still want to accept that responsibility?" Grace immediately answered, "Yes, I do," and Andrew, looking first at Grace's determined face and then at his shoes, also answered "Yes."

Hilda wondered why they came at this time, remembering Jane's question, *Am I bad enough to be saved?*

Do they have something horrible to confess? Probably not. If so, would they confess to me? She looked straight into their faces as she told them, "You have to confess your sins—not to me, but to God. You can do that silently."

Together, though it was midday, they knelt by their chairs. Foolishly, Hilda hoped Franz or the other children—*where are they anyhow?*—would not come in, for they might just think she was playing a game. They did not, and Hilda prayed first, hoping she was saying the right things. Comforting words. Words of wisdom. Grace prayed too, in words Hilda did not expect her to use; it was patterned after prayers of radio ministers. When Andrew prayed, he drew on expressions Grace had just used.

They rose. Clumsily, Hilda pulled her chair toward her; it screeched, a noise not in the mood of the moment. *Now I should embrace them both*, Hilda thought. *I ought to show them that I'm happy that they came to me of themselves, without prodding.* But without walking around the chairs, she couldn't get to them.

Then Grace burst into tears. "I don't feel any different than I did before. Did I do something wrong? Isn't there anything else I should do?" She stood there, looking lonely in the middle of the floor, holding a thin hand over her face, the movement pulling up her dress that was too short for her; her feet, large in proportion to the rest of her, set toeing outward.

Hilda went to her. She found it was not impossible to embrace a grown, or almost grown, daughter. It took her back to the days not so very long ago when Grace was a soft well-nourished baby, not more in need of physical expressions of love than she was now. Over Grace's shoulder, Hilda could see Andrew was outdoors on the way to the barn. Quietly, stroking her unmanageable, long hair, Hilda said, "You must not expect it to be something sudden. It takes a lifetime. Let's get together and talk about it often. Whenever you have a question. Or just want to talk. "

She decided that she and Grace would sew a dress that afternoon, from some cotton they had been saving for when they would be wanting it. It would be easier to talk while their hands were busy.

CHAPTER THIRTY: 1931

They brought homework, all diligently studying because their teachers had inspired them to close out the year well, or, perhaps, they wanted to make a good impression on the Weihnachtsmann.[29] Even Andrew found himself quietly interested in his history book. They competed for the kerosene lamp, all wanting it near their books. Climbing up on a chair, Hans brought a picture book and demanded that the lamp be pushed closer to him.

"Come now," Hilda said, "what makes you all so studious? What if I insist having the lamp because I want to see my crocheting? You, at least, Hans, can play with your toys, and we'll read your book tomorrow when the others are in school."

Hans protested loudly; then, realizing they were ignoring him, resigned himself to playing with his tractor. Making loud, moist Fordson tractor-noises—*nu-nu-nu-nu*—he tried to disturb the others, but finally giving up, he followed it around the room, keeping always on a black line that was part of the design of the linoleum.

Franz did not start his usual reading of the newspaper, but slyly making sure Hilda caught the look on his face, he got himself a handful of peanuts from their Christmas hoard.

Andrew was the first to notice. "I didn't know we had peanuts," he said.

"*We* don't," Franz answered, grinning widely. "*I* do."

They all looked up from their books. But Andrew persisted, "Aw, can't I have some?"

It was his chance, Franz knew. "Well, you have the lamp and can read. That ought to be enough. I have to do something too, so I have peanuts."

At that, Grace bent back over her book, but Andrew and Jane both left the

---

29   Santa Claus. Literally, the Christmas Man.

table, deciding that they had studied enough. Franz gave them some peanuts and, pulling up a chair, seated himself near the table where the lamp was.

"Now you've started something," Hilda said. "Now they know we have peanuts, and we won't have any left for Christmas."

"What's the difference," Franz said with a shrug, "whether they eat them now or later? At least they're fresh now."

"But Christmas isn't Christmas without peanuts in their shoeboxes," Hilda insisted. "We'll have to buy more, and that will mean we have to buy less of other things."

"Well, children," Franz said, "enjoy these, because you won't get any for Christmas. But," he added to Hilda, "it's better for them to have a little at a time instead of a big portion all at once when there's so much other rich food to eat. It seems to me there are many more appendix operations right after Christmas than at any other time."

"Why can't we light another lamp?" Grace asked, who saw through her father's device of getting light for his own reading but succumbed to the enticing smell of the peanuts.

"You know the answer to that," Hilda replied, squinting over the stitches she was counting in the pattern of her crocheting.

"By saving kerosene money, we might hurt our eyes," Grace persisted.

"Where did you learn that?" Franz asked.

"We learned that in school," Jane answered for her sister. "We learned that we must have enough light for our eyes."

"Well," continued Franz, "back in the old days, people didn't have even kerosene lamps. They didn't need glasses either."

"That's only because there was no such thing as glasses then," Grace informed him.

"Or people went to bed when the sun set," Jane added.

"Or they didn't read because books weren't printed yet," Andrew said, who had studied the invention of the printing press in school. He continued, "Those must have been the days—no reading!"

Franz laughed. "Maybe things were better then. But not all things. There were a lot of other things they didn't have either."

"Tell us about it," begged Jane, climbing onto his lap, so he had to put down his hard-earned chance at reading the newspaper.

There would be quite a bit of time to read after the children went to bed, so he laughed as he began, "From the way you asked that, you'd think I'm so old that I lived before printing was invented."

"Well, how *do* you know?" asked Andrew, to whom dates and years did not mean very much. "What other things were there?"

"I'll tell you," Franz said, "if Jane will give me a kiss," and Jane immediately slipped off his lap. "Come now," he said and smiled. "You kiss Ma every night after your prayers, and me you never kiss. Why not?"

"That's different," was her only reply.

"Don't you think I like to be kissed?" Franz chuckled. "Why, your mother kisses me often, and I like that. Ma, come over here and give me a kiss just to show them."

Hilda laughed, embarrassed for being embarrassed. "Why Franz, now, don't be childish."

"Okay," Franz said. "If no one will kiss me, I guess I'll read my newspaper again." He looked past the top of his paper to Andrew. "Or will you come here and give me a kiss, Andrew?"

Andrew turned his back. "Aw, men don't kiss men," he finally said.

Franz, grinning now, said, "Sure they do. In some countries, they only kiss each other, and wouldn't think of kissing women."

"I wouldn't either," answered Andrew. Then, brightening, he said in a singsong way, "But I bet Grace kisses Albert."

Grace looked up immediately. "I do not! I hate him!"

"Children," Hilda said. "You mustn't tease. And you mustn't say you hate anyone. Remember, Jesus said we should love everyone."

"Well, I don't like Albert. Make Andrew stop teasing me!"

But Andrew had started to skip around the table, with Jane following him, also chanting, "Grace and Albert! Grace and Albert! Grace and Albert!"

Franz put out his arm to stop them. "Let's change the subject," he said, and began to talk about the days before printing.

Soon it was time for the children to go to bed; one by one they asked to leave, until even Grace laid down her book. When they were all gone, he said, "I wish I hadn't talked about kissing. That was stupid of me. The children didn't know what to think. But I wonder why we, as a family, don't kiss."

"We weren't a kissing family at my home. How much kissing did your family do?"

"Not much. Sometimes the women did. They kissed visitors. Female ones. On the cheek."

Hilda said, "I remember how comforted I felt when I was hurt and Ma clutched me to her soft bosom. It lessened the hurt. But Pa never kissed me, or even hugged me. Not that I can recall. I didn't feel unloved, however. Kisses didn't seem required or expected."

They looked at each other and embraced. It felt comfortable, secure to them both.

Then, as they were putting things to rights before retiring, Hilda suggested she ought to have her eyes examined. "Sometimes I wonder why I have so many headaches."

"You weren't very wise," Franz said, "crocheting like that on fine things when we don't have much light. Can't you find something else to do?"

"What is there? I'm tired in the evening and want to sit too. And I don't like to sit with my hands folded in my lap. Reading wouldn't be any better. I'll be happy when we finally have electricity."

*   *   *

Franz put aside his newspaper that did not tell him much, other than of some turmoil—war—in some faraway European countries.

He had been reading of a man named Hitler who had great ambitions for Germany and was seeking to improve things, at the expense of lands around his. He claimed they belonged with his country—culturally, anyhow. When Franz listened to him on the radio with the volume turned up high, they could feel vibrations, even in their room across the sea. His German—some pronunciation and some words—were different from the German Franz and Hilda could understand and speak, but Franz was proud that he could hear him directly instead of having to read the English version.

With the sound reverberating, Hilda had found Jane hiding far under their bed, crying. "My friend Doris told me her father said that war is coming to our country, and we'll all be killed."

"Of course not. That's just rumor mongering," Hilda told her. But turning to Franz, she remonstrated, "Turn down the volume. You aren't deaf." Franz sighed as he complied, muttering about sensitive girls.

Sometimes he wondered about that Hitler. He felt a slight empathy for him and his people. *For aren't our own people of the same flesh as those? Removed, because of our forebears' wanderings around the continent before they came to America, by several hundred years? But of the same flesh nevertheless. Then again, what if what people say is true: Hitler is "cleansing" Germany of Jews—God's "chosen people"? Turning Germany into a "pure" race?* He let his thoughts ramble on: *I've only ever met one Jew. Runs a business. Seems normal. Decent. Actually, I'm not sure he is a Jew. He doesn't go to church, but neither do some other people.*

Hilda had not heard his thoughts about the European situation. She asked, "Have you any idea how long it will take yet?" Seeing his confusion, she added, "The electricity. How long until we have it?"

"They said 'spring,' at first. But I don't see how that is possible. The ground is frozen and they have to dig post holes before they stretch the wires. Then they have to wire the houses along the line. Obviously, they'll wire for people who can pay first. I'll be happy if we have it by next fall or winter."

"I hope they'll wire before I do spring housecleaning. I'd hate to do it twice."

"They aren't messy. What they do, you can sweep up. At most, they take off the sideboards. Have you thought definitely where you want your plug outlets?"

"Oh, Franz, I haven't any idea. How can I tell where I want to plug in things when I don't know what kind of appliances I'll ever have, or even what kinds there are?"

"We'll have to get only those few we will be sure of—maybe one outlet in each room, because the cost will be plenty as it is. We can put more in later, as we need them. I think I could do it—I watched them the other day."

*   *   *

All the peanuts were eaten before Christmas. Though they had agreed not to buy more, Hilda and Franz decided that the children's shoeboxes would be bleak without peanuts, so they bought more.

Franz found a small pine in the grove to cut. He placed it on the center table in the middle of the parlor, and together they dressed it with decorations: tinsel and candle holders they had saved from previous years, colored-paper chains and popcorn strings the children made in school and brought home. They reserved lighting the candles for Christmas morning when they would find their presents.

The children had paged through the Montgomery Ward and Sears Roebuck catalogs, marking toys and clothes they would like. Grace marked a large doll, explaining self-consciously, "All the girls I know get a 'last doll,' and I'd like to have one too, not to play with but to set on my bed."

Later, alone with Hilda, Franz wondered what to order. "You know, if we buy Grace that doll, to be fair, we would not be able to give her anything else for Christmas—did you see what it cost? Maybe we could buy her a small, less expensive one."

"But if it's not a large beautiful one, Grace wouldn't want it. It has to be a large one that's pretty set on her bed."

"By a large beautiful one, do you mean one of those that look like a movie star—what's her name?"

"Yes, Shirley Temple," Hilda said. "She's a pretty little girl in the movies these days."

"How do you know about the movies and movie stars?"

"I listen to the children when they talk about their friends who are allowed to go to movies."

"Do you really think, if we could afford it, we should give her a doll that looks like a movie star?"

Hilda sighed. "It's hard to know what's right. How do we decide between a doll that looks like a movie star and other pretty ones? All dolls are pretty.

'Shirley' is just a common girl's name. 'Temple' is probably also a common family name. Put them together, and they spell 'sinner.'"

"Maybe we, or she, could give her a different name."

"The doll would still have those dimples and curly dark hair."

"Well, we really can't give her anything else if we give her that doll," Franz said. "We have to be fair to the other children. So the decision is easy. She'll just have to live with it… Anyhow, 'last doll' sounds like some sort of tradition. Did you get a 'last doll'?"

"No, I didn't. But I was working, living with a stepmother when I was her age."

*   *   *

Very excitedly, the night before Christmas, the children put out the boxes that had held their new shoes last autumn. The younger ones complained that theirs were so much smaller than those of the older ones, but Hilda soothed them, "The Weihnachtsmann knows that and will measure what he puts into the boxes." So they all wrote notes inside their boxes and set them up in places around the Christmas tree. Then they went to bed, early, quietly, even the older ones, who knew there was no such thing as a "Christmas Man."

Franz and Hilda waited until they knew the children were asleep to fill the boxes and to bring the gifts out of hiding. "Do you suppose they found any of these things?" Franz wondered. "When I was a boy, I looked for my gifts; if I did find them, I was disappointed, for there was no surprise to look forward to on Christmas morning."

"It seems to me Liesebet found Christmas presents too, because she tried, once, to bribe me into doing something for her with that bit of information," Hilda giggled.

Franz, playfully catching her, whispered, "Careful, you'll wake them. And then they won't believe in the Weinachtsmann anymore."

They worked, leisurely measuring candy and nuts—peanuts, walnuts, almonds, hazelnuts, and Brazil nuts into the shoeboxes, slipping a small trinket among the goodies, and placing oranges and apples on top. The boxes were full, and soon the room smelled of them.

Then, pulling the Christmas-decorated store paper off the various toys, they placed them next to the appropriate boxes. Hilda folded the paper carefully, dropping from the rumpled mass, a rubber ball they intended for Hans.

"Watch out," Franz said, "that you don't burn any of our gifts when you burn the wastepaper."

When they were finished, they looked over the room with the personality it had only at Christmas time. At all other times, the parlor was just an extra room, not lived in except when company came, and they sat in their best clothes. Wishing there was something more to do but knowing there wasn't, they went to bed.

CHAPTER THIRTY-ONE: 1931

Christmas was often cold and blustery. This sunny morning was almost warm. Franz and Hilda knew the children were becoming restless and were waiting to hear them shake the ashes down in the stove. "It's almost sadistic of us," Franz whispered. "Staying in bed like this, and then making them eat breakfast and saying their pieces before we open the door."

"Eating breakfast first is for their good," Hilda answered. "Why, if they didn't eat breakfast, they'd stuff on sweets. If we don't have them say their pieces before they see their toys, we wouldn't get them together to do it later."

As soon as frying cracklings perfumed the air, the children got up, quietly but excitedly. "We get *both* cracklings and oatmeal today," Andrew noted. "Today must be a *special* day."

Hans headed for the parlor door and started to cry when told he would have to wait. He stumbled badly through his piece that he had to memorize for the church program. But when the time finally came, he was rewarded, as Franz let him come into the front room first, to help light the candles. They came out after a bit, opening the double doors to let the rest of the impatient family in.

The children ran to where they had put their boxes; and then, puzzled by their parents' prank of mixing them up, hunted in other places. Happily, Hilda listened to their squeals as they tried out their gifts, and ran their fingers through the nuts and candy in their boxes for that extra tiny gift sure to be hidden there.

When Grace looked at her gifts, she said nothing. Noting that, Hilda's spirits sank, regretting that they had not been able to get that large doll for her. She wanted to tell her how she felt, but she could not catch Grace's eye, so she did nothing. Surely, there would be a time to talk this over.

The children saved the goodies in the boxes for last. Andrew laid out the nuts from his, naming them as he found them: "Peanut of course, walnut, hazelnut, almond, pecan, nigger toe."

"Stop!" Franz was beside him. "Where did you get that name? The right name for it is 'Brazil nut.'"

"I don't know. That's what everybody calls it."

"Everybody who?"

"Kids at school. What's wrong with it?"

By this time, the two had the attention of the whole family. Hilda decided to join in. "How do you feel if the children at school call you a name? Or don't they tease you about going to the Meadow Church? Or about speaking Low German at home?'

"They don't dare. I'd beat them up."

Franz took over again. "Now you're defending two things we don't believe in: violence and name calling. You know about violence. Now think of name calling. If you had black skin. If you were a negro. How would you feel if people made fun of you by naming a nut after you?"

"I wouldn't like it. But, I wasn't calling it a 'negro toe.'"

"'Nigger' is even more down-putting. By speaking of a 'nigger toe,' you're making a double insult."

Until now, Grace had been silent. "I've never seen a nig—I mean negro," she said. "Are they really black colored?"

"I have," Jane said. "There were some very dark children in the hospital in St. Paul. They were nice, and nice to me. They weren't any different, except in looks."

Franz pointed out, "Here in our small community, we seldom see people who are different from us. But we have to remember that God loves everybody, no matter what they look like."

Now Hilda reminded them of the familiar song, "Jesus loves the little children; all the children of the world: red and yellow, black and white; they are precious in his sight."

Franz suggested they all sing some songs, starting with this one and adding the Christmas songs they all, even Hans, knew: "Stille Nacht," and "Ihr Kinderlein Kommet."[30]

They stood behind Hilda, who sat at the pump organ and knew how to play those songs by heart. She hoped Andrew—and the other children— would take the lesson to heart, but that their day wasn't spoiled by the admonition.

*   *   *

---

30 "Silent Night" and "Little Children Come Hither"

Too soon, it was time to get ready for church. It was to be a full day, the day they had stayed after church for, to practice the program. More goodies would be doled out in brown paper sacks to all the children.

The children reluctantly left their new toys: Andrew with a working steam engine that puffed real steam, Jane with a new rubber baby doll dressed in clothes made from scraps left from her own Hilda-made school dresses; and Hans with a red dump truck. Hilda noticed that Grace had begun—it looked unenthusiastically—to leaf through her gift: all of Louisa May Alcott's novels, including Little Women, that she had mentioned a few months ago. It was a good thing that they had taken their baths the night before and wouldn't need much washing up now.

The morning service was long. Hilda wondered why they had it at all, for the children got restless through the long sermon. They knew their part came in the afternoon and wanted to discuss their gifts with their friends, who must all have received something as well.

She found it difficult, after the excitement of the morning, to concentrate on what the minister had to say. Looking around the church, she saw new hats here and there, or a new dress. She, herself, had told Franz she did not need any new clothes, and instead, he had made a cedar chest for her, to keep her winter woolens. He was wearing the new blue necktie she knit for him when he wasn't in the house.

There was nothing in the church to suggest that it was Christmas. Some churches had Christmas trees right in the front, not far from the pulpit. Franz and Hilda agreed that a Christmas tree, not necessary even in homes, would be very much out of place in a church where the main idea of Christmas was the birthday of their Lord. Still, though there were no decorations, Hilda felt that the air of Christmas was there. She could almost smell pine, and something indefinable that was not even there. There was the smell of coffee—for they were going to have the noon meal all together—but the smell of coffee did not belong only to Christmas. That was the smell of Easter, of Pentecost, and of weddings and funerals as well.

People were friendly that day. They were always friendly, and surely not more now than always, for hadn't they all known each other since they were children, and weren't they, many of them, related at least distantly? But to Hilda, it seemed as if there was something special, and she hoped she could figure it out.

Reverend Schmidt had begun to preach some time ago. Hilda realized she had not listened for his text that she knew would be the Christmas story in one form or another. Not unusually good, for he was never unusually good; he was a farmer, as were most of the unpaid ministers. He hadn't had much more education than Hilda herself. He was a second cousin, and Hilda remembered playing some childhood games with him.

Now he was speaking to her, teaching her and her children the truths of the Bible, with a voice that was not quite pleasant, and a face that didn't inspire any particular religious respect. Yet, for sermons like this Christmas one, Hilda did not regret that her children should learn from this man. He was sincere, and had said to her once, "If we were as wise and good as God, we would *be* God. And I am not God." She had liked that statement and respected him for it.

Then he was through, asking them all to sing "Silent Night" together, and inviting them to eat the Christmas meal together in Christian fellowship.

The noon meal was served in the partly-heated dining hall, still damp from the frost that came through the walls during the week. The food was not good; so many different kinds of ham and sausage, of tvaybak, of potato salad, pickles and pluma mos[31]—all prepared in the peculiar style of the individual housewives—were jumbled together. Invariably, families preferred the flavor of their own cooking. Nevertheless, they enjoyed the meal; the men and growing boys ate heartily, for their appetites were always healthy, whetted by the seasonal weather and excitement.

It didn't take long for the women to wash the dishes, standing in front of the rows of steaming dishpans and chattering loudly—so loudly, in fact, that Hilda wondered whether they weren't a bit disrespectful toward their house of worship, even if it was in the dining hall. Then, their hands red and swollen from the hot water, they went into the church, sitting as a body near the back.

Singing had already begun. The children were sitting in the choir pews, all dressed neatly and sparkling with excitement. When they started their part of the program, Hilda felt herself on edge. *I hope my children will perform at least as well as the others. Some certain children are always called upon to do extra things, and they do them so prettily and with such assurance. My children are seldom singled out... Perhaps the other children push themselves forward. Surely my children are every bit as intelligent. I wish they would be more in the foreground. What should I do to encourage them?*

I hope one of my children will be a missionary some day. It might even be nice if one was a minister, although I can hardly imagine Andrew as one. It's impossible to tell about Hans yet. But if one of them was a missionary and went to Africa perhaps, or India, I would be so proud. I would miss him, of course. Right now, I'm glad they are all still with me, but if they were in fields like that, I would feel that my unselfishness in letting them go would also be a contribution... Yet, in my heart, is this wish a way to make up for myself, my own shortcomings?

31 A soup made of dried fruit.

Hilda forced herself to return her attention to the program.

Grace and Andrew were too old to sit with the young children and only got up with their Sunday-school classes to sing a number. She looked at her two youngest children, sitting with the group, now standing up to sing one of their Christmas songs, "Away in a Manger." They fit in easily with the rest of the children, not conspicuous, except that Jane was taller than the other girls her age.

Then Hans got up with a small line of boys; each boy in the line held a letter that, put together, spelled "BIBLE." Hans was grinning, holding his B crookedly. Hilda tried to see why he was smiling; and then saw that he was smiling in the direction of where Andrew was sitting. With the expression on her face, Hilda tried to telegraph Hans to stop smiling, for she was afraid he would miss his turn in speaking and have to be prompted. But he said his piece, a short one about "Birth of Baby Jesus," and walked happily away from the front of the stage.

Jane recited a longer piece, a direct quote from the Christmas story in Matthew, and did not look toward Andrew. But Hans was now openly giggling at something Andrew must be doing. Hilda wished they were in the old-style church, where one of the church elders came around to tap misbehaving boys on the shoulder. At least that was what Pa said had been done when he was a boy in the old country. In some churches these days, families sat together; their children were surely better disciplined than they were here sitting with their age groups. It was disconcerting, and Hilda felt the spirit of Christmas leaving her as she tried to decide just what to say to them when they got home.

The children's program was over. The men were in their hallway; she could hear from the rustling that they were packing paper sacks into the dishpans that the women had just used for their dishwashing. They walked into the main room, carrying the filled pans high, toward the front where the children were trying to hide their anticipation, yet looking immediately into their sacks to see what was in them. Soon the church smelled of peanuts and oranges, and the crackle of the sacks was everywhere as the children of visitors were also handed gifts.

When it was time to go home, they did not linger long to talk because it would soon be dark. Some day it wouldn't matter, for they would have electricity and could milk even after dark.

On the way, Franz, taking advantage of their being together said, "What was the big joke, Hans, when you were reciting?"

"Nothing," Hans answered, his mouth full of candy.

Hilda was happy that their father was taking care of it, that she didn't have to scold them this Christmas day.

Franz continued: "It's quite strange when someone laughs about nothing."

Hans did not answer, but Jane did. "I know—it was Andrew. He—"

Franz was firm, keeping his eyes on the road as he drove. "Jane, this is between Hans and me. Hans will tell me."

Hans was beginning to cry. With his mouth still full, he tried to answer. "Andrew was making faces at me. I couldn't help it."

Andrew said nothing. Franz waited a moment and then asked, "Andrew, were you doing that?"

"Yes." His voice was small.

"Why?"

"I don't know. Because he was looking at me, I guess."

"Do you think church is the place to make faces?"

"You make faces too." When she heard that, Hilda almost laughed. But she caught herself and refrained from saying anything.

"You know, Andrew, that there is a time and place for everything, and I'm sure you have never seen me trying to make the minister laugh by making faces at him. In a sense, while he was reciting, Hans was the minister."

Jane tittered. Andrew said nothing.

"What shall we do with you, Andrew and Hans?" Franz asked. "Isn't it a shame that such a thing should happen on Christmas day?"

"I guess so," was all Andrew said.

"Maybe you should spank us," Hans said.

Hilda bit her lip and faced forward so the children, or Franz who was taking it seriously, would not see that she was amused.

"Is that what you want?" Franz asked them.

"No," Hans answered, still solemn.

"What do you think, Andrew? What should we do?"

"I don't know." Andrew's voice sounded annoyed. "Nothing, I guess. I'm sorry."

They were turning into their driveway. "We'll finish discussing this while we're doing chores, Andrew. Now, hurry and change clothes, because it will soon be too dark to see."

In her heart, Hilda's thoughts went to Andrew. *This has been a hard day for him. I trust Franz to ease things when they're alone.*

*   *   *

Tomorrow would be the Second Holiday. They would go to the home of Franz's mother, to celebrate with his brother and sisters and their spouses and children. On the Third Holiday, they would get together with Hilda's Aunt Mary and their other relatives.

It was always a relief when the holidays ended, for although they were jolly, they were a strain. Invariably, they caught colds and overate. When the children, in spite of warnings and admonitions not to be too wild, had tired even themselves from romping and tussling, they all were happy to settle down to some days of ordinary living. They played with their new toys, trying to make use of the few days that the break from school left them. When the vacation was over, they looked forward to seeing their classmates again, though they staunchly said they dreaded the thought. Half seriously, they called school "the dance of the tomcats."

CHAPTER THIRTY-TWO: 1932

It was the second blizzard that February. Two weeks ago, and before the road was plowed, Mr. Faulk, the driver of the boxy, orange wooden school bus, picked up the children in his rickety sleigh that was held together with barbed fencing wire. He usually used it to haul farm goods and animals, and even manure. This time, he was thoughtful to put in a bed of straw for the children to sit on. All were warmly dressed, starting with "long-handled" underwear[32] and ending with heavy coats and large knitted scarves wrapped around their heads, exposing only their eyes. Hilda insisted that they also cover themselves with their old hairy horse blanket, from which Andrew pulled away and Jane complained, "Aw, it stinks under it."

All went well at first, Grace starting to sing "Jingle Bells" with the other children joining in. But Mr. Faulk somehow dropped the reins and climbed out of the box to retrieve them. The horses spooked and took off. Grace jumped over the barbed wire and out of the box, but Andrew, Jane, and two neighbor children stayed inside it, shouting "Stop!" in their high-pitched child voices—scaring the horses even more. Cross country, the children screamed. Mr. Faulk hobbled over the uneven corn stubble, with Grace far behind. The ride stopped abruptly when the sleigh caught on a tree stump and overturned. The horses turned to look behind them, and the children emerged from under pieces of the broken sleigh. Passersby picked up the children to take them the rest of the way to school.

Not really injured, though they had been crying, they were celebrities at school that day. Adults admonished them, "Next time, just say 'whoa' in an assertive voice. Screaming 'Stop!' only scares the horses." But amongst themselves, the children agreed, "I bet grownups would be scared and holler too." That was the day Jane learned the English words "tipped over."

---

32   Thick itchy woolen underwear, with long sleeves and pant-legs.

Now it was again storming for several days. Never so hard that they couldn't see the trees in the front yard, yet hard enough to close the roads and keep the children home from school. "I'm glad Mr. Faulk didn't get his sleigh repaired," Grace said, reminding the family of the runaway.

"I never want to ride in that old sleigh again!" Jane added. "Even if he repairs it."

Grace wondered, "Why didn't you jump out of the box?"

"Her legs aren't as long as yours," Hilda chided her. "She could have broken her bones. Remember, she's been very sick and needs to take it easy. Besides, your coat could have caught on the barbed wire and dragged you along. Then what could have happened!"

"Well, it didn't," Grace's rejoinder.

Hans, again left out of the fun, declared, "Me too. I jumped."

Jane, with her special status, decided to set him straight. "Hans, you're too little. And you haven't been sick. Besides, you weren't even there."

Franz, who had just entered the room, decided to deflect the subject to today's storm. "If we didn't have that windbreak, we'd really be feeling it. This storm is worse than the one two weeks ago. Probably as bad as the ones we had in Montana, though there weren't any trees, even miles away to break the sharpness of those winds."

Andrew had come in with him, breathing through his hand-knit scarf, frosty where he had exhaled his moist breath. Their cheeks and noses were red, Andrew's a softer red than Franz's leathery skin.

"Tell us about Montana again," Jane begged, before they removed their thick fleece-lined coats.

"Oh, you've heard about it so often," Franz answered, watching with a twinkle as boyish as Andrew's for when Hilda's back should be turned so Andrew could open his coat.

Hilda went into the pantry. Then Andrew quickly opened his buttons and let out a half-grown cat. It darted, frightened, underneath the table and crouched slightly to look out at them with wide-open, large-pupil eyes. Jane laughed, bouncing with excitement, and Hans crawled, squealing, underneath the table after it. The cat scrambled across the room and under the stove.

"What, a cat in my house? What is this?" It was Hilda.

"I'll take her right back," Andrew said. "I just wanted to bring her in so the kids could play with her a little."

"But you realize it isn't good for the cat. She'll get warm in here, and when you take her outside, she'll catch cold."

Grace pulled her out from under the stove and held her high, away from the screaming and reaching Hans.

"Then too," Hilda continued, "she'll think she can get in all the time, and soon she'll sit and shiver in front of the door when she could be so comfortable in the barn with the other cats. They don't have much sense, so we must have a little of it."

"And then we'll step on her," Jane volunteered, "when she sits in front of the door."

"Oh, you shut up," Andrew said. "Do you have to lay a little egg?"

"Andrew," Franz said, suddenly severe, "that's not the way to talk. You apologize." Behind him, Jane crossed her eyes and stuck out her tongue at Andrew.

"Aw, she always thinks she's so smart. It's none of her business anyhow." Andrew flung his sheepskin coat into the corner.

"Andrew"—it was Hilda's turn—"you pick that right up and hang it where it belongs. I just got through picking up all the clothes that were lying around. I don't want to have to follow you all day, just picking up after you!" She stood there, her hands webbed with an eggy-floury mix, for she was making cruller dough.

Andrew picked up his coat with one swoop and carried it into the unheated hall.

"And, by the way, "Hilda added, "remember that whoever brings animals into the house has to clean up after them."

"She won't do anything," Andrew said. "She just did."

"Sometimes when they're excited they need to go oftener," Hilda said. "Especially after they've just had some milk."

"She's purring, hear her?" interrupted Grace, who had the cat stretched out on her lap. Long, awkwardly on her back, with her forepaws in the air and her hind legs lying relaxed apart.

"Looks like we're in for it another day," Franz said, changing the subject as he looked out the window.

"Tell us about storms in Montana," Grace said, even though they had all heard about them before.

"You should tell us," Franz replied. "You were there."

"But I don't remember it. I can't remember any storms. All I can remember is going away and playing in church, and Grossma Heldin."

"Was I there too?" Jane asked.

"Sure," Franz answered, looking slyly at Hilda who, if she heard him, was pretending not to.

"No, she wasn't." Andrew raised his voice.

"Yes, I was. Pa says so." Jane started toward Andrew, but not quickly enough to avoid their father's restraining hand.

"That's enough now, children," he said. "You were there in spirit, Jane, though you weren't born yet. Now, let's not fight any more. We should rather be thankful that we can spend time together like this, instead of getting on each other's nerves just because we can't have school or go outside to play."

"The only thing that will help will be school," Grace said, looking up from her gentle massaging.

"Just because you *like* school," Andrew said, admitting his feelings.

"That's enough," Franz said. "Stop that quibbling. Find your books and read, or do something."

"Yes," Hilda said, "I could use some help. Andrew, you get the old rolls of wallpaper and start measuring some of the flower pots. Those tin cans don't look very nice—it would help if you would cover them with wallpaper. Grace, put the cat down and wash your hands, and help me with these crullers."

Then it was still. Hilda looked to her children, all working self-forgetfully; even the cat was enjoying its illegal comfort underneath the stove again.

Franz opened his writing desk, crowded with papers. He had his accounts almost figured out. Sometimes he welcomed the storms, to catch up on his paperwork, except when the storm was so bad that the animals had to suffer, or it took all day to do chores.

Finances were picking up; this winter, they were able to pay all the interest on the mortgage without borrowing more money, and even to make a small payment on the principal. On top of that, Franz had negotiated the purchase of a one-year-old Dodge car. The auto dealer hired him to repair the picket fence around his yard next summer, and gave him time to pay the rest of the cost month by month. The car worked well; it seemed the color—a dull gray—had helped lower the price.

The crullers sank to the bottom of the hot fat as Hilda slipped them into the deep pan, but they rose almost instantly to the top, releasing tiny bubbles from their edges. The smell of the fresh fat and the heat from it rose to her face, warming it. She stood over it, enjoying the feel. Quickly, the crullers turned a golden brown. She removed them deftly, letting the excess fat drain momentarily. As soon as she dropped them into a large bowl, Andrew came for several, not waiting for them to cool but tossing them back and forth from hand to hand until he could hold them with one hand. Hilda tasted one herself. It was good, its flavor almost nutlike.

The children were all eating, and the wallpaper of the flowerpots was becoming stained. Hilda decided that it didn't matter enough to spoil the silence with advice. Without saying anything, she brought several crullers to Franz, who had become so absorbed in his work that he didn't smell that they were ready.

He looked up with a smile when he took them and went back to his work, eating.

"I wish we had some rhubarb sauce," Grace said. "Crullers are good just by themselves, but rhubarb makes them even better."

Jane said, "I know somebody who likes to eat crullers with watermelon."

"Huh," Andrew retorted. "Where will you find watermelon in the middle of a blizzard?"

Hilda set them straight. "It's crisp crullers they eat with watermelon, not soft ones like ours."

"I like your kind best," Hans said, and was backed up by the others.

*   *   *

By the afternoon, the air had cleared somewhat. It had stopped snowing, and the wind blew only in gusts, so now and then it seemed quite still. The children decided to take out the sled. "It will be good for them," Hilda said to Franz as she helped them bundle up. "They need the fresh air. And when they come in, they will be better tempered."

"Just don't go all the way to the hill," Franz cautioned. "The grove is protecting us from the strongest wind. When you get beyond the shelter, it's pretty cold. Close to zero. You can have a lot of fun on the drifts."

When they were outside, Franz turned to Hilda with an excited smile. "If we're careful how we spend our money, we'll be able to get the machinery and animals out of mortgage. Next year, when the electric line comes past our yard, we may be able to get connected. You start thinking where you want outlets and what motor you want first."

Hilda laughed. "You know what I want first—a motor for the washing machine, and an iron."

"One thing at a time," Franz answered. "I don't think we can afford more than one thing each, and it would help me a lot if I could have a motor for the water pump."

"Well, then I guess I should get the washing machine motor. That gasoline engine must give off a funny kind of poison,[33] because I get a headache every washday if it's too cold to open a window, or if I forget to keep a window open. But some day, I want an iron. It's so hard to have to keep the stove hot, especially in summer, just to keep heating the irons. They're so heavy that even Grace says she has a backache from ironing."

"You be good and maybe the Weihnachtsmann will bring you an iron," Franz teased.

"Can we get an electric radio too?" Grace had not gone out with the younger children.

Franz had forgotten she was there, holding the cat again; it was tousled-

---

33 Carbon monoxide.

looking from Grace's tweaking and rubbing. "Our battery radio will hold out for some time yet. We must get the necessary things first. Even after we have all our needs, we mustn't become spoiled and think we have to have everything else too. Sometimes I think we have more than we need anyhow."

Grace bent back over the book she had on her lap along with the cat.

"Besides," Franz went on, "you should go out too. Get some fresh air in your lungs. You'll get hunchbacked sitting inside all day long. Take the cat out with you, and maybe teach the little ones how to play fox and goose."

Slowly she rose, surprising the cat onto the floor. It stood still a moment and stretched its paws forward, flexing even its claws, yawning widely and heartily. Then it sat down, licking the rumpled fur smartly into place.

It took Grace some time to find her clothes and get ready to go outdoors. As she went, Hilda called after her, "Better send Hans in soon. He must be about tired, and I don't want him to catch cold."

A few minutes later, when Hilda looked out the window, she saw them running the circle they had trampled into the snow, Grace enjoying herself as much as the younger ones. "Needs a little push sometimes," she said to Franz. "I almost wish I could be playing with them."

"Why don't you?" Franz laughed.

"I'd be sorry later. I'm on my feet so much that it would be stupid to run around like that. Besides, I get all the fresh air I need feeding the chickens."

"You've gained some more weight," Franz said. "That's what's hard on your feet."

"You have too," Hilda replied. Secretly, she had tried to curb her appetite. It all came from eating what the children left over, she knew. She couldn't bear to throw away food when they had to be so careful with their money, and the children refused to finish their food sometimes, especially the fatty edges on the meat. "But before I forget," she went on, "the chickens are getting fresh air too—there is a lot of space between some of the wall boards, and the barn is mighty drafty. I think that is why they don't lay so many eggs now. Some of them have caught cold, in spite of the warm mash I bring them."

Franz went out then, sending the younger children with their soaked mittens into the house, and taking Grace and Andrew with him to help stuff straw into the cracks of the chicken barn. When Hilda later went to feed the chickens, she saw that they had also spread fresh clean straw on the ground. The chickens seemed to appreciate the change. They were strutting contentedly around, picking at and scratching in the straw, and cooing softly to themselves and to each other. As if for their efforts, Hilda found one more egg than they had been laying during the past week. Laughing, she brought that extra egg to Franz. "This egg is yours for making the chickens happy."

That evening, they were in unusually high spirits. It had been good for them to be out. The children's cheeks were glowing, and they were better natured than they had been. By the time Hilda had supper ready and Franz, Grace, and Andrew had come in from chores, they were hungry for the fried eggs and potatoes Hilda had ready for them.

As they were eating, they heard the sound of a motor. Franz recognized it. "The snow plow."

Andrew defined it. "School tomorrow," he said. They were no longer snowbound. Then he was dressed, hurrying out to watch the snow plow. Flashing blue lights signaling its whereabouts; it chewed its way through the tightly-packed snow that had silenced the road. Jane wanted to go out too, and when she asked, Hans asked to go too.

But Hilda saw their tired eyes. "The only road you're going to is the road to bed. Especially you, Jane, because you'll have to get up earlier tomorrow."

Andrew was back inside before Grace and Hilda had finished washing the dishes. "It was a rotary," he announced. "That means the drifts are pretty bad when they have to get out the rotary."

"What do you mean, 'rotary'?" Grace asked.

Hilda saw that his older sister's question made Andrew happy. He proudly explained, "The plow is not the grader type that pushes the snow off the road, but rather chews into it like a food chopper or corkscrew and then tosses it off the road like a grain elevator. It looks like it is blowing it off the road. That's where the name comes from: the blades are round and they rotate," he finished.

All Grace answered was, "Oh." Then she turned to her book again.

"Well, since it is our last evening of this snowstorm," Franz suggested, "let's have some fun." He was standing with his back to the cook stove, looking into the mirror at the other end of the room, the mirror that distorted all reflections anyhow. In order to see into it, he had to stand with his feet set apart, and he was making faces. Hans laughed heartily, and Grace looked up from her book.

"Come," Franz was saying, "I'll give this nickel to whoever makes the worst face in the mirror."

They all came then, crowding each other, trying to see that their own faces were the ugliest. "Come on, Ma," Andrew was saying. "Let's see your face."

To oblige them, Hilda looked as cross eyed as she could. Then they all practiced looking cross eyed, trying to see themselves in the mirror as they did it, until Franz explained, "Of course, you can't see your own crossed eyes. They're looking at each other, not in the mirror."

Jane pointed out, "This time we're not in church—making faces at the minister!"

If they heard her, no one reacted.

Soon, realizing that the younger ones were so excited as not to be able to fall sleep, Franz decided that he had made the worst, and therefore the best, face and that he had earned the nickel himself. As he pocketed it, he avoided an argument as to which of the children had won the contest.

They continued making faces until Hilda suggested, "You should try to make the prettiest faces possible."

That, they decided, was not nearly so much fun.

The next morning, the boxy orange school bus was late. While they were doing chores, Andrew saw it going past the farm to pick up other children, so they knew it was coming. Hilda was about to call her three back to the house, for fear they would get too cold waiting at the end of the driveway in below-zero weather. As she looked, the bus appeared over the hill.

The day passed quickly; Hilda was amazed at how soon she finished her housework. How quiet the house was. Franz noticed it too, though all he said was, "Guess we're back in the old grind."

Hans felt it especially, not used to being alone. He asked, "What should I do next?" Hilda mixed flour, salt, alum, lard, and water to make clay for him to create animals. Then he brought her each animal—cat, dog, cow, horse, and a flock of chickens—for her to admire. Together, they set them all on a windowsill to dry and harden.

When the children came home from school, they were charged with the news they had heard in their classes, even while the teachers had asked them to please pay attention.

Grace announced, "Jacob was absent because he has measles. Have I had measles?"

Andrew interrupted before Hilda could answer Grace. "Joseph has scarlet fever. Have I—"

"Yes and no," Hilda replied. "You've all had measles, but not scarlet fever. Measles is a bad disease, but scarlet fever is worse. I hope you all stay healthy."

Jane, joining the school reports, offered, "James got a baby brother—at home, without a doctor!"

Hilda exchanged a look with Franz but only replied, "That sounds like good news."

Only about half of their classmates were back in school, because others lived on lesser roads that had not yet been dug out. Even the Lobers' road was not very well opened. Where the WPA had cut the road through a hill, the space was filled with snow, and in the lee of farm groves were large drifts as high as their school bus. Some men must have had to help dig through the drifts, for the rotary would not have been able to chew its way through otherwise.

*   *   *

Since Grace was a bright, conscientious student, Mr. West, the high school principal, sent a note to her homeroom teacher asking for Grace to come to his office during her study period. He had good news for her. A graduate of the state university, he had read in his alumnae journal of nursing-school scholarships for good students, and he encouraged Grace to apply. He offered to write a favorable recommendation. She would be expected to carry a full load of classes, and to work in the university hospital as an aide. Tuition, room, and board would be provided.

"Yippee!" Grace wanted to shout, but she simply blushed and found words to thank Mr. West. Then she could hardly wait for the school day to end to tell her parents. She hoped it would be possible for them to lend her a small allowance. Just for necessities. Like a toothbrush. She would continue to use baking soda instead of toothpaste, of course.

But she didn't have the scholarship yet. And graduation was still five months off.

CHAPTER THIRTY-THREE: 1933–1940

Grace entered the state university school of nursing. Classes and work challenged her but also kindled her curiosity and enthusiasm. Hilda thought it fit her. Her frequent letters home admitted her homesick feelings, so her parents and her siblings wrote back often. Even Hans. She graduated with honors and found employment in a modern suburban hospital. Soon she would set aside money for continued studies and for her siblings, should they need help toward their schooling.

Andrew became more involved with school when he enrolled in Future Farmers classes and extra activities. He raised sheep, tending the lambs when their mothers didn't care or didn't know how to nurse them. He passed on scientific and practical knowledge to Franz who, sometimes, agreed to try new methods and sometimes rebutted with what he believed was more practical or within their means. His friends, though few, were staunch and loyal. He did not date, at least not to Hilda's knowledge.

Somewhat impulsive, Jane's friendships seemed shallow and short term to Hilda. She sang in the school and church choirs and joined school clubs, too many to have time to satisfy their aims. Her weak leg kept her from participating in sports such as running or girls' basketball. She said she hated boys, especially those who imitated her limp. Nevertheless, she did well in her studies, and her marks were consistently good. She would put off baptism until her friends were ready.

Hans developed into an easygoing adolescent. He did well enough in school to satisfy his parents, and he was sought after by the basketball coach, as he was agile and growing tall. Girls liked him—his courtesy and friendly smile; boys enjoyed his jokes and usually harmless pranks. He sometimes found reasons not to attend church, to Hilda's dismay and, so far, said he would "wait" to decide whether to be baptized.

Franz found gratification from watching his livestock thrive and grain crops yield bountiful harvests. Though his horses cropped the pasture grass short, he loved them and found excuses not to shoot them when they could no longer work—"out of bullets; not today." Jerry and Minnie died, separately, of whatever old horses die of. Their bodies were picked up by the rendering-works company for dog-food or fertilizer. Hilda chose not to think about that.

Franz continued teaching a Sunday-school class of women, even while he questioned the object of the particular lesson. It became easier just to hide his disbelief. He visited his mother at the Sunset Home frequently and at length, sometimes over Hilda's protest when she was waiting for the groceries he was to bring home. His reply to her complaint was, *"Wenn du noch eine Mutter hast, so danke Gott und sei zufrieden."*[34]

Hilda worked hard, even when the children were old enough to help. Her garden produced prize-winning vegetables and eye-catching flowers, though she never entered them in the county fair. She believed her ma would approve of them. She continued tending her chickens, proudly keeping track of how many eggs they laid, but she no longer helped with milking or hay-making and such, since Andrew was there to help. Every Saturday, she baked tvaybak. When her work of the day was done, she crocheted bedspreads and tablecloths and pieced together elaborate quilts, using remnants from dresses she had earlier sewed using the trusty Singer. She made sure there was one for each child. Each Sunday evening, she wrote two or three letters: first to Grace and then to Pa and Muttah. When there was time, she also wrote Liesebet and Joe or John and Marie and, sometimes, Hermann or Marta.

As they celebrated their twenty-fifth anniversary, Hilda and Franz's marriage appeared happy and serene, and it was. Questions each had were kept buried; they chose not to rile each other's peace of mind. As far as they knew, the children—and any outsiders—were unaware of any disparity between them concerning their faith. They attended church regularly; Franz sometimes dawdled, causing them to be late, which made Hilda uneasy.

They continued friendly relations with Aunt Mary, now living in the Sunset Home and, of course, with Franz's siblings and both of their cousins. Sunday afternoons they visited them, or were visited by them for faspa.

They practiced the frugal habits they acquired in Montana, reinforced by the Great Depression. They cleaned their plates, and the plates of the children if they left food, so both Hilda and Franz found their belts tighten. Clothing, when worn out, became rags to scrub floors or clean machinery parts. Strong, colorful rags could be cut into strips that Hilda wove or braided into rugs. Spoiled food was palatable for the chickens or pigs.

---

34   "So long as you have a mother, thank God and be content."

Life was good. Life went on. Though both Hilda and Franz kept diaries, later readers might skip parts as being tame and tedious. To Hilda and Franz it meant a long and happy time ahead.

CHAPTER THIRTY-FOUR: 1940

She called her lumbago "*hexen schuss.*"[35] It began as a burning, aching sensation in her lower back, and Hilda ignored it at first. She'd had backaches before when she overworked, or caught a draft; they always passed after a few days of discomfort. This time the aching became worse, until Hilda left her housework undone.

"It's the hottest part of the summer," she complained to Grace, who got leave from her nursing job to come home to help, "and I'm cold and shivering."

Grace didn't say much but continued with her work, packing heated blankets around her mother's back. All she answered was, "No, it isn't summer yet. They say spring is the worst time of year to catch cold."

"Here I lie and let my children wait on me." Hilda moved impatiently and then was immediately sorry. That slight movement was very painful.

"Maybe it's time your children waited on you for a change," Grace answered, and was out of the room.

Now Hilda knew that her firstborn child was an adult and a competent nurse. *Is Grace going to have the same kind of life that I've had? Hard, physical labor? Worrying, or at least concerned, about her mother as I was about mine? My mother died very young. What if I should die now?*

The idea was almost pleasant. Hilda closed her eyes, imagining her body becoming a nothing, and as she was thinking, the pain in her back seemed to recede. Grace came in, stood over her for a little while, and then left. Hilda smiled, knowing that Grace would tell the others that she was sleeping now. *What would she think if she found me dead? Would she lose her composure? Grace seldom shows much emotion these days. In a way, I'd like to jolt her a little, make her laugh heartily and loudly or, if not that, make her cry brokenly and*

---

35 Attack by a witch. A witch's [gun] shot.

painfully. Perhaps, if I should die, Grace would break a little. Maybe my dying would accomplish that one thing.

Outside her room, Hans was crying. Next, Hilda heard the calm voice of Grace, soothing him. *They would get along without me all right. Grace would be good to her siblings. Fair and firm, yet loving and capable. But would she have to give up her nursing career for them? An old maid I know did just that. No, I don't want that. And Franz. He's independent too. True, he would miss me. I'm sure he loves me. But he would get along. He could marry again. Then Grace wouldn't have to give up her career. I don't want that either.*

She thought of herself as spirit only, and she pictured herself approaching that Heaven she had known since she was a child. She didn't know she was falling asleep until later when Grace's coming into the room, though still, woke her. It was late afternoon, with shadows beginning to merge.

"Can I get you something?" Grace stood there, her arms hanging down at her sides. *She's a nurse, she'll know what to do*, Hilda thought. *All nurses know what to do.*

"What would you like for supper?" Grace asked. "I don't know what to make."

"Anything," Hilda answered. "I don't think I want to eat. Give the others whatever they want."

Grace left, presently stirring something in a pan.

When supper was almost ready, Hilda knew she could wait no longer. Embarrassed at having her own child assist her with such things, she finally felt compelled to call her. But Grace was not strong enough to help her to the chamber pot, and Franz came to lend a hand. Pain and embarrassment caused Hilda to cry. When she was again in bed, her face wet with tears and perspiration, and Grace had gone back to the kitchen to finish supper preparations, she allowed herself to cry unrestrained. Then Franz appeared, his cheek laid against hers, not saying anything. After she subsided, he left, still not saying anything. He sent Grace in, with a bowl of schav soup—summer borscht—she had made. It was curdled; she had not known how to blend cream into the mixture of garden greens: sorrel, chard, onion, and parsley. Whatever was available.

She didn't turn on the light. Hilda was thankful for that, for she didn't want Grace to see her face. When she tried to sit up to eat, she found she couldn't; the pain in her back and hips was greater than the slight hunger she felt. "I'm sorry, Grace, it's good soup but I just can't eat," Hilda finally said as she eased back into the softness of her featherbed.

Then, looking into the face of her daughter, though the light wasn't good, Hilda could see that she had been crying. Her face was swollen. As she saw it, she felt her daughter's head, laid on the pillow beside her own, her arms across her own, weeping bitterly. Grace spoke as if she had been crying for some time, brokenly, painfully fighting for breath. All she could say was, "Ma, I love you so." That was all. When she said it, Hilda felt great happiness well up in her own chest, happiness so great that she almost failed to realize her daughter's pain.

It was a while before Grace had cried all her tears. When she was able to lift her head, Hilda spoke, angry with herself for being embarrassed, yet noting that her daughter was also disconcerted. "If you wash your face with cold water, it'll be more comfortable, and it won't show so much either." And Grace walked out the room.

Then it occurred to Hilda: *I should have answered, "I love you very much, Grace." But I didn't say it. I haven't said it for a long time to any of my children. I do believe the children realize I love them… I hope I'll soon have another chance to say that to Grace. Grace seems to need it more than the others. Just why, I wonder, but can't say.* Regret remained heavy in her chest. She prayed, *Give me another chance to speak my love, and the presence of mind to say it.*

That evening when Franz came to bed beside her, and after she thought he had gone to sleep, he turned toward her, gently rubbing her arm. "There's something I'd like to talk to you about," he said. "Something that's been bothering me for a while and, though I've wanted to talk about it, I never could quite bring it up."

Hilda tried to think what that might be, but she couldn't make her mind function.

"Maybe," he went on, "that's why you had to get sick. To bring me to clean up on this." He was leaning with his head propped over his elbow. "You are awake, aren't you? I don't know what's the reason for it, but sometimes during the past months I've been wondering whether I was truly right with God. And, at the same time, whether I truly loved you."

Pain, greater than the pain she had been enduring all that day, shot through Hilda, seeming to radiate from her chest into her extremities. It was more from the statement regarding his love than the expression of his feeling about God. For years, she believed that the state of one's soul was more important than one's personal life. *Love for God should always come before love for other people. Without question—though they are different kinds of love. Something about "agape" comes to mind. But that refers to God's love for us. What's the other kind of love, according to the Bible? Oh, yes, Abraham was willing to sacrifice his son for God. But he didn't have to. God intervened. Besides, this is about my husband, and me—not my child.*

I know. The Bible says you must leave father and mother to follow Jesus; it doesn't say you must leave your wife or husband. And what does that have to do with Franz's and my love for each other? In spite of those thoughts, the pain didn't lessen. *If only I weren't sick, so I could react to what he said… This is what it must be like to be paralyzed.*

"Hilda, do you hear me? Please listen," Franz said, and Hilda felt a tear drop onto her face from his. *Funny,* she thought, *that's the second person who's cried today. Or is it the third?*

"Forgive me," he was saying now. "Maybe it's just that we're getting older, and I was getting used to you… Oh, I don't know what's the matter. Sometimes my mind seems to be going around and 'round and 'round, and when I'm through, I haven't gotten anywhere. Sometimes I think I must be a little crazy." His sobs sounded rusty, as if from being seldom used, but when he stopped short, saying, "What do you want?" he startled Hilda, who felt her heart jump erratically.

"I can't sleep." It was Jane's voice. Hilda couldn't see without turning painfully.

"Why not?"

"I don't know. I just can't sleep."

Franz got out of bed to lead her back to her room. He muttered when he returned sometime later. "I sat with her until she went back to sleep. It's something when children act like old women who can't sleep."

When Hilda tried to speak, she found she was hoarse. "It's that time of life," she tried to say, but had to clear her throat and start again. "When girls are at that age, just before their bodies change, they are sometimes quite nervous. I was too."

"I hope she didn't hear me. Do you think she did?"

"Probably not. I think she was too concerned about her own troubles." As she spoke, Hilda could feel Franz relaxing.

He picked up where he had left off. The interruption had calmed him. "I shouldn't have started out that way, Hilda, because I don't mean to hurt you. I love you. These days have taught me more than ever what you mean to me. Maybe I shouldn't have said anything at all, but I thought if I told you about it, you might understand and help me with it. I do love you. You believe me, don't you?

"I'm not blaming you," he continued when she didn't answer, "because this feeling comes on me sometimes without any reason. Sometimes, on a beautiful morning when I'm peacefully milking the cows, I start to think about things—mostly you and religion—I don't know why I think about you and religion together, but I always do. Maybe it's because you have had peace in your own heart for so long that you don't remember what it's like not to have it. Maybe I'm jealous of you, and blame you for my own problem. Whatever it is, it's been bothering me for a long time. Maybe you didn't notice it… But of course, you did. How could you help but notice. Did you?"

"Yes, but ..." Hilda's dry mouth was saying, while she thought back on the years of doubt she had had in her own heart. *The doubt I never seriously expressed to him because I thought he wouldn't understand. The doubt I carried with me even into matrimony in spite of the love I felt for him. That same doubt was possibly the real reason for my not being happy in Montana. Possibly the real reason we lost our child. And losing our almost-finished home in the storm.*

She wondered that God had blessed them in so many ways in spite of her doubt. But she must answer him, and he was waiting with an apparent frantic patience beside her. "Yes, I noticed something," she answered, "but I had no idea. I thought perhaps you were working too hard, or that your becoming older made you more staid and less talkative."

"Maybe it *is* my age." His voice was low. "I forget sometimes that I'm not a boy any longer. But that still doesn't solve the problem of my salvation. What am I to do? I can't go to Reverend Schmidt—I know him too well as a human. You're the only one I can talk to, and I oughtn't because of what I've been doing to you."

"You've been good to me, Franz. Never have you not been good to me."

"Being good to someone isn't enough. You can be good to someone you've never seen."

"When, Franz—when did you stop loving me? What did I do?"

"Hilda, don't say that. That's not what I mean. You didn't do anything. And, Hilda, you misunderstand. I'm trying to tell you that your illness now has made me truly realize what you mean to me." His arm was trembling. "How selfish I've been. Now that there aren't so big troubles—we're able to make payments on the farm quite regularly—I have to find something. The greatest trouble I could ever have would be through losing you, or losing your love. That must be it. It must be. Hilda, sometimes I think about it a lot.

"Then I start wondering what it is to be a Christian, and whether that would make a difference. Sometimes I don't care at all, and don't feel worse for it. Then I see you, your complete faith, your ability to let that faith carry you and the children through things, and, as if it were a circle, I hold that faith against you. I guess my soul is sick."

When Franz, as though he was out of breath, stopped speaking, the stillness around them was absolute. In the next room, the old Russian clock ticked.

Almost fiercely, Hilda longed to throw her aching arms around his neck, to embrace him until it hurt him; but she wasn't strong enough. Instead, she lay there, trying not to move her limbs, and wondering whether words would come to her.

*　　　*　　　*

The illness, after it began to ease, left Hilda slowly. "I feel old," she said, laughing, though it wasn't a joke. "Inside, I want to run lightly and friskily, but my limbs don't get the message."

"Does it hurt?" Grace asked, reaching out as if wanting to help her walk, though Hilda didn't need help getting to the table.

"Not a pain," Hilda said, seeing the family gathered around the dining table, watching as if poised to jump up and help her too. But when she sat down into the chair they had pillowed for her, she sat heavily and clumsily, her body an overfilled flour sack with thin, loose leg muscles that could not bear her weight.

Grace's cooking had improved during Hilda's illness. The practice of being on her own, plus the honest criticism of her family who ate what she made, regardless of that criticism, had taught her much. Hilda enjoyed the meal because she was able to be at the table rather than in her awkward, half-up position in bed, and because returning health gave her an appetite. And because her daughter had prepared it with so much care.

Even the younger children were well behaved, as if she were company at the table. Franz sat across from her as always, and when she caught his eye, he smiled at her. *What does he think?* Hilda wondered, and wished they had finished their conversation that night she had been so sick. He had not brought it up again.

*   *   *

Now, that she was better, Hilda had time to think. *I wish Franz would talk with me. I don't want to be the one to raise the subject. He's referring only to trifles, my health, or subjects outside either of us.*

She did, finally, bring it up. "I'm sorry I went to sleep that night, the night you talked to me. I couldn't help it. It was the fever. I couldn't think."

"It doesn't matter," Franz said. "Often, problems aren't solved by talking about them, and this was one of those times. I shouldn't have bothered you about it."

"But it's in the open now. It's between us, Franz, and I'd like nothing between us."

Franz stirred. "Now, Hilda, it's not between us. I love you. I told you that even then. I was upset. Forget it."

I ought to thank him for that declaration. I never doubted his love before. It was expressed more in the air around us than in words. When that air has been denied with words, I feel I need more than words to neutralize it. I wish he'd say it again, that he loves me, but I can't ask it. Instead, she inquired, "Is your doubt concerning religion also settled?"

"No, Hilda, I expect it never will be. Sometimes, I don't care very much.

Maybe it will just resolve itself if I don't try to force it. Maybe my doubt is truer than the blind belief that many people have. Don't let it bother you. I won't let on to the children—you can answer their questions if they have any." He turned aside, as if to sleep.

"Franz, I can't just forget about it. It takes away some of my own assurance, because part of my Christian strength rests on your belief. The fact that you believe is my encouragement."

He turned back, completely awake. "Don't, Hilda. If you are confused, our confusion combined will be greater than twice what our separate problems would be."

"Maybe if we prayed, humbly, and sincerely," Hilda urged.

"How can I pray humbly," he asked, "when I don't feel humble? When I do try to pray, I can't. I can't think of anything to say. When I pray aloud for the benefit of the children, I'm only praying words. No, Hilda, I don't think it will come, except of itself. Maybe if we just forget about it, it will come to me some day. If not, it might not even matter. Maybe if I belonged to a Catholic church, let them do the work of figuring things out..."

"Is your doubt for Christianity in general, or for our church, Franz? Does something in our church set you against religion?" Franz yawned, but to Hilda it seemed deliberate. "Did something happen to set you against it?" she persisted.

"No, Hilda, I guess it's just church in general. The people in it. All human beings. Picking on little things, like Jane's white shoes—why should white shoes be sin and black ones not sin? I think people who find such little 'faults' are the real sinners, for presuming to know what is right. For being so conceited as to proclaim God's feelings about little things that are not worth his notice. It makes religion so material, and sometimes I can't see beyond it."

"I didn't hear about Jane's shoes. What happened?"

"When you were sick, she wore her new white shoes in church, and another girl stamped on them with her muddy shoes because 'it's a sin to have white shoes.' Jane came to me, crying, and I almost told her to go right back and stamp on that girl's foot. Then I realized that we wouldn't be any better. I want my girl to believe in Christian principles I don't carry out myself."

"Who was the other girl?"

"I don't know for sure, but I can guess. Maybe it's a good thing I don't know; I'd probably yell at her parents. Obviously, it's one of those who don't have anything better to do than to think about clothing. And we say we have a God we must worship 'in spirit.'"

Something inside Hilda wanted to cry, but something stronger told her not to. "Franz, Franz, we mustn't judge God by the humans who interpret him. *We* can still worship him 'in spirit' and let the people, who want to, believe they are worshipping him by conforming to certain material rules."

Franz responded, "Where is your missionary zeal? Doesn't the Bible say we are responsible, not only for our own souls, but those of our earthly brothers? Isn't that precisely *their* reason for admonishing us when we don't conform to their values? Who's right? They wear dark shoes, long stockings even in summer, and women don't cut their hair. But what does God care about outward appearance?"

"Maybe we're both right, Franz. Perhaps you and I ought to transplant some of our religion into the material life. It ought to be in all our life, oughtn't it?"

"Maybe we're both wrong."

"But, Franz, what then?" It was a condemnation, not a question. There might not be a "then." There would be nothing.

"I don't know. That's why I'm troubled. That's what leaves me empty. Since there is nothing to start with, I feel there is nothing to do but wait. Maybe God will reveal Himself and fill that emptiness, once I become still. There is that Bible verse, 'Be still and know that I am God.' Maybe that's what will happen. Or maybe I'll just get used to being empty."

"I wish I could help you—us," Hilda said. Suddenly, she could not remember what it was that had given her peace. Was it peace?

"It is something each person must work out for himself."

"That's not what the ministers say. 'No one can save himself' is what they say." Hilda wished she was a child again and could run to her parents for help. Authoritative help. The kind of help where she could ask, and they would answer, and she would believe and accept the answer they would give her. "If only Pa didn't live so very far away," she said. "He would know how to help us."

Franz brightened. "You know, he used to inspire me so. I was always fully carried by his sermons. I had 'blessed assurance' that song speaks about. By the way, I don't like any songs in that new songbook. They're not even Mennonite. We might as well join a tent-meeting Baptist church."

"I don't like that book either," Hilda said. "But the new songbook isn't the only thing that's different these days. I feel as if our church is less Mennonite than it was once. It seems different from what it was before we moved to Montana. Do you think it will drop the name 'Mennonite'?"

"Who knows? I guess we're old folks when we don't like change, like the switch from German to English, or from the old songs we learned when we were young."

Hilda went along with Franz's digression. "The words in the new songs don't mean anything. Have you ever read them over, just to see what they mean?"

"We always sing so fast that I can't think about them," he replied. "And when we're already singing fast, the song leader tells us to sing even faster. Anyhow, the words aren't worth singing slowly and thinking about. For example, 'Jesus is the sweetest name I know.' Why 'sweet'?"

"You know, Franz, some words in some German hymns aren't very deep either. But we learned them and got used to them when we were young. By association, they have come to mean something to us."

"Yes, there were those, but if we wanted to, we could choose to sing some that had meaning. Now we have no choice. They're all just emotion-exciting children's songs."

"That's what the church wanted. We voted, remember, and because the children aren't learning German any more, we decided to get an English songbook."

"But all English songbooks aren't like that, Hilda. We could have chosen a better one. We could have decided to get the same thoughtful hymns in English ... that's 'our church.' That's partly what I'm rebelling against. I hate to have our children learning that kind of religion. Singing those dumb songs at the top of their lungs because that's the way they're taught. I can't say anything, because if they carry my ideas to church, they'll be hounded by the others, the way they get their white shoes stepped on. Besides, I'm in a muddle myself. I know what I'm rebelling against, but I have no substitute to offer. If I should pass on how I feel, I would only pass on my own problems."

Hilda wondered, "Why do you suppose this new songbook is so popular in our church?"

"Because people don't want to have to think. They're all lazy and selfish."

"Now we're judging them."

Franz heaved a sigh. "Everybody does it."

"It wasn't this way when we were children, was it?"

"It may have been. I didn't think about it much when I was a child."

"Franz, I think it *was* different. It was in our home at least. Pa often talked religion with Ma, and we heard them. Pa was the leader of our church, and the leader flavors the beliefs of the church. It seems to be different now. I wish I had a chance to talk all this over with Pa."

"But Reverend Schmidt was brought up the same way we were. He's your relative, after all."

"But he isn't Pa, and each person is an individual."

"Do you know what you're saying? You're saying that our church is what our minister makes it, and essentially you're saying that to keep it from changing, we ought to have a dictator who keeps things just as they are. You're saying we ought to have a pope."

"Maybe we should, Franz. Maybe the Catholics are right."

"Just a minute ago, *I* was for Catholicism—to make it unnecessary for me to have to figure things out… Here's another group to think about: the Quakers. They don't have a preacher at all. It seems their meetings are silent, with someone maybe speaking up from time to time, in turns, but not even every Sunday. Some Sundays, the entire morning is silent. They listen to each other, and respect each other's views."

"It's something to think about. There are so many faiths, all believing they know the truth. If we were Muslim, I'd have to wear a veil—or is it a shroud?"

"A veil. A shroud is for covering dead bodies. But as a Muslim, I could marry more than one wife. Also as a Mormon."

"Would you like that?"

"Not really. Besides, I believe it's illegal in this country."

"Where would our religious freedom go," Hilda asked, "if we joined a church with hard and fast rules?"

"With it we'd get a certain peace. We wouldn't have the responsibility of making up our own minds. If we should then be wrong in anything, we wouldn't have to take the blame," Franz said. "I guess part of our Christian duty is to be responsible for our own thoughts."

"Really, however," Hilda said, "Pa wasn't the dictator in our church; yet, under his influence, things were done differently. If only we, even though we're just ordinary members, could be that kind of influence."

"What?" Franz reacted. "Just what kind of influence would we be when we don't even know our own minds? I guess I shouldn't speak for us both. I mean when *I* don't know my own mind."

"Franz, you just said that when we were children, the situation was better, so if we're convinced of that, we already know our own minds, to some extent."

"Maybe we wish we could keep things as they have been in a changing world. Isn't the only real religion the one that keeps up with the times?"

"Keeps up, yes," Hilda agreed, "but isn't 'carried along.' The Bible says, '*In* the world, but not *of* the world.'"

"Well," Franz said, after another yawn, "I'm going to sleep. I still think that time is the only thing that will give us our answer. If we try to figure out everything, we'll go crazy."

Hilda did not say anything; soon he was asleep. Perhaps his yawns had not been planned after all. She, herself, was far from sleep. Heavy hearted, she tried to think of a way to see her father, either to convince him to take the long trip from the West coast to visit them, or to find some way for her and Franz to go West. They had often spoken of taking a trip; the only one they had ever taken was the one to and from Montana, and since they both wanted to see the wonders of an ocean and would enjoy seeing her parents again, it would be a good thing if they could plan a trip to see them.

Her decision to try to talk Franz into arranging that kind of trip did not help Hilda fall sleep. Over and over, she thought of a time that she and Franz might have peace—that "blessed assurance" Franz had spoken of.

CHAPTER THIRTY-FIVE: 1941

A flatbed truck delivered their refrigerator. After they discussed what would be more needed—a refrigerator or lights for the chicken barn—Hilda and Franz decided that chickens would not need lights in summer. Perhaps, by winter, they'd have money for lights as well. They postponed the idea of a trip West.

The children scrambled to pour water into the freezer compartment to make ice cubes. Putting a pail into the refrigerator, Jane said, "We'll have to stop drinking so much milk. It takes up too much space."

"All the cream will have to be inside the refrigerator too," Franz reminded her.

"Can't the cream go on the cellar floor as it always has 'til now?"

"Why, Jane," Hilda said, "you know that's mostly why we got the refrigerator. The extra money we'll make selling sweet instead of sour cream is going to help pay for it. We'll have to pack things together a bit."

Hans kept checking to see whether ice in summer was frozen yet. Andrew buried his nose in "The Farmer," that had arrived in the day's mail. But when the cubes were solid, he also sucked on one as he said, "Ice in summer. Years ago, no one would have thought it possible, huh, Dad?"

Franz's reply was a wide grin.

Outside, the day was dreary, and when threatening clouds finally opened in the middle of the afternoon, Hilda decided to light the cook stove for warmth.

At that, Franz suggested, "Better turn off the refrigerator. It's cool enough for the food without it."

Believing him, still sucking on his ice cube, Hans begged, "Pa, don't. Please."

"I'm just teasing, Hans," Franz laughed, as he reached to hug his young son.

*   *   *

When the storm subsided, breaking enough to frame a red- and orange-streaked sunset, it left the air cool, and Franz said, "The rain is good, but I hope it will warm soon. The corn needs humid heat—not just moisture. If it does, I expect this year to produce a bumper crop."

He went on, "Little did we guess we'd be able to buy a refrigerator. When I think, just a few years ago we had to mortgage the animals in order to pay taxes, and that we couldn't even pay the interest on the farm mortgage, I can hardly believe we can buy this kind of luxury."

"Even so," Hilda answered him, "I'll feel a lot better when it's finally paid for. How long will it take?"

Franz pondered. "Our president is gradually drawing the country toward the war that's festering in Europe. He says he doesn't want war, but there's now a draft to increase the army. Our country is helping allies with war goods and food. Market prices are up; we now get two dollars for a bushel of corn. We're benefiting from war, something we abhor. Killing our people back in the old country will give us a refrigerator… By paying a little each month, with the good deal the hardware store gave us, we should have it paid for by Christmas. We'll have to pray for a good crop. And that we don't have to join the war in Europe."

Hilda realized he did not mean "pray" but had said it for the children to hear. She picked up on his comment about the draft. "There isn't a chance that *you* will be drafted, is there?"

"No, no, don't worry. As Mennonites, we are COs—conscientious objectors. Besides, they want young, unmarried men who don't have important work, like farming—boys, really, who can be influenced into going along with whatever the government plans in the name of patriotism."

*   *   *

After the older children had left for a band concert, and Hans was tucked into bed, Hilda again brought up the idea of a trip to the West coast. They had not mentioned it since the day they decided to buy the refrigerator.

Franz thought a bit before answering. "You know, I don't like to do anything before we know we can pay for it. We have no idea what crops we'll have this year until we've harvested. It's different for the hired worker: he gets his salary check no matter what."

"You've changed," Hilda remarked with a forced chuckle. "I can remember the time you mortgaged fifteen years of your life for a farm, and now you

225

won't do something like taking a trip unless you have the money in your hands."

"Why is that something to laugh about?" Franz asked. "I don't see that you have to rub in something that I learned very painfully."

Surprised to note that Franz took offense, Hilda quickly said, "I'm sorry. I didn't mean it that way. I agree with you. But we're not staying young, you know. Each year we get older, and each year it will be harder for us to enjoy long trips."

"One year won't make much difference in our ages," Franz answered. "It would make a difference in money, since a year from now we'll know what kind of crops we'll have this fall."

"And we'll have to see what kind of crop we have *next* fall," Hilda continued for him.

"Don't think I don't want to go," Franz said. "It isn't that at all."

"This would be a good year to go. My father's church is celebrating an anniversary of some kind. They'd be very pleased at our coming. Especially Muttah. She's quite convinced that we older children have never accepted her marriage to Pa."

"That," answered Franz with a sigh, "would be a good enough reason for me not to go. Everyone will be there, the place will be in an uproar. And in the plans and preparations and, later the cleaning up, we wouldn't get a decent chance to visit. Besides, we *haven't* accepted her. Maybe in our minds, but not in your—our—hearts."

"It's possible, if we went to see them, the acceptance in my heart—our hearts—would follow… But back to growing old: you *are* showing signs of aging," Hilda said, trying to keep her teasing light, "when you can't enjoy a celebration because of the excitement. Maybe you and I should just sit and fold our hands and wait for death to release us."

"All right, Hilda, I'll say this: I *am* getting older. Sometimes I *would* just as soon sit and fold my hands. Sometimes I want to sit and not have *anything* bother me—no children, no work, no thinking about the future. I want to lie down to sleep. To sleep as if I never have to wake up again."

"We all do at one time or other. I did even when I was a young girl."

"I mean it, Hilda. I'm tired." When Hilda looked at Franz's face after this word, she saw that it was worrying him and decided to say no more.

*   *   *

Some weeks later, he brought up the subject, saying with what sounded to Hilda as carelessness. "Let's go West, Hilda. What's the point of sitting, accumulating money, when we can't take it with us to the next life anyhow?"

226

"It's all right, Franz," she answered with the resignation she had been able to find. "You were right about a year not making any difference. We'll enjoy it more if we don't have to worry about eating the rest of the year. And we'll avoid the anniversary crowds."

"I went through the books, Hilda. We can go. Even if the crops aren't bumper crops, we can just let down on our mortgage payments a little. When we come back from the trip, we'll be refreshed enough to work harder. Andrew is old enough to sort of run things, and we can ask Emma and Anna to look in now and then to help Jane cook. And Hans can even help. Maybe Grace can come home on the weekend to give them a hand... We can go after the corn is too big to cultivate and before it's time to harvest the small grain. Let's go."

Then they learned that another couple was planning a trip West and would have room for them to ride along in their car. It would be cheaper than going by train, and less tiring, and more interesting because they could see more. They decided to go.

The children were not happy about it. "Can't we all go?" Hans asked. Behind him, Jane waited for their reply.

"We don't have that kind of money," Franz said. "You're young. You'll have your chance before too long." When the children realized the idea was hopeless, they said no more and helped with the work almost eagerly.

The weather was favorable. It rained when the earth became dry, and day after day they had sunshine. The corn grew. Two weeks before Independence Day, it was more than the proverbial knee high, which it should have been by July 4. It was dark green, and its stalks and long slender leaves were lush with moisture. In the garden, the vegetables were fruitful, weighed down with well-formed seed. Hilda and Jane worked, trying to can as much as possible. Jane could simply open some jars and serve fresh vegetables and fruits for their meals during those two weeks. She already knew how to fry eggs and meat.

But during one of the hot days, Franz came home from the field early in the afternoon. His face was coldly perspiring, and he went directly to bed. It was not like him, for he had wonderful resistance to any of the illnesses that periodically struck the family. The entire family could have the summer flu, but he, alone, would keep his appetite through it.

Hilda did not have time to go to him right away, as they were canning plum preserves that needed to be sealed immediately, and Jane's hands were not strong enough to seal the jars. When she saw him, he was crying, silently, from pain. "My back, he said. "I must have caught what you had."

"I'll heat water for the hot water bottle, and make you some tea."

But he did not drink. A half-hour later, she checked on him, felt his hot forehead. He was saying something that sounded like "goggley goober."

Behind her, Jane and Hans were giggling, repeating, "goggley goober."

"Go get some ice. Crush it and wrap it in a rag and bring it to me." They stood there, still giggling. "Go now!"

"When he gets better, can we tell him the silly things he said?" Jane asked her.

"Yes, but wait until he is much better and has his sense of humor back."

CHAPTER THIRTY-SIX: 1941

It was night, though not so very late by the slow, deliberate strikes of the old Russian clock, a wedding present. For years, it stood on its little carved shelf that had been re-hung from one wall to another when they moved: first to Montana, back to Minnesota, on to the new house, and then to this farm. When it was shifted as they rearranged furniture, the family would first look at the blank wall from which it had just been moved, to see what time it was. Once, in a playful mood, Franz hung a pocket watch at the empty wall, and they smiled as they looked where they expected the clock to be. That Franz.

He did that just two years ago. Jane had lost her last baby tooth. She had been quiet and afraid before, very still during the pulling, and very gay after. The tooth had been so loose it stood sideways. Funny how that child recovered from being a thin thing after surviving infantile paralysis, and after her baby teeth were pulled and that rotting poison no longer seeped into her body. She was now a healthy girl with always too-short skirts, one leg a little thinner than the other. Limped a little. Always would, probably. What a time that was, that polio. Worry on top of the financial worries.

It finished striking eleven. With its strange voice—not a pleasant bell but a sandpaper rasp as it raised its little hammer, poised it for a small moment, and then struck dully against a coiled wire spring that shivered noisily. Hilda thought it sounded like the voice of a chicken when it's contented: "Crahw, crahw." *Do chickens make their noises inhaling or exhaling? Do they sometimes inhale and sometimes exhale?*

Hilda turned in bed; it creaked. She gritted her teeth, wishing she could go to sleep before midnight so she'd be fresher in the morning. She wondered if the clock would be able to strike twelve times, run down as it was, or would it die trying? It might be interesting to find out. She could place a bet with herself about it—if she betted. Then again, as a Mennonite, she didn't bet.

Not even with herself. But what if she should go to sleep, or almost to sleep, and the clock woke her with another laboring attempt? Then she'd wait there, wondering whether it would be able to finish all twelve strikes. That happened before: just when she was drifting and floating and becoming nebulously and heavily a part of the featherbed, the clock struck, reminding her that she wasn't quite asleep.

She was wide awake, thinking how ever to go to sleep before it was again time to strike another hour. It would be better to get up now to wind the clock so it would not have to toil through those next twelve strikes.

It was only a few steps into the next room and up onto a chair. The clock wound easily; with the strong brisk turns she gave it, the works were quickly tightened.

"Ma, is everything all right?"

It was Jane, whom Franz had called an old woman for not being able to sleep. She oughtn't do that so easily—waking up at the slightest noise. She was standing there, clutching a corner of a blanket she was dragging after her from her bedroom. Her hair looked a little too thin; it was hanging raggedly down her back. Probably should wear it curled or fluffed. Her skin was good though, suntanned and unblemished.

But she must answer the child, waiting there. "Yes, everything's all right. Now go back to bed." The child obeyed and walked back into the darkness of her bedroom.

Hilda walked barefoot into her own room and climbed into her still-warm bed. It was a nice, wide bed, quite wide enough for two people. It was now the place she slept by herself, except when they doubled up for company. It didn't mess up anymore; now all she had to do mornings was to pull up the covers, and it would be made.

Once it had been funny to make it. She used to smile to herself as she started with the featherbed, fluffing it up first, and then putting on the sheets, remembering the previous night and how tender he could be, running his fingers along, up, and down her arm as she let it lie motionless near him. Remembering how she would sink slowly into nothing at his side, waking in the morning to make fire in the cold stove to cook oatmeal in time for the children to eat and catch the orange wooden school bus.

It had always been perpetual, something that would be every night. It was habitual, but it never was unthinking; it never lost spontaneity or warmth of feeling. It would always be without end of nights and sleep and delicious waking up, even when they were too tired even to talk much. Even that day he said he wasn't sure about things. He had been there. It had been painful, but he had been there.

Then it wasn't always. Hilda turned onto her other side, trying not to let herself think through that awful week again. The week he had morphed from a hale, healthy farmer into a feverish, hallucinating sick body: sometimes making sense and sometimes speaking gibberish that the children laughed at and declared they would tease him about later. After he recovered.

She had memorized that week. She had learned it with her heart and her body and her soul, and she would always be able to recite it minute by minute. Each time she was compelled from within to recite it, she would, at the same time, recite it as a whole, one wordless whole. A hole. As if it was a monstrous large and horrible painting that could be looked at with one glimpse seeing all, and with a long careful going over of each detail making up that whole—both views giving the same final message, in unison: dead … death.

*　　　*　　　*

They didn't call Dr. Fiddler at first. After all, she had gotten over her hexen schuss without a doctor. But by Sunday morning, when he was passing blood, she knew it was time. Franz had demurred, "We'll think about it." Dr. Fiddler's comment as the hearse/ambulance arrived to take him to the hospital was, "If we can get his kidneys to work …"[36]

That was an exhausting day. Grace came home, even though it was busy at work, to join her at Franz's bedside. Andrew bravely did all the chores, and the younger two—who knew what they were doing? Were they even old enough to understand what was happening?

In the evening, the nurses told them to go home to rest. So they did. At midnight, the neighbor—the one with the large turkey farm and a telephone, woke them, his car horn blaring. "Go to the hospital."

"Is Franz all right?"

"Just go."

Hilda woke all four children. Andrew drove. It seemed to be a very long ride. When they arrived, they knew. In fact, Hilda had known when she heard the car horn.

*　　　*　　　*

"Dead, death. Cold, dead, death." Just words, she repeated to herself. Words that didn't fit him, didn't belong to his smiling face that sometimes came into the house in mid afternoon to look at the clock because his pocket watch had stopped or because he wanted to see if she was baking cookies. Standing with his muddy feet in the hall so as not to track up the clean kitchen floor, and then peering around the door, hanging onto it to keep from falling from that awkward position. But smiling.

36　Penicillin might have cured his acute kidney failure, but it was not available for civilians until about 1945.

Dead. She did not say the word aloud; it was not necessary to say it aloud when she could hear it as well as if it was said aloud. She lay still in bed, aching to move, to run outside to scream at the silent trees, the barn squatted there across the yard, the pasture behind it, and the acres of healthy corn plants standing beyond the pasture. The corn he had planted. And cultivated. Aching, knowing that if she ran to scream, she would wake the children, and come back with her throat scratchy, her feet wet and cold, and with that same heavy dullness inside her belly.

Thinking, perhaps if she ran to the *middle* of the cornfield, the corn he had planted and was proud of, that had grown and now promised a bumper crop while he was dead—perhaps no one would hear her. Perhaps if she could scream and cry everything out of herself, or if she could vomit, the lump would break and leave her and let her sleep for a long time so she could wake up and sit in a chair and think about things as they were with the sun shining on them.

If only she hadn't touched him after he was dead. If she hadn't felt how inelastic his flesh was. How unresponsive, indifferent, cold. Clammy. Almost sticky.

If only they had finished that conversation about salvation. If only they had found peace in salvation—or if they could have found peace in emptiness. *Where is he now? In Heaven? Could he be? Could he be in Hell? What if he's at neither place? What if there is no place?*

The clock struck again. Merrily, with its new-rewound life. It quickly finished its twelve strikes, which made it again an hour until it would strike again. Hilda got up to put another blanket on her bed. The night was cool, and there was no one to help keep the bed warm. She yawned widely and hoped her stimulated mind would soon let her fall sleep.

Then she heard the sound of singing just outside her window. It was a group from church. How could they know she would be awake? How could they know they were singing a hymn she had always questioned? Actually, disliked. "Blessed assurance, Jesus is mine. Oh what a foretaste of glory divine." They sang all four stanzas. She hugged her arms around herself and felt as if she was in their embrace. It felt more like a clinch than an embrace. She pulled away in her bed, as if to get out of their grip.

But then she got out of bed, lifted the bedroom window, and called out to them, "Thank you." How *could* they know, anyhow?

*   *   *

Morning was brought to Hilda by Hans, the smallest one with his soft face that smiled gap-toothed as he stood next to her bed. She hugged the child and saw over his shoulder, Jane just standing and looking. *What do they think of, those children?* Hilda got out of bed, telling them both to crawl under the covers until she could light the oven and get the chill out of the air, and heard them soon giggling as they tickled each other with their cold toes.

She pulled up the kitchen window to see what the morning brought. The rosebush was in bloom. A nearby robin was singing lustily, echoed by another robin from a tree outside the fence. *How can the sky be so blue?* She wanted to shout, *How can the birds sing "cheerily, cheerily" when my Franz is dead?*

How inappropriate it is! The rain on the burial was as it should be. I'm glad it shrank and faded my good dress—ruined it. I never want to wear it again.

She looked beyond the farmyard. The tractor stood parked where it always was. From somewhere, out of sight, came the bawling of the calf, and an answering lower-pitched moo, probably its mother. Andrew's lambs were bleating. All was as it was. Same as yesterday. Same as last week. Same as when Franz was still alive—healthy. Not dead.

Hilda forced herself to turn away, back to the kitchen, shook the ashes from the grates, put in some dry corncobs, and poured on a few drops of kerosene.

It took only one match. Her thoughts continued, persistent: *What do the children think now? They all cried at the funeral, and before it, and afterward too, even the youngest. Andrew cried too, poor boy; all boys should have fathers, as all girls should have mothers. And Grace, fainting there in the hospital. She was the only one who fainted. She's an adult, has deeper understanding than the little ones. She hasn't experienced much death before. She's a nurse who will see death often. They say it's different to see the death of someone who is just a sick body, so unlike experiencing the death of one's own father.*

Breakfast was oatmeal, as usual. Luckily, the children liked it. Franz had eaten it only because he was convinced it was good for him. They were all up early. Even Andrew, who asked, as soon as he was in the room, "Ma, did you wind the clock last night?"

So he had heard too. "As a matter of fact, yes, I did. You heard me?" He would have heard too, if she had run out into the cornfield.

"Yes, I almost woke up enough to laugh." The other children laughed too, thinking of Ma getting up at night to wind a clock. It was good that they could laugh. Children must not mourn.

She pulled out the Bible. She had not allowed a break in their custom of reading it each morning—even though they had skipped it now and then. It was hard to read passages she remembered reading with Franz, and Hilda was sorry she had not passed over Job. But she tried to keep insulation between her feelings and her mind, numbing it. This week they read from Job: "Then Satan answered the Lord, and said, 'doth Job fear God for naught? Hast not Thou made an hedge about him and about his house, and about all that he hath on every side? Thou hast blessed the work of his hands and his substance is increased in the land. But put forth Thine hand now, and touch all that he hath, and he will curse Thee to Thy face.' And the Lord said unto Satan, 'Behold, all that he hath is in thy power, only upon himself put not forth thy hand.' So Satan went forth from the presence of the Lord.

"What do you think about the story?" Hilda asked, looking first at Grace and then at Andrew. Grace made a half smile and said, very softly, "It's a good story." Andrew put in, "Sounds as if the Lord had a job to do." "I think it's scary," was Jane's comment. "Ya, spooky," Hans added.

Hilda thought that was the best discussion they had ever had about a morning-devotion Bible passage. "Let us pray," she said. *I can't put into words what I actually feel. The children won't know, and it wouldn't help them to know that I don't feel any security that I'm trying to give them. I can't remember Pa expressing his emotions in his prayers after Ma died—at that time, I thought he felt nothing, or at least not as much as I felt. I hope that, some day, my children will understand me.*

"Dear God, my Father, You are the heavenly Father for my children who have no earthly father. Keep us, guide us this new day." While she spoke the words, she wondered if the children listened. If they did, did they understand the words, and if they understood, did they think about the words and get from them the direction they would need for the day? In her mind, she added, *Keep Satan from putting forth his hand on them.*

*　　　*　　　*

Somehow, the harvesting was done. Before she had even begun to worry about how she would manage the cutting and threshing of the grain, or the picking of the corn, people came to help. Before she even got past her immediate frantic grief, before she could get her mind off the now, or yesterday. They came—neighbors, relatives, members of their church—the men with their hayracks and teams, their pitchforks and shovels. One hauled trailer-loads of grain to the grain elevator in town. The women came too, bringing fresh tvaybak, jam, cheese, sausage, whole roasted chickens, and freshly baked apple pies. They stayed to help do the dishes and to package the leftovers if there were any, and they promised to come again until the work was done.

The harvest turned out to be the best ever. Market prices were also the best ever, the result of the country's imminent entrance into the war. Hilda's gratitude was bittersweet: why couldn't Franz have lived to see his bountiful harvest? Why couldn't he garner the profits, celebrate the good times with her? Why couldn't they both take that trip West? Now, instead, her parents had come for the funeral, and she hadn't gotten around to that talk with Pa that she so wished for, since talk had only been about Franz's last week, and about some practical plans that had to be made regarding the probate.

*   *   *

On schedule in September, school started; Jane and Hans advanced to a grade higher than last year. Grace returned to her hospital job, as she had planned. Andrew conscientiously worked the farm, seemingly not interested in continuing his education after high school. Everything moved along normally. Only Franz wasn't there.

"What should we have in our sandwiches today?" Every day that question. Jane made her and Hans's lunches for school each day. "Make some pork and bean sandwiches. Use the leftover beans and smash them with a fork. It'll be good on the fresh whole-wheat bread. And, first, put the butter in the oven for a while. It's too hard. We shouldn't have put it into the refrigerator. Oh, and don't forget apples. We still have some in the cellar." Hilda remembered an evening, before they had electric lights, when the children were afraid to go to the cellar for apples by themselves.

Andrew was waiting with his pail for her to go milking with him. After many years of not milking, except during the busy harvest seasons, Hilda now resumed, perhaps as much to get out of the warm air of the house as to help. After all, if it got to be too much work for her, they could sell some of the cows.

The cows had been inside the barn all night. The barn smelled of their breaths and of the manure that had filled the gutters at night. Andrew was shoveling it into a wheelbarrow, a new one Franz had bought last winter but was now so coated that its green paint was hardly visible. The cows reached toward her as she gave them each a pan-full of ground mash, and then immediately plunged their blunt noses into it, blowing its dust with their large nostrils, and looking up with the powder of it sticking to the moistness of their noses and the hair around their noses. In front of them, the beams were covered with rime, and the cobwebs, hanging raggedly, were also beaded. There were no spiders sitting on those cobwebs.

Silently, Andrew began to milk. With his strong, young hands, hard as most college boys' were not, he was squirting warm fresh milk into his pail, causing it to make foam that he would later give to the cats. He did not openly love the cats as the girls did, but he never forgot to give them their share of milk.

This would be a good time for them to talk. Hilda wondered what they should talk about, knowing that for him to stay within himself was not good, knowing in his mind were many complicated questions she would not be able to answer but that would be better asked, even of her, than unasked. Knowing that, she was unable to think of anything that would not sound as if she was prying. *What questions does a growing boy have that his* mother *can deal with? That he needs a* father *for?*

One cat—Hilda couldn't remember what the children had named her—came meowing along and sat opposite the gutter. She squirted some milk at her, the cat catching the stream expertly with its open mouth and licking up the milk that she spilled on its fur. She was immediately sorry. It was dangerous, as she had so often told the children, because the cat knew no better and would come rubbing against the feet of the cow and probably startle the cow. Be stepped on. She remembered how a screaming cat tried to bite the horny heel of a cow that was insensitively standing on the tip of the cat's tail, and how Hilda had had to kick the cow before it moved its foot, letting the cat run angrily away to lick the sore tip.

When they finished milking, Hilda walked ahead into the house, carrying two pails of foamy milk while Andrew let the cows out for some water that was already coated with a thin layer of ice. It was going to be a cloudy day; the wind was now blowing last week's snow around, snow it hadn't yet somewhere managed to anchor down. It would soon have new snow to blow.

She checked over the lunches Jane had packed. Secretly, she slipped a piece of candy into each lunch box; candy they didn't know she had. After they're gone, she decided, she would write a letter to Grace, who was bravely working hard and who had tried to pretend that she was not homesick. Often, after writing Grace, Hilda felt herself almost believing some of the words of comfort she wrote her.

CHAPTER THIRTY-SEVEN: 1945

"The farm is paid for," Hans shouted, as if he was telling it for the first time.

On the day they always said they would celebrate, Grace came home. She was wearing high heels, and her dress was short—in the latest fashion—though modest. She had cut her hair and curled it. It was clear to Hilda that her hospital job in the Twin Cities supported her well enough that she could dress stylishly and still put aside money in case Andrew or Jane should decide to go to college. Or Hans, some day.

They made a game of it. In a little while, after they had seemingly forgotten about it, Jane said, "Hans, do you know what?"

Hans answered, acting innocent, "No, what?"

And Jane shouted, again as if for the first time, "No more mortgage!" Then they both laughed wildly.

Hilda laughed with them at their game. "So what?" she said. "Why should that make you so happy?"

Jane, who looked older than she was and could easily pass for a girl of eighteen, said, "Nothing. It's just that the farm is paid for!"

"So," Andrew said, "now we can have everything we couldn't have because we had to save for the farm. Now you can't say 'no' any more when we want something."

They sat down to dinner, all of them today—without Franz, of course—and jointly recited their customary mealtime prayer: "*Komm Herr Jesu, sei du unser Gast; und segne was du uns geschenket hast.*[37] Amen." Food was special: fried pork chops with canned applesauce, boiled potatoes with gravy, fresh green beans, and a few new carrots. Skimmed milk to drink. To celebrate: chocolate cake for dessert. Only the chocolate and cake flour had not come

---

37   Come Lord Jesus, be our guest and bless what you have given us.

from—now—*their* farm. Still, who knew?—perhaps the cake flour had ultimately originated from their farm also.

Hilda thought of the many times she had had to say "no." When Franz lived, he had to do it, and she sometimes wondered whether he wasn't being a little too frugal. Always he said, "The mortgage. When that's paid for, we can do things, but if we let it go and lose the farm, we'll end up with nothing." After his death, and she had had to learn about writing checks, figuring interest, and budgeting grocery money, she had been forced to hold back, trying to be as fair as possible, apportioning money equally to the children, encouraging them to do as much for themselves as they could.

They raised chickens; Hans treated his as pets, while Jane hated them and their ways, caring for them only for the money she would get when she sold them. Andrew raised lambs, both as a project he started for the Future Farmers class before graduation from school, and because he liked them. He was careful not to name them, but he also did not offer them as meat for their table. The family never tasted sheep meat. The other animals—laying hens, pigs, cows, and one horse, Prince—were simply part of the farm, shared by the family like the machinery, the grain they harvested, and the trees that sheltered the buildings.

"We mustn't think," Hilda told them, "because we don't have the big mortgage any more, that we can start squandering our money. We'll have to continue being careful, to save a little for emergencies. If something unexpected should come up, we won't have hard times coming on us. What's more, don't forget that as Mennonites, our living should be simple. Being able to buy things we don't really need doesn't mean we should." She didn't look at Grace and her curls as she said it.

After they ate their meal, trying to keep a degree of thankfulness to God for their good fortune, Grace offered to do the dishes. "Of course," she added, "I won't mind if Jane offers to help me."

"Oh, you," Jane said, "that's nothing special. I have to do it all the time anyhow." She offered a loud sigh, making sure the boys heard her. "Sometimes I wish I was a boy. They never have to do it." She was right. Andrew had settled himself with the newspaper, after Hans took the funny section and was stretched out on the floor. Both of the boys ignored them, though to Hilda it was obvious that they were enjoying their positions.

"Sometime," Grace said, more loudly than necessary, "they'll say they *want* to help, as a special favor, just to show us that they appreciate all the times we've done it for them." But the boys chose to snub the psychology Grace was trying to use. Giving up, Grace turned to her mother. "Ma, why don't you take your nap? We'll finish up, and we'll even try to be quiet."

Now I am getting old, Hilda thought. *When my children tell me to take a nap.* She settled into the featherbed she had placed over the new innerspring mattress that her children had bought for her last Christmas, mainly with Grace's money, she suspected.

She still often thought of herself as *married, to Franz—no, a widow. A widowed mother of fatherless children. It was four years since he became sick so suddenly. And died.* But in those four years, she had not been able to get used to being a widow. Even at the meal today, she had not felt complete. It would have meant more to Franz than to any of them to celebrate having the farm paid for. *If only he had been able to live those days with us: the days of paying off the farm. The better times that made it possible for us to make larger payments— the better crops and the better prices. Of course, he didn't have to experience the war. Except the war hasn't touched us much anyhow—so far. Hans is too young, and Andrew is doing the necessary farm work, so he doesn't have to declare himself a pacifist, a conscientious objector to war.*

I still cannot believe in my heart that I will never see my Franz again. Surely one of these days he will come walking through the door to see what time it is, or to eat with the family. Sometimes, she caught sight of him out of the corner of her eye—but he disappeared when she turned to look directly at him. When she imagined him sleeping at her side in their bed, she refrained from reaching toward him, *in case he was there. Or not.* Always she would fall asleep as if that was a sort of escape for her.

Sometimes she wondered what she would do if he actually did return. *Would I act as if his being here was natural—normal, everyday? Would I be startled? Would I scold him for having been away?... I'm still doing everything as if Franz was still here. Still at my side; or rather, I at his side. My decisions are always what I think Franz would agree with. Sometimes my decisions aren't at all what I'd like to do; they're based on what I think Franz would have wanted. Even if I don't agree. If he was here, I'd argue against him.*

She got to the point in her thinking where she remembered his glowing health, the perfection of his body, but she could not think of his short illness that had left them all so helpless. *If only Grace had been able to do something, but she was only a nurse—not a doctor—and she said even now that at the time there was nothing that could save him. If he had gotten sick a few years later, when penicillin was available, there would have been hope. The fact was, he got sick when he did.*

To think of herself as a widow was to think of herself as being an extra person. *I'm a fifth wheel on a four-wheel buggy. A person hard to seat at the table, or hard to invite to people's homes because the man of the house would have no one to visit with. Or hard to place in a procession like a funeral when mourners walk two by two into the church. With whom should I walk? They sometimes have me walking by myself, sometimes with other widows. Or, when I want to go to* something, I can't ride like other wives with their husbands, but with my children, who should be, and would like to be, with others their own ages.

Ya, I'm a widow. That's for sure.

I wonder if the children, or anyone else, know about Albrecht. What was he thinking, coming to call on me so soon after Franz died? Why, it had only been six months. Oh, I know, my pa remarried so soon after Ma died. I will never forget how I felt about that. I know those times were different—but, all the same. She shuddered. *What an ugly man Albrecht is too. Smells of rotten potatoes. But even if he were handsome and smelled like apple blossoms, I can't imagine myself with any man other than Franz. Not ever.*

So, if I don't want the children to truck me around, I should learn to drive the Dodge. It can't be harder than controlling spirited horses. I did that well enough. Hilda remembered the one time she tried to learn to drive and took the car out to the stubble field. It bolted, choked, and dashed around in such unreasonable manner that she felt it was some living thing. She had stopped after a short time, grimly determined that she would try again and again until she had tamed it. But when she reached home and found the children lined up behind the barn watching and smiling, she declared, in defiance, that she would never touch it again. They encouraged her, saying she could surely learn to drive it, but she was not convinced enough herself, and she did not want to lay herself open to more of their concern.

Maybe I will, after all, she now decided. *Then the children can do their own things.*

Andrew, for example. He doesn't date like his school friends do. I don't know that he's had any dates at all. Of course, there's lots of time. Lots of the young fellows pair off much too young. Why, even Grace isn't married yet, and she's five years older than Andrew.

But she's a bit old. She did have callers when she was in high school. Franz didn't like her beaus, but instead of saying so outright, he imitated something about them. That was enough to convince Grace not to see them again. But, surely by now, she should have found someone.

I wish Grace had found work closer to home. If she did find a young man, he would likely not be of our own people. Franz and I were able to share our beliefs. Our questionings. We didn't have to compromise, for one of us to give up a strong faith in, say, Catholicism or Methodism. As a Mennonite, I ought to feel concern at my daughter's possibly leaving the Mennonite church; yet I don't feel anything more than a vague regret. It's more at Grace's settling so far from me that bothers me.

Whenever Hilda came to thinking about her church, she was also reminded of Franz's comments just a few months before he died. *He never spoke of finding a solution to his dilemma. He never again mentioned his confusion concerning his love of me. That didn't bother me after a while because he showed a love that didn't need expression. When he lay dying, between spells of delirium, he showed great concern for me and the children.*

He didn't mention his faith, or lack of faith. To be sure, when Reverend Schmidt went to speak with him that morning of his death, he asked outright whether Franz was ready to meet God, whether he was saved. Franz answered without hesitation that he was ready. But Franz might not have wished to discuss that with the minister even then. He probably didn't think he was going to die...

Once, Hilda shared her worries with Grace, although it was nothing like confiding in a husband. Grace told her quietly, "I have a Catholic friend who suggested that I have a mass said for my father. I did follow through. Sometimes when I walk by a Catholic church, I light a candle for him. I respect their ideas and find comfort in some of them." When Hilda heard that, to her surprise, she found comfort also.

It was during that conversation that Hilda opened up a memory that had sat heavy in her heart since the Christmas Grace asked for a large pretty doll to set on her bed. Hilda could not forget the sad look on Grace's face when she saw she hadn't received it. Now, when she brought up her regret, Grace only shrugged and said, "It's not important. Forget it. I have."

Hilda dozed off. When she woke, all that was left was a vague heaviness in her heart, and she was getting used to that heaviness. She did not expect it ever to leave her. She felt that she was learning to live with it, and even to enjoy certain aspects of life in spite of it.

CHAPTER THIRTY-EIGHT: 1947

"Read it to me," Hilda said, still at the table. "Let's hear what Jane's written"—her first letter home from orientation events at college—"so we can both know what's in it."

Andrew read. "*We had an all-school party last night, to get acquainted. We wore different-colored nametags to show which group we were in. We went around reading names on each other's tags. I met lots of nice kids, and one of them even asked me for a date already. We're going to a show Saturday night. Everyone goes to shows here …*"

Andrew read on. Hilda usually reread letters several times anyhow, to understand better, and to stretch out her pleasure from their exchange. Now she allowed her mind to wander: *At least they're not two-faced, my children. That's worth more to me than if they didn't go to movies at all. Of course, I'd rather they never went to them… Lots of young people who go to picture shows keep it from their parents.*

Hilda hadn't ever read the books that now were made into movies. She read English fairly well, for, though she had not gone to an English school, she had learned to read as she helped her children through their first primers. *I don't know what movies are like, or why books are acceptable and movies are not.*

Books the children read nowadays are a little too involved, she decided. *I ought to have kept up with them, but there's been so much work, and I had to help the younger ones as they learned the basics too. I'm glad the children have learned enough German to be able to read my letters to them. I know enough English so I can read their letters back.*

But the movies. What would Franz say to a letter casually mentioning that his daughter was going to the movies? Before he died, the idea didn't come up. The children were all at home, and none of their friends attended, so they never asked to go. Besides, they said the movies here in Mound Lake aren't any good. They're second rate because the movie house, not supported by most of the Mennonites, can't afford better ones... How do they know that? I wonder.

Six years ago, Franz was so against giving Grace a doll that looked like a movie star. Who knows—he might not care if he was still alive, Hilda finally decided. *Yet I don't know if he would have approved of Jane's attending an Episcopal college in the first place. He didn't mind Grace's choice of the state-supported university, because, while it wasn't actively keeping her securely within the Mennonite church, at least it wasn't luring her from it.*

The school counselor had told Jane that the college she picked is a good school. "Better than any of our own Mennonite colleges," Jane told her. What's more, they awarded her a scholarship that had to do with wanting a diverse student body. Jane, being Mennonite and speaking Low German, somehow made the college "diverse."

So, Hilda decided, *I'm all right with Jane's decision. I hope I'm all right. Besides, if the children haven't achieved faith by the time they're college age, they aren't likely to learn it in college. Sometimes, too, it's good to learn about other religions, if only to compare the advantages of one's own. But Episcopal—it is so like the Catholics; at least that's what I've heard. They baptize babies.*

Andrew finished reading the letter. He folded it, pushed it back through the opened end of the envelope and, without comment, began to read the newspaper. Hilda rose to do the dishes. There wasn't much to wash at noon: only hers and Andrew's. They usually ate a small lunch, saving the big meal for evening when Hans was home from school.

"What do you think about it?" Hilda forgot that Andrew was reading.

"What do I think about what?" Andrew didn't take his eyes off the paper.

"About Jane going to the movies. I guess I always knew that she went—Grace too—but I never could decide exactly how to think about it."

"Oh, I guess it doesn't really matter." Was Andrew just pretending to read?

"If I knew what they were like, I could probably say whether it was right or wrong to go, but I don't know what movies are like. I suppose I'll never know, because the world would set itself on end if I went to find out for myself."

Andrew did not respond.

"Do you know what they're like, Andrew?"

"I've never gone," he replied, and Hilda believed him because he had never really been out of town, and she knew he wouldn't go to the local cinema. "I guess it's all right. Grace says they're not bad. And she's careful."

When Hilda finished the dishes, she took a nap, a habit she had acquired, though sometimes she wasn't sure whether she did it to be alone to think or if she needed the rest. Usually she slept for a few moments and always she felt refreshed afterward.

When she rose, Andrew had gone outside to do necessary chores. Though by the calendar it was autumn, snow had not yet fallen, and the cattle were mostly outside, needing just a minimum of feed since they were cleaning up the corn that the picker had missed. Work was much easier now than it would be when the snows came, and it seemed almost as if Andrew was bored by it.

The letter lay where he had put it. Hilda picked it up and read through it carefully, wishing Jane would be more orderly with her handwriting. Or write more details. One paragraph was all she said about the movies, or about dates. She did not describe the fellow. Hilda decided to write her about that, for although she had faith in Jane's good judgment in her choice of friends, mostly, she wanted her to know she was concerned. Jane did not seem to take him very seriously, a fact that made Hilda both glad and sorry. Glad because he would undoubtedly be Episcopal, and she hoped that Jane would think twice before she married someone from another faith. Not that other faiths weren't good.

But she was sorry because she could not get used to the idea of a girl dating various boys. It might make her shallow, never taking boys seriously, and perhaps even hurting someone who might be interested in her. Hilda resolved to say something about that too, that Jane should not want to be hurt, nor should she want to hurt anyone else.

That thought nagged Hilda: in high school, and during the summer before leaving for college, Jane spent a lot of time with a young man named Robert something-or-other. He seemed pleasant, polite, decent. What was their relationship now? Did she just drop him? Was she a butterfly, flitting from boy to boy?

Jane described her classes in some detail and expressed wonder at the size of the assignments when she compared them with the work they had had to do in high school. She wrote that she was coming home in a couple of weeks. *I hope Robert knows she's coming … I hope Jane and Robert will fall in love and marry. It would be so much better for the youngsters to stay where they are at home… I know it's selfish to want to have them near me, and I know it's inevitable that they'll live their own lives…*

What a strange wish I had at one time, hoping one of my children should be a missionary. With all my heart, I'm happy that they aren't … yet I feel guilty about that… Before Grace was born, I considered that she would go into missions. It could still happen—missionary nurses are needed—but it doesn't seem likely. For now, Grace even mentioned that she was considering joining the Women's Army Nurse Corps. She hasn't asked for advice, and I know I can't give it to her.

As for Andrew, what if he wanted to go on to college? He's never seemed to consider it, and I haven't brought it up. Or have I...? I should have, I know; but he graduated from high school so soon after Franz died, and it was easier just to let him keep on doing the farm work. Surely, he would have told me if he didn't want to be a farmer all his life. He isn't shy, not with me—but he does seem shy with strangers. How is he with girls? I've never seen him with girls. Or have I?

Why did God give me children who grow so much beyond me and, to top that, require me to rear them by myself? Other people know how to lead their children, telling them what to do, expecting the children to do such-and-such, and actually see them obeying. Other parents succeed; they rear healthy and contented children, perhaps with fewer problems than my own.

I can think of only a few times that I tried to exercise authority, since my children are grown, and those few times they didn't only disobey, they convinced me they were right in their choices. Otherwise, they tell me their considerations and, when they've decided, they inform me.

All I can do is tell them I pray that their choices will be wise ones. Even when they talk with me about a problem, I find I don't know enough about it to discuss it. It scares me. How did I fail to keep up with them?

It's all happened since Franz died. When he was alive, they were still children, and their problems were those of eating ice cubes from the new refrigerator, of giggling in church programs, of naming the new batch of kittens. Now they don't go to the children's programs any more, and when they name the kittens, they take names from their textbooks, names like "Leukemia—Luke for short," or "Romeo."

*　　　*　　　*

When, a some weeks later, Jane came home for a visit, she had short hair. "How do you like it, Ma?" she asked, turning in a large circle.

"It's all right," Hilda said, though it bothered her, for she had always admired her daughter's hair. It was like Franz's—dark and shining with health. But she could not keep herself from asking, "Why did you cut it?"

"Oh, it was shaggy, and all the other girls have short hair too. My roommate cut it for me."

"You mean no one has long hair? Were you the only girl?"

"No—oh, there are some who never change their hair, but most of the girls wear theirs short. Besides, Ma, you didn't say anything about Grace cutting her hair."

"You don't know what I said to Grace privately, Jane. Now, I'm talking to you, not Grace. Remember, women's hair is their 'crowning glory,' according to the Bible."

"You sound as if you wanted me to be vain of my hair, Ma. Besides, don't feel too bad—it'll grow. It grows fast, especially when it's cut."

"Of course," Hilda said, since there wasn't anything to do about it now. "Still, I'm sorry it's gone. Must you be like the other girls there?"

*   *   *

Andrew came quietly in from chores. They had reduced the herds so Hilda would not have to help during the winter, except for the chickens that she considered hers. He seemed not to know what to talk about, finally teasing Jane lamely, "Does Robert know you're home?"

Jane snorted, "That creep? If he does, it isn't because I told him."

"That's a surprise, Jane," Hilda said, looking up from her crocheting. "I thought you liked him."

"I did, but I didn't know any better," Jane answered. "You know, that's what happens to people who always stay at home and never realize that the world is bigger than their home town."

"Well, thanks," Andrew replied. "I guess I know what class I belong to."

"Oh, I didn't mean that, but you'll have to admit it wouldn't hurt you to get around a little too."

"Look, Jane." Andrew stood, ready to go to his room. Hilda saw that his face had tightened. "You've been gone almost three whole months. My, what a lot you've learned! I'm so glad you even talk to me. I think I'll tell Robert that he'd better come here on his hands and knees if he wants to be lucky enough to talk to you." When he left the room, he closed the door behind him.

"Well, I wonder what's eating him?" Jane said. "Is he upset about something?"

"He works hard," Hilda told her daughter. "I think we should all appreciate that if it wasn't for him, we wouldn't be able to keep the farm. If we couldn't do that, we wouldn't be able to do a lot of things."

"That's too bad for him, though. Don't you think so, Ma? He should have the chance to go to college just as I do."

"There are a lot of things in life besides college, Jane. I—and your father—didn't have the chance even to finish grade school."

"I know that. But, still, things are different now. And, really, there's such a difference between people who get around a little and the ones who stay at home all the time."

If only Franz were here. He would have known how to talk to our daughter. But Hilda thought of something her father often said when she was young:

246

"It's the end result that counts. Often you can take several different roads to the same destination. Sometimes the longer ones are more interesting."

Jane pulled out a textbook she had brought home. "Ma, you just don't understand what I mean."

"I'm sorry, Jane; maybe I don't, but I try. Maybe you aren't trying to understand us here at home."

Jane did not answer but seemed to be reading.

Hilda wondered whether Jane had changed, or had the absence from each other made them more aware? She wondered about it a while. *Would it have been better to send her to a Mennonite school, or are all colleges alike?*

It was awkward to stop the conversation there. Finally she thought of something. "Are you studying for a test?"

"Yes, biology." She would have kept on reading, or pretending to read, if the telephone hadn't rung. "You answer, Ma; it can't be for me anyhow. And if it's Robert, just tell him I'm not home."

It was Robert. Hilda did not lie. "Yes, I'll call her."

Jane was angry. "Ma, why did you tell him—now it'll only be embarrassing."

"I'm not going to lie for you, daughter. You can fight your own fights, and if you don't want to see him, the kindest thing to do is to tell him so."

"Oh, Ma, that sort of thing just isn't done. It would hurt his feelings." But she answered the telephone, telling him she was terribly sorry but she was too busy because she had to study for a big important test Monday. That she really ought not to have come home at all but had because she thought she might get more studying done where it was quiet.

In the end, after she had hung up, she told Hilda, "Well, I guess he's going to come over for a little while anyhow. It makes me mad—all that waste of time, and I have to pretend to enjoy myself."

"Jane, what would you do if you knew someone was treating you that way, and only went out with you because he didn't know how to get out of it? Wouldn't you rather be told that right out, even if it hurt you a little bit, than to be fooled along, and maybe be made a fool of?"

"Ma, you can't tell a fellow, 'No, I don't want to go with you because you bore me.'"

"But you could say, 'I'm sorry, I think we waste each other's time going out, because there is a great difference between us, and between our interests.' That's not saying you're better than he is, because you're not. No one is."

"Well, maybe I'll tell him tonight. But I hate it. I hate to waste a weekend at home just telling someone I don't want to go out with him. I could have written it in a letter. It's easier anyhow. I can think about how I want to say it."

"And not give him a chance to talk?"

"Oh, he can talk; he can always write back."

"Well," Hilda said, "I'm glad you're going to talk with him. Where are you going?"

"We aren't going anywhere. There isn't time. He asked for a few minutes, and that's all he's getting."

"There's a basketball game tonight. Hans is playing. Have you seen him play yet?"

"Sure, I saw him last year, all the time."

"But, you haven't seen him since he's on the first five. He's very much better."

"Ma, how do you know? You never go."

"But I hear."

"Sure, he probably said so—he's that conceited."

*   *   *

Jane had to change her clothes, but before she was ready, Robert arrived. Smiling, he was his usual courteous self, and Hilda liked him. He reminded her of Franz when he was her beau, but she tried not to think of that as a reason for wanting her daughter to like him. She watched them go, he being genuinely glad to see Jane, and Jane casting back to her a kind of weary glance. Hilda wondered whether she had learned that from the dormitory girls. Robert didn't seem to notice.

It was late when they came home. Hans was already in, and he usually stayed out late after games. To make sure that it was Robert and Jane, Hilda went to the window. They were in his car, and Jane was in his arms.

Wide awake, Hilda wished she had not gone to the window. She did not want to spy on her children, though she knew she ought to know what they did and how they lived. Long after Jane came tiptoeing into the house, she could not go to sleep, wishing that Franz was there in bed with her, that he had his arms around her. It meant he loved her.

Next morning, when they were all up and had eaten their breakfasts singly, Hans, who had achieved the build of a tall basketball player, was the only one who dared to talk to Jane about the previous evening. "Say, what's the big idea," he said through the shaving foam around his mouth, "of going out for a big evening and not coming to see me play?"

"Huh," Jane shrugged. "There are other things to do in this world than to see a little brother play."

"Children," Hilda started to say, and then realized they were talking in fun. The realization bothered her. It was not a comfortable kind of fun. She couldn't learn to play that game.

Hans was walking over to Jane with some of the foam still on his face.

She squealed, enjoying it, but when he asked her, "What, for instance?" she did not answer.

It was not until afternoon that Hilda got a chance to talk to Jane alone. "Did you tell him?"

"No, Ma, I didn't. I'll write him instead."

Hilda thought again of seeing them in each other's arms and wished she hadn't looked out the window just then. "You're sure about it?"

'Yes, Ma, I'm sure. He told me he's going to be a conscientious objector, and I just think that's stupid."

"Did you tell him that? Did he explain himself to you?"

"No, what for? He thinks I agree with him, so what's the sense of upsetting him?"

Hilda knew she would cry if she said more. She thought again of herself and Franz and the fact that every caress she had ever given or received had been one of love. Sincere and deep love. At least, she was sure of it now. She longed to tell Jane to stop her present thinking and to give Robert a chance.

She wished she had the power. Would it help to pray that God intervened? Prayers like that had never worked for Hilda. *God did not save Franz. God did not do favors.*

CHAPTER THIRTY-NINE: 1948

Hilda cooked large meals again, for three children, when Jane came home for summer. Not for long, however. Jane would be returning to college. Hans, who said he needed time to think what he wanted to do with his life, was considering the possibility of being drafted. He had chosen not to be baptized and said in several ways that the Mennonite Church wasn't going to run his life: "Turn me into a conscientious objector." He helped Andrew with the farm work, following Andrew's directives but not taking initiative himself.

Jane had planned to take a summer job at a resort with some college friends. Then, at the last, she changed her mind, saying she'd like to help at home. She was very still, as if the year had tired her, and she needed a thorough rest before she would trust herself to talk. Even Hans couldn't tease a reaction out of her. Andrew did not try but spoke politely to her. Robert didn't call.

Hilda waited until the second afternoon, when Jane was outdoors sunbathing, before she spoke to Hans about her. Hans shrugged. "She probably thinks she's the only one in the world, and we should all bow down to her with respect."

"Hans, you are being just as selfish when you say that. It means that you don't care very much."

"Frankly, I don't. I don't see why we should worry about her when she hardly knows we exist." He turned to wash himself at the sink.

"Are you going out, Hans?" Hilda asked, realizing that he had stopped working for the day.

"Sure. I've got an early date."

"Who's driving?"

"I am. It's my turn."

"With my car." It was a statement, not a question, and Hilda felt something tighten inside her. That something was helplessness, because she knew she would have to give him the permission he had not asked for.

"Yep. I don't have a car like so many other guys have. If I had one, I'd use it. A couple of my friends got new cars for high school graduation."

Hilda responded, "If you had a father, you might have a car too— at least, you'd have the opportunity to earn one for yourself." She added, "It's better that way anyhow, because for boys to be given gifts as big as cars doesn't seem to be good for them."

But Hans was still talking. "Anytime you want to use the car, all you have to do is say so. I know it's your car." Then he went to his room to shave with his electric razor.

Angrily, Hilda considered selling the car, for she seldom got much use out of it. Since she had learned to drive, and was licensed, she did feel a certain independence. She didn't have many places to go, however. Church, for Sunday worship and the Tuesday quilting group, and shopping. She wasn't invited much for Sunday afternoon faspa, being a widow, except by Henry and Emma, and Amos and Anna. Franz's sisters did not socialize much; maybe they had friends from their church. Now and then, she called on Aunt Mary and Mother Lober, both of whom were living in Sunset Home. Otherwise, she never was much for tea parties.

Now she had the car, waiting there only for her children to drive it on their light-minded dates with girls they didn't love and had no intention of marrying.

But Jane was back in the house and talking with Hans, interested for the first time since she was at home. "Who are you taking?" she asked.

Hilda could not understand the name of the girl, but she heard she was from out of town.

"That dope?" Jane said, true to her new form. "What's the matter, you hard up or something?"

"She's a nice girl. Fat lot you know about her anyhow."

"She's just a kid. Does she still wear braces on her teeth?"

"So what?"

"Oh well, I guess it's none of my business."

"It sure isn't," Hans retaliated. Then his voice brightened, "But I bet you'll be mad when you find out who I'm double dating with!"

"Who?"

"Beg me a little."

"Oh, honestly, what a child you are."

Hilda had heard them teasing before, and though she didn't like to see her children upset each other, she felt almost satisfied that Jane didn't always have the edge over her brothers.

"It can't be anyone special," Jane decided. "You're just trying to make me curious, and I won't give you that satisfaction." She left, closing the door behind her, not waiting to ask Hilda who it was.

When Andrew came in for the evening, Hilda asked him if he knew anything about Hans's business, and Andrew, without concern, answered, "Sure I know, don't you? He often double dates with Robert and some other girl from somewhere out of town. The two girls are friends."

Hilda looked up at the clock, as if the time might help her to understand. "I thought Robert was in love with Jane."

"Well, I guess he has more sense than to waste his time on her. He's leaving for his voluntary service job soon. Or did you know that? You do know, don't you, that he's a CO?" Andrew added, and picked up the evening newspaper.

"Do you know where he's going for his service? What is he going to be doing?"

"Some place in Nebraska, or maybe Kansas. There's a Mennonite hospital there—I think it's a mental hospital—and they need orderlies. Boys, I mean men, strong enough to help control patients, or lift them. Or something." This time, Andrew held the paper higher.

Andrew did not date much, and when he did, he took out each girl only once. Hilda asked him about it several times, but each time he answered, "I don't see any point in wasting time and money on someone who doesn't especially interest me."

Guiltily, Hilda admitted to herself, *As long as Andrew doesn't marry, I'll be able to stay on the farm with him. I'll be a needed person, useful to him... No, I want Andrew to have a happy, normal life, and if he marries, I won't stand in his way. I'll move to a little house in town. Meanwhile, I'll enjoy life with him as it is, and make it plain that he can take his time finding a suitable helpmate. I'll also save money for that inevitable little house in town, so he won't have to hurry to marry some unimaginative girl, just because he needs someone to cook for him.*

But as for Jane, Hilda felt a sense of loss for her and decided to make use of the opportunity she now had to speak with Andrew privately. Ignoring the newspaper he was evidently using as a sign that he didn't wish to talk, Hilda spoke again. "Does Jane know Robert is dating?"

The newspaper hid Andrew's face. "How should I know? Everyone else knows."

"Is he going steady with this girl?"

"They haven't exchanged class rings, as far as I know, if that's what you mean."

"Well, does he date her a lot, or does he go out with different girls?"

"I don't know. Ask Hans. I think they date those girls every time they double date."

Hilda saw, again, Robert and Jane in each others' arms, some months before. Again she thought of herself and Franz ...

*   *   *

It was a pleasant summer. Rain fell when it was needed, gentle rain that Hilda could enjoy as she listened to it from her bed before it lulled her to sleep. The sun shone, causing the earth to bring forth vigorous and succulent vegetables and grain. "Of course," Hilda remarked laughingly, "the weeds like the weather too, and make me almost wish it was dryer so I wouldn't have to hoe so much."

As Hilda was hoeing the potato field for the third time—the last time, she decided—Jane came to help. She hoed for a while before she spoke; then, when the words came, Hilda realized she had been crying.

"Why did I go away to college, Ma?" she asked.

"You wanted to, remember?"

"I know. But I wish you had stopped me. I'm sorry now that I started."

"If I had had the power to keep you from it, you would have resented that."

Again, Jane hoed for a while before she answered. She was barefoot, as she always was in the summertime. Her shorts revealed that she had done considerable sunbathing at the college. As she turned to speak, Hilda noticed that her hair had become almost streaked from sun. "I've made a lot of mistakes. I wish I could blame someone else for them."

Hilda could not prevent herself from repeating a maxim her own mother had often spoken: "You should draw on past mistakes for present living, and be the richer for them."

"I know," Jane answered, "but there isn't much I can do now about some things I've spoiled."

Hilda decided to let Jane speak at her own pace. Conscious of each stroke, Hilda felt her arms working the hoe, while feeling relief that Jane should finally open up.

"I don't think I've learned very much," Jane continued, "at least not anything important. I've lost something by going away. I'm not at home any place. I could never adjust completely to the life most of the college kids lead. But after getting a little used to it, I feel restless at home. I'm sort of lost."

"What have you lost, Jane?"

"Oh, I don't know. Friends."

Hilda thought, *you mean Robert*, but kept to her resolve to let Jane speak herself, rather than urging her. "You haven't lost any friends who were worthwhile, have you? Surely, people who were real friends before are still your friends, aren't they?"

Jane was hoeing fast now, not looking up. "I guess that's true, but I still can't help feeling bad."

"Of course," Hilda added, "if it's our own fault that we lose friends, we should make the first move to reconcile with them."

Jane opened her eyes wide, but she turned away quickly. "I couldn't, Ma; this time it's different, even though it is my fault."

Hilda kept on hoeing.

Jane continued, "I mean, if I did make some kind of a first move, this friend would probably laugh in my face."

"That, Jane, would be your answer, and at least you'd know."

"Besides, I'm not entirely sure that I *want* to make up with him. I don't know what I want."

Hilda could not think of anything to say. Instead, she cleaned her hoe with the old knife she carried.

"You know who I mean, Ma. It's Robert. I found out that he's dating some girl from out of town. I never realized it would make any difference to me. Then I remembered how wonderful last spring was with Robert, and I could hardly wait for school to be out so I could come home to him. I couldn't write because I was embarrassed. Instead, I decided to wait until he came to see me. He never came. Maybe I should have called him as soon as I got home, but I didn't. Now it's too late. For sure."

"Do you suppose you could 'accidentally' run into him? If he saw that you were friendly, he might give you a chance to talk."

"I've been waiting for a chance—that's why I went to the band concert yesterday, but I only saw him from a distance, and I would have had to walk over to him in front of lots of other people." Jane was crying again. "I never realized how wonderful he was!"

"One thing you have to watch too, Jane, is that you don't endow him with qualities he doesn't have, just because he seems to be out of your reach. He's a human being."

"Yes, he is a human being—like a being with humanity. You know, he's a conscientious objector—not to get out of serving the country, but to actually help make the world a better place. He's going to work in a mental hospital and learn how to help people with mental illness. Maybe he'll go on to study, to be a doctor or psychologist or something. He told me that the last time I saw him, and I kind of sneered about that. I didn't actually sneer at him, and maybe he didn't notice, but inside I could just see him being a 'do-gooder.' And all for pennies! Do you know COs get paid just room and board, and a little pocket money for things like shampoo and stuff?"

Jane continued, "Now when I think about it, he really is a saint. A really *good* 'do-gooder.' While I'm sitting around college, drinking coffee and talking about poetry or the anatomy of frogs. I actually think I might even feel good about being a conscientious objector myself, except they don't take girls. But I might study psych, or nursing, or— I really want a different life from what I have now, Ma."

*　　　*　　　*

The letter came, as Hans knew it would. "Report to Fort Breckenridge for basic training." He would have a two-week furlough after that, and then be sent to "only God and the government know," according to Hans.

He showed the letter to Hilda, saying, "Well, here it is."

"Is this really what you want?" was all she could think to say.

"There isn't any alternative now."

"You're really willing to go to war, kill people you don't know? Who haven't done anything to you?"

"If that's what I'm ordered to do, that's what I'll do."

"Can you be a 'noncombatant'? I hear some soldiers have that assignment."

"No. If I'm going to be a soldier, I'm going to be a good soldier and do what soldiers do."

"But, how do you deal with our Mennonite pacifist tenets?"

"If you're going to quote the Bible, remember all the bloodshed. Those 'chosen' people went to war with God as their 'commander-in-chief.'"

"How do you reply to *Jesus*' teaching—'You have heard it said, an eye for an eye. But I say unto you, love your enemies, bless them that curse you, do good to them that hate you.'"

"I know, I know, Ma, I know. You don't need to go on."

"How do you answer—what your pa and I have tried to teach you?"

"Ma, I haven't heard you say anything about Grace joining the army."

"Grace isn't killing people. She's saving lives."

"So I'll save lives too, by killing killers."

What more could Hilda say? All she could bring out was, "I'll pray for you, son. Every day."

*　　　*　　　*

He was handsome in his uniform; basic training tightened the muscles he already had from strenuous farm work, high school basketball playing, and regular gym workouts. Looking at him, Hilda had bittersweet feelings: proud that he had found a calling he believed was right, but fearful that his life would be taken before he truly found himself.

He wrote home now and then, short letters not saying much, either because he was stationed at a place he was not allowed to disclose, or because he knew he couldn't share his thoughts or experiences with a family whose values he was leaving behind.

CHAPTER FORTY: 1949

Robert proposed, and Jane consented enthusiastically. How it happened was: Jane spotted him at the next Wednesday evening band concert and, although there were people around, she followed him to his car. This was, she had read in the paper, the last week he was at home before his induction into his alternative service assignment. If she waited, he would be gone.

She could feel her heart pounding; if it hadn't been dark, people might have noticed that her face was flushed. He had opened the door to his car and started at her touch. Whether there was anyone with him, a date perhaps, she didn't notice. If there was, whoever it was—boy or girl—dropped away.

"I'm terribly sorry," was all her dry tongue could say. Then, seeing his confusion, she tried to go on. "Not about startling you. I mean, I *am* sorry I startled you, but I'm sorry I lost you. I miss you … awfully… I'm so ashamed."

Taking her arm to lead her off the street, he looked hard at her before saying anything. Concert-goers streamed past, some chuckling and others bumping into them. "Kiss her!" said a voice they didn't acknowledge.

"Come with me? Where we can talk?" Robert asked. Jane forgot that she had her mother's car parked just down the street. She'd have to walk to town tomorrow to fetch it. So they went, driving slowly to a quiet place they knew of.

Once they decided, they were eager to marry as soon as possible—the next time he came home, whenever that would be. He'd let her know. Then Jane would go with him to his alternative service post, and look for work in that community. She'd also enroll at the local community college if it offered appropriate classes, and if they could afford it. They hoped they would be provided with a Quonset hut, a temporary building with a round roof that looked like a chicken barn but could be quite cozy.

Before they got the message to Grace, word came from her that she was, herself, married. Her letters were infrequent and short ever since she joined the Army Nurse Corps, commissioned as a lieutenant. She had been stationed at various hospitals—one in Texas and another in Colorado. Her work, busy and demanding, was tending to sick soldiers—mostly male and mostly with contagious diseases such as measles, mumps, and gastrointestinal upsets. So far, there had been no battle-injured patients for her to tend, and though it was possible for her to be shipped overseas close to battle fields, it hadn't happened.

One of her patients, a sergeant who had escaped measles when he was a child, had caught it when he was home on furlough. As usual with contagious illness, he was isolated; Grace and the other nurses had to wear cover-up uniforms that they left in his room before they washed their hands and went to see other patients. It was easier to assign one particular nurse per shift to him and send the other nurses elsewhere to work. Thus, Grace saw him every day for ten days.

It followed that, despite army rules prohibiting fraternization between commissioned and non-commissioned officers, Grace and her patient, named Hugo, developed a friendship that they continued after he was discharged from the hospital. They fell in love and persuaded the company chaplain to marry them.

Her letter home simply announced their marriage: *One of the things—I mean people—that has kept me busy is, I met a wonderful man. He's from Missouri, grew up on a farm just as I did. We like the same things, read the same kind of books. And, yes, Ma, he is a Christian.*

Our wedding was simple. We wore our dress uniforms, and our witnesses were a couple we know from the base. It would have been nice for you all to have been there, or for us to come home to our church for a big wedding with all the relatives, but we couldn't get time off. We'll come to see you when we have leave together. Meanwhile, here's a picture of the two of us.

Hilda, studying the face of her new son-in-law, judged him to be a good man: mature, outgoing, even good looking, although that should never be a requirement. In her letter to them both, she promised to pray for them and their happiness together. She enclosed a check for $25, aware that hosting a wedding here at home could cost far more. She suggested, *Buy something that you would like to remember your wedding with, since I don't know what you might want or need.*

Andrew shrugged and said, "Well, that's that."

Word of the two weddings reached Hans just before he was shipped overseas. To where, if he knew, he didn't say. He offered his best wishes to both sisters and promised to write again as soon as he could.

*　　　*　　　*

Colored leaves were still plentiful on Jane's wedding day, the sun bringing out the gaudy brilliance. It was a happy day, and if Grace and Hans could have come home, it would have been perfect. Grace sent a telegram that was, for her, unusually gay; wishing Jane all the best. It also mentioned pregnancy and discharge from the army in the works. Jane, in her happiness, did not notice, and Hilda decided that Grace's marriage had brought out a cheerier nature in her.

All the same, Hilda's heart was heavy during the ceremony joining Jane and Robert, not that she felt she was losing her daughter. In truth, she hardly thought about Jane. She wished Franz could be there to witness the marriage. Not looking down at her own work-worn hands and thickening body, but to the front where flowers outlined the form of the minister, she thought back to her own wedding. She imagined herself and Franz walking side by side, not touching, not even seeing each other because they were facing forward, but aware of each other. When they reached the front, her father spoke the marriage ceremony, wedding them for their lifetimes, which they were sure would be long.

Alone on the front bench, Hilda now felt that she was again at Franz's funeral, sitting on that same pew. Then, though she had had her children around her, she had been alone too. She had sat there, feeling dry from days of weeping, with the words, "Franz is dead" going through her head as if engraved on a wheel rotating in her brain. That day, instead of white satin bows on each pew and gorgeous garden wedding flowers at the altar, there were strong-scented funeral flowers—gladiolas—and a gray casket slowly being pushed to the front of the sanctuary.

At the time, she was certain the body of her husband was not inside that box. The feeling persisted after she saw the casket opened. Franz had never worn that suit, now furnished by the undertaker. She doubted he was even wearing trousers in that half-open box. After she touched him, and felt the clay that had once been his vibrant muscles, she was convinced that the body belonged to someone else.

For a long time, she felt that Franz might come back to her. Even yet, she sometimes heard a step that was like his, or a cough, or a form in half light, and immediately her pulse would quicken.

Now, she reminded herself, she was at her daughter's marriage, and the minister had already performed the ceremony and embarked on his sermon. He spoke English. The church offered German services for older folk like Hilda on certain Sundays; Hilda couldn't keep track of which Sundays those were. Jane could have arranged for her wedding to be held in German, but most of her friends had not learned German, and the church was filled with her and Robert's friends.

This was the same church building that Hilda attended as a child and had been married in. The same windows, pulpit, pews. But the gaslights had been replaced with electric lights, and the potbelly stove with a furnace. She looked to the front and wondered, *Why have they lighted candles? It's not dark outside. Well, I, guess it adds to a romantic atmosphere, if that is what they want.* There was talk, she had heard—she hadn't gone to the business meetings where it was discussed—that the church was going to move to town. Not the actual building; they would build a new, modern, brick edifice with Sunday-school classrooms right in the building, not in a separate one as it was now. *What will they do with this building? Raze it? Turn it into a chicken barn? That's abhorrent.* She shuddered, and almost looked around to see if anyone had noticed.

Hilda became aware of another difference: the music. Yes, the church now had a pump organ, no longer considered "unnecessary and therefore a sin," where her own wedding had been embellished with birdsong through the open windows. The couple had chosen some Christian music. To her surprise, a friend sang—in German, yet—*"Bist du bei mir, geh ich mit freude."*[38] For the recessional, the organist played *"Jesu geh voran."*[39] Hilda was glad they used those songs, and wondered if Jane knew they were favorites of hers.

The wedding dress fit Jane perfectly. It was the one Hilda had sewn and worn—how many years ago? She couldn't, at the moment, think. It had not required much altering at all. Jane was lovely in it, and Hilda's senses swelled with pride, or, rather, gratitude, that Jane had chosen to wear it. She looked fine, walking up the aisle, holding Andrew's arm. Her limp was so slight anymore, you had to look for it to see it. And Robert. How handsome he was in his new dark suit. It wasn't exactly black, maybe a dark blue. Black is for funerals.

But the minister—it was the new one, Reverend Hubner—was speaking. She tried to listen, for she knew that Jane was too excited to, and someone ought to remember enough of it to be able to tell her about it later. She postponed her musings.

---

38 "If Thou art with me, I go with gladness."
39 "Jesus, lead me on."

CHAPTER FORTY-ONE: 1951

Jane had been married more than two years and had given birth to a daughter they named Katherine. "Since your mother's teachings and example shaped you, Ma, I want to honor her memory," she had explained. Recently, a son, Robert—named after his father—was born; they called him Bobby. Grace's little girl, Linda, was a year older than Katherine.

Hilda wasn't sure if news of Jane's new baby had reached Hans when she had word that Hans had died. Jane, home for a brief visit, said, "Reverend Hubner told me he was sorry that we couldn't have his body sent here so we could have a proper burial. But I'm glad we don't have to see him. I'd rather remember him as he was—tease and all."

Hilda agreed, though her stomach and throat hurt. "We Christians make too great a fuss over funerals. When we should attach more importance to the soul than to the body."

The telegram did not specify how, or even where he had died. It left many questions unanswered. *Was he killed in action? In an accident? Of disease? Suicide? By mistake of another soldier? Rescuing a comrade?*

Is Hans a hero? Will we ever know? What does a soldier have to do to be a hero? What does anyone have to do? Is Hans a hero for saving another soldier's life? Was forgoing the option of conscientious objection heroic? If so, then can Robert and Jane be heroes as they face public derision for claiming conscientious objection to war? Is Grace a hero for caring for sick soldiers, even one with measles? Is Andrew a hero for working the farm for our livelihood? Are they all "Helden"?[40]

When she heard—and after the first shock—she felt a calm wonder at being the mother of dead children and the wife of a dead husband. She thought of Franz and Hans and that baby boy who would now be a grown man, carrying his father's name, had he lived.

---

40 Masculine German: meaning "heroes." Feminine plural is "Heldin."

Franz left his life with questions he stopped asking because he didn't want to work on them any longer. I was the only one who understood how he actually felt—the children still quote him as absolute authority on Christianity.

Cherub left life before he lived it. What might his questions have been?

Hans left his life possibly not asking questions. Or did he ask, and being wise, find his own answers? Or being wiser still, did he ask and was content that there are no answers? Using that same wisdom, did he enjoy life for what it was? Was he happy?

Who was Hans really? I don't know what he thought about; the girls he dated probably know the real Hans better than I do. I knew Franz better than his own parents did. Still, we were married, and I didn't know him until after we were married.

Putting together the background she and Franz had tried to give their children, and the way the world had changed, even in their own small community, Hilda tried to piece together who Hans was. *He should have been somewhat shy, but that was doctored out of him by his high school experiences. He should have been loyal to our church, but he often found reasons for not attending. Where did he get those ideas, that attitude? Franz and I surely never revealed any feelings like that, even when we personally rebelled against some of the practices of our faith. Did he ignore the whole matter of salvation? Was he bad at heart because he didn't acknowledge Mennonite tenets?*

As for conforming to Mennonite strictures, I know he attended movies, as did many of his friends. Sometimes he smelled of smoke, but whether he actually smoked himself, I don't know. And drinking—I know he didn't drink, for he never smelled of that. It could just as well be the fact that liquor was prohibited in the county as that the church frowned on it that he didn't drink.

Dancing? I know he tried, because he tried to teach Jane before she settled down. But watching them, I saw how clumsy he was at it and I knew that he had not done much, or enough, to do it well. Besides, in my heart, I wonder how wrong it could be to dance when there are worse things young people could do. The Bible even says we should praise God by dancing.[41] But that's a different kind of dancing. Reverend Hubner says that it's not the dancing so much as what it can lead to—"a vertical expression of a horizontal desire."

Girls. How well did Hans know them? Did he ever consider marriage? Hilda was thankful that he had not gotten any girl into trouble. At least she had not heard of any. She squirmed for admitting to herself what joy that kind of knowledge—physical love—had given her and wished, in a way that, before his death, he might have been able to know it also.

When Hans first left home, there was an emptiness, but no more than when Grace left, or Jane. His first furlough was pleasant; he looked well. Even when he

41   Psalm 150.

had a slight argument about pacifism with Jane and Robert, he good-naturedly switched the topic of conversation. Then they got on as if he was not in the armed forces, and there might not even be a war somewhere far away.

It hurt when he left the last time. He was quiet and almost tender to me. He didn't actually kiss me farewell, but to me it seemed that he would have liked to, and that was tenderness enough.

I'm sorry I didn't have a chance to talk with him quietly and naturally that last time. I had confidence in his promise to come home again soon, but I so wished he were assured of safety as a conscientious objector. He would still be alive.

I feel a certain respect for his not choosing that direction if he wasn't so led. After all, it was the physical danger that made me feel that way—Grace was in the army too, before the baby came, and she wasn't exposed to much danger. About her, I don't feel anything to regret. Perhaps it was even divine guidance, for that's how she met her husband, and isn't that what's made her happy at last?

I might find comfort if Hans had gone forward at a revival meeting, or had made a definite "step." But Grace did that, there in the bedroom with me, and she cried that she didn't feel different. Furthermore, Franz and I taught her and Hans and the other two children what the Mennonite church believed we ought to teach them. Along with that, we taught them tolerance of others and quiet, patient wisdom.

It wasn't as if Hans was brought up heathen and needed a sudden dramatic turning about. He probably, at his age, never even considered doubting what he was taught. Choosing to be a soldier instead of a conscientious objector might have been because he would have a regular salary instead of living for several years under a maintenance allowance. He would even have been able to go to college after that, though he never said as much. Except he died.

Yes, it might be a comfort to know that he was enthusiastic about the church. Maybe he would have found another church as Grace did. I have her letter in which she wrote that she and Hugo joined some other, ritualistic church. Whatever it's called:

I'm glad you're open minded enough, Ma, not to be upset because I left the Mennonite church. After all, Heaven would not be pleasant if only Mennonites were there. To me, the Mennonites don't have anything special that should make me want to be "true" to them. They used to be "different"; I guess they called themselves "being in the world, but not of the world."

Maybe I don't know enough about the world, but I see no difference between them and "the world." Sure, there are a few diehards who still think girls shouldn't cut their hair or paint their faces, but they are such trivial minds who worry about externals—and you can find them in any denomination.

There are other beliefs—like keeping ritual out of the church. Look how upset Mennonite people get when the usual "order" of the service is changed. If that isn't ritual, I wouldn't know what the word means.

Or pacifism: how prosperous many of our people are—because they cheated someone or because they didn't conform to the practice of helping others. That's as much a part of pacifism as not actually shooting someone is.

And, yes, look at all the gossip—think of how many people's souls are snuffed by gossip. I don't think Mennonites are guiltier than other churches, or small communities, but our guilt is greater because we profess to "love our enemies."

The way I think of your church, Ma, is the way you described it to me when Grosspa was minister. The way you and Pa lived. But I can't find your way of life in the Mennonite church, Ma, and sometimes I wonder whether you and Pa did. Did you?

What I mean is, I don't think it's different enough from other churches, to give it a reason for existing as a separate church. All this fuss about various sins—as if certain things are sin, without fail, and other things are good, without a doubt. Don't people have enough to do? Don't they have real worries that they have to start inventing some? Maybe we've all had too much to eat and ought to know what it's like to starve; maybe then we'd know what Christianity can be.

That's why I say that I don't feel bad about leaving the Mennonite Church—the Meadow Church. In fact, I'm leaving it because it doesn't exist anymore as far as I can see. That old church building is just a building for me. It's nice to go there, to visit with old friends, to sing together with them, and to remember old times. It's a chance to help other people, by giving money to the collections, by teaching Bible stories to the little children, and by being friendly and cheerful with other people. But that's just social, and you can get that in any assembly of like-minded people.

What I want from a church is worship. Worship of a God I believe in. That's why I like a darkened church; I always could think better with my eyes closed. That's why I don't care if I don't see anyone I know in church, because I find my social life elsewhere, and it doesn't matter to me who else is in church. I like to direct all my thoughts toward worship and adoration of God. I can find that the ritual (which, incidentally, is all word-for-word out of the Bible), at the very least, is in good grammar and beautiful poetry instead of in the stumbling, uneducated words of some minister, even if he is sincere. I haven't left the things you taught me, Ma, I've just left the church I once joined.

Hilda did not show the letter to the other children. It was part of her resolve not ever to betray their confidences. She was happy for Grace, that she had resolved a dilemma Hilda had struggled with her whole life. At the same time, in her heart, she was sorry that she and Franz had not been able to find a church for the children, a church that they could respect. Deep inside, she was sorry, taking it as a fault in herself that she hadn't been able to find something specific to believe in so she could pass it on to her offspring. She wept, bitterly digging her short worn-down fingernails into her hands, almost hoping that she could give herself a physical reason to cry.

Yet, weeping, she knew that Jane was happy in the church as she had taught it to her; she had left it temporarily but had come back to it. *Was Jane all wrong too? Were both Jane and Grace right? Or are we all wrong, each in our own thinking?*

Perhaps Andrew has found an answer. He seems to be most like his father and grandfather who, Hilda now realized, were very much alike. *But Andrew doesn't talk to me much about what he thinks. I wish he would.*

While she was weeping, Hilda realized she was crying for the death of Hans, a young healthy soldier, cut off before he could prove that life was worth living.

That's my problem: trying to agree in my heart with what I've learned to agree to outwardly. Other people are happily confident in their beliefs and go on from there. I'm caught by complicated details, the fine and secondary points; other people aren't. They seem not to stumble over basic ideas.

And she was weeping for her own soul. It was selfish. Hilda wondered again, *would—or should—it concern me if I don't still believe that there is a Hell where I will be punished for just such thoughts? Eternally weeping, wailing, gnashing my teeth.*

Answering Grace's letter, Hilda could not think of more words than to say, *I am happy that you have found a church in which you can worship. After all, as you say, it is not the denomination, but Christianity that counts.* She resolved to write her more when she could find the right words. *It's good at any rate,* she thought, *that Grace found Christianity to be her religion. She's at least one step further than her mother.*

For now, it seemed to Hilda, that satisfaction—knowing what one believed and being content with that knowledge—was the highest any person could go. *Perhaps that is what's meant by faith—that first submission one has to make. After a person has acknowledged the authority of a certain body, he will find it possible to agree to all the finer tenets also… If there were other churches in the community, perhaps I could find one I would fit into; perhaps I would even, like Jane, come back to my own.*

If I could learn not to care so much; if, like Franz, I could shut that question out of my life, and devote my energies to other problems I can find answers to. But did Franz actually shut it out of his life? Had it, perhaps, been eating away at his vitals, possibly even lowering his resistance to disease?

While she tried to sort out these memories from her feelings, Hilda was aware of a familiar pain in her chest. It wasn't severe, but it frightened her, for she didn't know what it was, or exactly where it hurt. During Hans's last furlough, she had the same pain. When she mentioned it, she was embarrassed when Hans laughed at her, calling her a hypochondriac. Maybe he was right. This time, again, the pain receded without her doing anything about it.

CHAPTER FORTY-TWO: 1951

"There's someone at the door to see you, Ma," Andrew said. "I don't know who they are."

Hilda sighed, irritated at being awakened from a nap, especially after a restless night. Looking out the window before she went to the door, she saw that they had come in a large, black car.

The older woman did not smile. "I'm Mrs. Olson. This is my daughter, Sharon. Perhaps your son, John, has spoken of her."

"I think so," Hilda said. "I don't remember whether he told me her name, but he did mention a girl from out of town." It was awkward standing on the step outside the door, but Hilda hoped they wouldn't stay long enough to make it worthwhile to come in. Besides, she had forgotten to sweep this morning.

The woman spoke again, standing slightly in front of her pretty daughter, who was holding back, not looking directly at Hilda. "We have something we must talk with you about. Could we come in?"

"Of course, I'm sorry. But you see, I didn't understand at first. If I had known"—Hilda began to lead them to the parlor—"I should have notified you when we heard. You see, our Hans was killed in action a few weeks ago. I was so upset that I didn't stop to think of his friends."

The woman waited a little, but the word had not softened her face. "Yes, we heard. News like that travels fast. That's why we have to come to you. Because we can't talk with him."

They did not speak for a moment. Hilda looked at the girl—Sharon, her mother had called her—who had found a thread on her skirt. She was trying to pull it off, but each time she wound it around her finger and yanked, the thread slipped, and she tried again.

"I guess it is silly to beat around the bush," Mrs. Olson finally said. "Your son, John, got my daughter into trouble. She is expecting his child."

The girl was still pulling at the thread. Now her face became a painful red color.

In her chest, Hilda felt a curious tightening, and it came to her that she would feel better when these people left. But it was her turn to talk; she should concentrate: "That can't be. He's dead."

"Yes, I know," the woman said. "He was home on furlough recently."

"Are you sure it's a pregnancy? Isn't it too soon to know? Girls sometimes skip periods, especially when they're upset."

"She's seen our doctor. He is sure."

Sharon could have been deaf, or invisible. She looked as if she wished she was.

Hilda turned toward the girl. "If you are pregnant, how do you know it's Hans's baby?"

"It can't be anybody else's." The girl's head was now bowed low.

Her mother took back control. "Are you saying she sleeps around? Is a harlot? Don't try to put the blame on my daughter!"

"I'm not. I don't know your daughter. Or you. I'm trying to understand—"

"I suppose you think my daughter purposely misled him?"

"No, no. But Hans isn't alive to defend himself. I'm sure if he were here, he would deny it."

"No one else could have. Right, Sharon?"

The blushing girl burst into quiet tears. Hilda almost couldn't understand her as she sobbed, "We only did it once. Just once, before he left this last time. I didn't want to, but he kept saying that he was going away and he loved me and nothing would happen because he'd be careful and he had safes along. So I told him, 'Just a little bit but not all the way,' but when he started, I guess he did go all the way."

"*Just once,*" Hilda thought. *Yet, she says he had safes along. How would he know he would get a chance to use them? Just once? Where had he gotten them? Is that what the army is like? Does the army hand out safes along with cigarettes? If he didn't do it before he left for the army? But my Hans, was it truly he?*

Suddenly, Hilda thought, *They're laying the blame on him because he's dead. How can anyone prove it was Hans? The girl might not have been true to him, she might have gone out with someone else. Who is this girl anyhow? Hans didn't even mention the girl's name, let alone that he was going steady with her.*

When she began to feel angry, Hilda felt better. "Well, whenever such a thing happens, it's just as much the girl's fault as the boy's. After all, girls can control themselves better than boys can. If they tempt the boys, up to a certain point, they can expect the boys not to be able to stop themselves."

Mrs. Olson raised her voice. "And how do you explain the fact that he had safes along, as if he had planned it all along?"

"That isn't hard, "Hilda countered. "Pregnancies don't happen that easily. They must have been doing it for a long time, and once such a habit is acquired, he took them along every time he went to see her. *If* he's actually the one."

"No ! No!" The girl had stopped sobbing. "Honest, it was *only* Hans. We did it *only* once."

Her mother believed her.

Hilda stood up. "That's what you *would* say. I don't know anyone *around here* who has loose morals. We Mennonites are very strict. I'd *expect* you not to admit that you did it more than once."

"Mrs. Lober—" The woman rose also. "All this doesn't change anything. The truth is that my daughter is expecting your son's child. We know. The doctor we went to is a doctor we can trust. And we refuse to have an abortion because we are Catholics. In fact, I am shocked that they even used contraceptives—"

Hilda laughed, loudly. She would not cry.

"Furthermore," the woman added, "we'll see who the baby looks like. We'll see then that John is the father."

"I'd have to see, too." Hilda knew her voice was weak now.

"Moreover, we are going to see that the child is baptized and brought up in a good Catholic orphanage, or adopted by a good Catholic couple. We are also going to insist that John do his share toward his child. He's dead; otherwise we would insist that he marry Sharon and join the Catholic Church. Or, if he refused, then some kind of monthly support from him directly, and he could choose to tell you about it or not… But now that he's dead, he can still do his share. You, of course, will be getting government life insurance from him, and I'm asking you to contribute that insurance to the support of his child."

Taken off guard, Hilda reacted, "What insurance? He never mentioned insurance to me." In her mind she added, *If he had insurance, and didn't tell me, it was likely he didn't want to worry me. He was a good boy. Lots of energy, but basically good.*

"Well, the army arranges for insurance for all their soldiers who die. And that money should go to their children. In this case, Sharon's baby."

All Hilda could think to say was, "You can't do that."

"And just why not?"

"You have much more money than we have. For us it would be a hardship; for you it would be easy."

"Look, if he were alive," the woman said slowly, as if she thought Hilda wasn't very bright, "he would have to support his child, right? All we are asking is the insurance money. We *could* ask for much more. After all, poor Sharon has to live out her life with this shame on her head. She has to bear the pains of pregnancy and childbirth. She has to quit college and lose her friends. What you're losing is only money. Besides, if he were alive, you wouldn't get any money from him. You would most likely have to help him get started in business or farming. So you're not even losing any money."

"He's not alive. If he was, he would know how to answer you."

"I guess we do have a lot to talk about, Mrs. Lober." Seeing that Hilda did not answer, she continued. "Come now, be reasonable. I could go to a lawyer. You wouldn't have a case. If we settle this quietly and out of court, it will save you money and both our reputations."

Dully, Hilda, remembering that Mennonites do not sue, answered, "I'll have to think about this. I can't make decisions in such a hurry."

"What is there to decide?"

Seeing that Hilda had nothing more to say, the woman turned to her daughter. "Come, Sharon, dear. We'll come back next week." Still in charge, she faced Hilda. "We'll bring one witness and you can furnish another, so we can make a written agreement. That way we won't have to have misunderstandings later. If we had to hire lawyers, it would cost. You more than us."

They walked out the door, the girl stumbling over a rug Hilda had made, her mother catching her solicitously.

Afterward, Andrew asked, "Who were those people?"

Hilda answered only, "The girl was Hans's girlfriend from out of town. They heard that Hans had died."

"She must have loved Hans to come see his mother now," Andrew said, as he put the day's mail on the table.

*   *   *

That night, again, Hilda could not sleep. *My boy, Hans,* she was thinking: *a grown boy and a dead father. Is he really a father? Is there such a thing as life insurance for all the soldiers who die? Could this be a kind of swindle?*

The insurance money, if there is such a thing, doesn't bother me; I'm almost glad that I can't get it to spend every month, knowing that I'd be getting it because he's dead. But I have to make sure that that woman doesn't get her hands on it, if there is such a thing.

What a world this is, she thought. *My parents came to this country because they thought here they could find religious freedom, happiness, privacy, opportunity. Instead, in this short time we are tied together into a big war, of which we know little and of which we, as Mennonites should know nothing. Our people are participating in politics, our boys are rebelling against the old ideas, joining the* army and getting themselves killed—and even living immoral lives, as if they had never heard of Mennonite beliefs.

When she took in that it was her own Hans, not someone else's boy who was now in trouble, she felt a pang through her entire body. *I know it's my fault. It's I—not Hans who was too young yet to have experienced significant thinking—I have failed in my duty. If I had taught him carefully enough, certain dos and don'ts so he would have obeyed even if he didn't understand at the moment, he wouldn't have gotten this girl into trouble … if he did. How much did he know about human reproduction? Where did he learn what he knew?*

I tried to teach him to think for himself, to consider me a friend rather than an authoritarian who's there to admonish him. I thought he, like the other children, would keep from doing certain things, if only out of respect for me and the memory of his father. That if I showed faith in him, that confidence would keep him from temptation.

I wonder how he became so ardent that he lost his self-control. Surely, he didn't inherit that from me or from Franz … if he did it. Could the girl have led him beyond his endurance? She didn't look particularly wild—not nearly so much as her mother.

Rebelliously, Hilda thought: *If Franz were alive, things would be different. The older children who can remember his influence better, turned out well… Grace? Well, her Linda was born soon after her marriage, but she did marry the father; I can let that go… And, Jane? She probably doesn't remember her father well, but at least she didn't get into such a predicament, and she found such a good husband…*

Has the war changed our customary way of life? Is it only our family?

If my mother hadn't died so young. If I could have learned to know the answers from her and Pa. Wildly, Hilda knew whom to blame: *Muttah. It's her fault that there's been that distance between me and Pa. That I haven't been able to resolve my own conflicts. And if I can't take care of myself, how can I be expected to rear children?*

Then she was able to relax and go to sleep. Everything would work out. She would be able to rest her conscience.

*   *   *

When Hilda woke the next morning, the unease was still with her: Hans. Almost she was glad for him that he had been able to taste of the joy that carnal knowledge might have given him before he died, even if it was illicit … *if he did it. For surely, his girlfriend was having masses celebrated for his soul. Wouldn't she?* Hilda submitted Hans to their church, at least for the time being.

I will focus on the infant in the future. My grandchild. If it is my grandchild.

I must see that baby… If there is a baby… I'll ask Grace to go with me. She surely remembers what Hans looked like when he was a baby. She'll also be able to look at the baby with me and see if it looks like Hans when he was a baby. I'll take along the snapshot of him after his bath. If it is indeed his baby, I should have some say in how the baby is brought up.

She recalled Grace telling her, somewhat sadly, "Ma, I'd like to have more children, but we can't seem to be able to." She remembered that early menopause ran in Franz's family—his mother and two sisters—even before age thirty. She thought again about Cherub, that beautiful perfect baby who never took a breath. *Why is it that some women who want and love babies aren't able to have them, while others have them against their will, or accidentally?*

If Sharon's baby is Hans's, wouldn't it be wonderful if it—he or she—could stay with the family? If Grace and Hugo would adopt it? Surely a reputable orphanage would prefer to place a baby with blood relations. Even if they aren't Catholic. Especially since the father is dead. Has given his life for his country.

That thought troubled Hilda—*why should a young man give his life in a war?*

*   *   *

When Mrs. Olson and her so-called witness came, with Sharon tagging along, to arrange for any government insurance money that might be coming from Hans's death, she pulled some legal-looking papers from a leather briefcase. The case looked like the skin of an alligator, or maybe a snake. The witness, a woman whose name Hilda didn't catch, said not a word throughout the visit. She could have been blind, deaf, and dumb. Or a dummy.

As neutrally and calmly as she was able to control her voice, Hilda asked, pen in hand, "What is the name of the orphanage?"

"You don't need the name of the orphanage. Just sign it to me, and I'll take care of it."

Hilda tightened her lips. "I'm sorry. This is a legal transaction, and I need to sign it to go to the orphanage." (*Not you,* she told herself.) "You said the money was to support the child. Surely you can pay your own bills."

Mrs. Olson was nonplussed. Sharon stood there.

"Since last week, I've been checking orphanages, and the one closest to your home is Our Lady of Perpetual Help. So that is who I'll address the money to." Hilda signed, directing the money to be support for Baby Lober. Her hand was steady and even without her usual—what she called—"elderly script." It felt good to put that problem aside, for now.

On their way to their car, Mrs. Olson stumbled over a small tree stump that should have been cut level to the ground. Her silent witness helped steady her. After they left, Hilda fetched Franz's old hacksaw and, using the energy of her pent-up emotions, she easily cut the stump.

She felt better: strong. *I tripped her. Twice. If there's no baby after all, the money will go to a good cause. This will end well.*

Before returning to the house after taking the saw back to its nail in the barn, she stopped to see Prince, her only horse now, watching her from inside the fence. Andrew sometimes rode him here and there on the farmland. Mostly for fun. She stroked his neck. "What a fine horse you grew up to be: gentle like your mother, Minnie, and spirited like your wild bronco father. How proud Franz was of you."

CHAPTER FORTY THREE: 1951–52

Days following the second Olson visit seemed tranquil, almost humdrum. Hilda, confident that she had dealt with them with dignity and without tears, was sure that the matter of money was settled. Franz would have been proud of her; he would not have done better.

Andrew was now busy tending the farm work, with occasional help from itinerant workers from other Mennonite communities. Young men followed the harvests, starting in the southwestern states and finishing in the northern states as grains progressively ripened. This time there was a young woman, a sister of one of the men, who also came in hopes of helping a farm wife with the work of cooking.

The men slept on clean new hay in the loft of the barn, using well-water to freshen their faces and hands, and any place behind the barn to relieve themselves. Evenings, Hilda could hear them yodeling and singing songs from country, folk, and religious to popular; one of them played guitar, the girl lending her clear soprano. Their voices were twangy but true.

It was not seemly for the girl to sleep in the barn, and Hilda offered Grace and Jane's room—not Hans's—to her. Hilda didn't notice anything particular about her. She was obviously of good Mennonite stock—not a smoker or drinker. Neither short nor tall, sturdy with dark, wavy hair tied back, and clear brown eyes. Her straight forehead indicated intelligence—a truism Hilda remembered hearing from her mother.

It was acceptable to have her around; she didn't get underfoot, and she didn't have to be told what to do every minute. She was quiet but joined the conversation at the table when the men came in for meals. After dinner, before she took a short rest, she helped clean up while the men went to stretch out on the grass and tell stories in the shade of the boxelder trees.

Hilda did not notice Andrew's interest in the young woman. When he told her, one evening after she and all the men had retired, that he liked her and was going to court her, Hilda asked, "Which girl are you talking about?"

The girl's name was Agatha. During the school year, she was studying at a Mennonite college in South Dakota to be a teacher. She would use money she earned in summer to pay her tuition. She had only a year left of school. Furthermore, it turned out, she liked Andrew.

After the harvest, South Dakota was not too far away for Andrew to make frequent trips to visit her, and Hilda saw that he seemed happy when he left, and happy when he returned. He wrote many letters, some containing poetry that he asked Hilda to check, not for grammar and punctuation since her English wasn't up to it, but for meaning or clarity. This was the young man who was the least scholarly of Hilda's children, who always complained when he was assigned writing compositions in school.

She was not surprised when he let slip their plans to marry, maybe after Agatha had taught for a year or two, or even right after she graduated. It would depend on whether there was a teaching job available locally, or nearby.

The year passed. He went to Agatha's graduation, where he learned that her parents seemed concerned that she might not put her years of college to use if she married a farmer. They were courteous but reserved. When an opening occurred in a local school, Agatha and Andrew agreed she would accept a position there, and then they could work out how she could be his wife and teach at the same time. They felt confident her parents would be satisfied by that arrangement.

"You can keep your bedroom," Andrew told Hilda, "and we'll sleep upstairs. This is a big house."

"No, not two cooks in a kitchen. It doesn't work out."

"You got along all right during last fall's harvest."

"That was different. I was clearly in charge and she was my 'help.' When you marry, she should have her own kitchen."

"I won't put you out of our house. Out of your kitchen. Agatha agrees with me about this."

"My Pa used to say, 'Relatives should live far enough apart that one cannot see the other's chimney smoking.'"

"That's a clever saying. But what would you do?"

"Andrew, listen. I haven't said this to you before. Maybe I should have, but I didn't want you to feel that I was pushing you to get married. It was easy—maybe too comfortable—just to let things ride. But I've always thought, even before your father died, that we would move to town when you got married. After he died, I still thought about it sometimes. Now that is what I will do."

"What will you do in town? Go to the movies? Shop?"

"I'll find plenty to do. I'll make a garden with lots of flowers. I'll walk to church, now that the church has moved to town. I'll go to the ladies' sewing circle and help make quilts for missions or for relief. And I'll have an indoor bathroom for the first time in my life."

"Maybe we can have an indoor bathroom here too. In fact, I've been thinking about that, and wondering whether we couldn't get a loan for it. You don't need to move to town to get an indoor bathroom."

"Relax, Andrew. I'm happy for you. You and Agatha should do what you want here, and I won't need to have you or her chauffeuring me to where I want to go. And you can always come to visit me in town."

"What do you mean, *chauffeuring*?"

"I won't need the car in town. You can have it."

*   *   *

Before the wedding, Hilda was lucky to find a soon-to-be-vacant little house not far from the center of town. It would suit her, she thought, but since it would not be available for several months, this would be an ideal time for her to take that trip to the West Coast that she had longed for so many years. She could see Pa and Muttah once more, this time for a happy visit, not a funeral. They were both said to be in good health.

A nephew, Amos's son, was driving to Oregon where he was going to look for work, or possibly to buy a truck-farm to raise chickens or strawberries. He welcomed Hilda for her company on that four-day trip.

*   *   *

The ocean did indeed sound much like the comforting winds in the Minnesota cottonwood grove. Now, Hilda wondered why she hadn't given much thought to that comparison in recent years. She sat on a stone, closed her eyes and listened. She took in the crashing of the waves against huge dark rocks, their tonguing up through openings between other piled-up boulders. With her eyes closed, it was hard to determine whether she felt transported to her childhood in her featherbed, listening to the winter wind. *Which sound is the authentic sound—the wind in the trees or the roaring ocean? Which one is the simile?*

She longed to stay in this place and ponder, but Muttah came near and reminded her that they wanted to go on to a market.

"I'm so happy to just listen to the ocean." Hilda said. "I could sit here for hours, just listening. Don't you like hearing it?"

"I've heard it before. The market will be closing soon. We have to go."

Hilda stood up and inwardly sighed. *That Muttah. Never in accord with me. We just don't feel things the same.*

*   *   *

She wrote postcards to the children: My parents' strawberries are large and juicy—much bigger than the ones in Minnesota. I wish I could bring you some. She did not try to describe the sound of the ocean. *How do you put a noise into words? It could be like trying to explain silence.*

Since moving to Oregon from their active farming-ministering life in Montana, Pa and Muttah lived a quiet regular life. They had a cow and a few chickens, and they raised strawberries and boysenberries. They went to bed early, and ate the same breakfast—coffee and buttered bread each day. Dinner was still at noon—meat and potatoes, as it had been on the farm—and supper was tvaybak with jelly, and milk to drink. Fruit, those delectable berries, sat on the counter, available to be snacked by the handful. Pa still read the farm magazines, and Muttah crocheted countless doilies. They continued the morning and evening devotions that they had practiced during their entire marriage, though they did not kneel on the floor any more but held their bowed heads in their hands.

They were always together; there never was a time for Hilda to carry on an extended conversation with her father. It just wouldn't work to start one with Muttah always at hand. She longed to share her burdens with Pa, now also the news about Hans's sin … *if he did it.* Perhaps she should write him. She should have written him long ago, that other question she had harbored all these years. Why hadn't she done that? She'd have to be careful how she worded the letter, since Muttah would be reading it too.

On the train going back home, she started a letter to her father. But the jiggling of the train and her own tremor made her ideas, her thoughts, appear as uncertain as her penmanship. She would have to recopy it, if she still felt the need to write at all.

*   *   *

The South Dakota church, decorated with flowers from Agatha's parents' garden, was filled with both Andrew's and Agatha's friends and relatives. Jane and Grace and their families arrived in Sioux Falls by train, fetched by Julius, Agatha's brother. Hilda, who hitched a ride with Andrew to the wedding, would ride back home with Henry and Emma, who now drove a modern Buick.

Sitting in the front pew, Hilda again reminisced about her own wedding, and Jane's. *How much this ceremony is like Jane's and my own—and different. The music this time is a pipe organ: not a pump organ. Not birdsong from the open window. The church pews are cushioned. Andrew and Agatha aren't sitting on hard chairs while the minister talks. They're standing, and the bride doesn't have to be concerned that her gown will wrinkle. They don't have to stand long, for the minister isn't preaching.*

The text he read was the same one Hilda's father and Jane's pastor had read, but this time she did not hear the word "obey." Nor that wives were to submit to their husbands. *Did Jane have to promise to obey Robert?* Hilda recalled that she hadn't been listening to that part of Jane's wedding ritual. This time, the husband was only instructed to love his wife, and the wife to love her husband. *It seems an improvement*, Hilda thought, *though I never really felt that Franz was a tyrant, even those times that I gave in to his wishes. Like his wish to move to Montana, and then his wish to move back to Minnesota, and then his wish to move to the bigger farm. Those were all his wishes, and I was reluctant. Well, maybe not reluctant to return to Minnesota. But it all turned out mostly for the good.*

Hilda almost missed hearing the next words, that Andrew could now kiss the bride. *That's a change. I don't remember that happening in Jane's wedding. I would have been mortified kissing Franz in public, in front of the entire congregation yet.*

Now the organ was playing a joyous song that Hilda didn't recognize. *Probably a modern song.* And the couple were walking arm-in-arm to the back of the church. People were clapping. *What a strange thing to do in church!*

It's just been a couple of years since Jane's wedding. Are things so different in South Dakota? Or have practices changed during those years in both churches?

Next, an usher invited her and Agatha's parents to follow the couple. They would all go to the church dining hall for lunch. Hilda smelled the coffee and guessed there would be familiar farm-style food.

After the newlyweds were given a happy sendoff to a secret somewhere for their honeymoon, the car—still Hilda's—decorated with flowers and pulling tin cans—rattled its way out of town. Hilda resolved to get the Dodge titled in Andrew's name soon, even though it wasn't exactly new anymore. Agatha's parents approached her then, visited briefly, and invited her to get together sometime to get better acquainted.

*　　　*　　　*

Jane said she and her family had to hurry to Sioux Falls to catch their train home, but Grace and her family had a few hours before having to leave. Finally catching a moment with Grace alone, Hilda confided in her: the accusation of a woman and her daughter.

Grace's first remark was, "I'm not too surprised."

"You think that is what Hans was like?"

"No, no. I mean that nowadays it happens. Especially when a soldier is about to be shipped to active duty. He wants 'proof' of commitment from a girl. Maybe he needs affirmation of life. Isn't that what sex is, in a way?... Also, Ma, what have you been thinking of me? Did you think my Linda was a seven-month baby? You know she weighed nine pounds when she was born, seven months after I was married."

"I have to admit I lost a few nights' sleep, Grace, but there was so much else going on, and when she was born, you were married to a fine man who loves you and whom you love. And I think you are happy together. As far as I can tell, Hans didn't love Sharon—that's her name—Sharon Olson. And Sharon doesn't—didn't love Hans, quite obviously. Her mother certainly didn't love Hans. Mostly they think about the shame of having a bastard baby."

"Maybe, if Hans had lived, he would have married Sharon on his next furlough."

"Now we'll never know. *If it is his baby* ... I guess I didn't really know my own son. But maybe he didn't do it. Maybe the girl lied to her mother about her secret life. It's even possible that there is no pregnancy and they are only trying to wrest money from the government."

Hilda recounted the threat of a lawsuit, and her own signing away of any insurance money that might come from the government on Hans's behalf. She took a deep breath and asked, "Grace, if there is a baby, and if the baby is turned over to an orphanage, will you go with me to look at it? See if it looks like Hans when he was a baby?"

"Why? Why not just let it go?"

"I need to know. Is Hans the father? If the baby looks like Hans, I will feel torn about him or her growing up in an orphanage. Orphanages can be terrible places. Like holding pens for pigs or cattle."

"I remember, when I was little, hearing ten or twelve orphans singing in church," Grace said. "Their caretaker offered the congregation to pick one to adopt. I begged you and Pa to adopt a girl for me. You looked sad when you refused."

"Ya. It felt like a livestock auction, or a rummage sale," Hilda added. "Anyway, I would feel awful if Mrs. Olson would change her mind and decide to bring up the child herself. She is a nasty woman. A horrible mother. I even feel sorry for Sharon, with that mother."

"So what will you do if the child looks like Hans? Or if the child looks like Sharon? Children don't always look like their father. *Or* like their mother."

"I don't know, Grace. I'm hoping it doesn't look like Hans. Then I can put it behind me. Turn it over to God."

"And what will you do if you think the baby *does* look like Hans? Adopt it yourself?"

"I'm too old. If I adopted a child now, I would be seventy-five when it would be ten. I don't know how long I will live. My heart sometimes beats funny, and my brain—or maybe it's my eyes—works strangely. I sometimes see people who aren't real. Aren't there at all."

"Oh, Ma. You never told me. Have you seen a doctor about those symptoms?"

No, it really isn't serious. Except I shouldn't even think about adopting a baby."

Grace put her arm around her mother's shoulder. "Look, let's not worry about something that may turn out to be nothing. Who knows, it may be a 'false pregnancy.' Or she may miscarry. Or she may marry someone and keep the baby. Or, as you say, there isn't any baby. So many different things... Have you heard yet? It seems to me the baby should have been born by now."

"No, I haven't heard. You're right. For it to be Hans's baby, it would be several months old by now."

"Well, Ma, why don't you check and let me know? If it does turn out that the baby was born and placed in an orphanage, I'll come with you to look at it. Then we can decide what to do, or find someone who can help us decide."

That night, Hilda was able to sleep, thanking God for her daughter, and trusting God to help her face whatever happened.

*　　　*　　　*

When local gossip brought the news that Sharon Olson had a baby boy, Hilda inquired of the orphanage at Our Lady of Perpetual Help if they had a baby boy up for adoption. The woman answering the phone was reluctant to give out any information, but from the way she sounded, Hilda figured they did. She called Grace, who agreed to come the next weekend.

*　　　*　　　*

Grace did all the talking. She introduced herself: "I am a married mother of one child who would like to have more children but am not able to. Could we see your babies?" Hilda allowed her heart to leap, just a little bit.

There were five. The oldest one was several months old. A boy. Awake. Hilda saw the soft, dark hair. Dark like Hans's. Not blonde like Sharon's. The skin, ruddy like Hans's, not pale pink like Sharon's. The earlobe, the nose. He looked at Grace and reached his hand toward her dangly earring. He was the image of Hans when he was a baby. Hilda looked at Grace. *What is she thinking?*

Grace was looking only at the baby. "What is the birth date of this baby?" she asked. The date jibed with Sharon's expected delivery date.

They stood looking. Grace spoke again, "May I hold him?" Hilda's heart leaped a little more.

As she reached for him and held him close, looking into his face, Grace continued. "Why was he given up?"

The matron stiffened. "We can't give you any information. The mother wants her privacy. There is no father."

"Well, I want this child. What do I have to do to adopt him?" Hilda's heart was wildly leaping.

"Are you Catholic?"

"Why, yes, as a matter of fact, I am," she lied.

"That's all we ask. That he be brought up in the Catholic faith. He's been baptized here."

"When can I have him?"

"You may take him now. We are overcrowded as it is … and we usually don't keep babies long. Except that he's a boy. Girls are easier to adopt out. Are you interested in another, older one, as a playmate for him?"

"Not today. Maybe in a year or so."

*   *   *

The baby was in Grace's arms as they left for her car. Hilda carried an extra diaper and a bottle of milk, all that the baby brought with him, besides the somewhat ragged shirt he was wearing and the blanket he was wrapped in.

"I didn't know you were Catholic, Grace. I thought you were Episcopalian."

"I'm not Catholic. But they'll never know. I live out of state, out of their diocese, remember. And he's going to visit his grandmother and learn about the Mennonites also."

"What will Hugo say? Does he even know where you are today?"

"Ma, I *have* talked the idea over with Hugo. Thoroughly. I've given the idea a lot of thought. I've prayed about it. I want this baby, no matter who the father is, even though in my heart, I believe it is Hans's. I already love him."

"I still have the old cradle. Do you want to take it?"

"Sure, Ma, and we'll stop in town for more clothes, diapers, bottles, and milk. I can hardly wait to show him to Hugo. And Linda. She's been asking for a baby brother."

"What will you name him?"

"I'll check with Hugo. How about naming him after his father? I always liked 'Hans' for a name. And 'Hugo' for a middle name… What fun we'll have!"

"One thing, Grace: don't tell my pa or Muttah about Hans. I don't know how they would take it. As for telling Jane or Andrew, use your judgment. I haven't told them anything about Sharon or the baby. Of course, maybe as he grows older, they'll notice how much he resembles Hans. Mainly, I'd rather not let it be known in town; it's nobody's business."

CHAPTER FORTY-FOUR: 1952–54

Hilda surveyed her new home. With Andrew at her side, she entered through the back-door hallway that led to the cellar stairs and kitchen. "I do like my new kitchen—my first one with electric oven, stove, and refrigerator. No more corncobs or cow chips." She whirled toward the sink, turned a spigot, and pulled at Andrew's sleeve. "Look, running water. Not a hand pump." Then, rubbing her hands across the smooth wooden counter space, she added, "This will be easy to keep clean."

She pointed to the cheery flowered wallpaper. "This even goes with the upholstery of my sofa and chair. See how sunny and airy the parlor is, with its two wide windows, one in each wall? That'll be good for my blooming plants."

Joining her, Andrew said, "The center table will have to stand against a wall. It would be too crowded sitting in the center of the room. Oh, and, Agatha is pleased that you left the pump organ on the farm for her to play. I hope you won't miss it too much."

"Ya, this room is too small for the organ, but I'll come to the farm and play it now and then. And listen to Agatha play. Otherwise, the eating room spills through the double doors into the parlor, so to say—or the other way around. If we expand the round-oak table when everyone is here, people can visit back and forth between the two rooms. I like the pantry right there, too. It's handy."

He turned to the bedroom. "I'm glad you have a bedroom downstairs. Not that you couldn't climb stairs to sleep up there."

Hilda added, "At least I can so far. But this one down here is convenient to the bathroom."

They looked into the bathroom: her first one, with a claw-footed tub big enough to stretch out in. "I hope you can get as nice a bathroom on the farm as this," Hilda said.

Andrew answered with a chuckle. "I guess we could come here to take baths."

Hilda's retorted, "Huh!"

They climbed the rather steep steps to two bedrooms upstairs. "It might not be comfortable for a guest to have to walk through the first one to the second bedroom," Hilda noted, "but, oh well, it will only be used for family visitors. The closets under the eaves are useful."

Last, they inspected the cellar, with its cool cement walls and floor, fine for storing canned goods and root vegetables. "I can imagine our boys, someday, riding their tricycles down here when we visit you," Andrew said.

Hilda added, "Or roller skating."

"I don't think boys do much roller skating. Usually it's girls."

"You're behind the times, Andrew. I saw a young boy skating on the sidewalk yesterday. Besides, don't count your boys before they're hatched," Hilda chuckled. "Who knows—you might have a passel of girls. No boys."

Turning from Andrew's blushing face, Hilda peered into the cistern filled almost to capacity. "I'll be tempted to waste water. I remember how frugal we had to be with water in Montana. Used well water for laundry and even baths. Turned our white clothing gray. Made our skin itch."

"Well," Andrew said, as he looked at his watch and started back upstairs toward the back door, "I'm glad things are better here. Let me know if there is anything you need me to do. I'm never so busy that I can't come to help out."

*   *   *

After Andrew left, Hilda took a closer look at details. Her new home needed work: painting outside and inside, and cleaning. The door hinges squeaked; you could never sneak through those doors. The kitchen floor linoleum was cracked and should be replaced before anyone tripped and fell. The parlor could use a colorful rug—a soft, warm one.

Not speaking aloud—speaking aloud would sound demented, should anyone overhear—she looked at the oak flooring of both front rooms. *Should I refinish those floors? Could my back and knees take the work? My lumbago hasn't bothered me much lately, but I've been careful not to overdo. Maybe someone from church could help and wouldn't charge too much.*

*   *   *

Her first evening in her new home, Hilda filled the porcelain bathtub with warm water—water heated by an electric heater. Not water she'd have to heat over the stove. She felt a little silly, filling it so full, but what of it? She wouldn't do it every day. She lowered herself into the bottom of the tub, listened to the overflow gurgling as the water she displaced rose almost to the top. She lay still for a while and then wiggled her toes and paddled with her hands, feeling the water splash gently at her chin. She sank down more, her head under water, and blew some bubbles, letting her hair drift around her.

Laughing aloud, she was glad she was alone. *Franz would laugh. But what would the children say?* When the water cooled, she considered adding hot water, but she looked at her wrinkled fingers and decided she could do it again some other time, providing the cistern had enough water in it.

She dressed and ate a little of the roast chicken Agatha had sent along for her, with a tvaybak and a tomato. It was still light outside. She found her hoe to steady herself as she walked around the back yard. Andrew had tilled about half; it was good black soil and would sustain a healthy garden. She examined a vigorous rhubarb plant and a bush that looked like mulberry right next to the border of her lot. If it bore good fruit, she'd make mulberry jam and mulberry-rhubarb pie.

She hoped no one would want to develop that now-empty neighboring plot; they might not want mulberries dropping on their land. Or droppings on their drying sheets from birds that ate the mulberries. Oh well.

*   *   *

Before long, neighbors called on her, bringing still-warm cookies or new tomatoes or cucumbers from their gardens. A member of the Meadow Church—now no longer in a meadow but in town and still called "Meadow" by the old-time members—offered her rides to Sunday worship and to ladies' sewing circle meetings. Oh, she could walk to church, she wasn't in such bad shape, but it was a bit far, about six blocks each way, and she could save her strength.

The owner of the hardware store came around to ask if Hilda was available to keep his blind, aging mother company and read to her. Hilda wasn't bold enough to ask how old she was but guessed she'd be close to Pa's age. She lived in an apartment above the store. He would pay her. Certainly, the pay would be good; it would help boost Hilda's Social Security status. As a farm wife, there was very little in her name.

It turned out that Hilda enjoyed the old lady who asked to be called by her name, Nata. Though she couldn't see, Nata could hear and speak very well, and recounted many stories about her life in the old country, not far from the Sea of Azov. Her stories echoed tales Pa and Ma had told of their childhoods.

"I was a young girl, attending the Mennonite school before emigrating to the New World. Some years before, Catherine the Great promised us immigrants from the north of Europe freedom from conscription, freedom to keep our Low-German language, and freedom to have our own schools. In return, we drew on our farming methods as we worked the dry land.

"She also expected us to be a kind of buffer to the Turks. Catherine kept her promise, and subsequent Tsars—Paul I, Alexander I, and Nicholas I continued the concessions.

"In May of 1818, Alexander I even visited the community in person and ate our tvaybak. My, how all the people—including our parents—cleaned house, swept the yards, and curried the horses to get ready. He gave a ruby ring to one of our elders; I don't remember who that was."

"How was it," Hilda wondered, "that the Mennonites were so proud to welcome the Tsar?"

"Even though we Mennonites aren't active in politics, we do follow Jesus' admonition to render to Caesar what is Caesar's and to God what is God's. Mennonites always pay taxes and follow the law, even though we don't run for office or swear oaths. Remember, the word 'tsar' is a shorter way of saying 'Caesar.'"

"But in the 1870s," Nata went on, "word came that our young men would be drafted, and our separateness would be put at risk. Soon hardship set in; supplies became scarce, and the schools and churches were threatened. I was hungry and cold; I remember warming myself by hugging the cow one cold evening. That was when my parents and others decided to accept the invitation from the United States railroad companies to settle in Minnesota, South Dakota, Nebraska, and Kansas. Some went to Canada."

"That's about when my parents, and Franz's, also immigrated here," Hilda said. "But have you heard of Americans, back in 1931 or '32—anyway, during the Depression—re-emigrating to Russia because they were jobless and hungry? Franz told me about that. He heard it in town. Russia was the USSR then, or part of it, and Stalin invited poor Americans—even negroes—to Russia where he promised them jobs, food, and school for their children."

"Yes," Nata replied. "Poor folk. And they were never heard from again. Nobody knows what happened to them during the 'terror' years."[42]

"I wonder if they were able to keep their Christian beliefs. Franz said the country wasn't particularly Christian."

"Actually, they were atheist. I think those émigrés were not leaving to keep their faith. They were emigrating for food. Maybe they didn't care one way or another about keeping Christian beliefs."

---

42 See *Remember Us: Letters from Stalin's Gulag, 1930–37* by Ruth Derksen Siemens; *The Forsaken: An American Tragedy in Stalin's Russia* by Tim Tzouliadis; and a film, *Through the Red Gate.*

"Well, we had a hard time during the Depression," Hilda said, "but we didn't starve, and we were allowed to keep our faith. I wonder what *we* would have done there, then."

"Depends on how strong your faith is, I guess. Back when I could see, I read a lot. I read that early Protestants, even Mennonites, were tortured and actually killed for their beliefs. And that wasn't in Russia. It was in Spain, I think. Or France. It could have been Germany. They were deemed heretics."

"I wonder if I would have been strong enough. Would you?"

Nata answered, "Probably not."

Hilda soon looked forward to the days when she was scheduled to visit Nata, and she took on additional duties: washing Nata's hair and combing it, and bringing her fresh, homemade bread. She hoped she could continue this job for a long time, though she was warned by Nata's children that Nata's health might fail any time.

*   *   *

Meanwhile, Hilda was busy at home. She set aside time each day to cut triangular pieces of cloth remnants for a quilt, and when she had enough to sew into a dozen star shapes, she pinned them in place on a large washed-out flour sack. Then she opened the trusty Singer to sew them all together.

As she sewed, she talked to herself, silently of course. *I don't mind being alone in the house. There do seem to be days when I don't see anyone; sometimes it's several days. The house is quiet, so I turn on the radio to hear the Old Fashioned Revival Hour, which has lively piano music and choir, or a doctor talking about healthy eating... I should cut down on butter. And I don't need more than one cookie for lunch.*

Maybe if I had an animal to feed or care for. But I don't want a dog; dogs are noisy. A cat? Well, always in the house? A bird? A singing canary would be pleasant. I'll ask the Sunset Home people where they got theirs.

Once in a while, it seems as if there are people in the room. Lots of people I don't know, people who don't say anything, and who disappear when I turn to look straight at them. I wonder who they are. Should I tell the children about them? Or the doctor? Maybe they'd think I'm losing my mind. Better not. Come to think of it, I did mention it to Grace that day after Andrew's wedding, but all Grace did was ask if I had told it to a doctor. She didn't push it.

Another thing is, sometimes I feel so tired. When I think about it, my heart beats oddly. So I don't think about it. And, my joints hurt, especially in the mornings, so I sit at the side of my bed for a while to adjust them. It's hard to pull on my stockings. The doctor gave me a cane and some pain pills that should ease the pain. He pointed out that they would be hard on my heart, so I oughtn't take too many. How many are too many?

*   *   *

After a year or so, Nata died in her sleep. Her children called Hilda with the news and brought her a last generous pay envelope. Hilda went to the funeral, puzzled that she didn't know the names of many of the mourners. Nata had been a member of another church, but, still, this was a small town, and usually everybody knows everybody. Not this time, however.

With summer coming, Hilda turned her attention to her garden. She filled it with seeds she had saved: tomatoes and cabbages, started in little pots before danger of frost was over. Other seeds—beans, peas, carrots, lettuce, and even sweet corn and potato eyes—she planted when the soil warmed. The children wondered when she would eat all that, but Hilda assured them that she would can what she couldn't eat herself, or what they didn't want, and give the rest to the church to distribute. Someone is always hungry.

*   *   *

Next fall, word came from Oregon that Muttah Heldin was ailing. That lump on her arm was the cause of it. It should have been removed years ago. Now, cancer had moved into her bones. She was not going to get well. At the news, Hilda sat in her rocking chair. She tried to think how she felt. There was just a heavy feeling inside her chest. She tried to picture Muttah. Smiling? Laughing? It didn't come. Muttah frowning? No, that didn't come either. Muttah just looking straight at her? Even that didn't appear.

The strange crowds of people massed beside her. Hilda rose; it was getting dark outside, and she turned on the light and the radio, and that woke Yellow Bill—"Bill" for short—her canary, who began to sing with the radio.

*   *   *

Both of Muttah's children, Hermann and Marta, and their children as well, came from Oregon and Montana on the train that carried Pa and the plain wooden coffin with Muttah in it. Liesebet and Joe came also, but John and Marie did not. Hilda told Jane and Grace they shouldn't feel obligated, but they and their families also came. They had not all been together since Hilda and Franz left Montana.

The funeral, held in the new Meadow Church, was a simple service, as Muttah would have wanted it, attended by some older folk who once knew her. Joe spoke a few words, calling her a good woman, and a quartet sang "Jesu geh voran." Hilda remembered that song had been part of Jane's wedding. Jesus leading throughout one's life, even to the end.

288

They buried Muttah in the old cemetery above the creek that still flowed, and across the road from the cornfield where the original Meadow Church once stood. Between her and Ma's graves was space for the eventual resting place of Hilda's father.

After a few meals and a few nights together at Hilda's house, cousin Henry and Emma's home, and Andrew and Agatha's farm—that old farmhouse could put up a lot of overnight guests—the Oregon and Montana people left to resume their lives and work. Pa stayed on.

CHAPTER FORTY-FIVE: 1954–55

How odd to be a child again. I am a child, but not a child, Hilda thought as she looked across the table to her father. To address him as Pa. Now, a month after he joined her in her little home, she took her turn to lay out today's clothes, prompt him to wash his hands before eating, and remind him of bedtime.

Not many people came to call. Only a few old timers were around, people who knew him when he was a farmer-preacher-healer. Those still alive—including his sister, Aunt Mary, who was no longer able to call on him—sat in rocking chairs in the Sunset Home. Her son, Peter, came now and then; with little to say, he'd sit for a while and then leave. Reverend Hubner, the pastor of the Meadow Church, or his wife, regularly stopped in, bringing the week's church bulletin and praying with them. During their short visits, they seemed to keep their hands on the doorknob, barely sitting down for a few minutes.

Hilda didn't attend Sunday services much these days, feeling uncomfortable about leaving Pa alone. When she suggested they both go, he didn't seem interested. They tried it once. His hearing was adequate in conversation one-on-one, but he said he couldn't follow the sermon. Hilda wasn't sure how much he could follow the radio pastor's preaching either.

She had given him her bedroom and her bedstead made of curlicued cast-iron painted blue, with its soft innerspring mattress. She had to puff climbing the stairs to an upstairs bedroom, but she didn't want to turn her parlor into a bedroom for him. She gave herself one concession: she used a chamber pot to avoid going downstairs during the night, and she secretly emptied and rinsed it every morning before he got up, along with the jug he used so he wouldn't have to get out of bed. He sometimes was disoriented, even though she kept several nightlights turned on.

He was always there—not that he was underfoot, but she felt inhibited.

She had gotten used to doing whatever she felt like doing: hoeing in the garden, stopping to chat with neighbors when they were outside, or hiking to the post office for a weekly letter from Jane or a monthly one from Grace. She wanted to give him a little push, to pull himself together. "Don't just sit there, go outside, take a walk, how about pulling weeds in the garden?"

Instead, he sat in the rocking chair, his feet maybe on the footstool, reading his New Testament or his hymnbook. Often he wept, wiping his eyes with his large white handkerchief. Sometimes he sang, his voice an old man's cracked timbre: "This world is not my home; I'm just a-passin' through. If Heaven's not my home, then Lord, what will I do? The angels beckon me from Heaven's open door, and I can't feel at home in this world anymore." It was an English song the young people in his church had sung. Usually, however, he sang old familiar German songs. His favorite was *"So nimm denn meine Hände und führe mich; bis an mein selig ende, und eviglich. ich mag allein nicht gehen, nicht einen schritt. wo du wirst gehen und stehen, da nimm mich mit.* "[43]

His singing inspired Yellow Bill, and Hilda wondered, *If I laughed about the duet, would he feel hurt?*

Pa seemed to perk up when young people called on him. Andrew or Agatha, or both together—with their twins Frank and James—stopped in frequently, and sat with him while he talked about early days, even about his life as a growing boy in the Ukraine. The boys listened too, bypassing the toys Hilda kept on hand in her house for their visits.

"My great-grandfather was born in Prussia near Marienburg in 1749. He and his children lived there until around 1820, when they moved to the Molotschna Colony north of the Black Sea.

"Winters challenged us. Our Russian stove, made of fieldstones and surfaced with cement, warmed the house. My mother used it for cooking and heating. It was so big you could sleep on top of it. Outside it was bitter cold. When cold weather started, I put on a warm union suit. By the time weather mellowed in spring, one sleeve would fall off, then another sleeve, and then a pants leg. In spring, when the water in the creek was warm enough for my first bath, the entire union suit would have fallen off."

"Didn't you smell?" Andrew asked.

He chuckled. "Nah, we all stank. You don't mind so much if everybody smells the same."

When Grace visited, she introduced her toddler, Hansle, while his sister, Linda, hung back behind her skirt. Their great-grandpa laid his hand on the child's head and said, "Fine boy. He reminds me of his Uncle Hans."

---

43 "Take Thou my hand, and lead Thou me, until my journey ends, eternally. Alone I will not wander, one single step; be Thou my true companion, and with me stay."

Whereupon, Linda came forward and asked him, "Will you pat my head too?" Grace did not mention that their son was adopted. She and Hugo had agreed not to tell Hansle himself, or Linda. Not yet, maybe not ever. They'd see.

Jane, who lived farther away now, juggling her studies with mothering, also came whenever she could. She told many tales about her classes and about the patients at the insane asylum where Robert worked. Their two children were active but well behaved, even though, with such busy parents, they spent lots of time with the hired girl.

Every day, Pa waited for Hilda to walk to the post office to collect his mail. One time, when he asked her to go, she said, "I'll go after I finish some ironing, now that my iron is hot. Just be patient."

"Patient, patient, patient," he sighed. "All my ninety years I have never learned patience."

"You certainly were patient when you had your cataract surgery," Hilda reminded him. "Ten days immobile in bed with sandbags on each side of your head holding you still!"

"That's different. A different kind of patience. You know. When you don't have a choice. You can be outwardly putting up with something and still be seething, impatient inside."

Whenever he got mail from John in Montana, or Hermann or Marta in Oregon, he seemed to brighten. He immediately dictated a reply for Hilda to write, since his tremor made his writing illegible. Hilda's own developing tremor was less bothersome mornings so the following day, before mailing the letter, she'd re-copy what she had written. His messages concerned the weather, and something he had heard on the radio. Each one ended with a paternal blessing, a kind of benediction that his children could think of as a ritual farewell.

Writing in formal German script was good practice for Hilda; her letters to her daughters were also written in German, but her grammar was sloppy. Really, just informal. She considered also writing benedictions to them, but decided, *That's not like me, so I won't start now.*

One warm afternoon, Pa surprised Hilda by shuffling outside with his little box camera to snap a picture of her and a neighbor while they were laughing about something—she couldn't bring to mind what. Surely something trivial or she'd remember. She did recall that the wind whipped their aprons high and mussed their hair. He joined their laughter and then shambled back indoors. There she found him later, again in his rocker, saying, "What if I had died in that moment of frivolity? How would I meet my maker?" He wasn't asking for an answer.

But what of the question Hilda had kept and set aside through the years? *Now he's here, and we can finally have that conversation I've so longed for. What would be a good time to bring it up? Perhaps after a prayer—but not after a mealtime prayer: the food would get cold. Bedtime devotions are also not a good time. The discussion might be too stimulating for us both, bring about wakefulness. Sunday might be a good day, in the morning after listening to a church service on the radio.*

The opportunity arrived. A radio preacher had just vehemently decried heathen beliefs: Islam, Hinduism, Jewish Orthodoxy, Atheism, Agnosticism, Animism, Catholicism—both Roman and Orthodox. Hilda couldn't catch, or remember, all the false religions he cited.

She decided to ask a non-leading question: "What do you think of that sermon, Pa?"

"Oh, I don't know. He was very fiery. He must be very sure of himself."

"He is a well-known Christian. His program is broadcasted on many stations all over the United States every Sunday. Lots of people are following him. Do you think he's right?"

"Well, there are all kinds of people. All kinds of beliefs. They all think they are right. They all have followers."

Hilda decided to be more direct: "We Mennonites think *we* are right. Or don't you think that?"

"Sure, the Mennonite Church is right for us."

Hilda tried one more time. "But even in the Mennonite church, people come up with strong assertions about faith that I think you don't support. When you were a pastor, how did you deal with those people, and what they claim?"

"I couldn't—didn't—deal. I let them think what they wanted. Maybe because, in my mind, I never knew if *my* beliefs were right. I never achieved total conviction. Certainty. I don't even know if there is a Heaven. Or where it is. If there is one, I want to go there. I think God understands." He yawned and stretched his legs as he put his feet onto the hassock.

Hilda saw that his eyes were closed, his mouth soon slightly open. She decided not to wipe the little bit of spittle that hung from his chin, for that would wake him. If only she could have asked him that nagging question when she was a child, or even last year. *How do you know if you are right with God? How can I know?*

*   *   *

He was weak. Didn't eat enough. Each day seemed like the one before, and Hilda could imagine it would always be so. But one morning, it wasn't the same. The house was quiet when she awoke. She had overslept. She came downstairs, pulled the cover off the birdcage, and talked to Bill. Right away, he jumped on his perch and chipped at his cuttlebone.

She poured some oatmeal, which Pa said kept him regular, into her enameled pan. She added water and a pinch of salt for taste, and set it on the back burner to simmer. Then she put on water to heat for coffee and set the table.

When the water was hot, she poured some over coffee grounds in the old pewter pot. She deliberately made noise, tapping her spoon against the edge of the saucepan, moving his chair across the hard floor. It screeched. Probably scratched the floor some more.

After a bit, she decided to knock on his door and then peer through a crack to see if he was sitting up. He wasn't. Boldly, she walked in and rubbed his arm, hoping he would not be annoyed by her intrusion.

Then she knew.

Do you call a doctor after someone has died? When you know for sure? Do you call the mortician? The minister? She decided to call Andrew; he would know what to do.

*   *   *

A small group gathered for his funeral. His children said they were busy harvesting, and, after all, had seen him not too long ago when he was alive. That was how they wanted to remember him. They arranged for flowers to be placed on the coffin, with the words "Beloved Father" printed in large gold letters on blue ribbon. Grace and Jane and their families did come, as much to stand beside their mother as to show grief for their grandfather. Henry and Emma Heldin, and Amos and Anna Lober also attended, for her sake.

Words at his graveside were read from a collection of his writings that he had kept through the years. His body was lowered between the graves of Katherine and Leah, as he had directed. The bouquet of flowers rested on the fresh ground now covering the site, level with the surrounding turf. The large tombstone, bought many years before, listed all three names. His death date would have to be carved after his name, later. Perhaps Andrew could arrange for that after the harvest.

Before she left the cemetery, Hilda wandered over to Franz's grave. She wouldn't talk with him, because she knew he wasn't there to hear, but she looked at his stone and thought of him. It had her name on it too, with her birth date, but with space for when she dies. A fill-in-the-blanks.

She thought of her dead sons. *We didn't bring Cherub's remains to the cemetery. Why didn't we? His grave is still on the farm—now Andrew's farm— above the creek. Well, Franz's death took over all my thoughts Maybe we could still move him. What would Grace, Andrew, and Jane think of the idea?*

But Hans's body can't also be buried here. Will he ever be found? Maybe not.

So the family isn't complete. Probably the other children will have their own family plots somewhere, some day. Perhaps not even here in this cemetery.

Weeds were growing over Franz's grave. She stooped to pull them, wondering, *Isn't it somebody's job to pull the weeds?* The ground had settled, grave-shaped. *That must mean the casket has caved in. Worms and decay. Dust to dust. Ashes to ashes ... but there aren't any ashes—just dust, worms, and decay. Well, the same thing happened to Ma's grave some years ago, and the cemetery people simply filled the hollow with more dirt and planted new grass over it. So that's what happens.*

As she weeded, she tried to sort out what she felt, what she believed she had been taught about the afterlife. *If there is a second coming, a day when Jesus returns to welcome all his believers, why does it matter if we're all within an acre of each other? All facing East as we raise our heads from the ground? Why East?*

Hilda wondered at herself that she didn't burst into tears.

CHAPTER FORTY-SIX: 1955–

All the out-of-town relatives had gone home. Andrew and Agatha were working on a last cutting of hay before a threatening rainstorm.

Hilda was again alone. Not the child of a living father, not the wife of a living husband, not the mother of children in the house. Just the keeper of a singing canary named Yellow Bill, in a little house in town. The sewer of little quilt blocks for the church mission circle. The hoer of weeds in the garden. Alone, except for the silent, elusive crowd at her side. She hadn't noticed them so much when Pa was with her.

She decided to allow herself a few days. She'd still sleep upstairs. It didn't feel right to sleep on the mattress on which he had died. Not yet. She'd keep it, though; it was too good, too new to replace; the waterproof mattress cover had protected it. Maybe, when he had time, Andrew could come turn it. She did open the two windows to freshen the air in the room. She emptied the clothes closet; a volunteer at the local secondhand store came to pick up the suits and even the everyday clothes. She would wash the floor and woodwork tomorrow. Not that they were dirty.

As for his Bible, his books, his letters—those he had received, as well as papers he had written? Well, they could wait. The cellar had room for them. One of these days, she'd look at them, or offer them to his second-family children. Muttah's children, Hermann and Marta.

Neighbors, friends, and relatives had filled her refrigerator with food— most of it sweet or starchy. Who did they suppose should eat it? Thinking about it made her stomach feel overloaded. She looked out the window to see how the garden was doing. It could use attention. The rhubarb plant had gone to seed. Overripe tomatoes had dropped to the ground; cucumbers had turned yellow. She took a spade and pail out with her to check on the potatoes and found that, even though she had neglected the weeds around the plants, the potatoes underneath were large and smooth. She felt her mouth watering for one, or maybe even two, baked potatoes. With butter. She picked up a few ripe tomatoes and found some cucumbers that were not overgrown, for a salad.

There seemed to be nobody working next door at the moment. The new neighbor was indeed building a house abutting the hearty mulberry bush, just as she had expected—dreaded—someone would do. *Why are they plunking their back door porch right up against it? Well, maybe not right against it, but facing it. Can't they see that the bush is there first? It's on my property; they can't cut it down. They'll find out: It won't be pleasant next summer when the mulberries are ripe.*

Who are the neighbors anyhow? Whoever it is didn't show up at my door before the funeral, nor at the funeral. They must be English, not Mennonites.

It was a new feeling. Hilda tried to think whether she was ever unwelcoming toward a new neighbor. *What should I do? Bring them a mulberry pie or a jar of mulberry jam when they move in? Would it be best to wait and see if they ever mention the mulberry bush instead of attracting attention to it by offering them jam? Maybe I should bring them something else, some fresh tvaybak. Perhaps we'll end up liking each other. Who knows?*

Back in the house, Hilda set her oven to bake. A big oven for just two potatoes, but so what? Sure, she could boil them, but who wants boiled potatoes all the time? She scrubbed the rich black dirt off them and admired their perfect shape. *Prize winning*, she decided. She pierced them, and placed them in the middle of the oven, so they could heat as the oven heated.

While they were baking, Hilda set the table. She found a clean white tablecloth, one she hadn't used since Pa had come to live with her, given that he tended to spill. She found her favorite plate and cup, and the knife and three-tined fork she always used. She thought of lighting a candle, but she didn't need the light. Besides, this wasn't a celebration. Just a kind of homecoming.

What to eat with the potatoes? Well, butter. The tomato and cucumber, sliced. Meat? There was some leftover baloney from the funeral lunch, but she wasn't hungry for it. She decided to skip eating meat. The two potatoes would be ample.

While waiting for the potatoes to finish baking, she considered reading her Bible. Then she decided not to. Who would know? She felt a sense of freedom, a little like the feeling she had at first when Franz left her alone with Grace on that trip to Lame Wolf. How guilty she felt when the blizzard kept her "free" for an entire week. But she was weary of guilt. Why should she feel guilty?

Aware that the house was quiet, though she could still hear the wind in the trees, it occurred to her that, during the time Pa lived with her, she hardly ever saw the crowd of nebulous people. If she had, she might have asked him if he saw them too. If he had, he might have known who they were. Angels? But angels were white, blindingly white. These were dark. Shadowy. Now they were again at her side.

She turned on the radio to the public radio station that usually played music. Sure enough, Bill joined in the music. She wondered, *Does Bill see them?*

*   *   *

Now, whenever Hilda went outdoors, there was no need to hurry back indoors to see to Pa. She found that she welcomed running into one neighbor, Mrs. Esau, who spoke Low German, but with a Kansas accent. They soon addressed each other informally as "du," or by name. Miriam had a recipe for sweet pickles, and Hilda gave her a dill pickle recipe, the one made in a stone crock that was ready to eat in just a couple of days. She covered them with a layer of fresh grape leaves from a wild plant tangled with a currant bush in the far corner of her garden.

Hilda asked about the new house that was being built, though she didn't mention how very close it stood to her lot (and to her mulberry bush). Miriam offered to introduce them, "They're nice people, though they're English and Lutheran; named Miller or Muller. Something like that."

Hilda declined. "I'd rather meet them more casually when I see them outdoors."

*   *   *

Henry and Emma came now and then. Emma followed Hilda around the house to look at her flowers thriving in tin-can pots on the window sills. She talked to Bill. Henry looked around, asking, "What would you like me to do?" Referring to the help he gave Franz after the tornado years ago, he said, "Build a fence?"

Taking his offer seriously, Hilda replied, "No, I don't need a fence here in town. There aren't any loose cattle to keep out."

Henry laughed. "It *is* a far cry from country living here. How about hanging your storm windows?"

"It's too early. We still have many warm days. Besides, I haven't washed them yet. But there is one thing." Hilda wondered if she should ask this: "Could you cut the branches of my mulberry bush that are hanging over the neighbor's property?"

"Sure. But, why? Don't you want them to have any?"

"No, that's not it. I'm thinking of the stains ripe mulberries will make on their porch steps—or droppings when the birds eat the mulberries."

"You know," Henry told her, "there are mulberry bushes all around town. Birds can bring purple droppings from anywhere."

"Still, I think it's good-neighborly to keep your branches from hanging over the neighbor's property. But, if you don't want to …"

Henry got up. "Of course I will. I'll go look at it now."

When he returned, he told her, "I looked at the bush, and at their building. I don't think their porch door will be facing your bush. It looks as if it will be at the side next to their house, not straight out to the back. They'll undoubtedly put a sidewalk toward the street, so any mulberries—or droppings from your bush—will fall on the ground."

"What do you suggest, then, Henry?"

"I can still cut the bush. Or not. Whatever you say."

"Oh, don't cut the whole bush. Just the branches that are hanging over the line."

"Do you know exactly where the line is?"

"I'm not sure. I didn't think of that, Henry. Maybe we'd better forget about cutting branches today. I'll ask Andrew if he knows where the property line is. Meanwhile, it would look lopsided if just one side was cut."

Emma chimed in, "I'm glad this is your most important concern. Here at your new place you could have all sorts of problems—water in the basement, leaky roof …"

"You're right, Emma. Thanks. And, Henry, I guess I don't have any job for you to do. Maybe you can sing to Bill and look at my flowers."

"Geraniums are pretty, but I never did like their smell."

"They do have a strong smell, but you get used to it. Look at my African violets: they're about to bloom. And here is my 'mother-in-law's tongue': they say it never blooms—but this one does."

Through her laughter, Emma said, "I should have one to give to my daughter-in-law. Can you give me a cutting?"

Then coffee was ready, and they sat down to some freshly baked tvaybak. Next July, they would enjoy fresh mulberry jam with tvaybak.

*   *   *

Hilda got better acquainted with Miriam, also a widow who relived past events in her life while pondering them. They took turns offering each other coffee. Hilda shared some feelings and opinions with her that she never told her children or even Franz. Some, but not all. She did not mention her amorphous visitors.

Miriam said, "Come to my church some time, maybe even next Sunday for communion. It's walking distance, just a block away. Are you able to walk that far?"

"I can, if I walk slowly and carry my cane. My joints work better in the mornings."

"I have the same problem. What are you taking for pain?"

"Usually aspirin. I'm not supposed to take too much, because of my heart, but I don't know how much is 'too much.' So I just keep taking some until it helps."

Miriam hooted. "I take lots too. We're the 'aspirin ladies.' We can write a song about us!" She twirled, a bit awkwardly.

It felt good to laugh with a friend. Hilda decided she'd go to any church with this lovely woman, no matter the church. It sounded like an interesting idea. "Well, then, sometime you must visit my church also."

*   *   *

For her visit to Miriam's church, Hilda chose her best dress, the one she wore to Pa's funeral, and her new hat with a perky flower on it. She had considered, for the funeral, whether the flower was a bit frivolous-looking, but decided that Pa's death was not to be mourned overmuch. He had longed to "go home." His funeral, a kind of celebration, had been recognition of his lifelong contributions to God, the church, and his family.

Hilda noticed the building had a large entry for everyone. Not separate men's and women's entry rooms. Inside the sanctuary, the men and women mingled, often in family groups. She thought about the advantage of women and men being separated so unmarried or widowed persons were simply with others of their gender—not unnecessarily seated next to or behind someone of the opposite sex.

On the other hand, when families sat as a group, the children were under their parents' supervision. She thought back to the day just last summer when a girl in the Meadow Church had played with a mirror that danced, reflecting light-spots around the ceiling and even into the preacher's face. It attracted Hilda's attention—and everyone else's. It interrupted the preacher, who said solemnly that the mirror should be put away. That ended it, but it took a while before Hilda could redirect her thoughts toward the lesson of the day.

The service in this church was familiar in that the ritual—if you can call what happens in a Mennonite church a "ritual"—was in the same order as that of her Meadow Church. The quite bookish sermon by the young dignified minister dealt with the frustration Moses must have felt, not being allowed to enter the promised land after being permitted to see it from afar.

Moses talked directly with God; he even saw God's face—or his back, depending on which account you read. At least that's what Hilda had read in the book of Exodus.

She thought of disappointments she had experienced. Her setbacks had been of an entirely different kind, not possible to compare with those of a leader of the Children of Israel. She knew she could talk directly to God, but sadly, her talks, her prayers, hadn't felt like how she understood Moses' conversations to be. Certainly she had never gotten what seemed like a clear answer from God, but something she had to figure out. It was far from seeing God's face, or even his back.

Again, since she couldn't talk directly with God, Hilda wished she could talk with Pa, the Pa she had known before he was old and feeble, when she believed he knew the answers. These notions, in spite of her new friendship, were not ideas she could talk over with Miriam.

After the service, the congregants did what churchgoers did in the Meadow Church: they lingered and chatted to catch up with each other's doings. Hilda had forgotten that Franz was once a member there, and that his sisters were still attending. This Mennonite church that Pa described was more liberal than the Meadow Church.

Then, Mathilda and Esther appeared and reached out their hands.

Mathilda said. "You must come to our house for faspa soon. We sisters live together now that our husbands have both died and our children are grown up."

"And I'd like you to come see me, now that I live in town," she replied. It occurred to Hilda that she and Mathilda had almost the same name. Could "Hilda" be a shortening of "Mathilda"?

As she walked home with Miriam, after thanking her for the invitation and remarking that the sermon had been most interesting, Hilda could think of nothing else to say. Miriam, however, said, "While you and your sisters-in-law were talking, I visited with some other people, and one of them told me that your Grace's youngest is adopted. Is that so?"

Surprised, Hilda asked, "Where did that come from? Why should that matter?"

"Oh, I don't think it matters. But everyone says how much that little boy looks like Grace, and even like Hans. His name is 'Hans' too, isn't it? And yet they say he's adopted."

"Well, if people ask, you can tell them that he is very much Grace and Hugo's child, and my grandchild." Hilda was proud that she was telling the truth here, without admitting to anything. "They named him after Grace's brother and my father in their memory." That was also the truth. "'Hans' is another name for 'John,' which was Pa's name. By the way, do you know where the gossip started?"

"All they said was, 'We heard that ...' You know how people pass on what they hear, or even just partly hear. Like the old whispering game. 'Telephone,' I think it's called."

Hilda resolved to pass on to Grace what Miriam had mentioned. Some day, she supposed, little Hansle would have to deal with the story of his birth. Maybe.

*   *   *

Mathilda and Esther followed through on their promise to invite Hilda to their place. Funny that now she would have her own relationship with Franz's sisters. When Franz was alive, whenever she was along, she had held back while they shared banter and serious news or family reminiscences. Somehow, since he died, they had never gotten together. It hadn't occurred to Hilda to call on them or to invite them. First, there were the girls' marriages; they had been invited to Jane's, and they had attended but stayed in the background. Andrew's wedding in South Dakota was too far for them to go to. They sent a present with a congratulatory card, but that was all. They acknowledged Hans's death in a letter of condolence, but they hadn't called on her.

Now, visiting them, Hilda brought them a jar of fresh currant jelly, made from the bush in her garden. Thanking her for it, Esther took it to their kitchen to open later. They would serve their own jam to her.

Looking around in their parlor, Hilda remembered Franz sitting in the chair he had usually occupied when they visited. She could almost see Franz there again. The portraits on the wall, of their solemn parents stiffly posed, showed familiar Franz features in both: the high forehead, prominent nose, strong chin, and direct gaze, though his mother's eyes were less intense. Hilda had never met his father, who had died before she met Franz, but she knew his mother, who was still living in the Sunset Home.

Mathilda returned from another room with a small stack of booklets, yellowing copybooks. "I was sorting through my things the other day and came across these of Franz's. Take them. Maybe your children will be interested in what school was like for him." Chuckling, she added, "Who knows, you may learn something about Franz you never knew before."

"I've learned," Hilda remarked, "that everyone has secrets. I'm learning some of my children's secrets now. Maybe some secrets should be kept."

"Don't worry, I looked through these, and there's nothing in them that you won't want to know."

"I think there isn't much more for me to learn about Franz, anything more strange than his love for perischki. I never could learn to like those sauerkraut and prune concoctions, but I made them for him because when we were courting, he told me they were his favorite food."

The sisters looked at each other. After a pause, Esther spoke up, "Nah, well, I think he was pulling your leg. None of us really liked it. Ma had learned to eat it when they were more or less starving in Ukraine."

302

"And," Mathilda added, "she cooked them as a sort of 'lesson' for us. She wanted us to learn what she had put up with in the old country. So she made them from time to time."

"He never let on," Hilda responded. "I made them special for his birthdays—not every year, but several times. He ate them greedily, I thought. He got our children to eat them too but, after he died, they never asked for them. And I never made them again."

"Forgive us for telling you. We really should have kept his secret," Esther grinned.

By that time, Hilda was laughing. Then, wildly, so hard that she could hardly catch a breath. "Oh, that's more than all right," she tried to say. "Now I don't feel guilty about not making them anymore. But I wish I could tell him that I now know he bamboozled me." She reached for Esther's arm to steady herself, and soon all three were holding each other up.

If their windows had been open, the neighbors would have wondered at the noise, and at what was so funny.

On her way home, a fair walk that Hilda managed, though she was tired and her hip joints were acting up, she mulled over what new perspective she now had about Franz's sisters. How different they were from those intimidating unknowns when she and Franz were courting. "Snide," she had thought of their comments about her father's ministry and her Meadow Church, comments some gossip had offered. "All those years when Franz was alive, I never got to know them for themselves. For myself. I wonder what new things I will learn about other people."

*   *   *

As she rounded the corner toward home, she came across people she had never seen before: man, woman, and half-grown girl. Shorter than she was, the man took off his hat and smiled. The woman, also smiling, reached out her hand in greeting.

Uh oh, Hilda thought, *not Mormon missionaries*. But she smiled and took the woman's hand.

"We're the Mullers," the lady said. "We've come to look at how our building is coming along. We've seen you working in your garden—it *is* you and your garden, isn't it? I could use some instruction in gardening."

Tired as she was from her walk home and her visit with Franz's sisters, Hilda knew this was her chance to be a welcoming neighbor. "Yes. I'm happy to meet you. How is your building doing?"

"We're quite pleased. We'll expect to move in before winter. We hope it won't be too much noise and confusion for you. And, by the way, our Liz here is a good lawn mower, aren't you, Liz?"

"I guess so," Liz answered. "I could use the money."

"So far, I've been mowing my own lawn, as little as there is," Hilda told her, "but I've been having trouble with my hips. Maybe we can work something out. I'll tell other neighbors too, if they'd like help."

Thus, all her concerns—about living alone, about the mulberry bush, and about "who are the new neighbors anyway?"—seemed to have faded away. Later she learned their names.

She wasn't alone. Not at all. Friendly neighbors next door. The lively bird, Yellow Bill, a songster indoors. And the silent, faceless people who came around most days to keep her company. They seemed pleasant enough. Didn't worry her. She knew she was content and would be at ease for some time to come.

CHAPTER FORTY-SEVEN: –1967

Thus, for a time, Hilda's days continued. She puttered in her garden, handing out her abundance of vegetables and flowers to her children, her neighbors, her church, or whoever would accept them.

She tended Yellow Bill, talked to him, and tuned her radio to music he would sing with, even if the music didn't especially please her. Yellow Bill was getting old: his feathers weren't as glossy as they had been. Hilda wondered, *Shouldn't they be white by now? Is his voice not as clear as it used to be? Or is my hearing worse?*

Mother Lober and Aunt Mary died within months of each other in the Sunset Home. Their deaths were peaceful; they hadn't suffered. They had lived long, upright, virtuous lives.

Hilda's bonds with Franz's sisters deepened, and she found she could call on them for help, should she ever want any. She enjoyed visiting with them as they raised her spirits, even when she hadn't been particularly downhearted.

Amos and Anna visited now and then, and Henry and Emma stopped by frequently, just to see how she was, and, by the way, to eat some of her good tvaybak. Peter and his wife, Elsie, whom Hilda never really got to know, also called on her. They had little to say, as if his mother, Aunt Mary, had said all there was to say.

All six had retired and moved to town. Amos walked with a cane, and Anna looked bent over. Henry no longer drove, because his eyesight was failing. Emma seemed the same as always: cheerful and helpful. Her hair, now snow white, had turned so gradually that Hilda didn't notice. Peter seemed smaller and looked pale, and Elsie, even smaller, walked in his shadow—what there was of it.

Once in a while, Hilda considered asking them all about that shivaree, so long ago, the night she and Franz were married. *Were they among the noisemakers? What were they thinking?* And she wondered, *Did Amos and Anna fall in love because they met at that cousins' meeting—or would it have happened anyway? Oh well, best to let it go.*

John and Marie, and Liesebet and Joe—still living in Montana but retired from farming—wrote regularly. They were not traveling much anymore. Hermann and Marta and their spouses always sent Christmas greetings.

Miriam Esau remained a true good neighbor, and they visited each other's churches for special events, or even regular worship. Now, Hilda needn't think of herself as a "fifth wheel" on the church pew. She wondered, *How would a fifth wheel on a pew look.?*

The Mullers were busy, both parents working and Liz at school; but Hilda's little lawn was mowed and walk was shoveled even before she noted that the work needed doing.

Hilda's health? Nothing to see a doctor about. Now and then, she was short of breath, but sitting for a while took care of that. Aspirin alleviated her aches and pains; if two tablets didn't do the trick, why, a few more did.

Her hair had turned white; if she were vain she would have been proud of its soft fluffiness. She wasn't vain. But she didn't like to look at the deep lines in her face, or at her hands that were dry, with short, ridged fingernails—an old woman's hands.

*   *   *

Afternoon naps were routine, but Hilda decided to change one thing: where to nap. She found that she slept too long in her bed: for hours—sometimes until sunset—when all she wanted was ten minutes or so. Therefore, she switched to resting on the sofa. She often spent that time counting her blessings, as the old song went.[44] It helped her relax.

This day, the couch was comfortable enough for an afternoon nap. Warmed by the sun shining at him in his cage, Bill was balanced on his perch and singing. The crowd of still, featureless people that often surrounded her again watched over her. She welcomed them this time. In the background, she could hear the ebb and surge of the ocean—or was it the winter wind in the cottonwood trees? She pulled her afghan up to her chin, her rainbow-colored one that she finished crocheting just last week. She delighted in its soft warmth.

The sewing machine stood open, the newly completed comforter still on the open lid. The pattern had a name; at the moment, Hilda couldn't think what that name was. It was perhaps the most painstaking quilt she had ever

---

44 "Count your many blessings. Name them one by one... See what God has done."

attempted. *I'd better wrap it in paper. Keep it clean until the next sewing circle meeting. In a while.*

I probably won't try again to make such a detailed one. She thought about that: *Who, among the many homeless people, would care how fancy a quilt was, so long as it was warm?*

She shifted to her side but decided not to get up just yet. For now, she just traced the life of that Singer from cold snowy Montana to two Minnesota farms and then here to town. *Just as I hoped, all my children, even the boys, sewed with it. Franz never did though. Why didn't he? Well, he was busy. But the Singer has held up. As I have.*

Not really sleepy, Hilda indulged in letting her mind wander some more. *I live here in my own house. Chose it myself. How long ago? At least a week? Maybe more like a month. Or was it a year? More than a year? Let's see: Pa was here a while ago, but he left. Was that before or after Andrew was married?*

Silly me. It had to be after, because I lived here when Pa moved in with me. After Muttah died. I've got that straight now.

Andrew got married and has two children, or is it three? Boy. Girl? No, twin boys: Frank and James. Nice children. Polite. Andrew's wife is Aganetha, or Agatha. Is Agatha a short name for Aganetha? I'll ask sometime. Some people use both names. One name for each girl.

The girls are mothers also. Grace and Jane. Good mothers. I hope they're passing on my parables to their children. Some of them, at any rate. I mean, some parables, not children... Sure they are. They always loved my stories. The ones I learned at my mother's knee. Or at least at her side.

Now that the war is over, Grace and her husband, Hugo—what a strange name. Not Mennonite but a good husband. Good father too—they're civilians now. What is it that they do? Well, Grace is a nurse. Takes care of me when I need it, but I don't need it now. They have two children. One is theirs: Linda. The other is somebody else's. Theirs really because they adopted. Named him Hans. Lindy and Hansle. They don't come here often enough. Grace doesn't write often enough either. Never did. That's how she is. But when she does come, she's good to me.

Now, Jane. A writer. Every week. I owe her a letter. I'll write when I get up. Her Robert—what a good man. A psychologist. Something like that. And Jane a teacher. A good woman. Their children growing up to be decent and devout. Katherine—like my ma—and what's their little boy's name? Oh yes, Bobby, after his father.

Well, all the grandchildren are fine and decent. I am so blessed.

But where is Hans? Oh, yes. He left. For war. Didn't come home. I wish he'd come, anyway, for a visit.

Wait. There was another child. He came before Hans—and even before Andrew and Jane. Didn't ever grow up. Didn't live at all. Named him Cherub.

He's one of God's cherubim. I'll see him someday if he's not too busy at the throne of God. Maybe the seraphim will give him a little time off.

At least Franz is around. Good old Franz. I can depend on him. He doesn't know if he's saved. Neither do I. So what? That makes two of us. Actually three, if you count Pa—he wasn't sure either. But he trusted God. I guess that's what we should also do.

Franz should be coming in soon. He's been out a long time.

Oh, for dumb. Here he is, right beside me. Been here all along.

With him here, I don't mind strangers in the house. Who are they anyhow? They've never introduced themselves. So silent. Maybe I should get up and offer them a cup of coffee and some tvaybak. I haven't been hospitable. They aren't unfriendly.

We can greet these people in the house together. Franz and I. In a bit, when I finish counting my blessings.

About the Author

Milly Janzen Balzer grew up in rural Minnesota, steeped in Mennonite lore. Her MA thesis was a collection of her stories. Following a Fulbright scholarship in Germany, she taught English. She lives with her husband and cat at Foulkeways in Gwynedd, Pennsylvania, where she bakes tvaybak and walks the trails.